MAN OF HONOUR

Upper Bavaria, 1704, the British army, illustrious and fresh from victory, stands proudly to attention, ready to fight for honour and glory. At the head of his company stands Lieutenant Jack Steel, admired by his men, the finest infantry in Queen Anne's army. Much praised for his courage, his strength, and his loyalty, Steel has come to the attentionof his commander in Chief, the Duke of Marlborough.

Tasked with rescuing a letter whose controversial contents could destroy Marlborough, Steel leads his men against the French, in skirmishes which will culminate in the battle of Blenheim. And along the way he is constantly threatened from within by the mellifluous Major Jennings, intent on destroying Steel and all that he stands for.

MAN OF HONOUR

Iain Gale

WINDSOR
PARAGON

First published 2008
by HarperCollins
This Large Print edition published 2008
by BBC Audiobooks Ltd
by arrangement with HarperCollins Publishers
Ltd

Hardcover ISBN: 978 1 405 64949 0
Softcover   ISBN: 978 1 405 64950 6

British Library Cataloguing in Publication Data available

Printed and bound in Great Britain by
Antony Rowe, Chippenham, Wiltshire

For Sarah

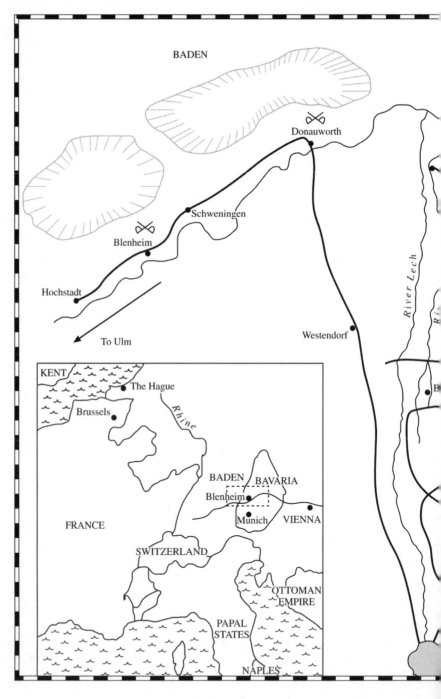

BADEN

Donauworth

Schweningen

Blenheim

Hochstadt

To Ulm

Westendorf

River Lech

KENT

The Hague

Brussels

Rhine

BADEN BAVARIA

Blenheim

FRANCE

Munich VIENNA

SWITZERLAND

OTTOMAN
EMPIRE

PAPAL
STATES

NAPLES

MARLBOROUGH'S CAMPAIGN ON THE DANUBE
July–August 1704

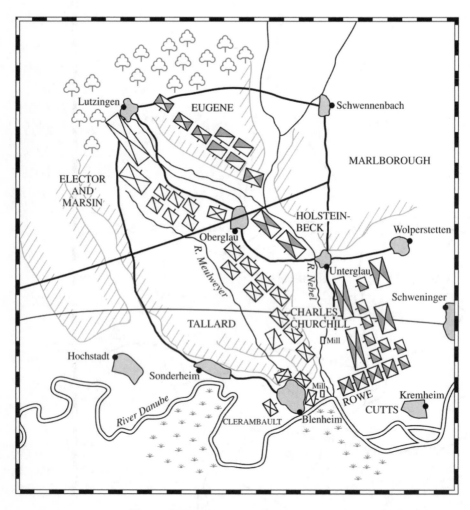

The Battle of Blenheim

13 August 1704

Illustrating the positions of the Allied and
Franco/Bavarian armies, before fighting commenced

PROLOGUE

Upper Bavaria, July 1704

They had come here by stealth to carry the war deep into the south. An army of many nations: English and Scots, Hanoverians and Prussians, Hessians, Danes and Dutch. They had but one purpose: the defeat of France and her ally, Bavaria. The French King, Louis XIV, they knew to be a power-mad maniac, styling himself the Sun King. It was clear that he would not be content until he possessed all Europe, from Spain to Poland. And so it was, on this sultry day in early July, as afternoon drifted into evening, that fate brought these many thousands of men to Donauwörth, a little Bavarian town with its ancient high walls and ramparts.

Above it, at the top of a steep slope, stood a fort whose hill, inspired by its distinctive shape, the local people had long ago christened 'Schellenberg'—The Hill of the Bell. It was abundantly and worryingly clear to all the soldiers who now stood in its shadow, that before any decisive victory could be won, before they could bring the French to battle, drive them back to Paris and remove forever the Sun King's threat, that this hill and its little fort would have to be taken.

1

ONE

The tall young officer stood a few yards out in front of the company of redcoats and stared up at the fort that towered above them on the hill. For two hours now he had been awaiting the order to advance and with every passing moment the enemy position looked more forbidding. Like almost every man in the army, he had the greatest admiration and respect for his Commander-in-Chief. But at this precise moment he had begun to wonder whether, truly, this entire enterprise might not be doomed to failure. He tried to banish the thought. To maintain some degree of *sang-froid* before his men. But as he did so, the first cannonball fell in front of the three ranks of red-coated infantry, bounced up from the springy turf with grisly precision, and carried away four of them in a welter of blood and brains.

'Feeling the heat, Mister Steel?'

The Lieutenant looked up. Silhouetted against the sun a tall figure in a full-bottomed wig peered down at him from horseback.

'A trifle, Sir James.'

'A trifle, eh? I'd have thought that you'd have been used to it after, how many years a soldier?'

'Nigh on a dozen, Colonel.'

'But of course. How could I forget? You earned your spurs in the Northern wars, did you not? Fighting the Rooshians. A little colder there I dare say.'

'A little, Colonel.'

'Can't imagine why you should have wanted to

3

go there at all. Narva, Riga? What sort of battles were those, eh?'

The question was not intended to have a reply.

'Well, Steel, what think you of our chances today? Shall we do it?'

'I believe that we can, Sir. Though it will not be easily done.'

'No, indeed. Yet we must take this town. It is the key to the Danube and the gateway to Bavaria. And to do that we needs must take the fort. And we must do it by frontal assault. There is no other way. You would say, Steel, that the rules of war dictate we must do it by siege. And you would be right. But we have no siege guns and thus our Commander-in-Chief, His Grace the Duke of Marlborough, dictates that this is the way it shall be done. And so it shall. We will attack up that hill into the face of their guns.'

He paused and shook his head. 'Our casualties will be heavy. God knows, Steel, this is not the proper way to win a battle. It will not be like any of the battles you saw with the Swedes, I'll warrant. Eh? Rooshians and Swedes, Steel. Indeed I can't fathom what you saw in it. No Rooshians today, Steel. Only the French and their Bavarian friends to beat. Still. Hot work, eh? Good day to you.'

Colonel Sir James Farquharson laughed, touched his hat to the young Lieutenant and trotted away down the line of the battalion, his voice echoing above the rising cannonfire as he shouted greetings to the other company commanders of the advance storming party:

'Good afternoon, Charles. Good day to you, Henry. We dine in Donauwörth this evening, I believe.'

4

Steel shook his head and smiled. Yes, he thought. He could see why Sir James would not understand the reasons why he should have wished to fight with the Swedes. That it would never occur to his Colonel to take yourself off to find a war. Soldiering for Sir James Farquharson was a gentlemanly affair. A thing of parades and banners. But if there was one thing that Jack Steel had learnt in the last twelve years it was that there was nothing gentlemanly about war. Nothing whatsoever.

He turned his head towards his men. Saw the lines being re-dressed by the sergeants and the corporals, the bloody gaps filled up from the rear with fresh troops. The dismembered bodies being dragged away.

'The Colonel seems happy, Sir. Do you suppose he thinks we're going to win?'

The surprisingly mellifluous voice belonged to Steel's Sergeant, Jacob Slaughter. Six foot two of Geordie and the only man in the company broader and taller than Steel himself. Gap-toothed, loose-limbed Sergeant Slaughter, who had run away to join the colours to avoid being sent to work in the new coal mines of County Durham. Towering Sergeant Slaughter who was so terrified of small spaces, who couldn't abide the dark and was unutterably clumsy in all manner of things. But who, on the field of battle, was a man transformed, as skilled and calculating a killer as Steel had ever encountered. A man next to whom, more than any other, you would want to stand when all around you the world had dissolved in a boiling surf of blood and death. Steel greeted him with a smile.

'D'you need to ask, Jacob? Sir James doesn't

5

think we'll win. He knows it. Our Colonel raised this regiment, his regiment with his name, from his own pocket. He wants us to be the finest in the British army. It's not just our lives that'll be at stake up there. It's his money and his pride. He needs a few battle honours. And it's up to us to give them to him.'

'D'you think we'll be going in soon then, Sir? I'm startin' to get a dreadful thirst.'

'By God, Jacob. That thirst of yours is no respecter of time and place. Here we stand, about to launch possibly the most desperate feat of arms to which you or I have ever been party—and quite probably our last—and you tell me you want a drink. I tell you, Sarn't, there'll be drink a plenty if we take this damned town. Don't you worry. I'll personally find you a cask of the finest Moselle.'

'You're as fine a gentleman as I've ever known, Mister Steel, and I'll take you at your word. But if you really mean it, Sir, I'd sooner have a barrel of German ale than any bloody wine—if it's all the same with you.'

He paused. His attention drawn by sudden movement towards the right of the line.

'Aye aye. Looks like we might be on the move.'

Following his Sergeant's gaze, Steel saw a galloper. A young Cornet of Cavalry mounted on a handsome black mare, racing at speed down the lines. Here then, at last, was the order. And not before time. They had marched, halted and been ordered at stand-to since three o'clock that morning. Now it was nearing six in the evening. Surely now they must go. The men were restless. They would not stand for much more delay, or they would lose their nerve. Steel looked about

6

him. Back down the slope he was able to see the massed battalions and squadrons of the main army, including the other ten companies of his own regiment.

Guidons and colours flew from their spear-topped poles, high above serried ranks of red, blue, grey, brown, and green as the allies assembled their might to follow into the gap that it was confidently presumed would be made by the storming party.

It was more evident than ever, he thought, what a rag-bag army this was. English, Scots, Irish, and an unlikely union of Dutchmen, Hessians, Prussians and Danes. Walk through their camp and you would find men communicating with each other by sign language, or attempting some laughable *patois*. Steel, ironically, had always found that the easiest language to use—that most understood by his allied counterparts—was the French of their enemies. He wondered how the allied army would hold together under fire. Oh, he did not doubt the Duke's capabilities with their own contingent. But how would so many foreigners suffer being commanded by an Englishman? Nevertheless, you could not help but admire the sight.

'A fine view, Jack, is it not?'

Steel's fellow officer, Lieutenant Henry Hansam, was standing beside him, holding open a small silver snuff box.

'Care for a pinch?'

Steel waved him away. Hansam took a good pinch and inhaled deeply before continuing:

'Although little good it does us. We are quite alone up here. They expect a miracle of us, Jack.

7

Nothing less than a miracle.'

He let out a loud sneeze, withdrew a silk handkerchief from his sleeve and wiped his nose. Steel spoke.

'Well, Henry. Can we manage it? Shall we give them their miracle?'

'We are the choice troops, you know. If we cannot take this position then most certainly it cannot be achieved. We are the chosen few. Forty-five times one hundred and thirty men, plucked from each English and Scots battalion on this field. The Duke himself has had a hand in our choosing. Naturally Sir James sends only his Grenadiers. And why not? It is the very purpose for which the Grenadiers were created. We are the "storm" troops. We have the height, the agility, the strength. And, by God Jack, you know we have the heart to do it.'

Steel cast a sideways look at their company. They were giants among men. Not one among them under five foot ten. They had been chosen, too, for their experience and skill with arms; their ability to move fast and to operate on their own initiative.

They were the finest infantry in Queen Anne's army and soon he would lead them forward, up the hill and, God willing, into the fort. To death or glory and the promise of a handsome bounty. Looking up again at the dark mass of the fort, Steel could not suppress a chill shudder of apprehension. He looked away and pretended to straighten his sash. Hansam sneezed again through his snuff, wiped his nose with the now discoloured square of silk.

Steel looked at his friend, who, along with him,

bore the title unique to the Grenadiers of 'Second Company Lieutenant'. With Colonel Farquharson keen to draw for himself the additional pay that came with the nominal command of their company, Hansam and Steel between them found that they now commanded the Grenadiers in the field yet without the status or pay of a captain. Nor had they any junior officers.

Their last Ensign, a weak-livered boy of fifteen, had left them at Coblenz—invalided out with chronic dysentery. As yet they had found no replacement. Steel spoke, quietly:

'Of course, there is the bounty money.'

Hansam raised his eyebrows.

'Of course, Jack. We cannot delude ourselves that the men will do it entirely for the love of Queen and country. Nor even, dare I say it, for love of the Duke. Keep them happy and they'll fight. Oh yes. They'll fight. For the bounty.'

'I was talking, Henry, about our own share.'

'Oh.'

Hansam paused, then grinned.

'Naturally, my dear fellow. Of course. We may profit too. Point of fact, I never did understand quite how someone as financially limited and indeed as frugal as yourself, had ever come to have started off in the Foot Guards. Although perhaps now I do see your reasons for transferring from that illustrious regiment to join our happy band.'

Steel nodded his head. Hansam spoke again, smiling:

'Perhaps, Jack . . . if we should survive, I might persuade you to accompany me to a proper tailor, in London. I mean take a look at yourself, Jack. Why, your hat alone . . .'

9

Steel looked down at the hat which he held in his hand. Unlike some Grenadier officers, he did not choose to wear the mitre cap, but preferred his battered, gold-laced black tricorne. In fact he habitually fought bareheaded. And anyway, at six foot one, as the second tallest man in the company, he knew that a Grenadier's mitre cap would have made him look less frightening than absurd. Besides, the most precious lesson he had got from twelve years of soldiering, nine of them with the colours, was that to survive as an officer you should not offer the enemy too obvious a target and yet at the same time must be sufficiently distinctive to be instantly recognisable to your own men.

'Well, Henry. It does let the men know where I am.'

Hansam laughed. For both officers knew that, with or without his hat, his men could hardly mistake Steel. Apart from his height, there was his hair, which rather than cutting short and covering with a full wig, as was the fashion, he preferred to wear long and tied back in a bow with a piece of black ribbon: another practical trick learnt on the field of battle.

'I say.'

Hansam was pointing along the line.

'We appear to be under orders.'

Steel could see that the galloper had reached the senior commanders of the storming party now. They had dismounted, as was common practice, to lead the attack on foot. He could make out Major-General Henry Withers and Brigadier-General James Ferguson, commanders respectively of the English and Scots troops of the assault force.

Beside them stood the determined figure of Johan Goors, the distinguished, middle-aged Dutch officer of engineers, well known for his opposition to Baden, to whom Marlborough had entrusted overall command of the assault.

The officers had gathered near, although not too close, to the 'forlorn hope', a band of some eighty men—volunteers all, drawn from Steel's old regiment, the First Foot Guards—whose unhappy task, as their name suggested, was to go first into the defences and discover by their own sacrifice where the enemy might be strongest. To put it bluntly, they would draw the enemy's fire on to themselves. Most of them would die. But for those who survived there would be the greatest rewards and celebrity. Immortality even. At its head Steel saw the unmistakeable tall and handsome Lord John Mordaunt. The two had served together for a time and Steel had been somewhat surprised last year when Mordaunt had been refused the hand of Marlborough's daughter. Perhaps the honour of leading the 'hope' now was some self-inflicted penance for that amorous failure. Or Mordaunt's last chance possibly to win the admiration of the man who might have been his father-in-law. From the right, a squadron of English dragoons now approached their line. Steel noticed that each trooper carried in front of him across his saddle two thick bundles of what looked like sticks, tied together with rope. The cavalry broke into open order and began to ride between each rank of the Grenadiers, handing out the bundles of fascines, one to each man. To the officers too. Steel took his own realizing how cumbersome it was. These though were the vital tools that they were to use to

11

cross the great defensive ditch that they had discovered lay in their way at the top of the hill, a short distance in front of the breastworks.

A thunderous roar made Steel turn momentarily and up on the gentle hill behind them he saw flame spout from the mouths of ten cannon. The sum total of the allied artillery had been stationed there, close to a small village set afire by the French in an attempt to impede their progress. Ten guns. That was all that they had to soften up the defences that lay above them. The balls flew over their heads and disappeared high up on the enemy position. Well, it appeared that at least someone in the high command was trying to prepare the way for their assault.

At the foot of the Schellenberg, all now safely across the stream, stood the formed ranks of the main army. English, Scots, Dutchmen and the men from Hesse and Prussia who had joined them at Coblenz. Steel watched as the evening sun glanced off the green slopes of the hill and the brown line of the basketwork gabions. Soon, he knew, this pretty field would be transformed into a bloody killing ground.

Instinctively, with the eye of the veteran, he began to calculate how far they would have to travel to make it to the defences. Four hundred yards perhaps. Hansam smiled at him.

'Well, that's it then. I suppose that we had better take our stations. No point in giving their gunners too obvious a target. Until we meet again, Jack, at the top of the hill.'

'At the top of the hill, Henry.'

Almost before he could sense the hollow ring of his words, he was suddenly aware of the reassuring presence of Sergeant Slaughter at his side.

'Ready, Sir? I think we're really off now.'

Steel felt the old emptiness in his stomach that always marked the approach of battle.

He knew that the only way to appear in control was to force your way through it.

'Very good Sarn't. Have the men make ready.'

Slaughter turned to the ranks.

'All right. Let's have you. Look to it now. Smarten up. Dress your ranks.'

They were standing six deep now, rather than in the customary four ranks. Six ranks to push with sheer weight of numbers as deep as possible into the fortifications and through the men beyond. But six ranks that would give equally such easy sport to the enemy guns whose cannonballs, falling just short of the front man, would bounce up and through him before continuing to take down another five, ten, twenty in his wake. Slaughter barked the command:

'Grenadiers. Fix . . .' he drew breath.

With one motion the Grenadiers drew the newfangled blades from their sheaths fumbling with the unfamiliar fastenings. Slaughter finished:

'. . . bayonets.'

With a rattle of metal against metal the company fixed the clumsy sockets on to the barrels of their fusils. A distant voice, the confident growl of General Goors, speaking in a slow and particular tone and loud to the point of hoarseness, rang out across the field.

'The storming party will advance.'

The pause that followed, as Goors turned to his front seemed an eternity. And then his single word of command.

'Advance.'

Along the line, the order was taken up by a hundred sergeants and lieutenants. Behind each regimental contingent two fifers began a tune that on the fifth bar, with a fast, rising roll, was taken up by the drummer boys. The familiar rattle and paradiddle of 'the Grenadiers' March'.

Then, with a great cheer, the line began to walk forward. Steel measured his pace. Not with the precision of the Prussians or the Dutch, who were always directed by their blessed manual of rules to walk into battle: 'as slow as foot could fall'. But rather with the singular, slow step of the British infantry. A gentle step, as their own manual directed, designed to ensure that the men would not be 'out of breath when they came to engage'. It was certainly an easy pace, he thought. But deadly. And under cannonfire quite the last way in which you would want to conduct yourself.

Walking forward now, as the enemy shot began to fly in earnest towards their lines, Steel felt his feet begin to sink into the soft ground. Weighed down by their bundles of faggots, the men soon found they could not gather pace. Four hundred yards, thought Steel. Good God. It seemed more like a mile now, stretching out before him up the hill. No hill now, but a mountain, from the top of which he saw guns belch more gouts of flame as the French artillery opened up with its full force. Ten, twenty roundshot at a time came leaping at them down the slope, finding a home in the ranks behind him. Steel heard the cries to his rear as his own men were blown to oblivion. He repeated a litany in his head: 'Face the front. Keep looking to the front. Don't be distracted. Don't, for pity's

14

sake, look back.'

He heard Slaughter close behind him, through the cacophany of shot, bark another, familiar command: 'Dress your ranks. Keep them steady. Corporal Jenkins. Your section. Keep it steady now, mind.'

Keep steady. It was madness in this hail of roundshot and grenades. But there was no other way. A cannonball flew past his left elbow. Steel felt the shockwave. Another roundshot came hurtling towards him and passed horribly close, before taking off the head of one of the second-rank men and continuing down the hill. To his left he could see Henry Hansam advancing at a similar walking pace. The drums were driving them forward now, hammering out their tattoo with frenzied rhythm. Momentarily forgetting his own advice, he looked behind. Saw Slaughter and next to him, his face covered in mud, his coat splashed with blood and brains from the man who had been killed beside him, yet still smiling through his fear, one of the infants of the company. A boy of barely sixteen. Steel grinned at him. He was a Yorkshire farmhand, if his memory served him right. Runaway, most like. He shouted through the cacophany:

'Truman, isn't it? All right lad?'

A bigger smile. That was good.

'Don't worry. You're doing well. Not bad for your first battle. Sarn't Slaughter, let's get up there and show them how it's done.'

Looking to his front he could see nothing but smoke and flying shot. The noise was indescribable. A familiar terror began to rise inside him. Like the sudden, illogical panic that

15

could sweep through you when standing on a precipice. Must stay calm, he thought. The men must not see that I am afraid. There was a cold feeling now in the pit of his stomach. Feet like lead. I am not afraid. He bit his lip until he could taste the blood. Good. He was alive. He would live through this. Just put one foot in front of the other and walk forward. That was it. Slowly he began to advance, and got into an automatic rhythm. Easier now. He raised his sword. It was the right time to say something now. The words flew from him.

'Grenadiers. Follow me.'

Again they started to climb the slope and with every pace more men fell, as more of the deadly black balls hurtled down towards them. Two hundred yards more now, he guessed. All they had to do was carry on and they'd be there. Just keep going. He was suddenly aware of a change in the rhythm of fire from the defences. Instantly, its cause became evident, as a hail of cannister shot— thirty iron balls blown from the cannon mouth in a canvas bag—slammed into the men standing to his left and took away a score of red-coated bodies. At the same instant a crash of musket fire signalled that the French infantry too had found their range. More men fell. Somewhere, through the drifting smoke to his left, another officer called out:

'Charge. Charge, boys. God save the Queen.'

Steel saw the man fall, but his cry was taken up along the line and as one, the men broke into a trot. Steel too began to run. Breathing hard now, the smell of powder drifting strong and acrid into his nostrils. They passed through a mist of billowing white smoke. When they emerged on the other side of the cloud however, a sunken gulley

16

appeared directly in front of him—from nowhere. Steel pulled up. He yelled at the men behind him to stop and found himself at the top of a muddy bank of a depth of four, perhaps five feet. Behind him the men came to a halt. All around him, and down along the line, he could hear the frantic shouts of corporals and sergeants. A corporal to his left was giving orders:

'Right lads. This is it. Drop your fasheens. Over we go.'

As the men began to throw down their wooden bundles, Steel wondered. This could not be right. It was too soon. This was no defensive ditch. Merely a sunken track. He turned to the Corporal:

'No, no. Don't use them here. This is not the place. Carry on. Follow me.'

The man looked suprised, but it was too late. The front rank had already thrown their precious rolls of wood down into the lane. Men attempted to clamber across, but found the distance too great and slithered off into the mud. At the same time, cannonballs started to crash into their ranks. The French gunners had adjusted their range and were aiming directly for the thin stripe of the track. Some of the men began to panic; unsure of whether they should stand, use their fascines or drop down without them into the gulley. The more athletic managed to cross the makeshift wooden causeway, only to find themselves all the more prone to the hail of roundshot. Steel jumped down into the ditch and half clambered up the other side, using the bank as cover. He heard Slaughter's booming voice.

'Keep to your ranks. Dress your ranks.'

For they were ragged now. And to the Sergeant

ragged ranks meant ragged discipline. Lack of confidence. Lack of nerve. Steel knew equally well that if their nerve went this soon, then the attack would just dissolve. But he could see too that, whatever Slaughter's instinct, this was no time for parade-ground drill. He called up to the big Sergeant.

'Jacob. Forget the bloody ranks. Get the men down here. Form on me.'

Startled out of his automatic manouevre, Slaughter checked and began to herd the men into cover. Quickly the half-company of Grenadiers descended into the gulley, followed Steel's example and pressed themselves hard against the cover of the far bank. Removing his hat, Steel peered gingerly over the top, up towards the fort. He could see them more clearly now. The figures in white coats up on the parapet. French infantry. They were standing quite still; drawn up in silence as if on parade. They made an eerie, unnerving contrast to the shouting mass of his own men that milled around him, pressing themselves into the muddy wall of the sunken road. Up on the fort Steel saw officers begin to shout commands. Saw the front rank of the French take one pace forward. He saw them reach behind and unbuckle a black pouch. Grenadiers. He knew all too well what was coming next. He turned to the men:

'Keep well into the bank. For God's sake, lads, keep well in and keep your heads down and you'll be all right.'

Two smooth black spheres, smaller than roundshot and sputtering flame bowled by the defenders underarm, like cricket balls, came bouncing into the makeshift trench. Steel looked

18

to see where they had landed and moved quickly away from them.

Men pushed themselves deeper into the muddy bank, trying in vain to make the ground swallow them up. The fuse of one of the round black bombs fizzed to a stop and failed to detonate. The other one though, which had come to rest by the far bank of the gulley, exploded in a hail of red-hot iron, instantly killing three of the Grenadiers and blinding another who lay shrieking in the mud, clutching at the bloody ruin of his face. Steel could hear the cries of other wounded men echoing from above, where behind them, among the second-wave assault troops on the lower slopes of the hill, more grenades had found their mark. There was only one thing to do now. He turned to Slaughter.

'We've got to get out of this death trap. Now. Come on.'

Looking out again above the rim of the bank, Steel tried to find a way forward. To the left lay the bulk of the storming party, mired down in the torrent of shot, not knowing whether to stand or advance. He saw men stumbling forward into the ditch. All was confusion. He thought he saw Goors himself fall. To his right though, there was no one. He and the Grenadiers were the very end of the line. The extreme right wing. For an instant a wild idea entered his mind. Might not the French, observing that the allied attack was going in on their right, perhaps have grouped their men principally towards that area? Surely that would mean that they would have weakened their own left flank. The flank that now lay obliquely to his own command. He peered through the smoke and looked hard up at the battlements. He could see where they ended—in the great bulk of the old fort—and could see too the cannon placed high on its ramparts pointing into what would soon be the flank of the attackers. But to the right of the fort he could see nothing but some hastily prepared earthworks. There were troops behind them to be sure. More white-coated infantry. But, if he guessed right, this was only a skeleton force. A plan was starting to form in his mind. Perhaps . . . He looked for Slaughter.

'Jacob. Have the men follow me. Tell them to remove their caps and keep their heads down and come on in single file. We're not going forward, Jacob. We're going sideways. We're going to move along the gulley. They can't see us here. But I know where they are. We're going to give the French a bit of a surprise.'

Slaughter smiled. He saw instantly what Steel was about and began to send word down the line. Steel beckoned to Truman.

'Go and find Mister Hansam. Tell him that we're going to stay in the trench. We're going to take the Frenchies in the flank. He'll know what I mean. Hurry now and tell him to keep his head down and to get the men to take their caps off.'

Slowly, bent double and making sure to keep his own head well below the bank, Steel began to make his way along the ditch. He looked back and saw that the Grenadiers were following suit. After twenty yards the ditch turned sharply back down the hill, towards the allied army. For a ghastly moment Steel panicked. What if he were wrong? What if this gulley did not lead parallel to the fortifications, as he had guessed, but away from the French and the battle? What then? Desertion?

20

Court martial? He began to sweat. There was nothing for it now though but to continue, whatever the consequences. He would take all the blame and exonerate Hansam. He would face the terrible charge of desertion in the face of the enemy on his own. Steel slipped on the muddy floor of the ditch, and swore. His thighs and back had begun to ache from the exertion of travelling bent over. They seemed to be taking an eternity to cover such a small distance. At length, after some eighty yards, they came to another junction. Steel saw that the main route of the gulley led left, back up the slope, towards the French lines. He muttered an imprecation of thanks to the Almighty under his breath. Heard Slaughter too, tucked in tight behind him: 'Thank God.'

They followed the line of the new ditch, climbing steadily as they went. Another fifty yards and the gulley came to an abrupt dead end. This was it then. Steel turned back, still crouching, and motioned the men to stay down. It was quieter here, away from the cannonade that was still taking its toll of the main force away to their left. He signed to the Grenadiers to sling their fusils on their backs, unbutton their pouches and withdraw one of the three grenades that it contained. Then indicated by sign language that, once they were within range of the enemy, they should ignite the fuse of the missile from the slow-burning match that each man wore strapped to his wrist. Creeping over to the southern side of the gulley he peered over the top. As he had suspected, some 200 yards down the slope, he could make out the plumes and horses of the allied commanders, concealed in a similar gulley. He beckoned to a Grenadier:

Pearson. Fastest runner in the company.

'Take yourself off to Marlborough. He's down there, see? Tell him that we've found a gap in the line. That I'm going to attack and the way is open. Got that? The way is open.'

The young man nodded and, crawling out of the ditch, was soon up and running for the allied lines. Steel crept back to the other side of the gulley. Then, taking a deep breath, he stood up, hauled himself up on top of the forward bank, placed his foot on the turf at the top, sprang out and straightened up. He found himself standing, horribly prone, not ten yards away from a stretch of crude, basketwork gabions, behind a shallow ditch. He had not realized that they might end up quite so close to the enemy lines. What was even more alarming though was the fact that he found himself staring directly into the terrified eyes of a French sentry. For a second both men stood stock still. Then, with one motion they both reached for their weapons.

The Frenchman fumbled with the lock of his musket. Steel, having returned his sword to its scabbard to travel down the gulley, pulled at a wide leather strap on his shoulder and grasped the stock of the short-barrelled fusil which was standard-issue to every officer of Grenadiers. His gun though, was subtly different. It had begun life as a fowling piece, whose ingenious maker had contrived somehow to create a weapon light enough to carry all day out in the hunting field. It was able to fire tight-packed game-shot or a single ball with equal ease and was cut to fit Steel alone. So that—whether his quarry might be a Frenchman or a partridge—when he raised it to his cheek it slipped as neatly into place as if it were an extension of his arm. To mount it was the work of less than a second. And he knew it to be loaded.

Feeling his heart beating hard against his ribs, he pulled back the cock with his right thumb. Felt the coldness of the barrel in his left hand and pressed his cheek close into the action. At that precise moment the Frenchman levelled his own weapon. Steel heard the crack of the man's shot, saw the flash. He felt the ball as it scudded past his cheek and that same instant gave the gentlest squeeze of his own trigger and felt the reassuring recoil as the piece jumped back into his shoulder. The Frenchman dropped stone dead, a bullet in the centre of his forehead. But the two shots had roused the other enemy sentries and the defences in front of Steel now began to fill with men in white coats who looked with dumbstruck amazement at their dead comrade and the apparently suicidal solitary British officer standing before them. Hoisting his gun coolly over his shoulder, Steel drew his sword from its sheath and turned to the redcoats in the gulley below him.

'Grenadiers. With me. Kill the bastards.'

He turned to face the French. Raising the sword above his head, Steel turned its point towards the enemy.

'Farquharson's Foot, follow me. For Marlborough and Queen Anne.'

Suddenly Slaughter was up beside him. A corporal joined them and other men followed. And then, with a great cheer, they were all up and running with him towards the French defences. Steel saw out of the corner of his eye, Hansam charging forward at the head of his half-company;

23

far beyond him on the left of the attack a milling mass of redcoats indicated that the main body of the assault was still floundering. The white-coated infantry, taken completely by surprise by the sea of redcoats that had appeared out of the ground, at last began to cock their weapons. A couple of them dropped their muskets and ran. An enemy officer appeared waving his sword and gesturing at the French Grenadiers. Five yards to go now, thought Steel. Three. At two yards the French opened up, with a ragged volley. Three Grenadiers fell. The remainder carried on and, reaching the earthworks, hurled their fizzing grenades deep over the defences exploding in a hail of flying metal and the screams of unseen men. Steel climbed on to one of the gabions:

'Come on. Follow me. Into them.'

Managing to scramble over the top of the parapet, and followed swiftly by Slaughter and a dozen British Grenadiers, Steel slashed blindly down with his sword. The huge weapon was, apart from his gun, the only thing he had brought out of his father's house. His first cut severed the forearm of a white-coated infantryman who collapsed screaming in the mud.

To his left he was aware of a flash of metal as a Frenchman, attempting to thrust home his bayonet into Steel's side, was beaten off by a Grenadier corporal who swiftly turned the deadly point and stabbed home with his own bayonet, deep into the man's gut. Another Frenchman, a huge sapper armed with a hatchet, attempted a swipe at Steel's feet but he jumped clear and brought down his blade, splitting the man's skull in two so that his head fell apart like two halves of a melon. A

24

French officer approached him warily. A man almost as tall as Steel himself, with the chiselled features of an aristocrat. For a moment Steel thought that the officer was about to challenge him to single combat. Then the Frenchman saw Steel's great sword and stopped. He nodded his head, presented his own rapier-thin weapon in a salute, close to his face, and brought it down with a flourish to his side, before making a shallow bow and backing away. Doing so, and with his piercing gaze still fixed on Steel's eyes, he called to what was left of his command. Then, quite suddenly, the defences were empty.

Steel looked left and right and through the smoke could see nothing but white-coated bodies. He turned one over with his foot: the coat collar and cuffs were all white, the pockets cut in the upright. He searched his memory. That could mean one of three regiments: Espagny, Bandeville or Nettancourt. All of them seasoned regiments of line infantry. What were they doing here? He had been told that the place would be garrisoned by inexperienced Bavarians. Steel looked around at his own men. There were a few British down. Three looked dead for sure. One was sitting clutching a bleeding stomach wound and another had lost an eye. But the important point was that, as far as Steel could see, no one, thank God, was standing before them. He prayed that Pearson had made it through to Marlborough. That reinforcements would be with them soon. Steel turned to Slaughter. 'Form the men up, Sarn't. See to the wounded. We're going to hold this place till help comes.'

Hansam appeared, covered in soot and mud, the

lace hanging from his coat. 'By God, Jack. That was hot stuff. Clever idea of yours. But what now?'

'I've sent a runner for reinforcements. All we can do is stand and wait.'

Both men were looking towards the left wing at the centre of the battle. Through the drifting smoke they caught glimpses of the fighting. Men engaged at close quarters; beating each other with musket butts. Clawing at faces, gouging eyes. Then, as their vision cleared they were able to make out a body of red-clad infantry, apparently making directly for them. Hansam spoke first:

'I sincerely hope that we don't have long to wait.'

Steel saw what he meant.

'Oh God. Dragoons.' He called out: 'Sarn't Slaughter.'

For the French too had seen the vulnerability of their open flank and now several squadrons of their confusingly red-coated dragoons, dismounted but as deadly as ever, were advancing with calm precision to retake the salient. But they were, he guessed, still just far enough away. Steel barked an order.

'Grenadiers. Form lines of half ranks.'

With hard-learned routine, Steel's men formed into three ranks. Hansam too was manouevering his platoon into formation and as the men moved quickly in response, Steel sheathed his sword and unslung his fusil. Taking up a position to the right of the formation, he shouted another command:

'Make ready.'

In as close as they were able to manage to a coordinated move, the second rank of each platoon of Grenadiers cocked their muskets while the front rank knelt down and placed the butts of their weapons on the ground, being careful to keep their thumbs on the cock and their fingers on the triggers. One of them, a recent recruit, dropped his musket and recovered it in embarassment. Slaughter growled.

'That man. Steady. Pick it up, lad.'

The rear rank closed up behind the second, their arms at high port and, as the manual directed, locked their feet closely with those standing immediately before them. Judging the distance of the closing dragoons, Steel continued.

'Present.'

In a single disciplined movement, eighty men eased their thumbs away from the cock of their muskets and at the same time moved their right feet a short step back, keeping the knee quite stiff, before placing the butts of their weapons in the hollow between chest and shoulder. The dragoons were almost on them now. Steel could see their faces: tanned and with thick moustaches beneath fur-topped red bonnets.

He waited. Thirty paces. Twenty now.

'Fire!'

The centre rank of Grenadiers opened up and as they began to reload the rank kneeling in front stood up and delivered their own deadly volley before turning neatly on the left foot and moving past the rank behind. As they did so the third rank brought their muskets down and through the gaps in the ranks to deliver a third salvo. This was the new way. The proper way to use the new muskets. This was why their 'Corporal John' had schooled them all so carefully. This, thought Steel, was real artistry. This was modern war. Seconds later he was proved right as the smoke cleared on a pile of red-coated bodies. The second rank of French dragoons, its officers and NCSs gone in the inferno of musketry, had come to a halt and stood staring at their enemy, unsure of what to do next. Among the British ranks corporals yelled orders:

'Reload . . . Re-form.'

Looking beyond the hesitant, decimated Frenchmen, Steel could now see more infantry in red coats advancing across the plateau. A second squadron with fresh officers.

He turned to Slaughter:

'Look. More of the buggers. Fall back on the gabions. We have to hold them, Jacob.'

He turned and peered towards the allied lines down in the valley.

'Where the hell is that relief force?'

Quickly the two platoons of British Grenadiers fell back together towards the parapet.

Steel looked for Hansam. Smiling, he shouted across to him:

'Can you do it, Henry? Can we hold them?'

'I'd invite them to surrender, Jack, but I think they might have other plans.'

Steel laughed, grimly, and turned to Slaughter.

'Right, Jacob. As you will. Let's show them how it's done.'

Again the Grenadiers assumed their three-rank formation and again, the red ranks began to close. Desperate, Steel turned to look down towards the allied lines. Pearson had failed. There was no one coming to help them. No last minute reprieve. So much for his brilliant plan. Their only way out was to take as many French with them to hell as they could. He strained his eyes in hope but was

28

rewarded only with horror.

'Oh, good God, no!'

Through the smoke, advancing up the slope towards their position, Steel began to make out tall, white-coated figures marching in close order. French infantry. A battalion. No, an entire brigade. Slaughter had seen them too:

'Christ almighty, Sir. How the hell? They've got round behind us.'

Steel flung himself back against the parapet and closed his eyes.

'I'm sorry, Jacob. This wasn't meant to happen.'

'Nothing's meant to happen in war, Mister Steel. It just does.'

Instinctively Steel started to turn the men. If one rank could about-face there might just be a chance to hold off the French in both directions. At least for a little while.

But he knew that it was too late. The white-coated infantry were too close. Steel cast down his gun and drew his sword. As he prepared for the worst, a lone, foreign voice floated up towards him from the white ranks:

'Hallo there, in the defences. Are you English?'

This, surely was the final insult. To be asked for his surrender in such a way. Well, that was one thing at least he would not concede.

'We're Scots. Most of us. And we hold this place in the name of Queen Anne.'

'Then thank God, my friend. We have come to save you.'

He couldn't place the accent, but as the man stepped out of the smoke, Steel knew instantly. These were not French but Imperial infantry and Grenadiers, like themselves. He began to laugh.

'Christ, but I'm glad to see you. We thought you were French.'

The Austrian officer looked aghast.

'No, my friend. We are not French. We hate the French. Excuse me. Captain Wendt, Regiment von Diesbach.'

The Imperial infantry were among them now and as they climbed in through the gabions Steel's men clapped them on the back. But the French were still advancing.

'Take position.'

Slaughter had seen the danger. Again the ranks formed, joined now by the long line of Wendt's men. The French, shocked by the sudden appearance of so many of the enemy, came again to an abrupt halt. This time, Steel knew, they would not wait for the volley.

'Fire!'

Three hundred muskets crashed in unison and the red-coated Frenchmen, caught in the act of turning, fell in scores. Then Steel was up and in front of his men.

'Now, Grenadiers! Now. Charge!'

With a great cheer the British redcoats rushed forward, smashing, bayonets levelled, into the remains of the dragoons. The second squadron did not stay to watch the carnage. Seeing his chance to press the advantage, Steel moved through the mêlée, waving his sword high above his head.

'Grenadiers. To me. We've got them, boys. Follow up. Follow up. Come on. Follow me.'

Leaving the wounded French dragoons to the tender mercies of the Imperial infantry, the redcoats ran quickly to join Steel and Hansam, pouring pell-mell towards the centre of the fortification. To their left more Austrians were now climbing unhindered over the breastworks. There must, he thought, be a good 500 on the plateau by now. Yet the day was not yet complete. Suddenly, in a clatter of sword and harness, and with a chilling cheer, a squadron of red-coated cavalry swept past their right flank. At their head Steel recognized Lord John Hay. Marlborough was sending in the Scots dragoons. Some said they were the finest horsemen in Europe. Steel watched as their sabres swung and chopped at the heads of the French infantry like tops of barley. The Grenadiers pressed on now too, along the slope and directly into the exposed flank of the main French garrison. Then with a great cheer the entire allied line—the British and Dutch who for nigh on two hours had suffered at the hands of the defenders, broke in over the parapet. And then it was over. The French line simply fell to pieces.

Steel glimpsed a senior French officer—a full General he thought—riding hell for leather down past the ruined fort, towards the town, pursued by five of his aides and a party of British dragoons. Isolated groups of French infantry began to surrender. Some succeeded. Others fell under the unforgiving bayonets of the allied infantry. Steel looked away. He knew what happened in the aftermath of an assault. It was unlike any other battle. No room for gentlemanly conduct here. He watched instead, transfixed, as the allied cavalry and dragoons careered down the reverse slope towards Donauwörth, in pursuit of the French who were dropping anything that might slow their progress: packs, muskets, hats, all were thrown off in the desperate rush for safety. Some of the

31

Frenchmen made it across the single narrow bridge. The less fortunate were forced into the waters of the Danube. Few emerged. He saw horses trampling men into the mud as the cavalry swung their sabres and the allies exacted their murderous revenge. Hansam patted him gently on the back.

'Well, Jack. I told you I'd see you at the top of the hill, and here we are. You know I am a man of my word.'

'We did cut it a little fine, don't you think?'

Hansam smiled, picking langrously at a soot-encrusted fingernail.

'Oh, I knew we'd do it.'

And so they had. Against all the odds and against all the rules of military logic they had done it. But at a terrible cost. Steel looked back down the hill towards the allied lines where the main body of the army was now preparing to advance. There seemed to be no grass any more. Just a carpet of bodies. Redcoats mostly. Among them men sat nursing wounds and wives and lovers looked for their men. Hansam sneezed and tucked away his snuff handkerchief.

'I'd better rejoin my men. They look set to chase the Frenchies all the way to Paris.'

As Hansam hurried off to secure the prisoners, Steel found Slaughter kneeling over the dead body of a Grenadier. Pearson. His face looked quite serene, despite the fact that a musket ball had passed into his cheek and blown off the back of his head. The Sergeant spoke quietly.

'Poor sod. He did bloody well. Saved the lot of us, I reckon. Close thing, Sir, weren't it?'

'I never knew a bloodier fight.'

'Nor me.'

Slaughter paused, pushing the dead boy's hair away from his brow.

'Do you think this is how it will be, Mister Steel? The rest of the campaign. The rest of the war?'

'I do, Jacob. This is how the Duke chooses to make war. This is war without limits. War such as even you and I had not seen until today. As savage and bloody and brutal a war as Europe has seen for nigh on eighty years. Since this place was built.'

Steel kicked the earth wall of the ruined fort. 'It is not the way that gentlemen like to fight. When that war ended gentlemen drew up rules for the conduct of war designed to prevent such a thing ever happening again. Well, Jacob. Today we threw away the rule book. Now it's up to men like you and me to make sure that there's still such a thing as honour on a battlefield.'

'We have to write our own rules, you mean, Sir?'

'Our own rules. Yes. That's it exactly.'

Steel looked down at the broken body of the young Grenadier that lay at his feet. 'If we must fight in such a way as this, Jacob, then at least let's do it with honour. God knows this life is short enough. We might as well take pride in what we do.'

He raised his sword and, stooping to pick up a length of neck cloth that lay on the ground, wiped the big blade clean of blood, before sliding it firmly back into the scabbard.

'And now, Sarn't, I believe there was the matter of a cask of wine.'

'Ale, Sir.'

Steel laughed.

'Ale, Jacob. Find what's left of the platoon and

be sure to tell Mister Hansam where we're going. I think it's time to see what the good people of Donauwörth have to offer us.'

TWO

General Van Styrum was dead. Cut clean through the skull by a French officer's sword the moment he reached the ramparts. Goors too had been sent to oblivion with a bullet through his brain and with him a score more of the army's senior officers. In all six lieutenant-generals were dead, five more wounded, together with four major-generals and twenty-eight brigadiers and colonels.

Steel counted off in his head the names of close on a hundred lieutenants and captains, among them some old friends. Names that now stood as undeniable proof of their death on the hand-written list of officer casualties pinned that morning to one of the beams of the wooden-framed inn which served as temporary officers' mess for James Ferguson's Brigade of Marlborough's army. To Steel's surprise Mordaunt had survived, though God alone knew how. His element of the Guards had been decimated in throwing itself time and again against the French breastworks until the men had to tread upon piles of their own dead and dying to advance.

The victors' entry into Donauwörth had not been as easy as they had presumed it might. The French garrison had only abandoned the defences when they realized that the allies' efforts to bridge the Danube were sure to cut them off from the rest of their army. Then they had run; a pell-mell rattle of a retreat to join the main army. That had been two days ago. The cautious, curious townspeople had welcomed in the British redcoats and allied soldiers, uncertain of their fate and with recent memories of the slaughter of another war fresh in their minds. They needn't have worried. For the time being even the roughest elements of Marlborough's army had had enough of killing. Besides, pursuit of the French and Bavarians would be impossible until the engineers had finished their bridges. So the soldiers settled down to a few days of unexpected rest. Most of the officers had managed to secure billets within the private houses of wealthy merchants. For the NCOs and other ranks more humble dwellings or stables and outhouses made comfortable enough barracks. The wounded, who had not been transported by wagon or walked or crawled back to the headquarters camp at N"rdlingen while the battle still raged, had been placed in tents outside the city walls, such were their numbers.

Steel knew that a third of them would not survive their horrific wounds. Even now, three days after the fighting, the burial parties were still at work and the bitter-sweet stench of death hung heavy in the air. It was the moment that Steel liked least in any war. That time directly after a battle, when he was as conscious of loss as much as any victory. This was a fallow period when the men might be capable of anything, from drunkenness to desertion—or worse. For those who had survived the attack—officers and other ranks—the few days of rest while the engineers rebuilt the destroyed bridge spelt a welcome chance to enjoy local food and drink, not to mention the soft sheets and sensual delights available at the city's whorehouses. Steel presumed that it was at one such establishment that he might now find most of his company, but he was not of a mind to try. They were not the type to let the lull persuade them that a better life lay away from the army. It was three hours since he had left Slaughter in command of the half-company on the improvised drill ground behind the city walls. The men deserved their simple pleasures and he knew that the Sergeant would keep them straight.

For his own part, while he was not averse to the diversions of the flesh, the horror of the last few days had dispelled any such craven desires within Steel. They had in fact quite the opposite effect that victory in battle would have normally had on his libido. And so, rather than seek out the upmarket brothels where so many of his fellow officers were currently being entertained, he had come with Hansam to sit in this tavern. To drink and talk and savour these precious few hours of freedom. Steel gazed long at the names on the casualty list. He thought of home, of the news of the death of these officers reaching into so many vicarages and manor houses. Of mothers and sisters disconsolate with grief and fathers who gazed rheumy-eyed out of windows and over empty fields. Turning, he crossed to a table and sat down beside his friend. He took a long draught of wine, scratching at the irritating bites on his neck. Perhaps tomorrow he would find somewhere to have his uniform cleaned. His shirts and stocks at least. At length he spoke:

'This is a sad moment for Britain, Henry.'

Hansam, who had been staring into his wine, deep in thought, turned to his friend.

'Sad, yes, but surely you must admit, it was a glorious victory.'

'I doubt whether the Tories back in London will see it that way.'

'You cannot be sure, Jack. 'Tis said that the enemy lost 7,000 and another 2,000 drowned in our pursuit. Every day more bodies are being washed ashore. And we have taken nigh on 3,000 prisoners.'

'But, Henry, what of our losses? Look at this butcher's bill. Six thousand men dead and wounded and 1,500 of them English and Scots. One and a half thousand men. I tell you, I never knew a day so costly.'

'And on account of it we have the town and all that it contains. We have stores, Jack, and a strong strategic base. And you know there was no other way.'

He turned to attract the attention of the pretty, buxom teenage girl who was moving deftly between the tables of red-coated officers, balancing in the crook of each well-muscled forearm two pewter pitchers of wine.

'Another one over here. Madame. If you will, Madamoiselle. *S'il vous plait. Une autre, ici.*'

He turned to Steel:

'D'ye know any German, Jack?'

Steel grinned and shook his head. Hansam tried again.

'Ah. Yes. That's it. *Bitte.* Wine, *bitte.*'

The girl nodded at him and smiled. Hansam turned back to Steel.

'There, that should do it. But, Jack. You

especially must know that there is no point in regret. There was no other way. We would have been held up there for a week. Ten days. With many more casualties, and far less glory.'

'Glory? We lost good men on that hill, Henry. Morris. Roberts. Perkins. I visited the wounded this morning in that butchers' shop they call the field hospital.'

'But we won the battle, dammit Jack. It's war. Just war. You of all men know that. Ours is a bloody business and that was a job well done. Besides . . .'

He was drowned out by a guffaw of laughter and furious applause from a nearby table. Steel looked across at the source of the noise. Major the Honourable Aubrey Jennings was clearly in his element. This was just the sort of opportunity for which he had been waiting. A real chance to puff his ego and spread word of his military prowess throughout the army.

Jennings sat at the head of a long table, surrounded by the eager faces of a dozen rosy-cheeked junior officers from his regiment and others of the Brigade. They listened with rapt attention to his exploits in the recent engagement. Boys of sixteen, seventeen, nineteen, all of whom had been at the rear of the engagement and were thirsty now for a flavour of the battle they had missed and which they would re-tell back in England, with a few key embellishments placing themselves in the centre of the action. That was, after all, the way to win the ladies. Jennings placed his hands on the table, sweeping them this way and that in movements of apparent strategic significance, knocking plates and cutlery to the

38

floor.

'And so we climbed past the first ditch and advanced on up the slope.' Jennings flashed his brown eyes to make sure they were still listening. They were his best feature. In truth his only attractive feature in a thin, sallow face with high cheekbones that gave him a slightly ape-like appearance.

Jennings had joined the army to avoid a minor scandal involving a simple serving girl. His father, whose memory he worshipped as that of a saint, (though in truth he had been far from saintly) had purchased Aubrey the commission as a Captain a few weeks before his death in a hunting accident in a new regiment being raised by his brother-in-law, Sir James Farquharson. The family estate—20,000 acres in Hampshire, mostly arable, had naturally passed automatically to Jennings' older brother. For his own small but adequate living he was forced to rely upon the revenue from some modest London property bequeathed by his mother and whatever he could glean, by whatever means possible, from his new profession. So, he thought, it had all come right in the end. If he could only keep himself from serious injury on the field of battle, he might return home a hero and then who would bother over the matter of a twopenny whore? Besides, the army suited him.

In Jennings' mind he had been born a soldier. There was something about the uniform that felt so reassuringly familiar. Something about the cut and the feel of it that transformed him whenever he put it on. It fitted his frame so well. He was not after all a muscular man, not athletic in the conventional sense, but he considered himself to cut a real dash in the scarlet coat of Farquharson's. It was true that Jennings looked every bit a soldier, and he certainly acted the part.

In the few months he had served with the colours he developed his own philosophy of war. Naturally, as he had observed other officers do, he tended to avoid the hot spots of battle. Why sacrifice yourself when good officers like him were always in short supply? He must be preserved. You might throw the men into the thick of it by all means. That after all was their purpose. They were expendable. Scum. No more than gutter scrapings. But officers like him were rare.

Jennings knew that officers were born to it and was assured by his Sergeant, a morally decrepit ex-highwayman named Stringer, whose company he tolerated, and who, when he was not out whoring followed him like an obsequious terrier, that the men looked up to him. Those who did not could be certain that he would make them suffer until they did. Either that or they would die.

The other sergeants he knew did not bear him any real respect, but they still looked up to him as an officer and that was tolerable. His brother officers he thought a mixed bunch. Fair-weather friends mostly whose affections were easily bought. The younger subalterns and captains he knew he could keep in his thrall with tales of high valour. The older ones he was able to charm with flattery and weasel words. Only one officer troubled Jennings. Steel was different. Steel was a problem. A problem that he simply did not understand. And when Jennings could not understand something there were only two solutions. Ignore it or snuff it out.

For his part, Steel had always made a point of avoiding Jennings and had taken pains to keep at a distance since joining the regiment. Of course with the Major's seniority there was no avoiding taking orders, although the Grenadiers were allowed to operate on their own more than any other company. Steel had hoped that with the correct degree of propriety he might be able to avoid any confrontation until either of them was killed in battle or transferred out of the regiment.

Now however, it seemed as if that hope might have proved in vain.

Listening closely to Jennings' boasts, Steel chewed on a piece of tobacco and tried to block the false words from his ears. But there was no getting away from the Major this morning. His blood was up.

'. . . One particularly big French Lieutenant lunged at me. I parried and thrust home and *voilà* . . . Another of King Louis' favourites had gone to meet his maker . . .'

Jennings slammed his fist hard down on the table. Steel spat the tobacco out on to the filthy floor and spoke under his breath.

'I'd like to help him meet his maker.'

Hansam smiled, and fixed Steel's gaze with a raised eyebrow:

'Now, Jack. Control yourself. Surely you do not dare to question the conduct of our brave Major?'

'You know Henry as well as I do. You were there. Remind me. Where was the good Major Jennings when we were fighting on the ramparts? He was standing at the foot of the hill with the colours and the remainder of the regiment. I tell you. He dishonours the memory of our fallen

41

comrades. You and I have not come 400 miles, have not marched down here through the Moselle and the Rhine to listen to some popinjay strut such falsehoods.'

'Jack. If you want my advice, you'd best to leave it. Allow him his moment. The truth will out when we engage the enemy again, which I trust will not be before too long. He's quite harmless. I tell you, in the next fight he'll get a French bullet through what little brain he possesses. Now where's that damned wine Madame. *Ici*. Here. Oh. *Bitte*. D'you think she saw me? I tell you, Jack the only unhappy people in this town are the regimental sutlers. And I can't say I'm displeased. Have another glass of wine.

'They take every opportunity to rob us blind, invent the prices on everything in the mess to double that you might pay at White's. And then, the moment we have the option to pay the natives for our grog what happens, the sutlers run complaining to the quartermaster-general with cries of "unfair" and not proper practice. Are you listening?'

But Steel had not been listening to Hansam for some time. He had ears only for Jennings, who had become still more eloquent in the account of his personal bravery at the Schellenberg.

Two of subalterns sprang to their feet vying to buy their hero another bottle.

'Well, gentlemen, what a fight it was, indeed. And now I reckon you'll all be in line for promotion. Terrible losses. Terrible. So many brave officers. But manage it we did. And with what an army.' He turned to a young, pink-faced Lieutenant.

'Eh, Fortescue? What think you of our allies? Prussia, Holland, Austria. We fight a war of allies. Of course I saw little of them on the ramparts . . .'

As Jennings droned on, Steel, distracted for a moment, began to wonder. It had been a feat to keep the army together in the face of such an assault. He had heard that there had been some dissent among the commanders as to whether or not to attack. He knew the whole enterprise to manage the Austrians and persuade the Dutch to Bavaria had been Marlborough's doing. The Dutchmen had a reputation for not shifting off their own soil so it was nothing short of a miracle.

Jennings' voice rose again above the hubbub of the room.

'. . . For all the use they are. The Dutch you know have never been good soldiers. And as for the Prussians . . . No give me an Englishman every time . . .'

Steel wondered whether Jennings had forgotten that he himself served in a Scottish regiment and if he was aware that Marlborough's army included more Irish and Scots than it did pure-bred Englishmen. The thought merely increased his anger. If there was one thing guaranteed to incur Steel's wrath it was officers who pretended their bravery. He had long suspected Jennings to be just such a soldier. Son of the brother-in-law of Sir James Farquharson, Jennings was *de facto* second in command of the regiment despite only recently arriving from home duty in London and quite fresh to the campaigning life. Steel knew that Jennings had paid his way into the regiment with substantially more than the usual 1,000 pounds required for a Captain's commission and clearly he believed that his money would buy him not only a company but glory too. Jennings' voice rose again:

'So there I was, standin' on the very parapet of the defences and I turned to my men. "Men," I says. "Men, come with me now and we shall write such a chapter in Britain's history as has never been seen. I intend to take this place and you shall be with me." And then, with a great huzzah we were upon them. I can honestly say that my blade did not rest until the job was done. And so many dead. What brave boys. Quite tragic . . .'

Jennings looked across to where Steel was sitting. Noticing the look of revulsion on his face and realizing that here might be an opportunity, he called across:

'Ah, Mister Steel. I had quite forgotten you. I was just enlightening these young gentlemen as to the nature of our late engagement. Gentlemen, Mister Steel was also there at the Hill of the Bell. Although I am not certain as to in precisely which part of the fight he took part. Perhaps you would care to enlighten us, Mister Steel. Were you with the pioneers, or the baggage, perhaps?'

Steel said nothing.

Jennings grinned and took a sip from his glass of Moselle.

'A fine wine this, d'you not think, Steel? Or perhaps you do not care for it. You would prefer something more robust. A bottle of Rhenish rotgut perhaps, or a nipperkin of molasses ale? I liberated this wine me'self from the cellars of the French commandant. You are most welcome to a glass, Steel. But do not feel obliged to accept. I do not suppose you are in a position to return my hospitality.'

It was too much.

'I'm not sure that I properly understand you, Sir.'

'You must do, Sir. For you forget, I am Adjutant of the regiment. I have sight of all the company accounts and unless you have rectified the matter, Mister Steel, your mess account remains unpaid from last month. And, as I recall, the month before that. Am I not right?'

Two of the subalterns laughed, briefly, then stopped, realizing that perhaps they had gone too far and that this was no longer a laughing matter. Then there was silence.

Jennings coughed and continued:

'Of course, should you be in erm . . . difficulty, I would be only too happy to oblige with a small money order. For a reasonable consideration, of course.'

He smiled, narrowed his eyes, looked directly at Steel and took another sip of wine.

Steel stiffened with rage. Hansam, who had observed the conversation, now closed his eyes and was surprised by the calmness of his friend's reply:

'I have no need of your assistance, Major Jennings. I am informed that I shall profit from my share of the bounty due to my part in the assault party. And surely you too will benefit from that action. Or was I perhaps correct in assuming that you had actually taken no part in the fight?'

The party of subalterns let out an audible gasp. Jennings reddened, although what proportion was from embarrassment and what from indignation was not clear.

'How dare you, Sir. You imply that I am a liar. Not merely that but a dissembling coward. Have a care how you trespass upon the reputation of a gentleman. As I am a reasonable fellow, I shall allow you to retract your accusation. Otherwise you must face my wrath, and the consequences.'

Steel pushed forward, knocking over the table and its contents. A wine bottle and two glasses smashed on the stone floor. The serving girl ran into the kitchens and the officers began to move away from the vortex of the argument. Steel spoke.

'You will retract that comment, Sir.'

'I think not, Mister Steel.'

'You will retract that comment, Major Jennings, and your previous slur on my character, or pay for your insolence with your life. Although it will hardly be a fair fight. Nevertheless, you might provide me with a few moments' sport. That is if you have the stomach for any fight. Which I very much doubt.'

Hansam spoke, quietly:

'Jack. Do remember, duelling is not lawful. You will be court-martialled.'

Across the smoke-filled room the other officers had now stopped talking. But to those who knew the two men their confrontation came as no surprise. They knew that Jennings had long marked out Steel for just such an opportunity. And they, like Jennings, were puzzled by this curious, charismatic young man who had exchanged a prestigious commission in the Foot Guards—a position many of them would have killed for—for a lieutenancy in Farquharson's unproven battalion of misfits.

It was plain to Jennings how he himself might profit from his association with his uncle's regiment. He knew that money was to be made

46

from the quartermasters' books. Loss of stores; natural wastage. That sort of thing. Good cloth, ammunition and vittels fetched a good price on the open market and there were plenty in the regiment willing to help him for a few shillings, even if it did mean their risking the lash. And Jennings was sure that he would be able to keep himself out of harm's way, as he had done yesterday. But people like Steel always seemed to be out to spoil his plans. Steel must be done away with and here was the opportunity, if somewhat sooner than he had expected. Jennings looked about the tavern and called to a red-coated officer.

'Charles. A moment of your time.'

The man, a tall, lean individual with fine-boned features and a nervous twitch in the left side of his face, Steel recognized as Captain Charles Frampton of the regiment's number two company. He knew him to be an ally of Jennings and watched as he now took his leave of his companions and walked across to the florid Major.

As the two men whispered, Hansam took Steel by the elbow.

'Jack. You cannot do this. Not here. Not in public. If you must, then issue a challenge. Have it done in private. Of course, I shall second you. But not here. This is to invite disaster.'

Steel pulled free of his grasp. 'Too late.'

Jennings had taken off his coat and handed it to the newcomer. 'Mister Steel, you are acquainted with Charles Frampton. You have your own second?'

Steel nodded at the newcomer.

Hansam stepped forward.

'Ah, Lieutenant Hansam. We are indeed

47

honoured.'

Frampton muttered into Jennings' ear: 'Careful, Aubrey. I hear that he is a damned fine soldier.'

Jennings stiffened and, still smiling at Steel, spoke in a similar whisper to his second. 'My dear Charles. Taking part in a few scraps in the Swedish war does not turn a man into a hero.'

'They say, Aubrey, that he accounted for forty Russians single-handed at the battle of Narva. And that after Riga the King of Sweden himself presented him with a gold medal.'

'Narva. Riga. What nonsense. Those names mean nothing. And now are we not allied to the Danes? Sweden's enemies. I hardly think that Mister Steel will want to boast much of his relationship with the Swedish throne. Besides. Killing a few Russian savages? That's not real war. Not the way gentlemen do battle.'

He drew from his cuff a crisp, white lace handkerchief and applied it gently to his delicate nose. 'And that is precisely what I intend to demonstrate.'

Jennings walked forward.

'Think now, Steel. Do you really want this end? Think on it. Do you really want to die in a tavern brawl? Were you aware perhaps that I had studied in London, under no less than the renowned Monsieur Besson? Perhaps you are familiar with him. He has taught the *arme blanche* in most of the courts of Europe.'

Steel did not reply. He merely drew his sword and assumed the *en garde* position.

Jennings instantly did the same. As Hansam hastened to Steel's side, Jennings' second walked to meet him. The two men shook hands and

48

retired a few paces behind their friends.

The room had fallen silent now. Tables and chairs were pushed aside and most of the officers who had not already left began to make their exits into the street until only a small group of unwary subalterns remained. The staff too had long retreated behind the bar. The silence was broken suddenly by the sharp clang of metal on metal as Jennings tapped Steel's blade.

Steel disengaged, circling Jennings' sword with a deft flick of the wrist and made a slashing cut across the centre to unsettle his opponent. But Jennings had seen the move coming and side-stepped, returning to the *en garde* with the tip of his blade pointing directly at Steel's side. He might have plunged it deep in, and the fact that he did not made it clear to Steel that he was only playing. Jennings spoke.

'Oh come now, Steel. That was but a poke. I would not make use of such a thrust but with a ruffian. Have you nothing better to offer me?'

Steel raised his arm to the tierce position so that his blade was pointing directly downwards at Jennings, leaving his own body apparently unguarded. Jennings slapped at the blade with a clang of metal on metal and levelled his own sword, which came within an inch of Steel's abdomen. Both men were sweating hard now. They pulled away for an instant, regaining their balance. Then circled and moved their blades around each other without touching. Steel's sword made a marked contrast to Jennings' lighter, standard issue infantry sword. But what it lacked in weight, the Major's weapon made up in speed. Steel recovered his blade into the cavalry *en garde*, ready to slice at Jennings, but as he did so his opponent made a neat side-step and brought the tip of his own sword swiftly into contact with the Lieutenant's arm, tearing the cloth of his shirt. Within seconds a thin red line had begun to darken the white cloth. Frampton spoke.

'A hit to Major Jennings. First blood. Continue, gentlemen.'

Steel, appearing unaware of the damage to his arm, although actually in acute pain, took care to keep his blade as it was—pointing heavenward and poker-straight. If only, he thought, if only he will make one small error. Then I shall have him. He knew how easily his great blade could fall and with what force. How, given but a split-second his cut would sever Jennings' sword arm and finish this business. But he could not find a way in. The man was too good. For all his foppishness and evident cowardice, it was clear that Jennings had not lied about his prowess with a sword. Steel began to walk to the right, encouraging his opponent to do the same until both men were circling slowly on the spot. Now. He thought. Now. If I can take the advantage. Just move for an instant to the left and then it will all be over. He prepared to make his move. Shifted the balance on his feet. Now. Now is the moment. The air hung heavy with anticipation. Now. It must be, now. But before Steel could strike the door of the tavern flew open with such force that its studded wooden surface banged hard against the wall.

The sudden noise broke the spell. Steel and Jennings stopped their dance of death and, frozen to the spot, turned their heads towards the light. Before they had a chance to renew the fight, the room had filled with a dozen redcoats armed with muskets. While two of them levelled their bayonets at the duellists, the others formed two lines through which another figure now entered the inn. A Colonel, a man in his late forties, clad in a neatly tailored dark blue coat, trimmed with red and gold lace. A Colonel on the British Staff.

The man strode forward purposefully towards Steel and Jennings, a grave expression on his face.

Hansam, moving quickly, pushed in behind Jennings to stand in front of the Colonel, attempting to block his view. He began to speak, quickly.

'Good day, Sir. May I present myself. Lieutenant Henry Hansam of Farquharson's. I imagine, Colonel, that you are wondering quite reasonably what exactly is taking place and I would not blame you one bit for entertaining such thoughts. What you see here, Colonel, what in fact Lieutenant Steel here was doing, Sir, was merely demonstrating to Major Jennings the relative virtues of the broadsword as opposed to the rapier.'

He wrested Steel's sword from his grasp and proferred it to the Colonel.

'This is the very sword in question you see, Sir. Quite a Queen amongst blades, would you not agree?' Hansam pushed the hilt of the sword closer to the Colonel's face, inviting inspection. 'It was made by Ferrara, Sir, d'you see?'

But the Colonel did not care to see the sword. Fixing his gimlet eyes on Steel's, he spoke. 'Lieutenant. Perhaps you would care to explain to me yourself exactly what is going on here. You are aware are you not of the penalty for duelling?

Particularly among officers of Her Majesty's army in the field. And you appear to have drawn blood.'

Steel looked at his arm. The shirt around the cut was stained a deep red. 'Sir. Yes, Sir.'

'Yes, Sir. A court martial, Sir, with death as the ultimate penalty.'

The Colonel turned to Jennings. And you, Major Jennings. It is Major Jennings, is it not? You too should know better than this.'

'I. Colonel . . .' Jennings thought fast. 'I have to say that I was provoked, Sir.'

'That is as may be, Major. But you are the senior officer present, are you not?'

The subalterns attempted as best they could to melt into the shadows. The Colonel did not wait for Jennings' reply.

'Why don't you just put up your sword, Sir, and we'll say no more of it. And what of you, Mister Steel. What of you? I think that you had better come with me. Your sword, if I may, Lieutenant.'

Steel took his sword from Hansam, reversing it so that he held only the blade, and handed it hilt first to the Colonel who, signalling to two armed sentries to bring up the rear, led the way out of the tavern followed by Steel and Hansam. Steel presumed the worst. Jennings of course could be exonerated. Related to Farquharson and with power in high places, there was little he could do, save perhaps kill his commander, that would merit any serious punishment within the army. But Steel was a mere Lieutenant, of lower origins and with neither property nor capital. Perhaps he might be made an example of, in this army where only the harshest lessons would set the precedent.

Outside in the busy, foul-smelling street, where

in the thin drizzle the townspeople mingled cautiously with the soldiers and the street vendors and tradesmen tried to go about their business as best they could and make the most of this sudden influx of customers, a troop of red-coated dragoons trotted past the group emerging from the tavern and Steel watched as a skinny urchin picked the pocket of an off-duty soldier.

Hawkins turned to Steel and to his surprise, gave him a wide grin. He motioned to the escort to leave them, returned the great broadsword to its owner and spoke again. This time though his voice had a quite different tone to that he had used in the tavern.

'I'm sorry to have alarmed you in that way, Mister Steel. Forgive me. Perhaps it was just as well that I arrived when I did.'

He looked at Steel's shoulder. 'You might really have got into trouble. Best get that seen to. Allow me to introduce myself. Hawkins. Colonel James Hawkins, late of Colonel Hamilton's regiment, currently on attachment to the Allied Staff.'

Steel had heard of this Colonel Hawkins and knew his reputation both in the field and out. It was said that as a younger man, during the wars of the Grand Alliance, Hawkins had taken the fort of Dixmude all but single-handed. His capacity for drink was also well known and Steel could see from his now somewhat corpulent build and ruddy complexion that the latter at least was certainly justified. But whatever his predilections, there was precious little that James Hawkins did not know about soldiering. For all his stoutness, he still cut a dashing figure and his round face seemed to wear a fixed smile, helped by the subtle line of an old scar which ran up the side of his left cheek and which at the same time concealed behind it any inkling of what his true thoughts might have been.

He looked at Steel and the crease of a smile changed to another grin.

Steel looked puzzled.

'Don't worry, Lieutenant. You are not on a charge. Though I can't say that I'm not tempted. You've led me a dance almost as merry as that you were leading our Major Jennings. No, I have sought you out not for punishment but for a quite different reason. Come. We'll go to my quarters.'

He turned to Hansam.

'Oh, Lieutenant Hansam. You may accompany us, if you wish. Come along. We do not mind. Do we Steel?'

With Steel and Hawkins walking at the front, the three officers walked together through the cobbled streets, mostly in silence although from time to time Hawkins made a comment about the inordinate amount of filth in the gutters, the changeable weather and variable quality of the local wine. They took first a left and then a right turn, ducking beneath the open galleries of the half-timbered shops and houses, until at length they arrived at a modest house whose merchant owner, wherever he might now be, had evidently spent some effort and no little money in embellishing its façade with neo-classical motifs in the latest style.

'My servant found it. It is a little *de trop*, don't you think. But still it's comfortable enough.'

Hawkins showed the two men into the hall and through to the parlour which showed similar signs of 'improving' design. He motioned for them to sit before the fire and poured three large glasses of wine.

'Now gentlemen. Or more specifically, Lieutenant Steel, to our purpose. The battle is won and you gentlemen, whatever Major Jennings might say, played a great part in its winning. It was a glorious victory, but mark you, at a price. In Vienna the Emperor talks already of making Marlborough a Prince. The Queen herself, I dare say, has written to him. We may have won a battle and strategically are in a good position. But gentlemen, in London we are undone. Fifteen hundred dead Britons does not make pretty reading. The Tories will say that Marlborough is finished. They will ask why so many men should have fallen to take one hill. And soon they will start to call for his dismissal. We need to move fast before any such harm can be done. We must persuade the Elector, by military might, to come over to us and abandon his French allies or we must frighten him into submission. For both we need an army that is fit to fight.

'But there is another problem. To advance we must be supplied. This town with its alehouses and courtesans may seem like the Elysian Fields to you gentlemen. But the troops are wanting. There is no bread. Flour cannot be got. Do you know how many hundredweight of bread a day this army requires merely to march, let alone fight? I will tell you. Sixty thousand men need 900 hunderweight of flour. Of course, we have our field commissary from the agency of commissioners of supply and transport. We have our agents also. And they're all admirable men in their field: Solomon and Moses Medina. And His Grace the Duke of Würtemberg has sent to his country for 200 wagons to help bring on the stores. But first gentlemen, we must have the stores themselves. It appears that flour cannot be got from the usual channels within less than three weeks. And without flour we have no bread and without bread', he paused 'without bread we have no army. Brigadier Baldwin has been instructed to get all the corn he can find and lay it in the magazines at Neuberg. But we need flour immediately, or the army will starve. And that, if you'll permit me, Mister Steel, is where you come in.'

Steel was perplexed. Having pardoned him for what was a court-martial offence, the Colonel now appeared to be commissioning him as some sort of quartermaster. Before he could ask however, Hawkins went on.

'You will assemble your half-company of Grenadiers, Mister Steel, and you will take yourself off to the little village of Sattelberg. It's around five days' march from here, south-west, across the Lech and past Aicha. I don't expect that you'll run into any of the enemy. They're much further north. Even the Bavarians. At Sattelberg you will meet up with a merchant. A Bavarian, by the name of Kretzmer. Nasty piece of work if you ask me and in the pay of both sides, unless I am mistaken. Which I rarely am. But I do have good reason to believe that he'll be able to sell you some flour. And that's what matters. At this moment I truly believe that I'd deal with the devil to get hold of enough flour to feed the army. You must of course check that it's good. Oh, don't worry. I know you're no expert. I'll be sending a cook with you—my own man—to tell the stuff.'

Steel's face had coloured. Hawkins saw it.

'A little more wine? It is rather stuffy in here.'

While Hawkins refilled their glasses, Steel stared intently at the painted black-and-white chequer-boarded floor and Hansam wandered across to the window, pretending to fix his gaze on the skyline.

Eventually, Steel spoke: 'Allow me, Colonel Hawkins, to make certain that I have this quite straight in my mind. You take me away from a matter of honour, in the face of my brother officers, in the face of the regiment and the brigade. You order me to abandon a duel, albeit illegal, which I fought as a consequence of having been grossly insulted and physically harmed. And you do so in order to put me in charge of a detachment of requisition of men from the finest company in the British army, to get flour for the army's bloody bread?'

Hawkins raised his eyebrows. He smiled bemusedly and thought about it. 'Yes. Quite so, Mister Steel. You are right. Have you a question?'

Hansam muttered something under his breath, but Steel continued. 'Yes, I have a question. Is this, Colonel, all the reward I get for my part in the taking of that bloody hill?'

He pointed towards the window beyond which they could see the outline of the Schellenberg, towering over the town. 'Is this then all my bounty?'

He slammed his glass down on the table. 'By God, Sir, I . . . I'll . . .'

Hansam, moved to action, placed a firm hand on his friend's arm.

Hawkins smiled. He had known for a while

about Steel. Had noted the mention of his name in connection with some matter of honour here, a modest act of bravery there. It was his job to take notice of such things. To mark out men who might otherwise not come to the attention of the Commander-in-Chief. For this was an army in the making and Hawkins' brief was to find the men to lead it. He had been waiting for this moment for some time and had known that sooner or later it would come. He had hoped that when it did Steel would not let him down. And he had not been disappointed. The Colonel spoke gently.

'Yes. I can see that my sources were quite right about you, Mister Steel. You have a temper that knows no concept of rank. In any other circumstances, much as I like you, I would probably have had you taken out and shot for insubordination and threat. But at the present moment, I can see that you are precisely the man we need.'

Steel stared at him, quizzically.

'You'll hear more? Oh yes. There is more required of you. Much more.' Steel frowned. Then began to laugh, shaking his head. 'Colonel Hawkins. Do not, please insult me afresh. You are playing with me and this surely is not the conduct of officers. What can you mean now I wonder? Do you perhaps wish me also to procure a case of perfume for your wife. Or perhaps a trinket for your mistress?'

Steel realized he had gone too far. Hawkins though, merely stared at him, and chose his words with care.

'Mister Steel, I have no wife. Or at least not any longer. And since she passed on I have not had

58

eyes for any other woman.' He paused, poured himself a glass of wine and took a long draught before continuing.

'I do, however have a proposition for you.'

Steel nodded. 'I am truly sorry to hear about your wife, Sir. And sorry too if I caused you offence. But believe me, Colonel, whatever you are come to offer me, I am certainly in no position to undertake favours.'

'This is no favour, Mister Steel. It is a direct order. From His Grace.'

Steel stopped and moved Hansam's arm from its grip on his. 'You come from Marlborough?'

Hawkins nodded, smiling.

'Then do please continue, Colonel.'

'His Grace is quite aware of your prominent part in the late battle, Steel. And of the advancement it might justify. Advancement which might be particularly alacritous should you feel able to carry off this other . . . little business.'

Steel nodded.

'You are aware no doubt that some ten years ago His Grace was imprisoned in the Tower of London on a charge of being a Jacobite. That of course we now know to be utterly false. Do we not, Mister Steel?'

The Colonel gazed at him hard, awaiting a reply.

'Do we not, Mister Steel?'

'We do, Colonel.'

'We do. Of course we do. Quite right again. However. And this is where you come in. When you encounter our friend the flour merchant you will find that he also has something else on his person for you to deliver to me. It is a certain

59

paper—a letter shall we say—which, were it to fall into the wrong hands would give certain parties at home in London the opportunity to engineer the removal of His Grace from command of this army. And that, Steel, is a state of affairs which I am sure you will agree would be no less than catastrophic.'

'Sir.'

'So now we come to the crux of the matter. What we would like you to do Steel, what His Grace requires you to do, is to relieve this merchant of his letter and return it to its rightful owner. If you do not then he will sell it to the French, who will pass it to the Duke's enemies, of which there are a good few. And that will be the end for Marlborough, the army and you. It's as simple as that. You'll do it?'

Steel was silent. He thought for a moment. 'May I ask what the letter contains, Sir? To whom it is addressed.'

'No. You may not ask that. But I shall say merely that it contains material sufficient to destroy Marlborough forever and perhaps even to condemn him to a traitor's death on the gallows.'

There was another pause. Steel spoke again. 'May I ask, Colonel, as to why you have chosen me for this . . . honour?'

'A good question. But it was not merely my choice. You are the Duke's man now. Your name came to Marlborough from London. From no less than his own wife. You were recommended I believe by someone in the Duchess's inner circle as a man who is utterly trustworthy and loyal to the Duke's cause. And as you know there are too many in this army who would not perhaps fulfill those precise criteria. Eh, Hansam?'

'Quite so, Colonel.'

Steel walked across to the window and gazed out on to the town below. So that was it. Steel had thought that by resigning his commission in the Guards, by removing himself from St James's, he might evade forever the attentions of the woman whose love had first found him a career in the army.

Arabella Moore was the wife of a Director of the Bank of England; a substantial landowner. She had done well for the younger daughter of a West Country parson. But lovely Arabella was fifteen years her husband's junior, and it had been clear for some time to those who spoke of such things in society circles, that for all his wealth and the evident care he took of her, in certain matters her dear husband was unlikely to satisfy his young bride's voracious appetite. Steel had been seduced in an instant by her ravishing looks and infectious gaiety. They had met at a dance in Edinburgh, at Mister Patrick's assembly rooms in the High Street.

Steel had been an impressionable youth of eighteen, she a high-ranking married woman of twenty-eight. Their summer flirtation had grown to become something more and on her return to London, Arabella had been only too happy to pay for her young lover's commission into the Guards. And so, for five glorious years, although careful to be discreet, they had enjoyed each other to the full. And in that time Steel had grown from boy to man, loving his mistress and his regiment with at first an equal passion but gradually realizing that while the bedchamber yielded delights that were gone in an instant, his love affair with the army had somehow blossomed without his knowing it into something altogether more enthralling.

And so he had fallen out of love with Arabella and had spent more time with his other love. Evenings in the mess and mornings at drill. As other men returned from the wars in Flanders and he thrilled to their tales, the parade ground duties which at first had seemed so grand, began to pall. Peace in 1697 seemed to set the seal on his fate. But Steel wanted action and, with a guile learnt from his lover, managed to engineer his way into an attachment to the command of the Swedish army, then newly embarked on a war with Russia. It had been clear though that something more drastic was required to distance himself from Arabella. He had thought that a move to Farquharson's and this new war might suffice. But now she had found him again and with that devilish skill he knew so well had placed him in such a position that he could not possibly refuse the honour offered to him. Recommended for the task directly by Sarah Churchill, his Commander-in-Chief's wife and the Queen's own confidante, he could do nothing but accept this unlooked-for mission, whatever it might bring. He smiled at the impossibility of his situation. How very, very clever she was. He turned to Hawkins. Hansam saw that he was smiling broadly.

'Of course, Colonel, I accept. What else might I do? I am honoured. So tell me, please. When do we start? How many men do I take? Can I choose them? Have you any more precise information? Have we plans? Names?'

Hawkins clapped him on the shoulder.

'Wait, my boy, patience. All in good time, Steel.

More immediately, I have arranged a meeting for you with Marlborough. He wishes to see for himself this man who comes to him so highly recommended. And then you will go. In four days' time.'

Steel raised his eyebrows. Four days. It was time enough, presumably, to gather his men. Hawkins went on:

'And you'll have company. An Ensign of Grenadiers, newly arrived from England. A Mister Williams. A pleasant lad. He's my late wife's nephew. Your Colonel's agreed to take him in. Be sure to take care of him, Steel. Oh, and try to behave yourself. It would do to forget that business with Jennings. You can be sure that you cannot avoid him on this campaign.'

He smiled to himself.

'Just remember that the man's a fool and consider the likelihood that like any fool who serves with the army, he'll meet a fool's death, 'ere long. Do not take the trouble, Steel, to take upon yourself a task which fate has so clearly marked out as a foregone conclusion.'

Steel smiled back at the Colonel. He was warming to the man, but was still unsure as to quite how to take his comment. Whether it was meant in jest or in deadly earnest.

Hawkins laughed. 'And now, gentlemen, we have a war to fight. And I am afraid that I must take my leave of you. Might I suggest that you repair to another establishment. I hear good things of an inn on the other side of the city, close by the bridge, at the sign of the running horse. At least there you are not likely to encounter the good Major. And Steel, you'd best have that arm looked at. You've a busy time ahead of you, and you know how the Commander-in-Chief is most particular about the condition of his officers. Especially those whom he chooses to engage in his personal service. We wouldn't want you to come to any harm before you've even set out.'

THREE

Saluting the sentry posted outside, Colonel Hawkins walked through the shade of the striped entrance awning and into Marlborough's tent. Inside the General Staff stood gathered in silence around their Commander-in-Chief. It was gloomy and unpleasantly humid, the airless atmosphere adding to the inescapable tension of what had evidently been a difficult briefing. Major-General Withers, Goors' deputy, now promoted to command of the Advance Guard, was rubbing nervously at his lapel. Beside him, staring intently at a map stood Henry Lumley, commander of the English horse. Marlborough's own brother Charles, who commanded twenty-four battalions, the bulk of the army, stood talking quietly to Lord Orkney, while in a corner of the tent, on a folding camp chair, sat the Margrave of Baden, his foot bandaged from the wound to his toe he had received at Schellenberg, with his own half-dozen commanders. Marlborough turned to greet the Colonel:

'Ah, Hawkins. Have you any news for us? Do the cannon arrive, at last?'

Hawkins shook his head.

'I am sorry to report, Your Grace, gentlemen, that we have no intelligence save that our last action very much disheartened the enemy. There is of course the important matter of victualling the army. For while our German friends', he smiled at Baden, 'will certainly march on with empty bellies, the British soldier I am afraid will not do without his bread. But I can report that we now have the matter in hand.'

Hawkins lowered his voice.

'There is another matter, Your Grace. That rather delicate matter of which we have spoken before and on which I must speak to you now in person.'

Marlborough nodded to Hawkins and addressed the company:

'Well, gentlemen. That it would seem is that. We are in agreement then. There is no other course of action. And as regards the more pressing matter of the attack on the town of Rain, you are all clear as to your duties?'

The British commanders nodded and quickly took their leave. Baden, it seemed for a moment to Marlborough, might be about to make yet another protest. But then, as if by some miracle, his face grew ashen-white and he closed his eyes. Clearly his wound was giving him considerable pain. Reopening his eyes and leaning on one of his commanders for support, he rose from the chair and with a hasty goodbye left the tent.

Marlborough relaxed and leant back against the table.

Only Hawkins now remained in the tent, along with a single servant clearing away the remains of the hasty breakfast which had preceded their meeting. Marlborough spoke.

'So then, James. I take it that you have informed the officer in question of his mission?'

'Lieutenant Steel, Sir. Yes, he is now fully apprised of what he must do.'

'Good. And you truly think that he can do it, James?'

'I am in no doubt, Sir. I've seen him fight. He is, I am convinced, one of the finest officers in your army.'

'He is something of an individual, I believe.'

'He transferred to Farquharson's from the Guards, his commission into that regiment having been purchased for him by a lady. He's of modest stock, Sir. The second son of a Scots farmer. He has no private income to speak of and he is hungry for patronage and promotion. An ideal man for the job.'

Marlborough toyed with a silver snuff box which lay on the table, opening and closing the lid.

'He is over-familiar with the men. Is that right?'

'I would not have put it quite that way, myself. Although he is perhaps more ready to take the advice of his Sergeant and he shares Your Grace's own concern for the welfare of his soldiers. "Eccentric" they call him in the officers' mess. But the men, and those who have served with him before, say that there are few better than Steel in all your army. And make no mistake, he's a shrewd one, Sir, and a wit. As you will recall, it was your own lady who recommended him to us.'

'That, as you know, James, is quite beside the point. It is my decision to employ Mister Steel in this matter and mine alone. My dear wife must be kept quite apart from the whole affair. For, should he fail in his mission. Should, God forfend, those who wish me ill get hold of that paper, the Duchess must not be implicated in the slightest degree.'

Hawkins sensed that it would be politic to change the subject. He looked up at the map, running his hand across the black squares which represented the towns and villages of the Electorate, which he knew might soon be nothing more than smouldering ruins.

'You are quite set on laying waste to Bavaria?'

Marlborough looked down and tapped the red velvet-covered baton—the symbol of his rank—on the small, polished oak table which had been placed against the wall of the tent.

'I shall dispatch men from this army to burn as many of the towns and villages of Bavaria as we find within reach. Just the houses mind you. We shall spare the woodlands and of course leave anything of the Elector's property. Seeing that still standing can surely only help to turn his own people against him. And the people themselves shall be safe, I will not have any of them harmed. It is mere coercion, not rape, but it is the only way. We must force the Elector's hand. It is of particular sadness to me in a country of such neat domestic husbandry as I have ever seen outside England.'

Hawkins shook his head. 'If you are set on it, then I cannot divert your mind. But this is not warfare as you and I have known it these past twenty years. And if you really want to know my opinion it will not have the effect you believe. The Elector will not turn, whatever you do to his country. And be careful, Your Grace. I know soldiers as well as you do. For all your care of this army, Sir, it is still made up to a large extent of brigands and cut-throats. We shall have to keep a watch on them.'

Sensing how sombre the mood in the tent had now become, Hawkins added with a smile: 'For I know how you hate anything that is not properly accounted for.'

Marlborough laughed. From outside the tent, above the general hubbub, they caught the sound of the drums and fifes of a regimental band striking up to keep the men in good spirits. 'Lillibulero'. Marlborough smiled and began to drum his fingers on the table top. It was a favourite tune.

'You still know how to divert me from my black moods, James. Thank God at least for that. But I am so tired. More tired, my friend than I can possibly remember.' He rubbed hard at his forehead. Pressed his temples together.

'My entire head aches to bursting. My blood is so terribly heated. I think that I shall call for the physician, presently. Did you know that I have had rhubarb and liquorice sent across from England. The Queen herself advised its use to Lady Sarah as a cure for the headache. But, even so, I am not fully persuaded. I am certain that by this evening I shall yet again be compelled to take some quinine. And you know how sick of the stomach that makes me. But even quinine cannot cure what really ails me.'

He looked into Hawkins' eyes with a child's gaze of hopeless yearning.

'You know to what I refer. All my troubles, James. What times have come upon me. And who now remains with me in whom to place my trust? Poor Goors is dead. He, you know, was my chief help in moments such as this. Others too are gone. Tell me who, save you, old friend, who can I now turn to?'

Hawkins placed a gentle hand upon his Commander's shoulder. 'Do not despair, Sir. You are merely unsettled by your headaches. There is hope. As you say, you yet have me. And there is George Cadogan, Your Grace. He has ever been true. And Cardonell too.'

'True, James. Quite true. Cadogan and Cardonell are a constant strength. Yet that is the measure of it. Just so. Two men and yourself, James. That is the sum of my family. How can I know who else to trust? How to know where my enemies may have placed their spies? God, how I long for this business to be over.'

Removing his wig to reveal his closely cropped hair, Marlborough draped it carefully over the stand made for the purpose that stood with his other personal effects on a small console table in the corner of the tent next to his camp-bed. Then he sat down at the table and, resting his elbows on its surface, buried his head in his hands.

Hawkins stared down at him and wondered at the vulnerability of this man in whom the nation, indeed half the civilized world had placed all its hope and trust.

Presently, the Duke raised his face and, pressing his hands, palms down hard against the table, flat on the polished wood, looked directly up at Hawkins.

'We must prevail, James. We must beat the French.'

He paused in the epic silence of his words, knowing that, even with his old friend he must instantly dispel any suspicion that they might not be able to do so. Marlborough continued:

'Oh yes, we shall beat them. That I do firmly believe. But first, I pray to God in heaven that your man Steel will be able to deliver me from the greater personal peril. Or else, truly James, we shall all of us be lost beyond redemption.'

*   *   *

Steel sat in the small tent and carefully inscribed the names of his dead men in the company roster with a neat, tutored script. His soldier-servant, Nate Thomas, sat just within the door flap polishing his master's boots.

Nate liked Mister Steel. Cared for him more than most of the officers in this army in which any gentleman might purchase a command but where precious few officers were gentlemen. Steel he knew to be a fair man. A man who, if he was cool at times, would always give reward where it was due. And he was a real soldier too. Not some trumped-up popinjay like so many of those who took it upon themselves to give commands. All the same, thought Nate, as he spat on the toe of Steel's boot before buffing it again, best to give him a proper shine today. For whatever might be Steel's odd habits, and although he was inclined to behave more like a sergeant at times, Nate knew that he must not have his officer looking untidy on battalion parade. He spat again and began to rub the polish into the leather with a round, even motion, decreasing the size of the circles to

70

produce a glass-like finish. He was staring proudly at his handiwork when Henry Hansam appeared in the entrance. He looked down at the soldier-servant.

'Hard at it, Nate? Making a good job of it. In truth, though, I shouldn't bother if I were you. You know that Mister Steel will have them filthy again two minutes after you've finished.'

He turned to his friend. 'Jack. We have a new travelling companion. Allow me to present Lieutenant Thomas Williams, lately arrived from England to join the regiment. More specifically to join our own company. I give you, our new Ensign.'

With a theatrical flourish, Hansam stepped into the two-man tent, holding open the flap so that his companion might enter. The newcomer was a young officer of perhaps 16 years old, with that distinctive, wiry build that came with the starvation diet prescribed by one of England's finest private schools and a complexion that most readily reminded Steel of ripe strawberries. What most marked Williams out however, was the even brighter hue of his new scarlet coat, as yet unblemished to the drab brick-red worn by the other officers and men of the army, dulled by the dust and mud of campaigning. His crossbelt was whitened to perfection, his cross-plate, sword hilt and scabbard shone fresh from the foundry and his hair was hidden beneath the rich locks of a clean, new full-bottomed chestnut-brown wig that must have cost the best part of a sergeant's annual pay. In short, thought Steel, the boy was perfect cannon fodder.

Steel smiled and rose to greet the new arrival.

'Mister Williams. Or might I say Thomas? Or

71

perhaps you prefer Tom? You must know at once, Tom, that we stand on no great formality in this company.'

'Thank you, Sir. My parents do call me Thomas, but you may call me Tom, if you wish, Sir.'

He was touched by this unusual officer's apparent interest, and surprised. It was one of the rare instances he had found since his arrival in this army of what just might prove to be real friendship.

The younger son of a gentleman farmer from Wiltshire, Thomas Williams, with his lack of ability to absorb either the classics or the Bible and his tendency to colour and stutter when the centre of attention, had seemed from the first an unlikely candidate for the church and so his father had purchased him a commission in Farquharson's Foot. Perhaps in a couple of years' time, if Thomas acquitted himself well, Mr Williams senior would find the additional £300 to raise his son to a full Lieutenancy. Perhaps the army might be the making of him. For the present, however, Tom found himself on the lowest rung of the officer hierarchy and his new comrades had lost no time in letting him know it. Here though, in this curious-looking, strikingly handsome Lieutenant of Grenadiers, with his strange clothes and the unorthodox hair, Thomas Williams sensed that he might have found a kindred spirit, or perhaps at least a guardian angel. He realized that Steel was looking at him very closely.

'Have we met?'

Steel stared hard at Williams' eyes. Looked at the long slant of his nose, the slightly weak chin and tried to place him. Eventually it came. 'Yes. I believe we have. I do know you now. You were with Jennings. At the tavern.'

The boy blushed and looked down at his gleaming shoes. Grasping nervously at his sword knot, Tom said nothing. Then thought the better of it:

'I wasn't exactly "with" Major Jennings, Sir.'

Steel smiled. Perhaps he had underestimated the lad after all. He knew how defend himself in an impossible position.

'Yes. That's good. Well said. And I assume, Tom, that, even if you were not "with him", you knew better than to believe any of his arrogant twaddle?'

Williams looked up, uncertain as to how to take this or how to respond. Was it yet another example of the sort of mess-hall ribaldry to which he was fast becoming accustomed? Were they trying to make him appear a fool yet again, as he had so often been caught out at Eton and only recently, on his first week in the army when a sergeant-major at the depot in England had quite deliberately put him out of step when on parade.

'I . . . I don't quite understand, Sir. I thought that Major Jennings was considered a hero. He said that . . .'

Steel exclaimed and cut in: 'You will hear Major Jennings say many things, Tom. And I dare say it is possible that some of them may well be true. So, if you choose to believe that he is the perfect martial hero he would have you think him, then you must consider that is precisely what our Major Jennings is. He is a hero as drawn on stage by the great Colley Cibber himself, or Sir John Vanbrugh. As perfect a hero as you or I might be likely to see

73

treading the boards at Drury Lane or Dorset Fields on any night of the week, for two shillings.'

Williams frowned.

Hansam chuckled. 'Now, Jack. Don't tease the lad.'

Steel nodded. 'I was forgetting myself. Hero or not, Tom, Major Jennings is a soldier nevertheless, and he will march with us and serve with us beneath the colours and he will stand with us before the shot on the field of battle and take his chances against the French just as we do.'

At the mention of battle Williams turned pale, then smiled, wanly. Steel, noticing his apprehension, attempted to ease the moment by pretending to brush something off his coat.

'Wait. There. Restored to glory. And there is more to soldiering than battle, eh Henry? What think you to the army, Tom?'

'I . . . I think it must be a very grand life, Sir. I think . . . that I shall very much like being a soldier.'

Both the Lieutenants laughed. Steel clapped Williams on the back.

'And I think that perhaps I'll ask you that question again shortly after your first battle. Then we'll see how you reply, Tom, eh? Now, come. Time presses. Permit us to stand you a dish of tea, or something stronger if you will, in what passes for the present for our mess. Nate. My boots.'

After Steel had pulled on the shining boots and finished adjusting the other elements of his dress, the three men walked out of the tent. Before them, reflecting the pale sunshine, lay a mass of similar white tents, laid out in symmetrical lines and grids: the entire British army encamped under canvas in its temporary home. It was as if, Steel thought, a small English town had been transported to the heart of Bavaria. Along the alleyways that ran between the rows of tents bewigged officers strolled in conversation while among them dozens of children—the offspring of camp followers—ran and played, sometimes pursued by their desperate mothers. Other women sat nursing babies or were busy washing and steaming the lice-infested clothes of husbands and families or cooking suspicious-looking rations in great iron pots. Soldiers sat beside their tents darning their uniforms and attending to minor wounds and the blisters and sores which inevitably followed from a long march. In separate lines, tradesmen and craftspeople sat before their own tents making good the accoutrements required to keep 30,000 men in a battle-ready state. And with this vision of industry and idleness came the unmistakable noise and aroma of camp life. The staccato clack of metal on metal, the whinnying of the horses, the shrieks of the children, sharp against an undercurrent of chatter and music and rising above it all the not altogether unpleasant stench of food, sweat, horses and humanity. Steel watched as carts filled with provisions rumbled past the lines while others standing ready for the wounded from whatever battle was next to come, were cleaned as best they could by the sutlers of the blood and gore left by their previous unfortunate occupants.

It was a scene being enacted throughout the south German states that morning, and across the French border, Steel knew, in the camp of every army: British, French, Hanoverian, Prussian, Bavarian and the rest. But here, he thought, something was subtly different. Here, he knew that before the tent lines had been laid, the site had been carefully chosen by keen-eyed civilian commissaries sent out by Marlborough himself. And close behind them followed the army: always setting off early in the morning, at sunrise—five o'clock or before—and halting shortly after midday, thus avoiding the greatest heat and making camp so that the night's rest gave the men the illusion of a full day's halt. Such was the care that the General took with his army, thought Steel. He knew too that the food and provisions now so evidently on display had been carefully stockpiled to provide for just such an encampment.

This was the new army. Marlborough's army. An army that made the old sweats mutter in amazement. For here was organization of a type never before seen in a British army on foreign soil. It was Marlborough who had made this army. Had fashioned it from the ragtag rabble that had emerged from the chaos of King William's Glorious Revolution and brought it through the Irish wars to this great campaign. It was true that back in London, the Duke still had his enemies who even now might be plotting his removal. But here on the march, with the army, 'Corporal John' was God. But he was also a soldier and a man, his vulnerable mortality no different from any who filled the ranks of his army. That was the reason the soldiers would fight for him. Would die for him—a hero's death if they were lucky. That was why they would march wherever he took them. To whatever lay over the next hill. To glory. And so, as the women cooked and sewed and the money changed hands, and the children played and the wounded died, the majority of the soldiers wondered how long they might count on being able to rest and how many more dawns they might see.

Hansam broke Steel's reverie. 'I see that we have our Prussian friends with us now.'

Steel too had noticed the arrival of the long marching column as it snaked its way past the lines of the British encampment. The distinctive dark blue coats of the Hanoverian and Prussian infantry, their tall Grenadiers evident in their own profusion of elegant, elaborately laced caps. These were their allies, marching to join Marlborough's red caterpillar. There must be, he supposed, several thousand of them. Perhaps ten battalions.

Hansam spoke again: 'You can't help admiring their style. Can you?'

Steel gazed across at the Prussian infantry, marching in precise formation, using the recently reintroduced, artificially high 'cadence' step, looking for all the world as if they were on parade at Potsdam.

'Style, Henry? That's not style. That's nothing more than blind obedience. Those men are more terrified of their own officers than they are of the French. Beaten regularly twice a week for the most trivial offence, they're underfed and generally abused. They march nicely and I dare say they fight well—to command. But in truth they're no more than walking muskets.'

Steel was no admirer of the Prussian system. Oh, he had seen it work in battle. Had watched the blue-coated juggernaut as it inched across the field through a hail of shot to smash its way through the enemy ranks. But he could not believe that this

77

was really the way to fight. Like automatons. Certainly you must have discipline and drill. That was the only way to persuade the men to stand in rank and take the shot when it came flying towards them. How else would men stand, save by drill and discipline. And musketry too required drill. That in truth was the real secret of the system of platoon fire that had wrought such destruction on the French in the late engagement. But Steel believed, too, that in the heat of battle there was still a time to give every man his head. Then you really saw what the British infantryman was made of. Certainly, the Prussians were no cowards. But driven on by their blind rote, they could never match the individual skill and ingenuity of a British Grenadier.

Nevertheless, there were, he knew, times when strict discipline was paramount. And now, he remembered, was just one such moment. Steel heard the clock in the nearby village church striking eight. Normally this would have been the time of the morning for the men of his company and indeed the entire battalion to have been engaged in their various routine duties. Sharpening bayonets at the farrier's wheel, oiling the mechanisms of the highly prized new muskets, checking their shoes and feet for signs of wear. But he knew that none of his men, nor any of Sir James Farquharson's Regiment of Foot had been among the redcoats sitting in the tent lines. This morning Farquharson's men had other business on their minds. Only the camp followers and children were excused from this parade. It was, he supposed, an entertainment of sorts. A diversion intended to enhance the moral welfare of the other ranks and to reinforce the position of the officers by example. A flogging. Steel turned to the Ensign.

'Well, Tom, you've certainly chosen your day to arrive. We've a spectacle for you. Although I am not sure how well you'll take to it. But first, come and meet your fellow officers.'

They approached the group of captains and lieutenants who were talking together before the mess tent at one side of the small headquarters square formed by the administrative tents of the regiment. Steel introduced Williams to each in turn.

'Gentlemen, may I present Mister Williams. Ensign Tom Williams. Newly arrived to the Grenadiers. Tom, may I introduce Monsieur le Lieutenant Daniel Laurent, our own Huguenot "refugie", who thinks it better to fight for us and his God than his own countrymen and theirs.'

The tall Frenchman bowed, aware, as always, that his presence might seem bizarre to any newly arrived officer.

'A *votre service*, Monsieur Williams.'

'Much obliged to you in turn, Monsieur Laurent.'

Steel smiled and continued. 'Observe too, Tom, how Monsieur Laurent retains the enviable manners of his nation.' Laurent laughed, and raised his eyebrows.

'And this is Captain Melville, late of my Lord Orkney's Foot. And this gentleman over here with the permanent grin, is Lieutenant McInnery. Seamus to his friends, of whom he would have you think that there must be very many.'

He lowered his voice to a stage whisper: 'Truth is, the poor fellow hasn't one.'

McInnery laughed, and bowed to Williams. Steel moved between them.

'Oh. And stay well clear of him, Thomas. He'll lead you into bad ways. Within a week you'll be penniless and ridden with the pox from some twopenny tart.'

McInnery shoved Steel hard in the shoulder. 'Jack. What would you have the poor boy believe. Honestly, you go too far. I have a good mind to call you out.'

Steel looked hard at the Irishman and smiled. 'But perhaps not today, though, Seamus. Eh?'

Steel's attention was distracted by the arrival of the duty officer, Charles Frampton, Jennings' crony. A bluff, Kentish man with no time for idle chatter but a seemingly unending capacity for wine which appeared to have no effect on him whatsoever.

'Gentlemen. I think that we might address the matter in hand if we are to get it over with before midday, do you not?'

Steel whispered to Williams: 'It seems, Tom, that our tea will have to wait. Although by the time this is finished I dare say you may be in want of something a little stronger.'

As the officers moved off to their respective companies, Steel looked about the makeshift parade ground. A square had been marked out by four flagpoles, to each of which was attached a square of red silk reserved for just such an occasion. On the farthest side of the square, directly in the centre of two of the poles a wooden frame had been erected using five halberds. Three had been tied together to form a triangle and a fourth then attached to the apex to act as a

80

buttress thus making a tripod. The fifth had been tied directly across the centre of the triangle. At right angles to it, between the other flagpoles, stood three companies of the regiment. Steel's, being that of the Grenadiers, was to the right and he now took his position at its rear. Nate helped him to mount his horse, a tall bay gelding. Steel looked at the bare structure of the whipping block and cursed. It never failed to astonish him that even now, with the army better fed and furnished than ever before, there were still some soldiers within its ranks foolish enough or hungry enough or just stupid enough to risk everything by stealing. And this was the army's answer.

Slaughter, who was standing to his front spoke without turning his head.

'It's a bloody shame, Mister Steel, Sir. A real bloody shame. Dan Cussiter is no more a thief than I am.'

Steel lent over to pat his horse's head. 'Careful now, Jacob. That's seditious talk. You know that the army no longer lives off the country. It is the Duke's work. Every major or captain has the responsibility of telling every man in his company that if one of them steals so much as an egg they will be either hanged or flogged without mercy. And should that be the case then you know the good Major Jennings will always be on hand to ensure that justice is carried out to the letter of the law and within an inch of your life.'

Steel sat up in the saddle.

Slaughter spoke again, although he was still staring straight ahead. 'Perhaps one day they'll reform this army so that them as is good stays from harm and them that's bad at heart get their just

81

rewards.'

Steel said nothing, but entertained similar thoughts. Perhaps when some were turned to dung on the fields of Germany, then those left behind might yet benefit. But he very much doubted it. Marlborough could do many things, but he could not interfere with the very infrastructure of the army; the fact that everything worked only by example. And that meant punishing some poor bugger today, whether or not he really was a thief. Steel's thoughts were lost in the growing thunder of a drum roll. Two men had been sentenced. As was the custom when the army was in the field, desperately attempting to preserve its manpower while unable to forgo military justice, only one was to be punished. So the two men had drawn lots to determine who would receive the flogging. The winner, a moon-faced oaf from number three company had been returned to the ranks and now stood smiling with grim satisfaction as he watched his partner in crime being led out into the square.

Cussiter stood between the Grenadiers of the escort with his head hanging down, staring at his feet, waiting for the inevitable. He had been stripped to the waist and his hands bound, ready to receive punishment, and the white of his thin flesh shone horribly stark and raw against the massed red coats of the parade and the grey of the unforgiving morning. A flogging was not the worst punishment that the army had to offer. There was death, of course, by shooting, hanging or breaking on the wheel—in which your bones were smashed with an iron bar before you were cut down and left in the dust of the parade ground to die slowly and in unimaginable agony, or until a merciful officer

82

put his pistol to your head and blew your brains to the air. There were other ingenious punishments to suit particular crimes. Steel was familiar with the rules, some of which had been laid down by Marlborough himself for each offence.

'All men found gathering peas or beans or under the pretence of rooting to be hanged as marauders without trial.' There were also clear distinctions between what merited 'severe punishment', 'most severe' and 'the utmost punishment'. Flogging, like the other common forms, was brutal and barbaric, yet Steel knew that there was really no other way. But it was hard to wipe from his mind the images of so many punishment parades and their various different methods.

There was the whirligig, in which the prisoner was placed in a wooden cage that was then spun on a spindle until he was so dizzy that at the least he suffered vomiting, involuntary defecation, urination and blinding headaches. At worst he would experience apoplectic seizures, internal bleeding and possibly death. Then there was the wooden horse on which the convicted man was compelled to sit astride while weights were gradually attached to each foot. It didn't help if your victim happened to be among those administering the punishment, as so often seemed to be the case. It was said that a prolonged spell on the wooden horse could bring about rupture and destroy forever your chances of fathering a family; Steel had seen men very nearly gelded by the revolting contraption. But nothing, felt Steel, no product of the torturer's ingenuity, could equal for sheer spectacle or barbarity, the horror of a simple flogging.

He wondered whether he was alone in feeling this way about what they were all about to watch. He knew that many officers shrugged it off with the casual nonchalance they might accord chastising a disobedient dog. Others though, he suspected, shared his qualms. Of course it was quite impossible to express such views. And Steel felt at times that perhaps it was a failing on his part. An inability to be quite everything that the men expected in an officer. Looking away from the tripod, Steel's eye found his Colonel.

James Farquharson was sitting uncomfortably on his horse at the centre of one of the companies, surrounded by his immediate military family. Close to him sat Jennings and for an instant Steel contemplated how they might eventually resolve their quarrel. Whether one or both of them might die in the resolution or whether both might not be killed by the enemy first. Jennings was an unpopular enough officer. Perhaps he would die by a British bullet rather than by one of their enemies'. It happened. All too frequently in fact. Who could say in the heat of battle quite from where the deadly shot had come?

A little back from the punishment block Farquharson still felt too close for comfort and pulling at the reins of his handsome grey mare he coughed, nervously.

'You know, Aubrey, I really do find all this so very tiresome.'

He belched and wiped his mouth with a white lace handkerchief he kept hidden in his sleeve.

'I suppose that I must really remain until the end, eh. Until it is erm . . . finished?'

Jennings smiled. 'I really don't see how you can

84

do otherwise, Sir James. It is after all your regiment. Not good for the men to see you go before the . . . erm . . . finish, Sir.'

'Quite so, quite so. It was merely that I remembered a prior engagement you understand. Staff business as it were. You were not to know. It is of no matter, no matter at all. How many lashes did you say?'

'A round hundred, Sir James. You yourself signed the warrant.'

'A hundred. Yes indeed. Dreadful crime. Quite dreadful. What was it again?'

Jennings turned back to the parade without answering. He knew the real reason for his commanding officer's desire to leave. And that it had nothing to do with 'staff business'. He did not in truth respect Farquharson any more than he respected Steel. Neither, in his opinion, was the sort of officer who was wanted in a modern army. Oh, it would suffice in the sort of army on which Milord Marlborough had set his heart. But Jennings knew that modern warfare needed a quite different sort of man in command. Ruthless, inspiring, pitiless. Certainly Marlborough had shown his grasp of the new warfare at Schellenberg. That was real war. War without mercy. But Jennings could see that their great commander, like the old fools who commanded the majority of his regiments, had no stomach for the sort of warfare he envisaged. The new breed of soldier needed nerves of steel and undaunted courage. And such a soldier could, naturally, only be commanded by men like himself. The square was almost complete now. The remaining officers of the regiment rode into place with their respective companies. Jennings was joined by Charles Frampton who had completed his immediate duties.

'Good afternoon, Charles.'

'Aubrey. Sir James. Bloody business this. Can't say that I really care for it.'

Farquharson smiled. Jennings spoke:

'Nor I, Charles, in truth. But it is what the army requires. Distasteful business though it is.'

'Oh, I did not mean that I disapproved of it. Not at all. Quite so. Absolutely necessary. No other way. I was merely hoping to have been able to have spent the morning at drill. Most important you know. Now. Where are we? Where is the dreadful fellow?'

Another rattle of side drums signalled the approach of the prisoner and escort. Dan Cussiter was a scrawny looking Yorkshire-born Private from number three company. According to tradition, he was led by two Grenadiers and Sergeant Stringer, whose weasel face was suffused with a grin. Stringer relished all punishment parades and liked to see the men suffer. He would walk round the frame soaking up every moment of the agony, and he looked up now at Jennings with the eager anticipation of a waiting terrier.

'Colonel, Sah. Permission to proceed with the punishment, Sah.'

Farquharson nodded to Jennings who in turn nodded to Stringer.

'Lay it on, Sarn't.'

Two drummer boys in their shirtsleeves had taken up their positions on the left and right of the ghastly frame. Their comrades continued the drum roll as the prisoner was led to the wooden poles.

Steel barely knew Cussiter. Certainly, he had seen him many times about the camp and on the march, but the man had never made a particular impression. He seemed somewhat anonymous, not at all the sort of fellow you might mark out as a potential criminal. Steel wondered exactly what he had done to deserve this punishment. Theft certainly, but of what and of what value? True, in the measure of things a hundred lashes was relatively light. Some men were sentenced to 1,000 lashes and more to be administered over a number of days or weeks. At least in Cussiter's case it seemed likely that it would be done in one session.

The drums stopped as the man was tied with one hand on each side of the central halberd and his feet spread out at the wide base of the triangle. A corporal pressed a piece of folded leather into his mouth, a precaution lest he bite off his own tongue with the pain, but also a gag to prevent him from screaming and thus further disgracing himself and the regiment. Stringer stood to the left of the frame and nodded to one of the young drummer boys.

'Drummers, do your duty.'

Steel watched as the boy raised the cat o' nine tails above his head and rotated it twice in the air as he had been taught to do by the regimental farrier. It seemed to hover in the air before the boy brought it down with a slap across the man's back. Steel watched as the white flesh began to seep red and winced as Cussiter's body arched away from the blow. Now it was evident why the fifth halberd was tied across the triangle. There was to be no chance that the prisoner might be able to sink his torso forward and avoid the lash.

Stringer's cruelly jubilant voice rang out across the silent parade ground: 'One.'

The boy's hand came up again and again the whip journeyed round his head before falling on the white back.

'Two.'

Now the drummer boy drew the tails of the cat through the fingers of his left hand, as he had been taught to do between each stroke, to rid them of excess blood and any pieces of skin or flesh which might have attached themselves. Again the whip descended.

'Three. Keep 'em high, lad.' The last thing they wanted was for the strokes to fall on the man's vital organs thus resulting in his death or being invalided out of the regiment.

'Four.' The cat whistled down again, the thick knots at the top of each thong cutting into the soft flesh of Cussiter's back.

It seemed interminable. After the first twenty-five strokes the drummers changed and with the new boy came fresh agonies for the prisoner as the strokes began to fall from a different side and with a different pace.

'Twenty-eight,' boomed Stringer, his face split wide in a grin.

'Twenty-nine.'

By the time they had reached fifty, the halfway mark, Cussiter's body was sagging down, but his head still seemed to be holding itself aloft. The drummers paused as Stringer stepped forward to investigate what seemed to be a piece of exposed bone. He addressed the Adjutant. 'Think I can see a rib sir.'

Steel looked. It was true. There was a glint of

something pearly white against Cussiter's bloodied flesh.

Jennings spoke: 'No matter, Sarn't. Carry on.'

There was an audible groan from the battalion. The battalion Sergeant-Major responded: 'Silence in the ranks there. Corporal, take names.'

Two of the officers opposite Steel also began to whisper to each other. This was certainly most irregular. The idea was not to lay the man open to the bone so quickly. The punishment should really be suspended. Jennings nodded to Stringer and the drummers began again.

'Fifty-one.'

Having had the blissful remission of a few seconds without the lash, Cussiter's back arched out in a new extreme of contortion as the next stroke descended with renewed fury. Blood splashed up with every cut now. The drummers were soon covered and it flowed in slow rivulets down the victim's back to form puddles around him in the dust. Even Steel looked away and wished the thing might end. In whatever way.

Looking across the parade ground to where Williams sat, he noticed that the young Ensign's complexion was now quite white. Farquharson's face too had turned ashen and it was evident that the Colonel was attempting to divert his eyes away from the spectacle.

Jennings, on the other hand, was staring with ghoulish fascination at the wreck of Cussiter's back. After what seemed an eternity the words came at last.

'One hundred.'

Stringer turned away from the bloody tripod and addressed the Colonel: 'Punishment completed, Sah.'

Farquharson, mute with emotional exhaustion, said nothing, but merely nodded. Jennings gave the command: 'Take him down.'

At the words the battalion seemed to relax as a man with a great sigh of relief that it was finally over. Hands fumbled at the ropes binding Cussiter to the halberds and he toppled sideways into the arms of a corporal, then steadied himself on his feet and attempted to walk away. It was a brave show, but in reality he needed two men to help him back to the company lines. Steel heard the clock tower chime. Half past ten. Damn waste of time, half-flaying a man alive. He would now most certainly be late for his appointment. But how could he have excused himself from attending without giving anything away? Not waiting for the other officers, Steel quietly told Slaughter to take over and turned his horse back towards the lines.

*   *   *

It was a good twenty minutes past the appointed hour before he found himself within Marlborough's campaign tent. It was quite a fancy affair he thought, as befitted the Commander-in-Chief. Its walls were lined in red striped ticking and on the ground were laid a number of oriental carpets. Several pieces of furniture stood about the walls. A handsome console table with ormolu supports and a camp-bed, draped with red silk, stood in one of the darker corners, while in the centre of the room lay a large, polished oak table covered in maps and papers and several chairs.

The Duke stood with his back to Steel, who had

90

been announced by an aide-de-camp, who stood hovering beside the tent flap. He was hunched over one of the maps, his fists pressed down on the tabletop. In another corner of the tent, apparently absorbed in leafing through the pages of a leather-bound book, stood Colonel Hawkins. As Steel entered he looked up and smiled before looking back at the pages. Marlborough spoke, without turning round.

'You are late, Mister Steel. Tardiness is not something of which you make a habit, I hope.'

'Not at all, Your Grace. My sincere apologies. The regiment was paraded for punishment. A flogging.'

'Never a very pleasant business, Mister Steel. But absolutely necessary. We must have discipline at all costs, eh? Be fair to the men, Steel, but be firm with it. That's the way to make an army. But now, here you are.'

The Duke turned and Steel recognized that face. Although it looked somewhat care-worn now, the brow furrowed as if by pain, yet still quite as handsome in close-up as he remembered. He had met the General only once before, at a court assembly, and doubted whether the great man would remember him. Marlborough, as usual, wore the dark red coat of a British General, decorated with a profusion of gold lace and under his coat the blue sash of the Order of the Garter. Most noticeably, rather than the high cavalry top-boots, favoured by most general officers, he wore a pair of long grey buttoning gaiters. He stared at Steel for a good two minutes as if getting the measure of this man to whom he had entrusted his future. Finally, he seemed satisfied.

'Yes. Discipline is paramount. We cannot allow the army to run amok can we. It's all they know, Steel. Good lads at heart. But how else to keep 'em in check, eh?'

'Indeed, Your Grace.'

'Now, Steel, to the matter in hand. Colonel Hawkins here tells me that you have been made aware of the importance of this mission. I merely wanted to commend you on your way and to hammer home beyond doubt the absolute necessity that you should succeed. This is no less than a matter of life and death, Steel. My death and now also your own.'

He smiled.

'If you fail in this mission, if the document you seek should find its way into the hands of my enemies, they will as surely break me up like hounds falling upon a hare. And be assured, Mister Steel, that if you do fail then they will most certainly do the same to you.'

He paused. 'I'm told, by my sources in London and by Colonel Hawkins, that you are a man to be trusted.'

He fixed Steel with strikingly cold grey-green eyes.

Steel swallowed: 'I very much believe that to be true, Your Grace.'

'It had better be, my boy.'

Steel felt a sudden impetuous curiosity which momentarily overcame his nervousness. 'May I ask by whom in London I was named to you, Sir?'

Marlborough laughed. 'No indeed, you may not, Sir. But I guess that you must already know. Shall we just call her 'Milady'.

'So then, Steel. D'you think you can do it? Can

you save my skin and this blessed war?'

'I shall do my utmost, Sir.'

'Yes. I do believe you will. Bring me the papers, Steel, and I shall ensure that you are given fair reward. D'you take my meaning?'

'Indeed, Your Grace. You are most generous. But in truth to serve you is honour and reward enough, Sir.'

Marlborough turned to Hawkins. 'You were right, James. He does have a silver tongue. I can see what Milady must see in him. And I hear that you can fight too, Steel.'

'I like to think I can acquit myself with a sword, Sir.'

'I'm told you have a particular penchant for duelling, eh?'

'Not really, Sir.'

'Real or not, I won't have it in the army if I can help it. Kills off my best officers before they have sight of the French. Waste of good men, Steel. Take my advice. Give it up.' He turned back to the map.

'What think you of the campaign thus far?'

'Donauwörth was a great victory, Sir.'

Marlborough looked up and raised his eyebrows. 'Indeed it was, Steel. But tell me. Was it enough? You know that my enemies decry the casualties. What though does the army feel?'

'It is war, Sir. Men are killed in any battle. The fact is that we took the position and drove off the enemy. It was a glorious day, Sir.'

'It is war, Steel. But this is a new war. Tomorrow we advance on the town of Rain. We shall besiege it and we shall take it, cannon or not. But you, Mister Steel, you will not be coming with us. You have your own orders and two days to prepare for your journey. Be swift and be sure, Steel. For if you are not, then we are all ruined.'

*   *   *

Aubrey Jennings sat in his tent writing up the company reports. It was the most tedious part of his job and normally he would have paid a junior officer to do the task. This evening though there was a general amnesty for all lieutenants and they had leave to visit the local village. So here he sat doing the job of a quartermaster, numbering off rations and issues of clothing, equipment, ammunition, and rum. Besides, he thought, it did allow him the opportunity for a little creative accounting. Who, after all, would know that the actual number of pairs of shoes delivered was 300 and not the 600 for which he had indented? The additional money would go straight into his pocket. Not bad for an evening's work, tiresome as it was. Jennings sat back in his chair, closed his eyes and sighed.

'God, Charles. I can't abide paperwork. We should have clerks to do such things. Never would have happened in the old army. You know I can't help thinking that we may have our priorities wrong. What need have the men for new shoes when there are hundreds of perfectly serviceable pairs being discarded? The men never needed regular supplies of new shoes before. Why now? What does Marlborough suppose it will buy him? Popularity? Of course he's right. But he doesn't have to sit here and write up the damned papers for the bloody things. I tell you, it's typical of the way this army is going. I don't like it, Charles. It's not what soldiering's about. Reforms yes, of course we need reforms. But not like this. Not reforms for new shoes. We need reforms for new men. New officers and a new code of fighting. I'm not liked you know, in Whitehall. I've been passed over. I should have command of a battalion.'

Charles Frampton spoke from a corner of the tent, without looking up from his book. 'You could always raise your own regiment, Aubrey.'

'D'you suppose I'm made of money, Charles. Don't be ridiculous. Waste my own money on clothing and feeding 600 men. No. I intend to rise by merit and persuasion. It is my right.'

There was a cough from outside the tent. Jennings looked up and then back down again at the ledger and took up his pen. 'Come.'

Stringer entered, leering.

'Yes. What is it Sarn't?'

'Have to report, Sir. Men are a bit low, Sir.'

Jennings looked up at the grinning Sergeant and put down his pen.

'Perhaps I had better go and raise their spirits. D'you think?'

'No, I wouldn't do that. No, Sir. Not if I was you, Sir. See, it's the effect of the flogging, Sir. Never very happy after a flogging the men aren't. There's talk as you should have had 'im cut down after fifty, Sir.'

'Oh there is, is there? Well Sarn't, see if tomorrow you can't listen a little closer as to where that talk is coming from and then we'll see if whatever big-mouthed miscreant is the author of that treason doesn't get a hundred lashes or more of his own for his trouble.'

Stringer grinned his toothless smile.

'Very good, Sir. I'll get about it now, Sir.'

Turning, he made to leave the tent, but before he could do so an officer entered, his red coat marked out by the distinctive green facings and grey waistcoat of Wood's Regiment of Horse. Jennings knew him as a casual acquaintance. Thomas Stapleton, a Major of no little repute, testimony to which was born out by the white scar which ran the length of his right cheek. Jennings knew him too from London.

He suspected that Stapleton, with his obvious allegiances, must be as disenchanted with the motives and ambitions of their great commander as he was himself. Wondering what business Stapleton might now have with him, he rose from the table to greet him.

'Major Stapleton. How very pleasant to see you again. To what do we owe your presence? A drop of claret perhaps. Charles.'

Frampton poured a glass and brought it across to them.

'Thank you, Major Jennings. That would be most agreeable.'

Stapleton had been blessed from birth with a speech impediment, pronouncing all his 'r's as if they were 'w's. It had the effect of making his already high-pitched voice still more comical. But there was nothing amusing in the expression he wore as he accepted the proferred goblet of wine from Frampton. He took a sip and got to the matter in hand.

'May I speak plainly?'

'Major Stapleton. You may rest assured that you are among friends here. You know Captain

96

Frampton?'

Major Stapleton nodded and then frowned: 'Indeed. Nevertheless, Major Jennings.'

He raised his eyes towards Frampton. 'If you would be so kind.'

Jennings turned to Frampton. 'Charles. I'm afraid that I must ask you to leave us, briefly.'

Frampton walked slowly across to the entrance and Jennings, realizing that Stringer was still standing by the entrance to the tent, motioned for the Sergeant, too, to leave. Once both men had gone, Stapleton began:

'Major Jennings. You will have heard, no doubt, that a wagon train was lately ambushed near Ingolstadt by a party of Bavarian cavalry.'

'It is common knowledge, Major. Yes. But it was I believe of little consequence. It contained personal possessions mostly. No ammunition. No supplies.'

'Quite true. Personal possessions certainly. A quantity of silverware and plate, fresh uniforms for the general officers. In fact the majority of it was the personal property of the Commander-in-Chief. What you were perhaps unaware of however, was that within those wagons was a chest of highly personal documents and correspondence belonging to His Grace the Duke of Marlborough.'

Jennings grinned. 'How personal, exactly?'

'The chest contained certain papers. Letters from his wife and so on.'

'How very droll. Go on.'

'The point is, Major, that finding no supplies of any military value, the Bavarian Colonel who captured the train sold on its contents to one of his countrymen, a merchant.

'You will not be surprised I hazard if I tell you that said merchant, an inquisitive, inventive sort of chap, having glimpsed in one of the letters what seemed to him familiar armorial bearings, spent many hours perusing the papers.'

He took a long draught of wine.

'Within a letter from the Duke to his wife, the man found concealed a very different piece of correspondence. A letter to Marlborough from the court of the exiled King James at St Germain. A letter thanking our General in the most friendly terms, for his concerns as to the Stuart pretender's state of health and also for his enduring loyalty.'

Jennings was staring now. Smiling.

'You begin to understand what this might imply?'

'Perfectly. Do continue.'

'Naturally, our Bavarian merchant, being a man with an eye for self-advancement, thought to return the letter to its owner—at a price—and therefore some days ago sent an emissary into our camp. In short he has arranged to sell it back to Marlborough for 500 crowns. And this, Major, is where I come in. Or rather, where you come in. I am informed that you and I are of the same political persuasion.'

'I am a Tory, if that is what you mean. And a true patriot.'

'Indeed. And being of that persuasion I venture that you would be as keen as I to see my Lord Marlborough replaced as commander-in-chief of this army?'

'You hardly need ask, Major. The Duke's ambitions will be the ruination of the army. He does all from self-interest, rather than the good of his country. If given his head he will sacrifice as many men as it takes to advance himself to the highest office. He must go.'

'You will be aware too that the Margrave is discontented with the Duke's conduct of the campaign. I have today learnt from one of Baden's men on Marlborough's staff that the Duke and Colonel Hawkins have contrived to send an expedition to procure the letter. It will leave within the week under the pretext of foraging for flour. It is to be led by an officer of your own regiment. A Lieutenant Steel.'

Jennings continued to smile.

'You will appreciate, Major Jennings, that we have here an unmissable opportunity to bring down Marlborough and rescue this war for the Tories. Bavaria is no place for the army. Nor Flanders. It is, as my Lord Nottingham would have it, the only theatre in which to wage a war against the French is in Spain itself. It is vital that we put an end to the campaign before we are committed any deeper to this foolhardy expedition into Bavaria. Here is the answer. You will lead a counter-expedition to beat Steel to the merchant. I have arranged for Baden himself to ask Sir James for your temporary transfer to his forces as liaison. With luck Steel will know nothing of it; you will leave a full day after him. But you will not be hindered by wagons as he is. Take a parallel route and you are certain to reach the rendezvous ahead of him. You will meet the merchant, a Herr Kretzmer. Pass yourself off as Steel and procure the letter in exchange for the money.' He smiled, as if struck by a sudden thought and spoke very quietly.

'Of course in an ideal situation you might see to it that Herr Kretzmer no longer had any need for the money and return it to me. Or rather to the funds. Now that would be splendid. But no matter. It is spoken for. Simply procure the papers and on your return we shall send the traitorous document to London. The Queen will have no alternative but to dismiss Marlborough and banish his meddlesome wife from court. You and I shall be greeted as heroes, and our standing both in the army and the greater world will be without limit. Will you do it?'

Jennings raised his glass. 'How can I possibly refuse?'

Reaching inside his coat, Stapleton drew out a bulging leather purse and placed it heavily on the table alongside the company ledger book.

'This purse contains precisely 500 crowns. Herr Kretzmer will be expecting not a penny less.'

Jennings looked at the purse. 'Rest assured, Major Stapleton, you may trust in me to get your papers. I will gratefully accept your reward on my return. But, believe me, I go to my task wholly in the conviction of the justice of our cause.'

As Stapleton left the tent, Frampton re-entered.

'Well, Charles. It seems that my prayers, had I but said them, have been answered. And all at one stroke. Not only do I elevate myself to greater position, but I rid the army of the curse of Marlborough and in the same action destroy Steel. It is a conceit so perfect that I might have thought of it myself.'

Frampton said nothing. Merely nodded in assent and poured himself another goblet of claret. Jennings ran his hands down the side of the leather purse, feeling the outline of the coins within. At length he called out: 'Stringer.'

The Sergeant appeared at the entrance of the tent.

'Sarn't. Better start saying your goodbyes. In three days' time we are to leave the main body of the army and journey south.'

'South, Sir?'

'South, Stringer.'

Jennings smiled. 'We're going to save the army.'

FOUR

Dawn picked at the land with shafts of pale yellow light and a gentle wind blew across the ripe crops and down into the valley of the River Lech. Steel could hear the men outside beginning to stir. The familiar sounds of mess tins and cooking pots as the soldiers assembled what rations they could find for a makeshift breakfast. Half sitting, half lying against a bale of straw in the barn of a deserted farmstead, Steel shivered and wrapped his cloak tight around his sinewy body, reluctant to admit that all too soon he, too, would have to move from what for the past four hours had passed for a bed. It had been a damp and thankless night.

The horses, for some reason unsettled in the empty stables, had kept him awake into the early hours with their whinnying and twice the nervous picquets had raised the alarm. Each time Williams, as jumpy as the mounts, had come in to report, only to leave embarrassed and uncomfortable. There had, of course, been no real danger, but

Steel knew that the men were on edge and, while gently chiding Williams, indulged them. For if the truth be known, he more than shared their apprehension. They were deep in enemy territory now. In the very heart of Bavaria, Swabia to be precise. Even as they made their way through the pleasant, peaceful farmland, Steel knew that over the hills, within a few miles, villages were being burnt by his own army.

It was three days since they had left the main camp. Today was the 14th July, a Sunday. The flat plain of the meandering river valley of the Lech had given way after a day to more wooded terrain. They had crossed the river by bridge at Waltershofen and five miles on had entered the thick forest which covered the countryside to the west of the brewing town of Aicha. The woods were full of biting insects that lost no time in feasting on fresh, northern blood. It had taken them a day to get clear of the trees. But the rank, red sores from the mosquitoes still raged on their skin.

They had now arrived on the flood plain of the Paar, where high plantations of hops signalled that they were entering the heart of the Bavarian beer-making country. They had left behind neat little villages sat in lush valleys rich in arable crop and cattle and entered another countryside of higher hills with mountain tops visible beyond, capped with snow. A wild country that reminded Steel of the land that lay to the west of his family home, far away towards the Western Isles. Yet, for all the familiarity of the breathtaking scenery and gentle, bucolic images which surrounded him, with every step they took further away from the army and into enemy territory, Steel sensed the increasing possibility that they were walking into danger.

The door of the barn swung open and a tall figure was silhouetted against the growing light.

'Ready to move, Sir? Found you some coffee. Can't say what it tastes like, though. Never touch the stuff myself.'

Having no servant with him, Steel was happy to allow Jacob Slaughter to minister to his needs. He had left Nate with Hansam's half-company back at the camp to guard his kit. You never knew who might take a fancy to it. Now the big Geordie peered down at him through the half-darkness and offered his officer the part-filled tin cup.

'Thank you, Jacob. Most thoughtful.' He took a long drink from the mug and let the thick, acrid liquid trickle down his throat.

'Can't say that I'm keen to see this dawn, Sarn't. But it brings us one more day closer to our return, eh? How are the men?'

'All present, Sir. Sixty-three of our lads, and myself and Mister Williams. Though I don't know as I'd say that they were all quite "correct", if you understand me. Carter and Milligan are complaining of sores on their feet. Tarling looks like he might be coming down with the ague and Macpherson's cut hi'self in the hand, on his bayonet, Sir. Cleaning it. Mister Williams is already standing-to. He's a good lad. Keen as mustard. Just what we need.'

This then, thought Steel, was his escort with which to bring back the flour for the army and the precious treasure whose loss would bring Marlborough's ruination. He chanced another sip of the steaming brew and winced at the taste.

103

'We'll need to move fast today, Sarn't. Word will have got out that we're here.'

They made an easy target in their obligatory scarlet coats, with the wagon train strung out along the road. They marched in full order, as if they might have been on duty at St James', and Steel felt the gaze of a hundred imagined enemy eyes observing their every step and waited for the first shot to ring out from the tall trees that flanked their progress. Steel stood up, carefully, handed Slaughter the empty mug and folded his cloak. He brushed himself clean of the straw and mire from the floor and followed his Sergeant out into the cold dawn.

In the little courtyard the men were gradually assembling, stamping their feet and blowing on fingers.

Slaughter announced his presence: 'Henderson, Mackay, Tarling. You others. Stand-to. Officer on parade.'

The men moved more smartly into line and formed three ranks.

'Form them up, Sarn't.'

'Marching formation. Move to it.'

Within minutes the men had changed formation. Steel looked down the column of march. Forty wagons, strung out in line. Enough to carry 300 quintails of flour. That would keep the entire army in good supply for a day, but well divided and distributed, it might last for a week. Time enough for the command to find another source. He saw that each wagon was now flanked by a four-man escort. 'At the command, the column will move off. Forward march.'

The sleepy civilian waggoners whipped their

beasts into action and the red-coated column again began to move east.

*   *   *

They had been travelling for barely three hours when, reaching the top of a hill they saw the road stretch away before them in a shallow valley before climbing again steeply. And there, at the top of another hill, lay the distant roofs and gables of a village.

Steel, unused to riding with a supply train and impatient to increase the pace, pressed his thighs together and urged his horse, a chestnut mare that he had purchased in Coblenz and christened Molly, forward and down the slope. Dust rose from beneath her hooves and as she took up the pace to a gentle trot her harness added a high note to the rhythmic clank which marked the passage of a body of armed men.

For a moment, Steel stopped and turned in the saddle. He looked past young Williams and over the heads of the men then, turning back, dug his heels into Molly's flanks before pulling a wad of tobacco from his pocket. He placed it in his mouth and began to chew. Steel's only desire was to accomplish his mission as quickly as possible and return safely to where the army might next be encamped. Wherever that might be. He felt restless. In need of action. This was not the place for him, up here at the head of a marching supply train. Perhaps if he were to march with the men. He reined in his horse and slid from the saddle. Spitting the tobacco from his mouth into the roadside and grasping the reins, he slipped easily

105

into time with the column, alongside Slaughter who grinned at him with pleasure.

'Come to join us, Sir?'

'Needed a change, Sarn't. Just that.'

Slaughter pointed off to the left. 'There it is again, Sir. More smoke. Men don't like it. They was all talking about it last night.'

Over the last two days, as they had marched, they had become increasingly aware of tall plumes of smoke rising against the sky, visible from some distance. The men had wondered at them and suggested a number of explanations. That the French were burning crops, lest they fall into allied hands. That bridges and barges were being destroyed to impede their progress. Even that they indicated some great battle whose glory they had missed. But Steel knew what they really meant. Before they had left Hawkins had intimated one more fact to him and he in turn had passed it on only to Hansam, Williams and Jacob.

Marlborough was going to burn Bavaria. No one, God willing, soldier or civilian, would be killed. But in a last effort to force the Elector to quit his pact with the French, he would send out troops to lay waste every town they found. Steel was secretly appalled at the thought. Yet he understood how it fitted perfectly with the logic of the sort of warfare on which Marlborough had now embarked. This was total war. War waged by, almost, any means. So the horsemen would come with their burning torches and they would be ruthless, though yet with an edge of clemency.

Still, the rising grey-black clouds provoked him to a shiver. What effect would this have upon the native population, forced from their homes and rendered penniless? What reception might he and his men now expect as they made their way through this pleasant country whose neat fields and townships had lately so delighted his eye. He suspected that at best, should they find a village still intact, they would not be made to feel welcome. At worst, well who knew? Visions of ambush filled his mind. Of erstwhile lawful people taking the law into their own hands to revenge this outrage. Of redcoats with their throats cut in their sleep. Who could know what unexpected dangers awaited them? He moved to the side of the sweating horse and, unbuckling the saddle-bag, withdrew a worn and folded sheet of paper.

It was a map, given to him by Hawkins before they left. But while it showed the major towns and rivers, precious few of the villages were marked on it. Steel knew from the position of stars that he was still going east, with the Lech at his back and the other, smaller river they had crossed, the Paar, to the south. And that he realized, must mean that they were headed in the right direction and that one more day's march along this road should bring them to their goal and then they could return to what they did best. Steel was no spy or secret agent. He was a soldier. Just that. He wondered that Hawkins had marked him out for this mission, then remembered Arabella. And with that memory came the sensation of a feather bed and a vision of her face. He spat tobacco husk on the ground. Christ but she was devious.

'All right, Sir?'

'Thank you, Sarn't. Quite all right, thank you. Just impatient to get this job done.'

'And get back to the army, Sir?'

'Precisely, Jacob. The sooner we finish this business, the quicker we get to the French.'

Steel swatted at a mosquito that had settled on his cheek, for they were marching parallel to a small stream and a marsh, and the insects were beginning to discover this new quarry.

'And the sooner we beat the French the quicker we shall all return north and away from this vermin-infested country.'

Slaughter kept quiet. He knew when Steel was in one of his rare moods of ill humour and recognized the moment. They came on fast and you could never predict them. Perhaps the coffee had unsettled him. He would have to remember that. Steel continued, addressing Slaughter but talking to no one in particular:

'We have to find the French and give battle. And soon, otherwise we shall be sucked deeper into this country and our lines of communication stretched still further. But it would appear that at this precise moment not even Marlborough really knows where they might be.'

*   *   *

Two miles to the north, another red-coated column came to a halt. At its head, astride his grey mare, their officer too was reading a map. Aubrey Jennings was lost. Hopelessly lost. They had set off from the camp a day after Steel and, as advised by Stapleton, had taken a route parallel to his and to the north, by way of Wiesenbach and Eiselstredt. Inhospitable little places with tongue-twisting names and their people hidden behind shutters that creaked as they peered to glimpse the redcoats clanking through their cobbled streets. Outside the towns and villages the country of lower Bavaria was pleasant enough terrain, though hardly anything to rival the South Downs. Farmland mostly, but as they marched they found the landscape scarred increasingly by burnt-out farmsteads and peasants standing in the field, staring at them with hateful, weary eyes. From time to time Jennings was aware of a column of smoke trailing up skywards from another burning settlement. Clearly one of the opposing armies was at work hereabouts and it made the Major nervous. So nervous indeed that his attention had been deflected from their route.

'Sarn't Stringer.'

'Sir.'

'We'll rest here for ten minutes. Have the men fall out.'

'Very good, Sir.'

As Stringer shouted at the musketeers, and one by one the weary soldiers unslung their knapsacks and sat on the verge, Jennings looked back to the map. He was sure that they had passed through the village of Nieder-Berebach, but for the last four miles nothing had seemed to correspond to the geography which would have followed such a route, as stated on the plan. A river to his left he took to be the Paar. But why then did it not divide in two as was shown on his map? Now a bridge lay across their path along the riverbank and that, most certainly, was not marked. At this rate they would arrive at the rendezvous with Kretzmer long after Steel. And that must not happen.

'Sarn't Stringer. How far would you say we have covered today?

'Today, Sir? Around ten mile, Sir.'

Yes. That is my reckoning. This river, Sarn't. The Paar, is it not?'

'Really couldn't say, Sir. Not lost are we, Sir?'

Jennings scowled at him. 'Lost? How could I be lost, Stringer?'

Jennings looked back at the map and tried turning it on its side so that the river as shown on its criss-crossed face lined up with that which lay before him. This was useless.

'We shall proceed along the line of the river, Sarn't. Due east.'

'If you say so, Sir.'

'Is it not due east?'

'If you say so, Sir.'

'Don't be so dashed stubborn, man. Tell me this is due east.'

'This is due east, Sir.'

'Thank you, Stringer. And thus, if we simply follow the river we can turn to the right within two miles and march towards the south. We shall make camp for the night and, God willing, shall reach Sattelberg and our rendezvous with the flour merchant Herr Kretzmer by early tomorrow.'

'If you say so, Sir.'

Jennings sighed and gave up, deciding that it would be best if they were to stop again after two miles and reassess the situation.

He sat down on the bare stump of a thick tree and, making sure that he had his back to the men, drew from his pocket the purse given to him by Stapleton. Here in his hand it felt heavier than in his coat. He fingered the bulges in its sides, tracing the outline of the coins. Unable to resist the temptation, he spread back the string, opened the mouth of the purse and pulled out one of the gold pieces. He turned it over in his hand, slowly, lovingly.

A cough made him raise his head, with a start. Stringer stood above him. He had told the Sergeant of the nature of his mission, although not of the precise detail of the precious papers. It was a good idea though to let the man in on the urgency and importance of the affair. Jennings knew that Stringer was a vital ally and suspected too that he might be an implacable enemy. Unabashed, he continued to flip the coin between thumb and forefinger.

'You see, Sergeant Stringer, I am that unluckiest of men. I am the younger son. I do not inherit. All that I have is a pitiful allowance and that is it. My brother takes everything. You of course do not have such troubles. I once had expectations. Considerable expectations. But a young man soon learns his lot in life. Better to have had no hopes at all than to suffer bitter disappointment. You for instance, have only ever had to shift for yourself. Your family had nothing.'

'Not quite nothing, Sir. My ma had a good little business when I was a nipper, selling mackerel in Honey Lane Market. Four for sixpence. But then she sold some bad fish and lost that job and we was poor and then she began to thieve. One day they caught her stealing silver lace from a shop in Covent Garden. They 'anged her till she was dead. Hanged my mother for six yards of lace. An' I was left alone. Never known my father, see, Sir. That's when . . .'

'That's when you fell in with a bad lot, eh?'

Jennings was tiring of the Sergeant's history.

'And you've been a rogue ever since.'

He laughed in what he took to be a spirit of camaraderie. Stringer did nothing to dissuade him.

'Not any longer, Sir. I'm a Sergeant now, Major Jennings.' He pointed to the silver lace which adorned his coat. 'Respectable. Silver lace, Sir. And they won't hang me for it, neither.'

Jennings nodded. 'A respectable rogue then. And your mother would be proud. But a rogue, nevertheless. You cannot ever escape yourself, Stringer. In the end we all come to know our true selves. Whether at heart each of us is truly good or bad.'

Stringer, unsure as to how to reply, said nothing. Jennings looked again at the bag of gold coins and wondered. Would it be so very bad if a few were to go missing?

Stringer read his thoughts: 'The Kraut would notice, Sir. He's a merchant. They're like that. Canny with money.'

Jennings, surprised by his lack of offence at the Sergeant's remark, let it go. Then he thought about it. Stringer watched him.

'Yes. You're right. And it is not mine to take. It belongs to the party and it has a purpose far greater than my own pocket. Besides which, when I give it to Herr Kretzmer in return for the papers, my star will be so far in the ascendant that 500 crowns will be nothing.'

Stringer smiled, secure in the knowledge that if his master enjoyed good fortune then surely some of that luck would be visited in turn on him.

He was contemplating his coming prosperity when a dull thud, like air being squeezed out of a bag, made him turn his head in time to see one of

112

the men flinch back from the impact of a musket ball which had struck his chest. There was a crack as another shot rang out from the trees to their left.

'Alarm. To arms.'

The shots were coming fast now but few hit their targets. Jennings, ducking his head, peered into the darkness of the wood, but he could see nothing but the flash of musketry. 'To arms. We are attacked.'

Quickly the redcoats jumped to their feet and gathered their muskets from the pyramid in which they had been piled, but not before more of the balls had found a target. Jennings saw four of his men go down as the sporadic fire increased. They were getting better, the enemy. He drew his sword, and looked for Stringer.

'Sarn't. Load as quickly as you will. Have the men fix bayonets. Form two ranks.'

'Load your pieces. Fix . . . bayonets.'

Hurriedly the men obeyed, ripping open the cartridges, spitting the balls down the barrel and rattling their ramrods. But more fell under the relentless fire from the yet unseen enemy. They were starting to form a unit now. Dressing ranks, even under fire. Jennings scoured the ground. Twelve men at least were down. More, he guessed, hidden beyond the ranks before him. Three of them, wounded, were being helped to the rear of their makeshift position. There was not a moment to waste. He barked a command.

'Make ready. Present.'

Sixty muskets came up to shoulder level.

'Fire!'

Jennings' company spat flame and was

113

enveloped in thick white smoke. He heard the smack as their balls hit trees and tore leaves from branches, splintering wood and with it the more pleasing, softer thud as they bit into flesh. One man, in his haste to fire, had forgotten to extract his ramrod which had gone sailing across the field and embedded itself in a tree. Stringer rounded on him:

'Wiggins, you careless bugger. Rear rank. Ware, you take his place.'

There was no use for a man with no ramrod in the firing line. Wiggins would just have to remain at the rear until he could retrieve a musket from a dead friend. Jennings guessed that he would not have too long a wait. With steely precision the redcoats reloaded.

Stringer had divided the remaining men into two platoons now and Jennings knew what would follow. The Sergeant's voice carried towards the wood.

'Number one platoon, fire!'

Again a volley crashed out from the British line. Half as strong as the first, but with a purpose. From the trees the enemy returned fire and began to reload and then Stringer barked again:

'Number two platoon, fire!'

The second platoon squeezed their triggers and evidently caught the men in the trees off guard, for there was a momentary break in enemy firing.

But it did not last long and Jennings realized that such revolutionary tactics, which could work so well in open battle against an enemy who needed to pause to reload, would not have the same devastating effect against men who fired individually.

The men in the trees had begun to shout with excitement now, scenting victory. Stringer growled at the line:

'Steady. Keep it up. Steady fire, lads.'

We must retire, thought Jennings. Form a defensive line. That was it. He wanted them shoulder to shoulder. Heel to heel.

'Fall back. Regroup on me.'

Slowly, as they fired, the redcoats began to close up their shattered lines.

How the devil could whoever was firing at them keep up such a steady, withering fire? These must be regular troops, Jennings thought. Surely. But what regular infantry ever deployed in such a manner, using the trees for cover? Not showing themselves on the field? This was not the way to wage war. But, he thought, it was making a bloody mess of his company. The line was looking horribly ragged, with men falling every minute. The wounded crawled to the rear, legs broken, sides torn by musketry, arms hanging limp.

Jennings screamed out over the noise of gunfire: 'Dress your lines.'

Stringer echoed him: 'Close up. Close up, you buggers.'

They were down, he reckoned, to only around forty men now at all capable of returning the enemy fire. Jennings watched as, slowly, emboldened by their success, their assailants at last began to emerge from the cover of the wood. The men wore no uniforms. Some were in shirtsleeves, others in a variety of civilian dress, over which they had slung cartridge bags. They carried hunting guns mostly, although some had what looked like French or Bavarian issue muskets, topped with bayonets. Banditii, thought Jennings. Brigands. And they looked as if they meant to offer no quarter. He had been unlucky enough to run into a party of the bandits whom he had been told plagued these hills. Not only that but, by the look of it, he was outgunned and now in real and mortal danger of losing the encounter.

He looked for Stringer and realized what they must do. It was their only chance. A full-blooded infantry charge that might just catch the civilians off guard and send them scurrying off in terror. That, at least, was what he prayed.

'Sarn't. Have the entire line fix bayonets. We'll give them the steel.'

'Fix . . . bayonets. On guard.'

Most of the men had already done so, but the few who had not now screwed the steel socket bayonets into place over the corresponding nipple on their musket barrels.

'Now men. For Farquharson's. For the Queen. For . . .'

Jennings was on the point of giving the command when, from his right and slightly to the rear a thunder of musketry crashed out. A disciplined volley that through its smoke betrayed the presence of regular soldiers. And, it appeared, they were on his side.

He watched as the bullets thudded into the ranks of the peasants. The volley did not do as much destruction as it would have to men caught in close order. But it was enough. The marksmen and the farmers began to move back. One man stared at the bright red stain spreading quickly across his shirt, unable to comprehend his own destruction.

Jennings heard a single, distinctively English voice cry out: 'Second rank, fire.'

Another crackle of gunfire and the smoke grew more dense. Before him, Jennings watched as the peasants began to run.

Jennings wondered who he had to thank for their salvation. He glanced to the right and through the cloud of white smoke saw a line of red coats, then he turned back to his front, looking for Stringer. He saw him some yards in front, anticipating their next move and Jennings raised his sword high above his head and circled it through the air. Their rescuers might have stolen his thunder, but by God, they would not take all the glory from this field:

'Now men. With me. Charge.'

With a yell the front two ranks sprang forward to follow the Major and took the fight into the trees. Jennings felt the blood coursing through him as he leapt a tree trunk and pushed through the standing bracken. To the left and right he could see the bodies of dead peasants. There were wounded too. One man, propped up against a log, looked up at him with pleading eyes and held a trembling arm towards the Major while clutching at his bloody stomach with the other. Jennings ignored him and ran on, jumping the brush which covered the floor of the small wood. And then they were on them.

Glancing to his left Jennings was aware of a musketeer plunging his bayonet deep into the back of one of the retreating bandits. He saw the steel tip emerge from the man's stomach, glistening red, and then the redcoat retrieved his weapon and before the man had slid to the ground had set off in pursuit of another.

Stringer appeared at his side, grinning and with a dripping blade.

'Just like stickin' pigs, Sir, ain't it?'

Jennings stared at him. He returned Stringer's smile and looked ahead where two of his men, intent on revenge, were smashing the head of one of their attackers to a pulp with the butts of their rifles.

'Get on there, you men. Leave that one. He's dead. Get after the others.'

The wood was not deep and emerging on to the other side, Jennings could see the survivors streaming away down the hill to its rear. Most of them had thrown down their weapons in their haste to escape. Several of the redcoats were kneeling down now, attempting to pick them off. But at this range Jennings knew there was little chance.

'Re-form. Let them go, lads. They know when they're licked. Well done, boys.'

As they returned through the wood, its floor slick with blood, Jennings again passed the corpses of their attackers. At the tree stump, the man with the pleading eyes was dead now. He lay there, gazing open-lidded up at the gaps among the branches. Jennings wondered for a moment who this would-be assassin might have been. He looked to be in his mid twenties. Might he be someone's husband? Would he be missed at supper tonight in some miserable farm or perhaps around a sad campfire? It struck Jennings for an instant that, should he fall, should it be his form lying dead here rather than the farmer's boy, then no one would grieve for Aubrey Jennings. Save perhaps

118

the whores who plied the dark lanes between the Strand and Drury Lane and no doubt by his tailor in the Temple and those several other tradesmen to whom his bills also remained unpaid. It was a sad thought. No widow. No weeping children. Not even a parson to honour his name on Sunday. It seemed unjust that he should not leave someone with a broken heart.

Reaching the edge of the copse, Jennings looked to the left and through the clearing white smoke made out a single red-coated form.

He walked towards the young British officer, and doffed his hat in salute:

'Thank God, Sir. Aubrey Jennings, Major. Farquharson's Foot. I am in your debt. You came not a moment too soon. In truth, I thought we were done for.'

His wide smile changed to a look of incredulity as he realized that the redcoat officer who he had taken for a captain, was none other than Tom Williams, who beamed back at him. Jennings looked towards their rescuers. Saw the mitre caps and groaned.

'Oh it was nothing, Sir. It's Mister Steel you should thank.'

Jennings, frowning hard, turned and saw the familiar features. He said nothing.

Steel slung his gun over his shoulder:

'Major, you know that you owe your life to young Williams' sense of hearing?'

Jennings bit his lip. 'His hearing?'

'He had ridden a little way off from the wagons, Major. Told me he'd seen a wild deer and reckoned he might bag it for the pot. I told him to stick close to us but he rode clear of the sound of the wagons and then it was that he heard the gunfire. Your fire. He came tearing back to us, and here we are.'

Steel did not bother telling Jennings how hard a decision it had been to abandon the wagons temporarily on the road with a skeleton guard as they marched at double-time to his rescue. Nor of his disappointment to discover that it was none other than Jennings for whom they had risked their security. For what troubled Steel more than either of these matters was what the devil Jennings was doing there.

'Indeed, Steel. It would seem that I do owe you thanks. Who were they d'you suppose? Not regulars, certainly. But why should the peasantry be provoked to attack?'

'Haven't you noticed the smoke, Major? They're being burnt out of their homes. All their possessions destroyed. And it's our men who are doing it. What would you do in similar circumstances?'

Jennings demurred. 'They're peasants. No more. They deserve everything we gave them. A dozen of my men dead, a score more wounded. And by nothing more than damned peasants.'

'If they're peasants, Major, they're peasants good enough to take on the British army and damned near win. Would it be presumptious, Major Jennings, to ask how you come to be here? Are you come for us? Are we to be recalled?'

Jennings sensed the concern in Steel's voice: 'Oh no, Steel. We are come for you but you are to proceed as ordered. We are merely here to assist you.'

He paused, aware of the irony. 'Colonel

Hawkins asked me to follow you. He had been given intelligence that there were considerable numbers of Bavarian troops operating in this area and feared that you might be hard-pressed.'

Steel smiled, as determined not to let go the truth of their situation as Jennings was to ignore it.

'It would seem then, Major, that what we have is a case of the apparently helpless coming to the aid of the rescuer.'

Jennings looked at him, stony faced.

Another thought entered Steel's befuddled brain. 'Colonel Hawkins sent you?'

'Indeed.'

Steel was not sure whether to feel reassured or insulted. Did Hawkins not consider him capable of carrying out the task? Or was there truly a threat of greater numbers? And it struck him that it was curious that the Colonel should have sent Jennings rather perhaps than Hansam to his relief, when he was only too aware of their bitter enmity. He frowned and nodded at Jennings.

'It is as well that you are here. It would not do to fail in this mission.'

Jennings smiled at him, strangely, and cursed under his breath. For with their rescue came the bitter truth that there was now little chance of his reaching Kretzmer before Steel and relieving him of the papers.

'No indeed, Steel. That would not do at all.'

'So now we should press on to Sattelberg?'

Jennings pondered: 'No, Steel. I think it better to make camp here for the night. Best to put ourselves in order before we enter the town, eh?'

He paused beside one of the enemy corpses and turned over its white face with the tip of his boot.

121

The man was no more than a youth. Barely eighteen.

'These men may have been peasants right enough, but we beat them in the fight and we should show the rest of them why. Discipline, Steel. The iron discipline of regular, steadfast infantry. You can't beat it. We can't have the populace as a whole thinking the British army a bunch of ragamuffins. Wouldn't do at all.'

Steel frowned. 'But, Major, I must protest. You know of the urgency of this mission.'

Jennings looked hard at Steel. Could he know the true reason for his coming here?

'I am well aware, Mister Steel, of the urgency of your quest. That we must return as soon as we can to the army, with the flour. Nevertheless I am your superior officer and I elect to pitch our camp here for the night. Herr Kretzmer I am sure will wait for us until morning.'

Steel glared and turned to Slaughter, who was busy binding the wound of a young Grenadier.

'Sarn't. Have the men fall out and make camp. We're resting here tonight. Major Jennings' orders.'

'Here, Sir?'

'Here, Sarn't. Get to it.'

Jennings walked slowly over to the body of another dead peasant. The neat, black-scorched entry wound left by the musket ball in the man's chest belied the bloody mess where it had exited his back. Jennings kicked at the corpse and stroked thoughtfully at his own chin. He needed this delay to decide on his next course of action. Obviously the original plan to pay Kretzmer before Steel's arrival was as dead as the man at his feet. He

122

would have to act on his initiative alone.

*   *   *

He was still hatching a plan a half-hour later, when Stringer approached him.

'Beggin' your pardon, Sir. But me and some of the men was wondering if you'd like to share in a piece of chicken, Sir. Found all legal and proper, Sir. Property of . . . no one in particular.'

Jennings smiled. 'How very kind, Sarn't. That would be most agreeable. And as it belonged to no one in particular then no word of it any further than our own little circle, eh? Now tell me, how do you intend to cook your chicken? Will you fricassee it or do the men prefer a ragout, d'you think?'

Steel watched the Major and his fawning Sergeant walk across to where a platoon of his musketeers were gathered about a fire over which they had suspended a stout straight branch between two cleft sticks. This was surely Stringer's doing, he thought. He would have coerced the men into parting with some of their hard-won plunder, legal or not. As for the rest of them, he and Williams would make do with the bread and cheese he had carried in his pack for the past two days. Slaughter, he knew, had a bottle of rum.

There had not been time to bury the dead before nightfall. They had moved them though, covered them with what leaves and branches they could find in the half-light and laid them out under the cover of the trees that grew along the riverbank; the stench would blow with the wind away from the camp. It was not ideal, but that was

123

ever the case with war. You simply had to make the best of your lot. He reached into his pocket for a wad of tobacco and placing it in his mouth began to chew. He had sent Slaughter back for the wagons, with a full platoon. The light was fading and empty as they were, there was nothing to be gained by chancing their loss. Walking across the camp, he found Tom Williams by the bridge, staring up at the sky.

'I think that's the Plough, Sir. Am I right?'

'I think you are, Tom. Well done. We'll make a woodsman of you yet.'

'Good to have Major Jennings and his men, Sir, don't you think?'

Steel spat a mouthful of the acrid tobacco juice on to the ground.

'Yes, very good. Very good of Colonel Hawkins to keep me in his thoughts. Judging by today's experience we will soon be glad of the extra men. But time is of the essence, Tom. We should not delay.'

Even as he spoke, and tried to tell himself to think nothing of it, Steel could not comprehend what had possessed Hawkins to send Jennings to his aid. Nor why the Major should have elected to spend the night here, among the corpses, when the town was so close at hand. And later, as he drew his blanket tightly around his still-clothed form and lay trying to chase sleep, while the gentle sound of the running water rippled through his consciousness, he found the thought still nagging at his mind. It was insistent as the intermittent hoot of an old barn owl that had come to sit in one of the high trees by the riverbank, gazing down greedily at the wide-eyed bodies of the dead.

124

FIVE

The two men gazed at the tall column of smoke that climbed up lazily into the sky. Steel spoke:

'Well, at least we know we're not alone, Jacob. Three thousand horse dispatched as far as Munich with orders to burn and destroy all the country about it.'

The Sergeant grimaced and muttered under his breath.

'Still. Best not tell the men, Sir. They don't like it. Goes against the grain. Doing that to civilians. And it can't help us neither. If you ask me, Mister Steel, we're walking into trouble.'

'Better to be here, Jacob, than kicking our heels with the rest of the army in the trenches besieging Rain. Or worse still out with the damned dragoons burning innocent civilians out of their homes.'

'I'm blessed if I can fathom it out, Sir. I mean what are we doing here? Why send us, Grenadiers for God's sake, the best of all the army, to find provisions?'

Steel shook his head and said nothing. I wish I could tell you, Jacob, he thought. But there are some things which even you cannot know. He looked ahead.

At least this village, whose white-painted houses now began to rise up ahead of him as they crested the slope, appeared as yet to have escaped utterly the ravages of Marlborough's dragoons. Sattelberg. The rendezvous with Kretzmer.

'Look, Sarn't. No sign of burning here, at least. Perhaps they've stopped. We shouldn't find any

125

trouble.'

Slaughter nodded and smiled. But in his heart, Steel knew that it would not be in Marlborough's way to finish this thing so soon. A few burnt townships would not be sufficient to make the point. If he really believed that these tactics would coerce the Elector, Steel knew that his commander would conduct a sustained campaign of terror. This was only the beginning. He grasped the pommel of his saddle and with a swift motion hoisted his leg up on to Molly's back. Whatever his personal feelings, he also knew that to lead a column into a village required any officer to look the part.

Steel goaded the horse into a trot and rode along to the where Williams led the column. 'Looks a pretty little place, Tom, don't it?'

They had started from their bivouac an hour ago, travelling more slowly now, on account of the wagon train. Not that they had woken late. It had taken a good two hours to bury all the dead, from both sides. It was around nine in the morning now and, as they grew closer to the village Steel noticed in the neighbouring fields the cattle grazing happily and carts standing half-filled with harvested produce.

'Villagers seem to be at their breakfast, Sir.'

'Perhaps they'll save some for us, Tom, eh?'

As the redcoats entered what appeared to be the place's major street a single sheepdog, who had been standing in the middle of the highway, barked a greeting and ran off to the left.

Steel looked up to the windows, waiting for the usual inquisitive faces to appear. For the children to run to greet them with taunting rhymes and begging gestures. Waiting for the doors of the houses to open. For the women to stand on the thresholds. For his men to whistle at the pretty ones and mock the ugly and the old. Would they be treated, he wondered, with condemnatory silence, or openly jeered. He hardly thought it likely they would have a warm welcome. What they received though exceeded all his expectations. The column advanced still further into the half-cobbled street, until it was almost at a tall stone cross, in the very heart of the little community. Still, though the half-timbered houses stood neat and silent in black-and-white perfection, the bright summer flowers pretty in their painted wooden boxes, no doors were opened. Steel raised his hand in command.

'Company, halt.'

Everything was just as it should be. Beside a well-maintained water pump sat a clean pail, ready to be filled. Smoke curled up from the chimney of the inn to his right and from those of several other houses. He fancied that he caught the faint smell of cooking on the air. Cabbage. And something else—a strange aroma.

On one side of the village square, beyond the cross, stood a small church, a solid enough structure of stone and wood in the local style. He looked around to find any other building of authority. The church would do. Surely the priest would know what was going on. Grasping his pommel, Steel dismounted and, drawing his fusil from its sheath on the back of his saddle, he slung it over his shoulder.

'Mister Williams. Stay here. I'm going to find someone. Sarn't, with me.'

With measured step, Slaughter at his side, eyes searching the windows and surrounding lanes, Steel walked towards the church. Pushing gently at the door, he found it to be open. Inside was a cool haven. It was a simple basilica of plain stone, enlivened by two large and unremarkable oil paintings of obscure Catholic saints in grizzly attitudes of martyrdom. At the far end stood an altar whose gold ornament and richness of decoration were in profound contrast to the dun-hued stone. The place reeeked of incense and damp.

Steel yelled into the cool gloom: 'Hello. Monsignor?'

His words echoed around the stones. The place was quite empty.

Nodding to Slaughter to follow him, he turned and walked out, back into the square.

Jennings had ridden up and was talking to Williams. Steel walked over to them. 'No one in there. No priest. No one. Where the hell is everyone?'

Jennings gazed down at him with the supercilious disdain of someone to whom that conclusion had long been obvious.

'Yes, I do wonder.'

He took a handkerchief from his sleeve and dabbed at his nose.

'So, Mister Steel. What do you suggest that we do now? As you rightly observe the place appears to be deserted. Where, d'you suppose, is our contact?'

Steel, more bemused than irritated, shook his head. 'I have no idea, Sir. Really. I can't fathom it.'

'Well we'd better find someone. Let me try.'

He turned in the saddle towards the rear of the column.

'Stringer.'

The Sergeant came running, eager-eyed, from across the village square.

'Sir.'

'See if you can find someone in this godforsaken place. Anyone. Take . . . a platoon and search the houses. One by one. Kick down any doors that are locked.'

Steel turned to Williams. 'Tom, rest the men here. Have them sit down. Ten minutes.'

Ignoring Jennings' raised eyebrows, he looked at Slaughter. 'Come on, Jacob.'

Steel unslung his gun from his shoulder and, holding it at the ready, began to walk with the Sergeant, up the road which led away from the church to the left, and from where he could still hear the sound of the howling dog. He looked down at the dusty cobbles. There had been movement here recently. The earth, which would normally have lain in a dust across the round stones, had been displaced so that they shone in the pale sunlight. A lot of movement by the look of it. Following the line of the exposed cobblestones he looked up the road, tracing the path of those who had gone before. Houses flanked either side of the narrow street and at the top, at the edge of a field, stood a large structure, simpler than the rest. A barn.

He turned to Slaughter. 'Come on. Keep your eyes open.'

Slowly, the two men made their way up the hill. From below they could hear the splinter of wood as Stringer and his men kicked in the doors of locked houses. As they neared the edge of the village he looked at Slaughter and nodded in the direction of the timber-framed barn.

Quickly, Steel pushed open the door of the building and was barely over the threshold when he retched. Instinctively, although the place was quite dark, he closed his eyes. It was all he could do to avoid vomiting.

The smell was vile, but what met his gaze was far worse.

The barn was filled with bodies. Men, women and children, piled high upon one another. There must have been six score of them. All ages. And all were quite dead. He knew that without even troubling to look. Whoever had done this thing had been thorough. Not a sound came from the place save the buzzing of the flies that hovered and settled on the lifeless forms. Sattelberg had been a small farming township, with a population of barely 120 souls.

And here they were. Murdered in cold blood and left to rot.

Left, rather, thought Steel, with the specific intention that they should be discovered. This, he knew, was not the work of any of Marlborough's men. But that was precisely what those who had done it wanted those who were meant to find the bodies to suppose. This had been meant to look like the work of British soldiers, but whoever had really done it had certainly not been counting upon their handiwork being discovered first by a company of genuine redcoats.

Yet, Steel asked himself, what sort of men could have done such a thing? This sort of atrocity had not taken place in Europe for almost a hundred years. Not since the wars of Gustavus. Could this really be the way that his own age would now go to war? The assault on Schellenberg had indeed made him think. But this new horror was quite another thing. He looked down at the bloody cadavers. Saw the leg of a young girl, not yet ten, he thought, protruding at a sickening angle from beneath the torso of a half-naked woman streaked with dried blood, presumably her dead mother, her arms still wrapped around the child. He forced himself to walk deeper into the gloom. Saw the body of a boy, the top of his head blown off, and that of a girl in her teens, a gaping hole in her back marking the exit of a musket ball. Tripping over outstretched, lifeless limbs to make his way back to the door, he found the corpse of the priest, tumbled into a corner. He had died from a sword cut to his head.

Steel staggered to the door. What sort of men killed innocents in this way? Not men at all. Mere beasts. Choking again on the stench, he pulled a handkerchief from his pocket and held it to his face. Calling out into the street, he struggled to get the words out of his dry mouth.

'Sarn't Slaughter. In here. Burial detail.'

Slaughter walked towards him and entered the barn. For a moment he stood speechless then, covering his mouth with his hand, spoke in a quiet voice:

'Holy Christ, Sir. Sweet mother of God. The poor bastards. Who the bloody hell did this? Not the French, surely? Not soldiers? Eh?'

Steel gazed at the corpses and managed at last to speak. 'Well, I don't think, Jacob, that it was our men. And it surely couldn't be the Bavarians

131

themselves. This surely is the reason why Major Jennings was attacked by those peasants. It can only have been the French. D'you think?'

'I'm learning not to think in this war, Mister Steel, Sir. Christ. Will you look at them. The poor wee babbies too. Holy Mother. It's inhuman. Inhuman, Sir.'

'And that's just what we were meant to think, Sarn't. And anyone else who might have found this. This wasn't meant for us. But you've seen the smoke. Let's say you were Bavarian and that you found this. What would you think? Who would you suppose had done it? What would you do?'

Slaughter froze. 'I . . . I'd say that it was us that had done it, Sir. The English. Or at least them Dutch dragoons that's been burnin' the villages. I'd swear to kill any redcoats that I saw. Oh Christ. I see, Sir. The bastards.'

'Of course you'd think that. And of course you'd want to kill the bloody English, wouldn't you? And you'd come looking for any of us you could find.'

They turned and left the charnel-house, stunned momentarily by the sunlight.

Jennings was advancing towards them up the street, his face a mask of anger. 'What the devil's going on, Steel? We can find no one down in the village. We've got work to do. There's no time to dally here. Where's the bloody agent? Have you found him? What're you doin' up here?'

Then he noticed the open door of the barn. 'I say, what's in here?'

Jennings walked up to the door, pushed it open to enter and instantly wished he hadn't. They heard the sound of him puking on the floor and, after a few moments, he emerged, wiping his mouth and ashen faced. He dabbed at his nose with the cologne-scented handkerchief and reached into his waistcoat pocket for his snuff box. Tucking a pinch of the brown powder into each nostril, he sneezed violently and then, after a few moments, turned to Steel.

'Good God. How revolting. Vile. Who? What d'you think? Must have been those brigands, eh?'

Steel shook his head. 'These people are Bavarians, Major. Same as your "brigands".'

'Not the French?'

Steel nodded. Jennings struggled to regain his composure.

'Of course, we had better burn the place. Burn all the bodies, eh? Poor buggers. Sarn't. Organize a detachment. Burn the barn.'

Steel stared at Jennings, hard. 'Sarn't Slaughter. You will disregard that last order. No, Major. We are going to bury them. All of them. And then, after we file our report when we return to the camp, someone will be able to come here and find them and then they'll all get the decent Christian burial that they deserve.'

Jennings opened his mouth to protest, but seeing the look in Slaughter's eyes, he thought the better of it.

Steel continued: 'We can't bury them individually, of course. That would take far too long and we don't know who's still watching us, do we? Sarn't Slaughter. See if you can find some shovels. There are bound to be some around here. Have the men dig two pits. Over there, in that field, to the west of the barn. And they'd better be quick about it. I don't like this place.'

Steel turned and walked back down the hill in

133

silence, followed at a short distance by the fuming Jennings. Reaching the square, he was struck by a sudden, ghastly thought. He turned to Williams.

'Has anyone seen the agent? Tom? Take half a platoon. Visit every house in the village. See if you can find me a fat Bavarian. Any civilian, living or dead, who looks as if he might have been a man wanting to sell me some flour.'

Williams stared at him. 'But, Mister Steel, Sir. Where are the villagers?'

'Up there. Dead. All of them. Now find that bloody Bavarian.'

Where the hell was the man, surely not in the barn? And what of the precious papers?

He signalled to a group of a dozen Grenadiers.

'You men. Come with me. See that building at the top of the street. It's full of bodies. Bring them out and be careful with it. And while you're about it see if you can find someone in there. We're looking for a fat man. A Bavarian merchant. I'll give tuppence to anyone who finds him.'

The young Ensign, stupefied, began to get about his task and as Steel was about to walk back up to the barn, Jennings caught his arm. He spat out his name, smiling.

'Steel. Why don't I try and find Herr Kretzmer too. You stay here and see if you can get this mess cleared up.'

Steel was silent. It occurred to him that if Jennings were to find Kretzmer himself then the man might mistake him for Steel and offer him the vital papers. What, Steel wondered, would the Major make of them? It was imperative that he find Kretzmer. How though, he wondered, might he decline Jennings' offer. To do so would be to

134

disobey what amounted to a direct order.

He was still wondering when the cellar door of a small one-storey house directly behind Jennings banged open against the ground and up from the basement, like some demon emerging on to the stage of one of Mr Pinkeman's famous plays, a white-faced figure emerged. The man was a civilian, his pallid features topped off by a dusty brown wig, his ample form straining against the buttons of a dark red velvet coat and somewhat under-generous pair of cambric breeches. From the state of his clothes and the straw in his wig, he had evidently contrived to get into some place of safety when the French had fallen upon the hapless villagers. The man caught sight of the red-coated soldiers and smiled, hopefully.

Jennings, unaware of the newcomer's presence, stood grinning at Steel, still believing him to have been outfoxed. Steel smiled and coughed, pointing slowly towards the door.

Jennings turned around. Steel spoke:

'Gentlemen. I think that we may have found our man.'

He nodded to the newcomer. 'Herr Kretzmer?'

The man nodded. Jennings turned, unable to believe this latest stroke of bad luck. Steel continued, speaking in French.

'Lieutenant Steel, Sir. You have, I believe, a quantity of flour that I am charged to purchase on behalf of Her Majesty's army.'

Kretzmer smiled. 'Thank God you are here. The French. I was terrified. It was dreadful. I managed to hide myself in the cellar. I just heard the screams. Did they kill them all?'

'Everyone.'

135

Kretzmer looked at the ground. Wiping his eyes with his hand he shook his head.

Steel spoke: 'Come, Herr Kretzmer. Let us do business. You have the flour?'

Kretzmer, ever the businessman, looked Steel in the eye and nodded. 'Yes. I have the flour. If you like it.'

Jennings cut in. 'I'm sorry, Herr Kretzmer. Aubrey Jennings, Major, Farquharson's Foot. I am Lieutenant Steel's commanding officer.'

Not quite yet you aren't, however much you might wish it, thought Steel.

Jennings continued: 'We have business, Herr Kretzmer. Shall we?'

Kretzmer led them across the village square to a tall stone building that stood by the church. He took a large iron key from his pocket and turned it in the lock, then opened one of the two doors. Inside they saw sacks piled high upon one another. There was enough flour here, thought Steel, to keep the army fed for at least two weeks. He called across to the cook, sent by Hawkins.

'You there. Cook. Come here. Time to work for your keep.'

It had become common practice for civilian contractors to mix in sand with grain or flour. The only way to tell if it was right was to open a sack at random and the only person sufficiently skilled to estimate the likelihood of it being representative of the entire consignment was a cook.

Sitting himself down at a low table that stood in a corner of the store, Steel watched as the man slit open one of the bags, allowed a little of the fine white powder to trickle to the floor and then put his hand in. He put it to his lips.

'That's flour, Sir. Fine flour, Sir. As good as any we've had.'

'Fine. Well that's good enough for me. Herr Kretzmer.' Steel motioned to the merchant and produced a purse. 'You may count it out if you wish.'

The merchant, his sad eyes now bright with greed, sat down on a hay bale and undid the drawstring on the purse before emptying the contents on to a small bench table. Eagerly, expertly, he counted out the coins and flipped them back into the purse.

Jennings watched attentively and turned to Steel.

'Best get the money put away once he's finished, before the men have sight of it. Never good for them to see money, eh, Steel? But I don't suppose that you see very much of it either.'

The door opened and Stringer entered.

'Major Jennings, Sir. I think you had better come. It's Murdoch. He's asking to see you, Sir. Reckon he won't last much longer, Major.'

Darting an anxious glance back at the two men, Jennings followed his Sergeant from the room. Alone now with Kretzmer, Steel watched as he finished counting the coins, then turned away. Now, he thought. The dying wish of Private Murdoch, wounded in the fight with the peasants, to see his officer had given him what might be his only chance.

He crossed the floor of the store and stood at the bench just as the man dropped the last coin into the purse and drew the string. Then, saying nothing, Steel placed his fists on the bench and slid one hand deftly over the purse, wresting it easily from Kretzmer.

'And now, Sir. I believe that we have other business. You have something else for me. Something for which I am also contracted to pay you?'

Steel produced another bag of gold coins from his valise.

Kretzmer pretended surprise and smiled. 'Yes, Lieutenant. I have your papers. Come. I will take you to them.'

*   *   *

High up on the lush, green eminence which overlooked what had been the peaceful village of Sattelberg, Major Claude Malbec, second in command of the Grenadiers Rouge, the most unruly, immoral and consistently victorious regiment in King Louis' army, knelt down on the dew-sodden grass before his men and reflected on the little vignette that had unfolded beneath him. He smiled. He had not expected his quarry to be cornered quite so easily. He twisted an end of his moustache and considered his good fortune. Following the fight at Schellenberg, he had been sent here with his battered command by his senior officer, Colonel Michelet, with orders to find a Bavarian merchant bearing some papers vital to the war effort. Not plans or orders, he had been told, but personal papers of some significance to the Duke of Marlborough. It was a prestigious mission and Malbec was honoured. They had arrived earlier that day, but of the Bavarian there was no trace. Some of the townspeople said they had seen such a man. But no one knew where he

138

was now. It had occurred to Malbec that they might be hiding him, but even under interrogation the men had denied knowledge of his whereabouts.

The massacre had been a little twist of his own, fuelled by his rising frustration at having failed in his mission. In truth though, he thought it now a stroke of inspiration. How it would incense the Bavarian peasantry against the British and their German allies and as word of it spread throughout the countryside, it would also undo any ill-feeling against their own leader and the French wrought by Marlborough's burnings. True, a couple of his men had expressed their opposition to the killings. But for the most part there had been no problem. Besides, however much his commanders and those back in Paris might decry what Marlborough was doing, it was no different, in fact less severe, than the devastation the French themselves had wrought upon the Palatinate in Lower Bavaria barely twenty years ago. What hypocrites, he thought, in the high command. How long would they ever survive in the field? What did they know of the cruel reality of war?

Acting on a hunch that sooner or later the British would arrive to find the merchant, Malbec had taken his men off to this hill. And now his perception had paid off. He watched as the tall redcoat officer, who, with his strange appearance, looked curiously familiar, emerged from the building with the fat Bavarian. Together the two men walked across the square and the German descended steps into the cellar of a building. He re-emerged carrying a small chest. Malbec watched as the man unlocked the wooden box and carefully withdrew a small package. This must be what he had been sent to take. Now all that remained was for him and his men to relieve the British of their prize.

*   *   *

Standing in the town square, Steel looked away from Kretzmer for a moment and up towards the barn. It seemed to him from here as if his Grenadiers might have already filled one of the shallow grave pits dug in the field behind the building. Several of them, he could see, bareheaded and in their shirtsleeves, were starting to pull out yet more of the bloodied bodies. He turned back to Kretzmer and saw that he had extracted a bundle of papers from the chest. Steel was just stretching out his hand to take it, when he heard the first shot. A musket ball whirred past his head and struck the wall of the tall white house behind him.

'Christ.'

Steel ducked instinctively to the ground, as he did so pushing over the merchant on to the cobbles.

'Get down.'

To their left he heard a word of command in French and then more guns spat fire. Up on the hill four men went down from the Grenadiers.

'Cover. Take cover.'

Keeping his head down, Steel pulled Kretzmer up from the ground and dragged him behind a water barrel. As other shots rang out across the street, ricocheting off stone and wood, he called towards where, from the corner of his eye, he had seen Slaughter execute a similar manoeuvre.

'Ambush. Take cover! Sarn't Slaughter. Are you all right?'

'Fine, Sir. Never better. D'you think that'll be the French then, Sir?'

'Well I don't suppose it's the bloody Foot Guards. Tom? Everyone else unhurt?'

'Sir.'

'Evans has caught one. Think he's dead, Sir.'

'Where the hell are they? Anyone know?'

Slaughter answered: 'There's some behind that big house over on the right, Sir. A hundred yards, maybe less. Some more behind you, near the church.'

How the hell the French, if that was indeed who they were, had got into the village God only knew. But here they were and, unless he did something about it, Steel realized that slowly but surely, most of his men were going to die. And then, if these were the same men who had massacred the villagers, any who surrendered would almost certainly be butchered in cold blood. He thought fast and looked up from his position on the ground and around the village, assessing strengths and weaknesses.

The wagoners were cowering beneath their vehicles and the horses were whinnying in the traces. Three narrow roads led off the village square. One leading up the hill went to the barn and the corpses. As far as he was aware, despite the casualties, there was still the best part of a platoon of Grenadiers up there, under Corporal Taylor. Thirty more Grenadiers were in one of the roads off to the right with Slaughter and the remainder close to him and Williams. Of Jennings

141

there was no sign. Steel knew that they had laid the wounded men from Jennings' company in a large house further up the hill towards the barn and presumed that the Major might still be there with what men remained fit to fight. He would have to make do with the Grenadiers. Better that way, they were men he could trust. He shouted across the street.

'Sarn't Slaughter. You take care of the lot to my rear. We'll do what we can up the hill. See you back at the camp. Good luck.'

He realized that Kretzmer was still with him. The merchant, shaking like a leaf, was stuffing the bundle of papers inside his waistcoat and trying to make himself invisible behind a barrel. Steel had no idea of the strength of their enemy. Certainly the fire had been strong initially, although since they had taken cover it had become more sporadic.

There was nothing for it. He turned to Williams.

'Tom. I'm going to take ten men and create a diversion. When you can see where they're firing at me from, take the rest and rush their position. You should only have thirty yards or so to run. They won't have time to reload. Prime your grenades before you go and throw them when you're ten yards out. Got that? Ten yards, then hit the ground. Wait for the explosions and then in you go with the bayonet. Right?'

'Sir.'

Williams' eyes were alive, the adrenalin pumping through him.

Steel looked around at the men crouching behind the barrels.

'Tarling, Bannister, Hopkins. Come with me. The rest of you, go with Mister Williams.

Grenades boys. Send them to hell.'

Steel looked at his men, then down at Kretzmer, who was whimpering. Steel cursed:

'Oh Christ.'

He tugged at the man's sleeve. 'Come on. Venez avec moi. And run like blazes.'

Leaping from the cover of the wooden casks, they erupted into the street, Steel dragging the fat Bavarian at his side. Instantly the enemy musketeers opened up. Head down, legs like lead in a lolloping run, Steel, his arm firmly around Kretzmer's flabby waist, cast a look over his shoulder. He could see two ranks at least, maybe more. White coats and brown moustachioed faces topped with bearskin hats. French Grenadiers. A half company or more. Regular infantry. Could these men really have been the authors of the crime in the barn? Steel was making for the safety of an open door in a half-timbered house across the street when he felt the balls from the first volley smacking the air around his head. He sensed that one of his men had gone down, but had no idea who. And then they were inside the door. Looking out into the street, Steel saw Bannister lying face upwards, a hole through his temple, and looking down the street he could see the French reloading, priming their pans. Come on, Tom. Where the hell was the young Ensign? In an instant it would be too late. Then, not a moment too soon and with an animal roar, Williams and his ten men appeared from behind the wagon. They charged down the street straight towards the French Grenadiers, the young officer, his sword drawn leading the way, his face split in a rictus of anger. Steel watched as the French, their loading

143

not yet completed, start incredulously as the ten Grenadiers came straight for them. It was lunacy, eleven men charging nigh on five times their number, drawn up in line three ranks deep, their flanks secure against two sides of a street. But this was a madness for which the French had not allowed.

Steel watched with fascination as their expressions turned to alarm and then surprise as, at ten yards out, the Grenadiers stopped short and hurled their fizzing black iron balls. Then the full horror of the situation hit the French. He looked on at the different reactions. Some men turned and ran. One threw down his musket. Others stood rooted to the spot and watched in silence as the black orbs glided through the air towards them. Their officer, standing at their side, his sword raised ready to command another volley, stood open mouthed. Williams and his men threw themselves down on the cobbles, covering their heads with their hands. And then the bombs exploded. All of them.

For once not one sputtered out and the French Grenadiers were ripped apart by shards of red-hot metal that tore at skin, sinew and bone, cutting their evil way through heads, necks, limbs, and torsos. The street disappeared in a cloud of black and grey smoke and gouts of blood. Some fragments of the grenades hit walls and tore shards of masonry and pan-tile free, sending them showering down on the enemy troops below.

Steel, who had closed the door against the blast, opened it cautiously and surveyed the scene. Gradually, as the smoke cleared, he made out a tangle of bodies and body parts lying across the street where a few seconds before the French had been drawn up. Williams pushed himself up from the road on his palms and got to his feet, coughing away the debris in his throat and brushing the dust and brick from his coat. He was followed by his ten Grenadiers, some of whom had begun to laugh. And Williams too found himself laughing with relief. For where the Frenchmen had been, lay nothing but a heap of dead and dying men. Through the dusty air Steel glimpsed the forms of perhaps a half-dozen of the white-coated infantry running for their lives and behind them, supporting each other, another five wounded. But of the rest nothing remained save broken bodies. Steel emerged from the house and, still steering Kretzmer, making sure not to let him go, led his remaining men towards Williams.

'Well done, Tom. Couldn't have made a better job of it myself.'

He patted the boy on the back. Williams turned round. He was staring wildly and his mouth hung wide open.

'They. They just disappeared. We did it. We killed them all. We did it. Look, Sir.'

Steel knew the reaction. The absolute shock of the first battle. He knew that the only thing to do now was to carry on. Move to the next killing ground.

'Yes, Tom you did it. And bloody well. Now take your men and follow up. Get into cover over there and see if you can find out if there are any more of the buggers in the place.'

He looked down at a dead Frenchman. Now there could be no doubt as to who had committed the atrocity. The man was a Grenadier. French,

145

wearing a dark brown bearskin cap which bore a brass plaque with a distinctive cipher which Steel had seen once before.

'I know that uniform. This is the same regiment we met at Schellenberg. I was told there were no enemy in these parts. What the hell are these buggers doing here?' He turned to Hopkins, Tarling and another man, Jock Miller.

'You three, come with me. Let's see if we can help Sarn't Slaughter.'

At that moment he became aware of the crack of gunfire from the street leading off to the right where he had sent Slaughter. Quickly, with Kretzmer still in tow, they ran across the square. There was firing, too, coming from further up the hill, by the barn. Taylor. He would have to wait. Entering the narrow street, Steel found Slaughter and his men pinned down behind a makeshift barricade of barrels and furniture. Steel, Kretzmer and the two Grenadiers dashed for cover and slid down next to the Sergeant. Slaughter was hot with the battle, and his face was decorated with a long, shallow cut across the forehead. Steel pointed to it.

'All right, Sarn't?'

Slaughter put up his hand and wiped away the blood.

'It's nothing. Just a graze. Bastards took us by surprise, Sir. We've three men down, but we managed to throw together some cover.'

Steel poked his head half an inch above the parapet of a chair leg and glimpsed another line of French Grenadiers. Another fifty, perhaps sixty men. Christ, they had come in some force to do their filthy work. A company at least, and the men up on the hill. The end of the street exploded again in another volley of French fire. The British crouched as low as they could as the musket balls zinged through gaps in the flimsy wooden barricade. Two men cried out as they were hit. Another fell dead without a sound.

Slaughter spoke. 'Begging your pardon, Sir, but do you think we might get out of here now. It's starting to get a bit hot for my liking.'

'My sentiments entirely, Sarn't.'

Steel looked to his right where, as he had dropped down, he thought he had seen an open doorway. Sure enough, there it was.

'Right, Jacob. I'll take ten men and outflank them. We'll go through that house. You stay put. See if you can keep them at the end of the street with ragged fire. When you hear me shout, have the men stand up and rush the Frogs. Use your grenades and then give them the bayonet. You know what to do. They won't see you. Trust me.'

Slaughter looked at Steel. He had never had cause not to trust him and he certainly did not intend to start now.

'Right you are, Sir.'

'Go to it, Jacob. It's time to make them pay for what they did to those poor bastards up on the hill.'

The Sergeant looked grim and nodded his head. He drew his bayonet from its scabbard and slotted it on to the end of his fusil. Steel edged towards the house.

'Hopkins, Miller, Tarling. The first seven of you men. Come with me.'

Still crouching, he led them into the house and prayed that there would be a rear door through which they could exit into the next street. Inside, full plates of food on the table and a child's doll lying on the floor bore grim testimony to the violent end of the house's former inhabitants. Steel did not pause to think. Pushing Kretzmer into a chair, he put his finger to his lips and waved his hand parallel to the floor in an attempt to tell the man to stay there and wait for his return. He needn't have worried. The sweating merchant, confused and terrified by what had happened earlier in the day and now aware of the full horror of which he had so nearly become a part, really didn't look as if he wanted to go anywhere.

Moving into the kitchen Steel found what he was looking for and cautiously edged the door open. The street beyond seemed empty. Carefully unbuckling his belt, he laid it down on a table, unsheathed his sword and slung his fusil over his shoulder. His men did the same. There must be nothing about them to make any noise which might alert the enemy. The Grenadiers, bareheaded now like their Lieutenant, knew the drill that he had taught them so doggedly and soon each man was left with only his gun, with its bayonet fixed and two leather pouches, one with ammunition, the other containing two grenades. Each of them touched a slow match at the embers of the fire which still burnt in the grate and threaded it carefully through a buttonhole in his coat, where it would smoulder until needed to ignite the bombs.

Waving his hand slowly along the line of the street, Steel motioned the men to follow him and left the house. He could hear intermittent sputtering musketry from up on the hill that could only mean the burial detail was still holding out.

Perhaps too Jennings, wherever he was, had managed to assemble enough men for a spirited resistance. The Grenadiers stuck close to him, following the line of the wall. This was how he had taught them to fight. To use their initiative, hugging whatever cover they could and above all being absolutely silent.

From the parallel street he could hear the sound of Slaughter's men delivering sporadic fusil shots and the occasional crashing volley in return as the French brought all their weapons to bear on the barricade, splintering wood and tearing through fabric with lethal ferocity.

Steel and his men moved slowly, with an almost feline stealth, along the line of houses, being careful not to linger between any two buildings. Within minutes they had drawn parallel with the French line. Three houses faced directly on to their flank. That would be enough. Making a circular sign with his hands to signify a grenade, Steel dispatched three Grenadiers into each of the buildings. They would know where to position themselves to give a sweeping field of fire over the Frenchmen. Steel and the last man, Hopkins, entered the centre building and climbed the narrow stairs. He moved at a crouch across a large bedroom and positioned himself beneath a half-leaded window. The Grenadiers waited only for his command.

Steel took a long breath. He calmed himself for the moment and with painstaking precision brought up his gun. Slowly, he eased the latch on the window and swung it open, at the same time pulling back the cock of the fusil. Like all of his men he had already primed the pan. Steel reached into his ammunition pouch and drawing out a cartridge, bit off the end before pouring the powder down the barrel and spitting in the ball. With his left hand he took the ramrod from its socket and gently prodded the bullet home. Now he was ready. Edging forward to the sill, he took careful aim. The officer was his. Steel fixed him tight in the sights. He was a handsome young man, barely twenty perhaps. An Ensign. Williams' exact counterpart. Again the thought crossed his mind. How could these men have done such a thing? Now was not the time to ask. Steel put his finger against the trigger of his gun and, comfortable with the familiar fit, began to squeeze. With a sharp crack and a puff of white smoke the image disappeared before his eyes and then all was chaos. Looking down at the street Steel could see the young French officer lying dead on the cobbles. Eight more Frenchmen lay wounded, dead and dying around him. The remainder, apparently with no officer now, had turned their eyes towards the three houses from which the Grenadiers were firing and had begun to take aim at the windows, but before they had time to fire a rain of black grenades fell into the street. The French ducked instinctively, but there was no escape. The sputtering fuses burnt deep into the packed explosive and the lethal metal shards did their job. All but two of the grenades exploded and the street became a mess of smoke and blood.

From his right, Steel heard a great cheer as the twenty men with Slaughter charged up the street and into any of the French who remained standing. Confident that the Sergeant would finish them off,

Steel rattled back down the stairs and out into the street. There was no need for caution now. He could still hear musketry from high on the hill but there was something else he had to do before going to the aid of Taylor or Jennings.

Crashing back into the house where he had abandoned Kretzmer, he found the man exactly where he had left him, frozen to the chair. Two Grenadiers stood guard over him. One of them, Tom McNeil, grinned at him.

'Thought we should make sure no harm come to him, Sir.'

Steel smiled. 'Very good, McNeil.'

He turned to Kretzmer. He had to act now, before Jennings returned, if the Major were still alive.

'Now, Herr Kretzmer. We have some unfinished business to conclude.'

'Sir. Yes. I have your papers.'

Reaching into his pocket, Kretzmer held out a small package to Steel. It was wrapped in brown paper and tied with string. Quickly, still holding the gun, Steel fumbled with the twine and managed to slip it off. Placing the package on the table he deftly opened one side and slid out what appeared to be the first of several pieces of parchment. It bore the ancient royal seal of the Stuart monarchy and a Paris address and was addressed clearly, in a long spidery hand, to the future Duke of Marlborough. Yes, these were the crucial papers.

Steel pushed the second purse towards Kretzmer who weighed it in his hand. He smiled and had just slipped it inside the capacious inner pocket of his coat when the door opened and

Jennings appeared. He was sweating and his face was flushed with the exhilaration of victory. There was blood on his sword. Kretzmer winced. Steel pocketed the papers.

'We've done it. They're on the run. It was a damn close thing though. Lost a few men. What happened here? See any action. Oh, I say, Steel. You appear to have cut yourself.'

Steel wiped his hand across his cheek and felt the blood. 'We saw them off.'

Jennings stared at Steel, then saw Kretzmer.

'So, do we have what we came for, Mister Steel?'

'The flour, Sir? Yes, we have the flour.'

'Then our business here is done, Lieutenant, is it not?'

'So it would seem, Sir.'

Jennings looked at his sword and noticing the blood, picked up a linen tablecloth which lay across the top of a chair and wiped it clean before sheathing it. He turned to Steel.

'Now, Lieutenant, you will take yourself off up the hill and ascertain as to whether your burial detail has finished interring those poor villagers. Then you will find another burial party from the Grenadiers and bury the dead from the later encounter.'

'Sir?'

'You have a problem, Steel?'

'I am to find the burial party from the Grenadiers alone.'

'Why certainly. My men are far too exhausted for such work. They have just fought a battle, Steel. Besides, you pride yourselves on being the biggest and the fittest men of the army. Most

152

certainly you shall find the burial party from the Grenadiers. Now if you please, Mister Steel.'

Steel, feeling the rage rise inside him, managed a nod towards Jennings and left the room. The Major relaxed in triumph and turned to Kretzmer.

'Now, Herr Kretzmer. I have a question for you. You came here with something more than flour, yes?'

Kretzmer eyed him carefully. Unsure how to answer.

'Yes. That is true.'

'You have a paper. A parcel, for which we are to pay you.'

'Yes, Herr Major. But you have already done so. The Lieutenant . . .'

Jennings brought his fist hard down upon the table. 'Damn the man to hell!'

Kretzmer shied away from Jennings' fury.

'I am sorry, Major. Was that not right? He knew about the paper. He had the money.'

Jennings stared at him. 'You fool. You stupid, stupid little man.'

For a moment the terrified merchant thought that Jennings might be about to hit him. Instead, the Major turned on his heel and began to walk quickly from the room. At the door he paused and hissed back at Kretzmer:

'Tell anyone of this, and you're a dead man.'

Outside in the town square, red-coated soldiers were busy collecting weapons and equipment from the dead. Jennings walked towards them, his hands curled tight by his side in clenched fists.

Since being rescued by Steel he had not held out much hope of being able to purchase the papers. So now, he thought, he would have to go to the trouble of putting his plan into action. He scanned the figures in the street and at length found the man he was looking for: 'Sergeant Stringer.'

'Sir?'

'I have a proposition for you. I propose to make you a very rich man.'

The Sergeant flashed a smile.

'You will recall our conversation on the matter of Captain Stapleton's gold and the fact that I was to pay Herr Kretzmer to procure the papers?'

'Sir.'

'There has been a change of plan.'

Stringer's weasel eyes narrowed.

'As Mister Steel contrived to speak to Herr Kretzmer before us, it would appear that he has taken the papers for himself and thus we can no longer buy them from that gentleman. In short Herr Kretzmer is no longer of any use. Lieutenant Steel, on the other hand, is vital to our plans. And here is the rub. If you are with me in this, Stringer, which I perceive from your expression you are, we must contrive some means of relieving Mister Steel of those papers. The gold of course now belongs to me. Or rather us. For if we return to Major Stapleton with the documents he will expect the gold to be forfeit. And who will say that we did not pay Herr Kretzmer?' Stringer furrowed his brow in thought.

'Mister Steel, Sir?'

'Mister Steel, Stringer. Our only problem is Mister Steel. What would you say we should do to solve that problem, Stringer?'

The Sergeant thought again and then, as the solution came to him drew close to Jennings' ear:

'Kill him, Sir. Settle him for good.'

'Yes, Stringer, I do think for once, that you may be right.'

SIX

Steel eased himself forward in the saddle and shifted position. Damn this leather. Surely, he should have learnt by now that anything bought as a bargain on campaign would quickly prove to be an utter waste of what little money he had. He moved again, carefully, lest the men should notice. There was a particular piece of the hard hide, just below the cantle, that kept on digging into his thigh and chafing the skin. He swore quietly and turned to the rider on his right. They sat at the head of the great column that wound for more than half a mile behind them through the sun-dappled Bavarian countryside.

'You know, Tom, I sometimes think that we'd all be better off marching with the men than stuck up here on horses. What d'you say?'

'My uncle says that the first duty of an officer is to maintain respect, Sir. Without respect, he says, there is no such thing as an officer.'

'And a very wise man your uncle is, too. But what do you think?'

'I think that I agree, Sir. I think that we should ride.'

'Then I dare say that you and your uncle may be right. Although as you'll learn, Tom, there is a good deal more to being an officer than merely keeping the men in order. They've got to trust you. How can they trust you if all they ever see of you is

155

your horse's backside? Eh? They may call Marlborough 'Corporal John'. May even thank him nightly in their prayers—if they say them—for all he does to comfort them. But we must never forget, Tom, that they're all scum at heart. They are a parcel of rogues and mercenaries. Lewd and dissipate creatures all. Where but the army would they find clothing, pay, and food? We give them all they could want. And in return they give us their lives. Marlborough knows it. You know it.'

The young Ensign smiled. Over the past week he had grown to like Steel and to value his companionship and advice freely given.

They had been on the road seven days now, the last two of which had been passed in loading the flour which would take Marlborough's army to battle. The wagons were increasingly heavy and their pace slower by the day. Steel wished to God that they could get back to rejoin the army. His tasks, both evident and secret, had now been accomplished and the sooner he could convey the papers safely back to Colonel Hawkins, the better. At present the little bundle weighed like a lead ingot against his chest.

He turned back to Williams:

'Quite a man, your uncle, wouldn't you say?'

'Uncle Septimus? Oh, I mean, Uncle James, Sir. Yes, he is rather.'

Steel laughed.

'What did you call him?'

'Er. Septimus, Sir.'

Again Steel laughed. Louder now. 'Well, I'll be buggered. Septimus.'

Williams blushed, concerned that he had betrayed Hawkins.

156

'I shall remember that. Don't worry, Tom. I shan't tell anyone else. It'll be our joke. Septimus indeed.'

They rode on in silence, Steel smirking at his amusing discovery, their harnesses jangling with a quite different note to the metallic rattle of the bayonets that marked the company's every step. Behind them came half a platoon of the Grenadiers, led by Slaughter, and then the first of the forty flour wagons, on which travelled the regimental cook. Each of the wagons was flanked now by just two men apiece. One wagon had been commandeered for the wounded and after that rolled the agent's carriage. For with their dragoons now ravaging the countryside and in light of the attack upon Jennings' company by brigands, Herr Kretzmer had asked if he might travel with the column as far as the allied lines.

Behind his coach rode Jennings. He had toyed with the idea of travelling in the carriage with Kretzmer and tethering his horse to the rear rail. How much more convenient and comfortable. But the Bavarian was piss-poor company and hardly a conversationalist, and Jennings had elected to ride.

Behind him came Stringer, at the head of the remaining marching infantry of Jennings' company, which made up the rearguard.

Following the encounters with the peasants and the French, they had changed formation in case of ambush and were returning to the camp by a different route from that on which either of the redcoat columns had entered Swabia. It took them a few miles further south, around the town of Aicha, and then curled up to the north-west and back again across the Lech. But it would be less

157

obvious to anyone who might have been tracking their progress. It had been Steel's idea and Jennings for once had accepted his advice. He knew the man prided himself on his fieldwork. That Steel had a nose for danger and that he made up what he lacked in more cosmopolitan attributes with a knowledge of country ways. For all his own farming background, rural matters were as foreign a country to Jennings as that in which they now found themselves. To him, Steel was a rustic, defined by his supreme lack of appropriate behaviour. Why, it was evident even in the way he fought. That business in the village for instance, he thought with disdain. What sort of fighting did Steel call that? Throwing bombs and picking individual targets. That wasn't real soldiering. Nor was it particularly effective. Oh, Steel might have frightened off a few of the enemy. Might have left a few dead in the street, but that wasn't soldiering. Jennings, on the other hand, had lined his men across the street and given fire by countermarching ranks, in the proper, prescribed manner. The French had returned his fire in the proper manner, and then both sides had retired, with honour.

Of course he had lost men. More men than Steel's precious Grenadiers. Eleven dead and badly wounded from his remaining two score and ten, to be precise. But what of it? There would be no taking cover for his men, by God. Jennings' men would stand and fight as all true British soldiers should. Not hide and dart about like Steel and his band of bomb-throwing misfits. In a real battle, Jennings knew, Steel would be useless. Here though, the country boy was so evidently in

158

his element that Jennings was only too happy to use him. He indulged himself a pinch of snuff and laughed inwardly, secure in the knowledge that it would after all, be the last command that Steel would ever have.

*   *   *

Steel thought it curious that, since the confrontation at the village, they had observed nothing more of the enemy. His mind was troubled by the massacre; haunted by the vision of the dead children and the priest with the half-severed head. He was concerned too by the fact that in the ensuing skirmish so many of those responsible had escaped, including, he presumed, their commander. But there were deeper concerns too. What had those Grenadiers been doing there? They were a curious regiment. Not one that he had seen or known of before Schellenberg. Why, he wondered, had they been at the village and why had their commanding officer been so keen to engage their column?

And of course there was Jennings. His presence weighed heavily on Steel's mind, as persistent and increasingly troublesome as the nagging pain of this damned saddle. The road wound on lazily through the rolling Swabian landscape and they settled into an easy rhythm. Grey-brown alpine cows gazed at the unlikely column from the fields and minute by laborious minute the sun grew more intense. At the small town of Klingen, where the road divided, rather than ride north on the road to Aicha, they branched south across a shallow river and soon began to climb again, more sharply now.

Steel pointed.

'Tom. D'you see that?'

They looked south, directly along their proposed line of march. Both men had seen the pall of black smoke that rose high above the treetops and climbed until it disappeared in low cloud. Steel caught the faint scent of fresh charcoal on the air.

'Our men or theirs, Sir?'

'Hard to say. But I wouldn't have thought that Marlborough would send his raiding parties quite this far south.'

As they reached the crest of the next hill, Steel, who had now ridden slightly in advance of the head of the column, looked down into the valley and saw what appeared to be a considerable body of people on the road below, coming directly towards him. Unsure what to make of it, he motioned for Williams to join him. 'You've got good eyes, Tom. What d'you reckon to them?'

The young Ensign peered down.

'They look like civilians, Sir. A fair number of them too. Men of all ages, with women and children, and not a few animals. And carts, Sir. Loaded up with God knows what. What can it mean?'

'I'll tell you what that means, Mister Williams. That means that either those French bastards who did for Sattelberg are up there and this lot are on the run from them in fear of their skins, or it means that our own dragoons are out doing their job. And while I don't like either explanation, I pray to God that it's the latter. In truth, Tom, what you see there is part of all that's left of that town up ahead. See the smoke? That'll be their homes.

160

Poor beggars. Where d'you suppose they'll go to now. And what do you think they'll think of us?'

They would soon find out. There was no avoiding the refugees, over a hundred of them. Doubtless a fraction of the total population, Steel thought, unless of course the others had already been put to the sword.

The miserable crowd grew closer. They were a unsettlingly broad social mix, forced into common suffering. The paupers together now with the merchants, each one of them carrying whatever they had been able to salvage. The richer ones pulled carts—for the horses must have been driven off into the fields and the cattle set free or butchered.

The two columns of carts and wagons only just had room to pass side by side on the narrow road. They passed one another in silence, save for the bleating of goats and the howling of babies cradled in their mothers' arms. Steel looked down at the faces of the dispossessed Bavarians, streaked with tears and set grim with anger and despair. This, Steel thought, is the true face of our war. This picture of misery. The death of civilization.

Hardly had the townspeople passed them, when Williams broke the silence:

'Look, Sir.'

A dust cloud told of the approach of a column of horsemen. Steel shaded his eyes against the sunlight and peered into the distance. There was possibly a full troop of them, he reckoned. Perhaps 150 men. For a moment he panicked. They wore red coats certainly, and they looked like dragoons. But were they English, Dutchmen, or French? After their encounter at Sattelberg he did not want

161

to take any more chances. Raising his hand in the air, Steel reined Molly gently into the side of the road.

'Halt.'

The column came to a clanking, grinding stop. Steel spoke again:

'Grenadiers. Forward.'

From behind him, Slaughter and the forward half-platoon of Grenadiers marched in double-time until they were directly to his rear, formed in two ranks.

'Make ready.'

Steel heard the men cock the locks of their guns and knew that the first rank would now have fallen to their knees, placing the butts of their weapons on the ground with the second at the ready close behind. That should do it. The cavalry, to his consternation, continued to advance towards them at a walk and finally came to an abrupt halt. At the moment of doing so, every trooper of their first three ranks drew his sword. Very neat, thought Steel. Whoever you are, you are good. The officer at the head of this red-coated cavalry, probably Steel adduced, from his lace, a Captain, rode forward with his Lieutenant and another trooper. All three looked grim faced and confident. Like the rest of the troop, the trio were covered in dust and soot and looked utterly exhausted. Steel noticed the broad orange sash around the Captain's waist. So, they were Dutch. He could guess only too well what their mission might have been. Having reached the head of the column, both of the dragoon officers doffed their hats— short caps of light-brown fur—and their gesture was returned by Steel and Williams. The Captain, a brawny, moustachioed man with two days' growth of beard on his swarthy skin, spoke first, in thickly accented English:

'Captain Matthias van der Voert of the regiment of dragoons van Coerland, in the army of the United Provinces, Sir. May I enquire who you are and what business you have here?'

'Lieutenant Jack Steel, Sir. Of Sir James Farquharson's Regiment of Foot, in the Army of her Britannic Majesty, Queen Anne. I am here on Lord Marlborough's business, Captain. We have a consignment of flour to be delivered to the army. Vital provisions, you understand.'

A thought entered his mind. 'Perhaps you might be able supplement our escort?'

The Captain gazed down the line of wagons and saw the thinly spread force of ill-at-ease infantrymen.

'I see why you might ask me that favour, Lieutenant. You're a sitting target like that. But I'm afraid that I really cannot be of any assistance. I am under orders to continue through this country, with my men. We cannot be diverted from our task.'

'May I enquire then as to the nature of your task, Captain?'

'We have orders to burn any sizeable village or town in Bavaria that we find still inhabited and to turn out its people into the countryside. It is, I understand, to be done at the express command of your Lord Marlborough.'

Steel nodded his head. It was just as he had presumed. He pointed to the column of smoke.

'That then, I imagine, Captain must be your work up ahead.'

'We burnt that town last night, Lieutenant. Cleared it, so to speak. There's nothing much left. Except the inn and an old church. No one there but an old innkeeper and his daughter. Very pretty. He's ill and she wouldn't move him. But they're quite harmless. Good beer though, if my men have left you any. The girl says that her father's something to do with the English. His relative lives in England, or some such thing. You may find out more. Please, persuade them to leave, if you can, Lieutenant. Our orders were simply to move the people on and burn their houses. We want no part in killing civilians. We left them alone there, just burned the houses. That's what we were told to do.'

He looked genuinely concerned, but was obviously ultimately confident that he had carried out his orders to the letter.

'They should leave. We're not alone here, this country's full of troops. Ours and theirs. Dutch, English, French. I wouldn't stay there if I were them. An old man and a girl. What can they do? They're dead meat, Lieutenant. Or worse.'

Steel was suddenly aware of a commotion from the rear of the column. He looked back along its length and saw that Jennings was trotting towards them. He was mouthing unintelligible words. The Dutch officer saw him too.

'You have another officer?'

'My superior. Our Adjutant. He prefers to travel towards the rear.'

The Dutchman shook his head. The English army never ceased to amuse him. Pleasant men to be sure, but such amateurs. They wage no war for seven years and then they march into the continent

164

and blithely expect to take command. Someone had even told him recently that the English were now claiming to have invented the new system of firing by platoon which the Dutch infantry had been using for at least five years. He laughed and Steel smiled back. Jennings grew closer.

'Mister Steel. What's this? Introduce me.'

'Major Jennings, Captain van der Voert of the dragoons, in the army of our friends in the United Provinces.'

Jennings flashed a disarming smile at the Dutchman.

'My dear Captain. How very fortunate. Now we shall all travel together. The country is teeming with French troops and brigands of every description. My own command was attacked and we have lately fought an action against Frenchmen of the foulest sort . . .'

Van der Voert cut him short.

'Major, I am indeed alarmed to hear of your encounters. But I am afraid that we cannot be travelling companions. We have specific orders, direct from the high command of the allied army. We proceed due west, Sir, and canot divert from our course.'

Steel interjected:

'The Captain is under orders from the Duke of Marlborough himself, Sir. He is to lay waste Bavaria.'

Jennings stared at Steel, tight-lipped.

'Then clearly we must not delay the good Captain from his duty. Good day to you, Sir.'

The Dutchman nodded.

'Herr Major, Lieutenant. I am afraid that we must leave you. We have pressing work, you know.

Your Lord keeps us busy.'

Steel grimaced. The Captain touched his hat and the others followed suit, then he turned with his men and rode back to the troop. Closing with them, he barked a gutteral order and with an impressive single movement, the dragoons returned their swords to their scabbards. Jennings, without a word, turned his horse and trotted back towards the rear of the column. Steel turned to Slaughter.

'Stand the men down, Sarn't.'

He watched the Dutch Captain lead his men off the road and into the fields so that they might ride past Steel's column to ease its passage.

Steel looked at Slaughter:

'Come on, Sarn't. Let's get to the bloody town before that inn, if it really exists, burns down.'

He sighed. 'Christ, Jacob. I hope we find the army soon. I'm not sure how much more of this I can take.'

'Sir?'

'Major Jennings, Sarn't. You know well enough what I mean.'

Slaughter smiled.

'I know, Sir. And I know that we shouldn't still be down here. We need to get back to the regiment. And if we don't get back soon I reckon we'll not just miss whatever battle there is. We'll miss the whole bloody war.'

*   *   *

The town of Sielenbach, when they finally arrived there, was nothing less than Steel had expected. A smoking, charred ruin of what had once been the

166

pride of its citizens. The redcoats advanced carefully up the long main street, pausing briefly at every road junction to look both ways, before crossing and peering into the ragged rooms of every ruined house to make sure that no one had indeed been left to die.

Steel knew that the men were tired and, worse than that, thirsty and low in morale. For them this whole expedition had been an inexplicable loss of face. They had covered themselves in blood and glory at the Schellenberg, only to be sent on this sutler's errand. Steel, they would have followed anywhere, given the prospect of action, but now they were deep in the Bavarian heartland, guarding a wagon train of flour. They had rescued a senior officer and a company of musketeers. Had beaten off an attack by as ruthless a bunch of Frenchmen as you could ever encounter, with no help it seemed from that same officer, their own Adjutant, who had himself recently carried out a ruthless and undeserved punishment on one of their number. They had discovered a terrible massacre and buried the dead, including women and babes, and now they saw towns being put to the torch by their own side and the ordinary people, people like themselves, being forced out into the countryside. Steel knew his men would be wondering what was going on and right now the last thing he wanted to do was answer questions.

The Grenadiers looked up to Steel and believed in him as much as they did in anything. They knew his war record, that he had served with the Swedes and come through that hell unscathed. There was something very special about Mister Steel. He was lucky and, like all soldiers who were deeply superstitious, they thought that perhaps some of his luck would rub off on them. But at the end of the day, he would always be an officer. Steel, too, felt the distance between them at times like this. Oh, he knew that he could rely upon Slaughter to keep them in order. But unless they rested—really rested and found their humour once more—he knew that he might all too easily have a mutiny on his hands.

For better or worse, Steel had taken the flogged man, Cussiter, into his half-company on the day following his punishment. The man had come to him personally and begged to be admitted. Cussiter had real spirit and Steel knew instinctively that, given time he would make a fine Grenadier. But Cussiter was also full of hatred, in particular for Farquharson and Jennings. Given the mood of the men, who knew what slight provocation might be needed for Cussiter to give way to his feelings. Here in the heart of enemy territory, where anything might happen, no one would ever be the wiser. It was better surely to pre-empt any trouble. Get to the damned inn—if it still stood. Stand each man a flagon or two of the local brew and let them get some rest. Soldiers were easy to handle, if you knew their ways. It was all very fine for Colonel James (or was it Septimus) Hawkins to tell his nephew that the key to being a good officer was to maintain respect, but Steel knew better. Keep them in good humour and they'd fight for you. Provoke them too strongly and you were as much a dead man as the nearest Frenchie.

Steel reined in and jumped down from the saddle. Best now to show solidarity, get down among them and lead by example. Besides, his status as an officer on entering a town might as well go to blazes here. He was hardly expecting a reception committee from the Mayor. Slaughter looked at him, equally cheerless.

'Begging your pardon, Sir, but was you proposing that we would spend the night here? In this godforsaken blackened hole?'

'That I was, Jacob. That I was. This is Sielenbach and it seems to me to be as fine a place as any to kick off your boots.'

Then, almost as an afterthought, he added:

'And remember. As far as we know the inn is still standing.'

Slaughter smiled. He said nothing, but began to walk with a new spring in his step.

'The men seem dispirited, Jacob. I am not wrong?'

'Never more true, Sir. There's talk at all times of what they're doing down here now and you know as well as I do, Mister Steel, that when a soldier lets those words cross his lips then them other thoughts cannot be far away.'

'Cussiter?'

'Oh, the lad'll be fine, Sir. But it's not just him as is grumbling.'

Slaughter paused, thoughtfully.

'Best to stop here, as you say, Sir. And, just so you know, I'm keeping Dan Cussiter as far away as I can from our friend the Major. If you know what I mean. Bit of bad luck Jennings being the other officer to come with us. If you don't mind my saying so.'

'No, Jacob. I don't mind you saying that at all.'

The crash of the men's boots echoed on the dry, soot-stained cobbles and resounded through the empty streets. There was no other sound save the rattle of equipment and the trundle of the wagons as the column slid noisily into the town.

There were no dogs barking here, nor even any birdsong. The smell of burning timber hung heavy on the air.

It was the height of the morning now, a sunny summer day, when normally the street would have been alive with noise as tradesmen and townspeople went about their business. Today, though, Kirchenstrasse stood empty, the tall, proud houses that had lined its sides no more than burnt-out, smoking ruins, like the stumps of so many blackened, rotten teeth. In places the fires still smouldered, the embers a mocking reminder of the vanished comfort of their hearths.

Possessions lay littered across the cobbles where they had been abandoned or forgotten in the headlong rush of a populace eager to escape further horrors. Clothes, shoes and bags lay everywhere. Dolls and other toys, scorched and filthy, along with larger items. Chairs, wooden boxes, musical instruments. Naturally, anything of particular value left behind by the townspeople had been taken by the Dutch. There were a few exceptions. A gilt-framed painting of Christ in Majesty lay in a gutter and a grandfather clock stood incongruously in the centre of the road junction, where its owners, having tried desperately to save their most precious possession, had been forced to leave it. Books lay strewn around and everywhere sheaves of paper blew through the deserted streets.

At length they came in view of the church. As the first building that they had seen in the place that had not been reduced to cinders, it stunned them with its simple majesty. Rounding the corner and entering the square, where the church façade rose high against the brilliant blue of the sky, Steel saw that close to the basilica stood another building. The inn was indeed still there, just as the Dutch Captain had told him. With its gaily painted timberwork and bright blue gilly flowers growing in pots, it made a grotesque contrast with the devastation that lay all around it.

'Sarn't, I think we'll stop here.'

Slaughter turned his head to the right:

'Column, halt.'

'Stand the men easy, Sarn't Slaughter. Allow them fifteen minutes rest.'

Williams rode up, and with him Jennings. The Major seemed indignant:

'Mister Steel. We have stopped. Tell me why?'

'Why, Sir. Because this is our bivouac for the night.'

'The night, Steel? But it is barely three o'clock of the afternoon. We surely have two more hours to march?'

'The men, Major, need to stop. And this is as good a place as any. Indeed it is better, on many counts. And it has an inn.'

Jennings looked across the street where a painted sign with a running grey horse hung above the inn door.

'Well, Steel. If you are convinced. Although I don't suppose for a moment that they'll have anything half decent.'

He turned to face the column.

'Sarn't Stringer. Where the devil is the oaf? Stringer. My bag.'

Jennings dismounted and strode across the square, followed by the ever-attendant Stringer, who had retrieved Jennings' bag from the coach.

Steel called after him:

'Oh, Major. There's a landlord who's old and sick and his daughter. Look out for them.'

He glanced at Slaughter.

'I do hope that the Major finds the accommodation to his liking. Come on, Sarn't, we'd best get this lot sorted for the night. We'll leave the wagons here on the street. There'll be no traffic through here in the next few hours. Oh, and Jacob.'

'Sir.'

'Find the men somewhere to sleep. There's what looks a likely field over there, behind the church. Tell the Grenadiers they might have two flagons of ale apiece in the inn—if it's to be had at all. Tell them I . . . tell them Lord Marlborough will stand the cost.'

'Very good, Sir.'

'Oh, and Jacob. Just so that you know, I shall be joining you out in the field. Jennings is in the inn—with his monkey—and nothing on earth could possibly persuade me to sleep under the same roof.'

*   *   *

Across the town square, Jennings pushed open the door of the inn and stepped inside, closely followed by his Sergeant. Rather than the dirty wine glasses and half-empty tankards of ale that he had expected to find still on the tables where the last customers might have left them, he was surprised to find the interior neat and tidy. The parlour was deserted, although a fire had been laid in the grate and a pile of plates stood on a dresser, ready to be set.

'Hallo. Anyone? Hallo.'

A door opened at the back of the room and a girl walked in. Jennings knew real beauty when he saw it and it took only a moment for him to decide that by whatever means, before they left this place, he was going to seduce her.

She addressed him in the local dialect.

'Good day. Oh. You are a soldier?'

'Yes, English, Miss. Major Aubrey Jennings, Farquharson's Regiment, at your service.'

He gave a low bow and removed his hat.

'You are English? Then I speak to you in English.'

Her voice was wonderfully gentle. A sweet contrast to the harsh, masculine world he had just left outside. Her words though were bitter.

'Tell me, Sir. Why should I trust the English? Your men come here and burn our town. Why? What have we done? We do not make war on you. Why? Why?'

Jennings, taken aback, said nothing. Then a thought entered his mind. Quite brilliant. 'Dear Miss, excuse me, you have me at a disadvantage. I do not have your name, Miss . . .'

'Weber. My name is Louisa Weber and this is my father's inn.'

'Dear Miss Weber. I have come to apologize. On behalf of his Grace the Duke of Marlborough, I offer you and your fellow townspeople his Grace's most sincere apologies. We encountered some of your friends on our way here and have attempted to recompense them for any damage that has been done. Obviously the village is beyond redemption, but we must do what we can. I beseech you to believe me, on my honour as a soldier and a gentleman that this was no doing of the English. It was the action of our Dutch allies and will be punished with the death of those responsible.'

For a moment the girl stared at him. Then she took his meaning.

'Oh. No, I. I did not want that. No killing. But the Dutch Captain explained to me. He said that they did this under orders from your Duke. That this was done to injure the Elector Max Emmanuel. To make him leave the French. That it is the English who ordered our town to be burnt.'

'I assure you, Miss Weber. It was not. We have caught the men who did this, the Dutchmen, and they are even now travelling under armed escort on their way to Donauwörth to be tried under court martial. Be certain, they will be hanged.'

The girl looked at the floor.

'I am sorry. I did not want them to die. The Captain seemed such a nice man. A real gentleman.'

'My poor dear. How much you have to learn, particularly about soldiers. I shall teach you. We may some of us be officers but not all officers can be said to be gentlemen. You must understand that some men are not to be trusted. That man was no gentleman.'

He moved towards her, placing a hand upon her shoulder at the point where the cotton of her blouse met the tempting, downy softness of her pale skin. She flinched and then relaxed under the warmth of his touch. It had been so long since anyone had done that.

'Dear Miss Weber. Louisa, if I may. You may trust an Englishman. You most certainly may trust me. Now come. Show me where I might rest tonight. I will pay of course and also for any food and wine you might be able to offer my men. We have had a long and arduous march in pursuit of your oppressors.'

*   *   *

Steel had inspected the Grenadiers' bivouac for the night, a pasture to the rear of the church in the shade of a few apple trees. He left his own kit there with Slaughter and walked back towards the square. He had commended his gun into the particular care of the Sergeant, but the great sword still clanked at his side and in the ghostly stillness of the abandoned streets, he placed his hand on the scabbard. It seemed almost sacriligous to hear such a sound in a place so newly marked by war. At the edge of the square and down the length of the main road that led into the town from the north, the laden wagons stood in the late afternoon light with their drivers. Some of the wagoners had taken the dray teams out of their shafts and were watering them at a nearby trough. Steel had ordered Williams to position two sentries on permanent guard on the wagons and a picquet of three men at each of the roads leading into the town. That accounted for half of their entire force. The others he expected, as had been arranged, in the inn. They would have to be careful of course, he, Williams and Slaughter, that

175

each man consumed only his allotted ration of ale. For while Steel's plan could work well as a preventative measure, it could also all too easily, he realized, be turned against him.

He walked up to the inn and pushed open the door. It was a sizeable place which, before the late catastrophe, might have made a good profit from the pilgrim route which Hawkins had told him, ran through these hills. The interior reeked reassuringly of stale alcohol and pipe smoke. The room was quite empty and Steel made his way across to the open staircase which rose to the upper floors. He was contemplating whether he should ascend, when he heard a low groan from a half-open door at the rear of the room. Pushing it open, he peered in and saw the figure of an old man, tucked under a blanket in a large wooden chair. He appeared to be mumbling in his sleep.

'He's my father.'

The soft voice, in a gently accented English, startled him and, turning, Steel instinctively placed his hand on the hilt of his sword. The girl spoke again.

'I'm sorry. I did not mean to alarm you.'

'I'm not alarmed, Miss. You just took me by surprise.'

She was exquisitely beautiful, with piercing blue eyes and hair like spun straw. Steel was entranced.

'You are English? Yes?'

'Yes. That is, I'm from Scotland, Miss. But . . . yes. You might say I am.'

He was unsure as to whether she had understood him. It was really not important.

'Captain, Lieutenant. Sir.' She looked in vain for his badge of rank.

'Lieutenant, Miss. Lieutenant Jack Steel of Farquharson's Regiment, in the service of Queen Anne.'

He gave a short bow. Louisa smiled and again, he was frozen by her beauty.

'My name is Louisa Weber, Lieutenant. You are welcome here. This is my father's inn. Your other officer, Major . . . Jennings, told me that you have found the men who did this horrible thing to our town. That this is not your doing, but the work of the Dutch. I try to understand.'

Steel nodded and wondered exactly what Jennings had said to her. How he had explained that they had 'found the men'.

Louisa knelt down on the floor beside her father and draped her arm lightly about his shoulders. She whispered something to him in German. Words of comfort on a day where none could help. She looked up at Steel, her beautiful eyes filled with despair.

'My father is sick. We must throw ourselves on your mercy. My father has a cousin in England. Living in Harwich. Perhaps you know it. It is a fishing town. His cousin is a merchant. A very rich man, I think. Perhaps, if we could get passage back to England, I could give you money, Lieutenant. I have already told this to Major Jennings. He says it will be fine. I told him my father's cousin will pay. It is now the only thing to do, I think. We are ruined here now.'

Steel felt truly sorry for her. She was right. The town had ceased to exist. The dragoons had left only the inn and the church standing but what use was an inn with no prospect of customers?

'Of course, Miss Weber. Of course we will do

177

everything that we can to help you. And your father. And please, we will not take your money. Whatever Major Jennings might have said. Please.'

How very typical of Jennings, he thought, to have accepted her offer of payment. He extended his hand to help her to her feet and as he did so, the door on to the square opened and Slaughter entered. Clearing his throat, he called through to Steel who he could see through the door to the back room.

'Mister Steel, Sir. I was wondering if now would be the right time for the men to get that ration of ale. We're fair parched.'

Steel appeared. 'Quite the right time, Sarn't. Send them in.'

He turned to Louisa, who had followed.

'Miss Weber. I take it that you can provide us with some ale? We have the money to pay for it. And whatever food you have to hand would be most welcome. If you could find a little wine, I would be very grateful.'

Happy for this semblance of normality, Louisa busied herself with attending to her guests.

The Grenadiers gradually filled the inn. They removed their caps as they entered and, piling their arms by the door, sat in groups at the tables. Within minutes the place was alive with noise. Steel watched Louisa as she moved among the soldiers and saw the change in her. How animated she had become. How very much more alive. He kept a low profile, sitting on his own in a dark corner beside the inglenook fireplace, although happily acknowledging any of the men who passed. Louisa had found him a pitcher of good Moselle and, although he could have drained it within minutes, he was pacing himself, anxious to keep an eye on the men. Slaughter, although he had taken his place within a group of senior other ranks, was exercising similar prudence. But neither man need have worried. One table was engaged in a game of cards. Another singing a round-work, whose ancient folk lyrics they had replaced with something rather more ribald. Steel watched the men relax for the first time in days and guessed that his tactic might have paid off. Slaughter caught his eye from across the room and nodded discreetly. Now, being convinced he could relax himself, from his shadowy obscurity Steel indulged in glimpses of Louisa as she made her way through the fug, serving the tall steins of sweet, dark brown ale, Dunkel, which in this part of Bavaria was the staple beer. From nowhere, too, she had conjured up a stew—thin but hot and satisfying and there was good black bread to go with it and ham and slabs of cheese—without the customary weevils.

The men, conscious that an officer was present, and that he was paying the bill, made no attempt to molest Louisa. He saw her smile, her pretty face lit from within and wondered unexpectedly how convincingly Jennings had entranced her with his unctuous words and promises. Then, catching the thought, puzzled how he could be jealous of that man, and why. He had only known this girl less than an hour. Had hardly spoken to her. And yet there was something about her that felt somehow . . . comfortable.

He saw Williams enter the inn and look about the room. A table of Grenadiers looked up and grinned. As the new boy of the company, the Ensign was still an object of fun, even though he had won his spurs in the skirmish with the French. Steel called across to him.

'Tom. Over here. Come and join me in a glass.'

Williams sat down and Steel filled two glasses.

'Any sign of our friend the Major?'

'None, Sir. I presumed that he might be in here.'

'And Herr Kretzmer?'

'No, Sir. Although he might be in his carriage.'

'So, Tom. I promised that I would ask again after your first battle. How do you like soldiering now?'

'I have not revised my opinion, Sir. Although, in truth, I must admit being unsettled by what we discovered at Sattelberg. Surely, Sir, that cannot be a true picture of war?'

'No, Tom. War is not often like that. But the truth about war is that you can never be quite sure what will happen next. Sattelberg was bad. But take it from me, in your time as a soldier you will see worse. Far worse. And yet there are times, too, when you will know that there is nothing like it in all the world. It is the most exciting and the most tedious of lives. A challenge and a drudge. And if you stay with it I will guarantee that there will not be a day in which you will not encounter something that will either make your soul leap with joy or your spine shiver with dread apprehension.'

*   *   *

Three hours later Tom Williams was still lost in dreams of soldiering. Steel helped him to his feet. Tom had, Steel thought, perhaps indulged in just a little too much wine. Most of the Grenadiers had

180

left the inn now, bound for the dubious comfort of their field bivouac. As the last few made their way towards the door, one with the words of a song on his lips and the rest with muttered thanks to their officer, Steel called to Slaughter.

'Sarn't. Will you be so kind as to help Mister Williams to his quarters. Place him close by me. Not so close though that should he awake in the night he might make the mistake of taking my kit for a latrine.'

Slaughter laughed.

'I thought he looked a bit groggy, Sir. Unused to the wine, I suppose, and there's hardly anything to him. I'll see to him, Mister Steel. You take your time.'

Slaughter had watched his officer all evening and had seen how he gazed at Louisa. He had known Steel long enough to understand what that look meant. Well, perhaps there would be time for love, if that was what he wanted. He recalled one drunken, desperate night in Flanders, after a day on which they had seen too many good men die, when Steel had told Slaughter about a girl called Arabella. About regrets and missed opportunities and what he had hoped life might hold for him. The following day of course, nothing more had been said. But the Sergeant had not forgotten his officer's confidences. Maybe this girl would follow them now. Perhaps she would be the one to offer Steel the life he craved. Cradling Tom Williams' comatose form in his great arms, Slaughter stepped from the inn and Steel found himself alone. He walked across to the door of the Webers' private quarters and gave a gentle cough. Louisa turned and saw him.

181

'I suppose that I should move Herr Kretzmer.'

Steel nodded in the direction of the Bavarian, who, having purchased a bottle of fine French brandy from Louisa, had crept away from the soldiers to occupy the chair lately vacated by her ailing father and proceeded to drink the contents. Louisa did not mind. Herr Kretzmer came from a different world to the Grenadiers and he did not mix easily. She was happy to indulge her countryman. Together, she and Steel gazed on his sleeping form.

'Leave him if you wish, Lieutenant. I will put a blanket over him and if he wakes up he will know which room to go to. Don't worry. He's as harmless as a puppy.'

Steel laughed.

'Thank you, Miss Weber, for all your hospitality. May I settle our account in the morning? We rise early.'

'As I do, Lieutenant. And please, call me Louisa. You are most welcome. It really felt as if the town were still . . . alive. I . . .'

She was suddenly lost for words. Instinctively Steel walked across to her. Gently placing an arm upon her shoulders, he looked into eyes which brimmed with tears.

'Please. There is no need to worry. Tomorrow, you will come with us. Bring whatever is important to you but please, don't worry. We will take care of you now. There is nothing more to fear. This is not an end, but a new beginning.'

She nodded, smiled, and for a moment Steel thought that he could detect in her eyes a spark of something more. Now though, he sensed, was not the moment. Steel withdrew his arm from her shoulder.

'Now, you must get some sleep. Tomorrow we march north. And you start a new life.'

*   *   *

Jennings was looking for drink. Following Kretzmer's departure, he had spent the best part of an hour in the church, deep in thought, if not in prayer. Then, feeling the pangs of hunger, he had sent Stringer into the inn to sniff him out what wine and food he could. He had chosen to eat his sparse supper alone, in the candle-lit gloom of the church, while his Sergeant sat outside on the steps. Now though, the man had reported that the Grenadiers, Mister Steel included, had retired for the night to their bivouac. Now at last, thought Jennings, he could enjoy the comforts for which he had paid. A real bed with clean sheets and perhaps before that a little more sustenance. And then, of course, there was the girl.

Leaving the church he walked quietly into the street. Stringer was waiting outside, leaning against a wall of the basilica. Seeing Jennings he straightened up. Now, in the moonlight, the town presented a truly eerie prospect. The night was chill and even Jennings felt a sense of unnatural unease. He walked over to the Sergeant.

'I want no one admitted to the inn on any account. No one. D'you take my meaning, Sarn't?'

'Sir. Yes, Sir.'

Quickly now, Jennings moved to the inn and eased the latch of the door. It was unlocked. Inside, the room stood empty and dark. All the candles but one had been extinguished and the

183

tables cleared. A light from the door at the rear betrayed the fact that the house had not quite gone to bed. Doubtless there he would find his brandy. And the possibility of other pleasures.

He walked softly across the wooden boards, holding his sword close to his side and pushed open the door.

'Miss Weber. How charming.'

Louisa gave a start and turned abruptly.

'Oh. Major Jennings. You gave me a fright. I am sorry. I was dreaming.'

'Of course. So like a woman. I was wondering if you might have a glass of cognac? Or indeed any fortified wine? I have had a busy night. Writing reports and so on. It would settle my nerves. No time for those in command to indulge themselves with the men.'

Louisa flashed him a sympathetic smile.

'Yes, Major. Of course. I think that we have some good French brandy. Allow me to get it for you.'

Moving further into the room, Jennings noticed Kretzmer asleep in the chair and instantly saw his opportunity. How very obliging, he thought, of the fat Bavarian.

Louisa had turned her back to him now and was stretching up to the high store cupboard where they kept the good stuff. After all the Major would pay. She sensed that he was suddenly closer and felt his breath on her neck as he spoke:

'You will recall, my dear, our conversation earlier. Our bargain. Your safe conduct to the English army. We agreed on a sum, did we not?'

Louisa turned to face him and found it difficult to avoid contact. She held the bottle between

184

them.

'Your brandy, Major.'

Jennings backed off a short way.

'You do recall though, Miss Weber . . . Louisa. The sum of which we spoke?'

She nodded. 'Yes, Major. But since then, things have changed. Lieutenant Steel has promised to take me to your army. He says that it will not cost me anything. That he will protect me.'

It was the worst thing that she could have said, and it sealed her fate.

'Mister Steel told you that, did he? Let me remind you, Miss Weber, that we struck a bargain and by my code of conduct, a bargain once made, cannot be undone. So, Miss. Unless you want us to leave you here to the tender mercies of the French, you'll pay up.'

He paused and smiled at her.

'Although, there is of course, another way. A way which would both save your hard-earned money and provide us both with a pleasurable diversion.'

Louisa blanched and looked at Jennings. Could he mean it? Was he really asking her to sell herself to him in exchange for their passage north?

'Major. You cannot mean what I suppose you to, surely?'

Jennings nodded and smiled.

'No. You cannot mean it.'

He was breathing harder now.

'Oh, but I do, pretty Louisa. I do mean it. So very, very earnestly.'

He saw her look of utter revulsion.

'What? No? Then, by God, I'll have you for nothing.'

185

Louisa opened her mouth to scream, but before she was able to utter a sound, his hand, rough and stinking of wine and filth, had been clamped hard over her lips. She tried to bite him, but her teeth could not reach the flat of his palm. Jennings pushed his body hard up against her and growled into her face.

'Now, my pretty girl. You and I are going to have some fun. And if you scream or try anything else silly, all I have to do is call to my Sergeant—you remember him, he's outside now—and he'll slit your father's throat, from ear to ear. And I'll blame it all on this one.'

He jerked his head in the direction of the sleeping Kretzmer. As he watched her eyes widen with terror at the realization that all was hopeless, Jennings instantly became yet more aroused and decided that it would be safe to remove his hand.

'So tell me. Where's your precious Mister Steel now? No? I'll tell you. He's fast asleep in the field with his men. He won't hear you. He won't help you now.'

Jennings stretched out his hand and inserted a finger in between the lace of the neckline of her white blouse and the soft flesh of her shoulder.

'Now, Miss. If you please. Your shirt.'

Louisa shuddered and froze. Jennings moved his hand further in, beneath the material and lifted it off her body, pushing it down her arm, then did the same on the other side. Then, with one swift motion he pushed down with both hands and she was naked from the waist up, horribly exposed to his gaze. Not bad, he thought. For a peasant. Her hand reached for a knife which she had remembered lay on the table behind her. But his

186

was faster. Their fingers collided and the blade clattered to the floor as Jennings caught her by the wrist and with his other hand slapped her hard across the face, making her whimper.

'You stupid German cow. Remember what I said, Miss. One word. One more stupid thing like that and the old man dies. Now. Help me.'

He reached for her thighs. She struggled, instinct taking over from reason. But his grip was an iron vice.

'My, you're a game one.'

He was used to this, she thought, through the red mist of terror and outrage which clouded her reason—the natural reaction which had kicked in to make all that would now happen appear unreal. He knew what he was doing. Had done it before. How many times, she wondered? How many women?

Jennings fumbled beneath her skirts then, impatient, ripped them to one side. He probed clumsily with his fingers and finding what he wanted, quickly unbuttoned his breeches. Desperate, lest she should utter a sound and condemn her father, Louisa bit hard into her own hand. Jennings, smiling with pleasure and hatred as he pushed at her, grunted out staccato words:

'Remember. Tell them I did this and I kill your father.'

After the horror and humiliation of what had just occurred, the act itself took less time and effort than she had imagined. She felt Jennings shudder and relax and she recoiled from the stink of his foul breath as he nuzzled his head into her neck in a ghastly parody of genuine lovemaking. She felt unspeakably defiled and desperate to rid

187

herself of this man. To somehow achieve the impossible and cleanse her sullied body.

Then it was over. Jennings straightened up, buttoned his breeches and adjusted his dress. His eye was caught by the gleam of candlelight upon the small knife that lay on the floor. Picking it up he looked down on the cowering, half-naked girl. It had been in his mind to slit her throat, but as he stood there another idea struck him. Something more deliciously cruel. He pocketed the knife and pointed to Kretzmer.

'Now. Quickly. Help me with his breeches.'

Louisa stared. Surely the man was not so perverted that he intended to force her to couple with Kretzmer? She watched, traumatized, as the Major pulled the knife from his pocket and winced as he used it to make a careful, but not too deep cut in his own hand. Finished, he placed its sticky handle in Kretzmer's palm, before withdrawing it and letting it fall again.

Then, and with no little effort, Jennings picked up the fat merchant, who all the time had remained comatose, and lifting him under his arms from the back, dragged him across the floor towards where Louisa stood, white, half-naked and trembling.

'Come on, whore. Get on with it. Undo his buttons.'

Hardly aware now of her actions, Louisa reached out and deftly unbuttoned the front of the merchant's breeches. As she finished and they fell from his corpulent form, Jennings pushed the man towards her, so that the two of them tumbled to the floor, sprawling, the half-naked girl pinned down under the Bavarian's dead-weight. The impact brought Kretzmer round to semi-consciousness and Jennings bent down and placed the man's fat hands on Louisa's breasts, smiling at her as he did so.

'Thank you, my dear. I trust that you enjoyed that as much as I. Or did you not? And remember. One word of the truth and your father dies.'

He slapped Kretzmer on the face, hard, knocking him into consciousness. Bewildered, the merchant pressed down instinctively on his hands to raise himself off the floor and in doing so found that he was embracing Louisa. He was lost for words.

Jennings turned to the door and, making sure that the grotesque sexual vignette was still perfectly arranged on the floor, shouted into the night, at the top of his voice.

'Guard. Guard. Quickly. To me. Assault. Alarm.'

And from the empty streets of the dead town there came at last the sound of soldiers, hurrying to the rescue.

SEVEN

Slaughter met Steel at the door of the inn. The Lieutenant's eyes were wide with anger and fear.

'Where is she? Is she all right?'

It was a stupid question and he regretted it instantly. The Sergeant gave him a gentle smile. He put a hand on his shoulder, half in comfort, half to prevent him from advancing any further before his mind had time to settle. He knew well what his officer was capable of and knew that in the heat of the moment the Bavarian would not stand a chance.

'Come on, Jacob. Let me through. I must see her.'

'Perhaps not just yet, Sir. She'll be all right. She's a tough girl.'

'Jacob. I mean it. Let me pass. I've got Taylor with me.'

At the mention of the man's name the Sergeant let his grip relax a little. Matt Taylor, a Corporal of the Grenadiers, had a little knowledge of medicine, chiefly of the herbal kind. Slaughter knew that Steel approved of that. Over the months, Taylor had become the elected apothecary of the company. It was only fitting, for before conviction for fraud had forced him into the ranks, he had served three years of a seven-year apprenticeship to the Worshipful Society of Apothecaries in London and had studied botany at the Physick garden at Chelsea. Since then Taylor had used plants and roots to cure everything from colic and scurvy to toothache, the soldiers' curse, and even the malaria which often followed from mosquito bites.

'Very well, Sir. Come on, Matt.'

The three men walked quickly through the inn and into the back room. Jennings stood by the door, his back against the scene:

'I did what I could, but it was too late. The brute had had his fun already. It was really all too sordid. Poor dear girl. Can you deal with it, Steel? Not my area I'm afraid.'

Jennings smiled and made his way towards the door of the inn. Steel froze in the entrance to the back room. The air stank of sex and sweat. Louisa sat in the far corner of the room, her ripped clothes pulled up around her, her face bruised, staring wildly. She was sobbing gently. Kretzmer was sitting in the chair in the opposite corner of the room. His hands and feet had been bound and a bruise that had half shut his eye and a cut on his cheek bore testimony to his treatment at the hands of his captors. Steel turned to Taylor:

'Matt. See what you can do for her. Be gentle.'

He marvelled at his own stupidity. To have left the girl unguarded at night in the presence of so many men. The Grenadiers were not a concern, but why had he not considered the others? Jennings' men or the waggoners and the cook. Why, had he not considered Kretzmer?

'Christ, Jacob. I'm a bloody fool. We should have posted a guard on her. A deserted town and a company of redcoats. I'm a bloody fool. It's my fault.'

'If you think that, Sir, then you are a bloody fool. It's no one's fault. She'll be all right. Matt's with her now.'

Steel watched as the Corporal bent to talk to Louisa, whispering to her as you would to a frightened or wounded animal. He saw her initial terror turn gradually to calm and then stood to one side as Taylor brought her out of the room and carried her gently up the stairs. Taylor turned back to him:

'It's all right, Sir. You can leave her with me now. Get some sleep.'

Turning back to the room, Steel gazed at the Bavarian with utter revulsion. In other circumstances he would have killed the man out of hand and taken the consequences. But he knew that as it was, in front of the men and particularly in the presence of Jennings, who would use any opportunity now to bring about Steel's ruination, he had to behave by the rules. And the rules stated that Kretzmer would be taken with them under guard back to the camp where he would be given a fair trial. Only then, if there was any justice in this world, would they be permitted to hang him. It would be a long wait.

*   *   *

Morning brought another bright day, the promise of unremitting heat and with it the sickening memory of the events of the previous evening. Steel climbed the stairs to Louisa's room and knocked at the door. Slowly it opened and Taylor's face appeared.

'How is she?'

'No better than you may imagine, Sir. He was that rough with her.'

'Should I speak to her?'

'I don't see why not. I don't have any German, Sir, but in the night she did say your name a few times. In the fever.'

'Thank you, Taylor.'

Steel walked across to the bed where Louisa lay dressed in a cotton nightshirt beneath fresh white sheets, her blonde hair framing her head like a halo. Taylor had done a good job of cleaning her up, although she still bore a heavy bruise where she had been hit hard on the the face and without looking too closely, Steel could see there were others on her neck. She opened her eyes, looked at

192

first alarmed at the presence of another man in the room, but then realized who it was.

'Oh. You. Lieutenant, I . . . Do you have him. Do you have . . .'

She stopped herself, quickly remembering what she must not say.

'I'm sorry, Miss. I shouldn't have come. It's just that I. Forgive me, but I was genuinely concerned. I feel . . . responsible for this.'

She smiled. 'You? How could you?'

'I should have placed guards. Should have had men I trust within the inn. Who knows what might have happened had Major Jennings not come in when he did.'

At the mention of Jennings' name Louisa's eyes widened and her face, which up till now had been restored to colour, turned pale.

'Are you feeling all right. Shall I call Corporal Taylor to return?'

'No, No. I'll be fine. He is a good man, Lieutenant. So gentle.'

'I'm sorry. I did not mean to suggest that what has happened was of no consequence. It . . . matters to me very much indeed. It is just that if he hadn't come in . . .'

'Yes.'

She half-closed her eyes.

'I know. But why? Why did he?'

Steel could see that she was confused. That would be Taylor's potions, no doubt.

'Herr Kretzmer will hang, Louisa. Have no doubt of that. We have him prisoner.'

She opened her eyes but did not smile. Saying nothing, she merely stared at the wall. Tears began to run down her face and Steel moved forward. He went to put an arm around her shoulders and then stopped himself.

'I . . . I'm sorry. I was only going to . . .'

She smiled. 'No. Please. I would like you to.'

Gently, Steel placed his arm in its filthy red sleeve upon her shoulder and thankfully she buried her head deep in his chest and began to sob. Steel held her closer and thought with revulsion of the last man to do so. An obscene excuse for a man.

She looked up at him.

'Oh, Jack. I don't know who to trust. He said he would kill my father and he will.'

'He won't. He can't. How can he? We have him. Kretzmer can do you no more harm, Louisa. Trust me.'

'He told me that too.'

'Kretzmer? Yes, but I mean it.'

He looked at her and thought that he could see in her eyes, along with what he might now perceive as love, a nameless fear.

'What is it? What's wrong?'

Louisa turned away and said nothing. How could she tell him about Jennings? As long as the man remained alive her father's life would be in danger. And there was something else. She had felt something just now. Something she had not expected.

From the street outside they could hear the sound of the redcoats gathering up their kit and anything still to be had and which might be carried in the way of food and drink. The day was passing. There was more, much more to say, but now was not the moment.

'We must leave here soon. You must go to your

father. Can he manage it? Can you?'

'I think so. I will look after him. Go and get your soldiers ready. I promise we'll be ready within the hour.'

Puzzled and not a little shaken, Steel left the room, passing Taylor as he went. 'Stay with her. Look after her and help her with the old man. Make sure they take what they need. And, Taylor, thank you.'

He wondered if the man had guessed at his growing attachment to the girl. Whether he would tell the others. Steel thought he knew him well enough to be sure that he would not. He walked down the stairs and out into the sunshine of the square. Much as it irked him, he had to acknowledge Jennings' role in Louisa's rescue. Slaughter had been first on the scene and there could be no doubting his word. He had discovered Kretzmer, his trousers around his ankles, standing above Louisa's half-naked form. Jennings was holding him firm and there had evidently been a struggle. The Bavarian had a bloody nose and a cut lip and Jennings was bleeding from his hand, wounded, it seemed, by a knife that lay upon the floor. There was, of course, no question of Kretzmer's guilt. The facts spoke for themselves.

They had bound Kretzmer's hands with rope and placed him, for want of anything more secure, in his own carriage, tied to the door and with a gag knotted across his mouth to drown the tirade of protest with which he had assailed them since he had recovered from his encounter with the floor— and two subsequent punches from Jennings.

*   *   *

Steel watched the Major now, as he crossed the town square to inspect his men, an unlikely hero, followed by Stringer, the lapdog. It was seven o'clock in the morning. It was a great deal later than they would normally have started their march to avoid the heat of the sun. But the events of the previous night had upset his intentions, and not just because of what had happened to Louisa. Contrary to his plan, most of the men had contrived to find rather more ale than he had intended and although only a few had actually been drunk, the rest did not find that the morning, with its various demands and duties, entirely suited their dulled senses.

Nevertheless, Steel had decided that they would leave within the next two hours. They might, he guessed, cover six miles in the day. He was about to rejoin the Grenadiers in the field when he thought the better of it. Time perhaps for one more thing. Something which he had not envisioned himself doing on this or any morning. Steel did not consider himself a religious man. Certainly he had grown up in a God-fearing Scottish Episcopalian household, where Sundays were observed and church attended. But he had not carried it through into adulthood. And yet, like all soldiers, when he was out on the battlefield and the air was thick with shot, Steel was inclined to believe that something or someone was keeping watch over him. His long-dead mother perhaps, or what other men might have called a guardian angel.

He pushed open the small five-foot-high entrance panel in the great church door and entered, his boots resounding on the polished stone floor. Sword rattling at his side, Steel walked towards the high altar and stopped the instant that his eyes caught the figure of the Madonna holding her son.

A woman and a dead man. He had seen it many times in the aftermath of battles, when a wife or a camp follower would find her husband or her lover on the field and, convulsed with grief, cradle him in just this way. He had heard the sobbing and knew the sound of the misery embodied now before him. The grief of all the world seemed bound up in this one image. He walked closer to the statue and tried to remember what it was you were meant to do. He had forgotten how to pray. Kneel. Yes, that was it. Holding on to his sword, he bent one knee and lowered himself down slowly on to the cold floor and bowed his head. That felt right. And now, what to say, after so long? He began, half-whispering, half merely thinking aloud.

'Dear God, if you do exist. Or whatever you might be. I am not asking for a miracle. Keep me safe in the battle that is surely to come, just as I know you will protect my men. And look down on Marlborough. Bless his victory and let us live. If I am to die, then let it be quick. Don't let me be maimed or blinded. But most of all, if you do exist, I pray you, let us win.'

Steel heard the door creak open behind him and, worried lest one of his men should discover him, rose quickly, his scabbard scraping on the floor and filling the empty basilica with its echo. He turned to see Slaughter advancing towards him, grinning.

'Sorry, Sir. I didn't know you were a godly man.'

'I'm not, Jacob. But there are times when anything is better than nothing, eh? Reckon we need a bit of luck at the moment. Right now I'd swear on a ruddy rabbit's foot if you had one.'

'Luck, Sir? Well, perhaps if that's what you want to call it. I'd call it fate myself. Oh, I credit you there's something bigger than us. Stands to reason. But all this?' He pointed around the church at the paintings of the saints, the carved tombs and the side chapels.

'All this is a bit too Papist for my liking, Mister Steel. Fate. That's what it is. You've to make your own way in life. But fate's what decides whether you live or die.'

Both men looked for a moment towards the altar. Steel broke the silence.

'Ready then?'

'As ever will be, Sir. Men are assembled in the square. Grumbling a bit, but that's the ale, mostly. They're happier than they were. The wagons are all rigged and ready to move. But it doesn't seem right, Sir, having poor Miss Weber sitting with him. I mean, after what he did to her.'

'No, Jacob, it doesn't. But there is no room for her to travel with the driver and we must keep Kretzmer in a closed carriage. He knows he's for the drop. If it were up to me I'd shoot him now. But that's not the way. There's nothing for it. The bastard can't go in a flour wagon and he can't very well travel with the wounded.'

He turned and together they walked down the nave. At the door, Slaughter turned his head back towards the altar, which was lit by a brilliant beam of sunshine through one of the clerestory windows. He spoke.

'Funny, ain't it, Sir. The power of that statue, if you get my meaning. I mean, what does it d'you think? What makes people come here from all over, just to make a wish on a piece of painted wood?'

'I wish I knew, Jacob. I wonder if any of them ever come true.'

*　　*　　*

Steel watched the great bird circling in the sky above them. What, he wondered, would they look like from up there, this sorry column of men and wagons trailing back along the dusty road? Nothing of interest to a black kite, he was certain. The bird wheeled again, high into the blue, climbing free of earthly tethers. Steel longed for such freedom. Merely to be free of this tiresome command would be sufficient. It was two days now since they had left Sielenbach. They had continued south at first, before turning right, towards the east. Then, re-crossing the Paar at Dasingen, they had started up the long, straight road north, which would take them back to the army.

Steel watched the bird again as it grew closer to the ground now. Perhaps it had finally spotted a likely prey. Riding in his place at the head of the column, he wished for once that he was not with his men.

He could hardly bear to imagine Louisa locked in the stifling coach with Kretzmer. From time to time Steel rode back to make sure that nothing was amiss, and their progress had been damnably slow. The road was dry and rutted. Recent rains had turned the earth to mud, which, pushed by passing traffic into ridges, had been baked hard in the sun. Now, unless the wheels that crossed it were iron-shod, they would eventually break on the clay. And even such carts as those provided by Hawkins could be easily unsettled.

On the previous day, two of the flour wagons had veered off the road. On the first occasion the men had managed to heave the wagon back. On the second though, the vehicle had overturned, spilling half of its contents into the roadside ditch and breaking both of the legs and crushing several ribs of the driver, who was now travelling in the wounded cart. Taylor had said that he doubted the poor man would last another day.

They had moved what could be salvaged of the spilt flour on to the other wagons, but the accident had cost them a precious two hours.

Steel tried to calculate the time remaining before they would reach the allied lines. This morning they had found the river Ach at the little town of Au and had been following it ever since. According to the map they had another eight miles before they reached the crossing of the Lech and then another day's march back to Donauwörth, if indeed that was where Marlborough had now taken his army. Hawkins had intimated that there might be some movement in the main body while Steel was away on his mission. He realized that his best recourse was to dispatch Williams in search of an outlying cavalry picquet from their army, once they grew closer to the theatre of operations. He turned to the boy and pointed at the wheeling kite.

'Look, Tom. D'you see it. Up there.'

Together they watched as the bird swooped down into a field, diving on its prey.

Steel turned to Williams.

'Tom, I think that tomorrow I may send you on an errand.'

'Sir?'

'I was contemplating dispatching you to find the army. D'you think you could manage it?'

'Of course, Sir. I'm quite certain of it.'

'Then you're a step ahead of me. We're heading back towards Donauwörth now, but in truth I'm damned if I know where His Grace might be at present. You'll just have to keep your head low and nose around until you see some redcoats.'

'And then make sure that they're our redcoats, and not the French, Sir.'

'Quite so. You would think that someone might by now have realized that it would be a great deal easier to fight a war—to actually kill your enemy—if you were able to tell at a glance whether or not they were on your side. Certainly, we British wear red coats, just as the French foot have their white and grey. But are not our friends the Danes now too in grey?

'And the Austrians retain a different colour of coat for every regiment. Sometimes I pity our commanders almost as much as I pity the men they command.'

The boy laughed and Steel with him. They had grown closer over the days and he was anxious to give the lad as much action as he could before they returned to the camp and prepared for the great battle which was surely soon to come.

'How much further now, Sir, do you suppose, until we are within striking distance?'

'I would think in the region of another six miles. The remainder of the day's march, God willing. I intend to stop for the night at a place called Bachweiden, if I have the name correctly. Rather too many "achs" and "bachs" hereabouts for me. From your uncle's map it appears to sit on a small river, so we should be able to water the horses. The men might even bathe, if they wish. They deserve a rest.'

*   *   *

They arrived at the little town at a little before five o'clock. It was a pretty place, with narrow cobbled streets which wound around a gentle hill and the half-timbered houses they had become used to in Swabia. As Steel had predicted, it sat above the confluence of two rivers beyond a gently arced stone bridge over the wider of the two. He halted the column before the bridge. The town looked deserted.

Williams approached him:

'Shall I take a party on reconnaissance, Sir?'

'No. I think we'll stop here for the moment. I don't like it.'

Williams followed his gaze across the bridge. Steel was right. The streets were quite empty. The young Ensign shivered as he recalled the carnage of Sattelberg. Steel saw him and read his mind.

'No, Tom. I don't think this is the work of the French again. We're too far north here for them. Our own army, or at least our scouts might be just a few miles up that road. The French would never dare come so close.'

But in truth Steel was not sure whether he believed his own words. He could detect no sign of life in the dusty streets and the houses stood with empty windows gazing blindly. There was the occasional crash as a door slammed or a shutter banged against a wall, caught in the breeze.

'Sarn't Slaughter.'

The man came running from the front of the column. Steel dismounted.

'Sir.'

'Follow me. Bring your men and make sure their weapons are loaded.'

As Slaughter relayed the orders, checked the flints and the powder, Steel handed Molly's reins to Williams.

'Tom, you stay with the column. Major Jennings is bound to try to interfere. He'll want to move on, most likely. Blame whatever you need to on me. I shan't be long. Bring the rest of the Grenadier company forward into the town and leave the Major's men as a rearguard. We don't want to be taken by surprise again.' He slipped his gun from the leather saddle-bag across Molly's flank and, having loaded it, advanced at the head of his Grenadiers across the bridge and up the single narrow street—barely the width of one and a half of their wagons—that led from it into the town. Still there was no sign of life. Slowly the redcoats made their way up the cobbles and into the heart of the town.

As was usual in these parts, Bachweiden was centred on a small square, with an arcaded market building on one side and on the other a church with a single spire. As Steel and his men moved between the houses, the clock on the church tower above them chimed the hour. It was the time at which work would stop and the tradesmen and workers of the town would be returning home to their families. But today there were no tradesmen. No families.

Nor thankfully, thought Steel, was there anything to suggest that this had been the scene of any violent struggle or a massacre. There were no howling dogs. No stench of rotting corpses. Nothing. He turned to Slaughter.

'What do you make of it, Jacob?'

'I'd say the place has been abandoned, Sir. There's no one here. I can feel it. They've all buggered off. Frightened of them Dutch dragoons, if you ask me. Place doesn't smell of death, Sir. If you know what I mean.'

Steel knew. There was an aura and an odour—honey-sweet and sickly—which hung around such places as Sattelberg. He hadn't caught it here. He nodded.

'Well we can't search every house. I say we stay. Post picquets on the entrance roads and change the guard every hour. The men can take it in turns to bathe in the river. Keep them near the bridge, and make sure that the horses get watered. We'll move the wagons into the main street. Tell the men to find what shelter they can for the night and make sure that there's no looting. Oh, and Slaughter, tell Mister Williams to bring the carriage up to the square. I want that Bavarian bastard where I can see him tonight.'

As Slaughter hurried off, Steel sat down on the edge of the fountain. He laid the gun down beside his leg and rubbed at his eyes. He had almost accomplished what he had been sent to do for Marlborough and Hawkins. They were very nearly back with the army. Soon perhaps he might return to normality. Soon too he hoped they would face the French in the longed-for battle. Would that be an end to the war? He doubted it. Steel hoped it would not be, if that were not too dreadful a hope to nurture. War was his world. War brought him to life and he knew that would ever be the way.

He thought about what he had become and what he had come from. Of the family home and the farm and the happiness that filled them before his mother had died. He had been just eleven, poised on adulthood, ready to go to Eton and filled with hope for the future. Her death had changed all that. Or so it had seemed. In fact it had not been her death but the loss of an expected fortune from his uncle that had ruined the family and ensured that rather than school, his lot would be a miserable private tutor and an apparent destiny as a clerk in his uncle's Edinburgh law firm. Steel had gone to work there at sixteen and that was what Arabella had rescued him from. And from temptation. For, coached by his fellow clerks, Steel had already begun to pilfer trifling amounts from the company books to pay for life's little pleasures. Her arrival had taken him away from the inevitable fate to which that would have led him, and for that at least he would always be grateful. She had reopened his eyes to the beauty of life. Had reminded him that there were things truly worth having. Worth fighting for: love, honour, integrity.

And now there was something else for which he was fighting. He was fighting for the army itself. His army. Every battle strengthened it as an army of which the new Britain—Queen Anne's Britain, could be truly proud.

Steel knew that however sound a job

Marlborough might make of building his army, it was up to men like him, officers fighting in the field, to put the flesh on those bare bones. They were living at the dawn of a new era and Steel knew that what he wanted more than anything else in the world was to have a part in it. Although, perhaps now, he thought, there was just one more thing that he wanted. But she would have to wait.

*　　　*　　　*

The rumble of iron-rimmed wheels over the cobbles signalled the arrival in the square of Kretzmer's carriage. Steel got to his feet and walked across to where it had pulled up in front of the stone pillars of the covered market. Jennings, his horse at a trot, rode a few paces behind.

'So, Mister Steel. Where have you brought us now? Another deserted town? D'you suppose there will be more cadavers to be found here?'

He sniffed the air.

'Perhaps not. But no people, for sure, hm?'

Steel bristled.

'I couldn't say, Major. But I would hazard not. We are not far from our own lines.'

'Oh, are we not? And how d'you come to that? By my reckoning we are a good ten miles from the army, if not more. Or are you lost, perhaps?'

'I intend to send Williams out as soon as possible. It is my belief that he will find the army directly to the north. At no more than five miles distant.'

Jennings smiled and dismounted.

'Well, if you are so certain and the army is so close, why the urgency? We have time in hand,

206

Steel, and an open town. Abandoned and thus legitimate booty for all to take. From what my Sergeant tells me its cellars and pantries are stuffed to bursting. Why not savour the moment? The army will wait until tomorrow.'

'Do I have to remind you, Major, of the importance of our mission. Every day we delay will cost the army dearly. By tomorrow the lack of rations will start to tell. It is imperative that we return with the supplies as swiftly as we may. Williams must go forthwith.'

'Do I have to remind you, Mister Steel, who commands here? In my opinion it would be far from prudent to send the boy off before morning. We have ample time. We rest here. That is an order, Steel.'

'Very well, Sir.'

Steel knew how to play this game—strictly by the book.

'Ensign Williams has the column, Major. I'll have him order the men to find billets with as little disruption as possible. The town may look abandoned, Sir, but I am certain that the Duke would not want us to indulge in plunder. I shall give orders for a moderate amount of subsistence foraging, with an inventory of all that is taken. And shall I also arrange the accommodation for Miss Weber and her father?'

Jennings sighed.

'Yes. As you will. Do what you want with them. I've had enough of her.'

He turned and walked back towards the main street, calling for his Sergeant. Rank had undisclosed advantages, thought Jennings. It was vital to his purpose that they should spend the night here. Jennings knew Steel to be right, that the army was at the most a half day's march from them. He knew that this would be his last opportunity to acquire the papers. Here, he thought, it could be easily contrived. Steel might be clever, but he was no match for Jennings and his Sergeant. Stringer was a natural assassin, as silent as a cat and as swift and sure as a butcher with a knife in the dark. He turned and looked back at Steel, who was opening the door of the carriage and wondered whether the Lieutenant had any inkling that tonight would be his last on earth.

*   *   *

Steel peered into the carriage. Inside, he could make out Kretzmer's lumpen, sleeping form, still bound and gagged. Opposite him, horribly close to her assailant, sat Louisa. She too was asleep, as was her father. Closing the door gently, Steel thought it best to leave them. He stationed a Grenadier at the carriage and walked across the square to a small terrace from which he was able to observe the bridge and the road into the town. The wagons were slowly moving in for the night although perhaps a score of them still lay on the other side of the river.

Down in the reedy shallows he could see a half-dozen of his men. They had thrown off their clothes on to the grassy bank and were jumping about like children, stark naked, laughing and splashing each other in the simple unaccustomed joy of cold, fresh water. Watching them like that, stripped of their uniform, robbed of any vestige of military life, Steel felt more than ever like their adoptive father. They were his family. He knew their ways, their foibles, the reasons why they had joined and how they had come to be here with him. In his care. He felt a responsibility for them and prayed that they would, all of them, the good and the bad, get through whatever trials the coming days would hold.

He was watching one man, John Simmons, a towering Glasgow navvy, as he attempted to duck a fellow Grenadier under the water for a third time, when something caught his eye upstream. A glint of sunlight on an unexpectedly bright object.

It happened in an instant, just thirty yards from where his men were playing. At a point where the river rounded a sharp bend overhung with trees, they came into view. Fifty, no sixty cavalrymen, spurring their horses directly along the river bed, straight towards the bathers. One of the picquets fired at them but missed. The noise gave the alarm but too late.

The water erupted in white spray under the hooves as they beat out against the sand and stones beneath and Steel felt sick to his stomach as he realized that the glint he had seen had been sunlight glancing off the polished steel blade of a drawn cavalry sabre. And then, with a great shout, they were upon the naked Grenadiers and the nightmare unfolded before him. His men never stood a chance.

He had a passing impression of colours. Of pale blue coats, glittering with silver buttons and braid, red hats resplendent with fur and feathers and elaborate, fur-trimmed cloaks slung from one shoulder. Hussars. These were the new cavalry employed by the French. The cavalry they had modelled on the Hungarian light. Fast, skilled and deadly. He had never encountered hussars before but they were all he had expected, and more. The great curved sabres rose and fell and he saw the pale white bodies of his men go down in a sea of blood. Saw Simmons, his face half-severed by a single stroke standing incredulous, grasping at the place where his eye had been, until a second sweeping cut from a grinning hussar took him down. Another man, McCartney, stood clutching at his bare chest which had been laid open by a razor-sharp edge of steel. A third man bubbled and gasped as he collapsed in the pink froth. The horsemen rode round and round the naked soldiers, hacking at their bare flesh in a scene of nightmarish biblical horror, drawn straight from a painting by one of the Italian masters. Steel watched as the naked men clawed and grabbed at the legs of the merciless riders. Watched as one by one they went down into the shallow water, not to rise. Steel snapped away from the vision and yelled down towards the bridge.

'Cavalry. Ware cavalry. Grenadiers. Form on me.'

Followed by the guards from the carriage and a handful of other men who poured from the deserted houses and alleys they had been searching around the square, Steel ran headlong down the main street, towards the bridge.

Emerging on the upper stretch of the riverbank, behind the low, lichen-clad wall which ran along the waterfront, he looked about to assess their strength. He saw Carter, Macpherson, Mackay, six others. He glimpsed Williams running towards

210

them.

'Mister Williams. Sarn't Slaughter. Form along the entrance to the street. Three ranks deep.'

'But the wagons, Sir. Look.'

Williams was pointing down the road towards the remaining flour wagons which had not yet crossed the bridge. Steel could see there were still at least a dozen, perhaps fifteen of them. Half of the hussars, having finished off the Grenadiers in the river, had charged directly towards the transport and were now attacking the drivers and whatever of the escort they could find who had not already fled across the bridge and into the town.

Steel watched as the unarmed civilians threw themselves from their seats. Some, begging for mercy, were butchered in cold blood. Others attempted to run into the trees at the roadside or waded into the river, only to be ridden down by the blue-coated cavalry and spitted on the riders' outstretched sabres, like vermin. Some of the hussars were armed with short axes and Steel watched as they hacked mercilessly into the running civilians. Many of the horsemen, he noticed, were grinning. He turned away.

'It's too late for them.'

Then he realized that a half platoon of Jennings' men, the rearguard, were down there with the train. He looked and saw that they had been caught in a semi-circle of hussars, behind the last wagon. Form square damn you. He willed them to do it. It was their only chance. And then he noticed that none of them had fixed their bayonets.

'Dear Christ.'

He saw one man, presumably a sergeant,

211

attempt to take control, trying to form them into ranks before being cut down with an axe, his head severed from his neck at an angle. Steel knew their fate. The hapless redcoats managed to get off three random shots before the cavalry rode in and simply cut them to pieces. To his horror Steel realized too that the wagon directly behind the dying group of redcoats was that bearing the wounded. The poor devils would be killed where they lay. Sure enough, one man leapt from his horse and began to walk among the wounded. Between the wooden poles of the wagon, Steel saw his axe rise and fall with relentless repetition. He looked more closely at the cavalry and saw long pigtails and swarthy, moustachioed faces. What the hell were French cavalry doing here, so close to the allied lines and so far away from their own army? And then he noticed something else. There, among the slashing fury of the blue-coated hussars, was another uniform quite out of place. A man dressed all in white. An infantry officer, his head crowned with a fur cap. An officer of French Grenadiers. It occurred to Steel that perhaps there might be a connection between the man's presence here and their encounter with the French Grenadiers at Sattelberg. Perhaps it was the Grenadier who had brought the horsemen here. Could the French have discovered the existence of Marlborough's letter? It was possible. Word was that the allied camp was as rife with spies and informers as the French.

Putting his hand to his chest, Steel felt the reassuring presence of the package and turned back to Williams.

'Form up the men here, Tom. Three ranks if

212

you can manage it. You can be sure that they'll come for us next. And I dare say there'll be infantry not far behind. Have you seen who's with them?'

He pointed out the white-coated rider.

'Sarn't Slaughter. Three ranks. Alternating fire. However you care to do it. Just keep those bloody cavalry away from the town. And have them fix bayonets. Quick.'

Dashing back up the street towards the square, Steel began once again to shout into the traversing alleyways, desperate to gather to him all the men he could.

'Grenadiers. To me.'

Three redcoats had joined him as he ran and from the top of the hill another dozen of his men, Corporal Taylor, along with Tarling, Cussiter, Milligan, Henderson, Hopkins, came running to meet him. He shouted to Taylor.

'Is that all of us?'

'Think so, Sir.'

'Where's Major Jennings?'

'Han't seen him, Sir.'

Damn that man, thought Steel. They needed everyone now. And to be honest, Jennings was as good a fighter as they had. He spotted another seven of Jennings' men, including Stringer, and called to them.

'You men. Sarn't Stringer. Follow me.'

At the top of the street he turned and counted his small force. Eighteen in all.

'Right. This is where you stand. This is as far as they're going to get. Corporal Taylor, Hopkins, Tarling, you other men. Form up here. Three ranks. Load up and have a second round ready. Be

213

sure to check your flints and fix your bayonets. Oh, and if you see Major Jennings, tell him he's wanted on the bridge.'

He positioned the men himself so that they were standing right at the top of the narrow street, facing down in the direction of the bridge. Three ranks deep, front rank kneeling, with six men in each rank—a hedge of bayonets and loaded muskets.

'Now listen all of you, and listen well. You're our final hope. Our last chance. Do nothing until you see me running up the street, then, quick as you can split in two and move to the sides. Half to the right, half to the left. We'll be running straight for you, so make it quick. The minute we're through your ranks, you close up. You'd better be ready. They'll be right up our arses. Taylor, you're in charge. Cussiter, you come with me.'

At the double the two men raced across the square to the carriage.

'Herr Weber, Miss Louisa. Out please, if you wouldn't mind. We're going to find you somewhere a little less exposed.'

He turned to Cussiter.

'Take them into that house over there. Make sure that they're safe. Stay with them.'

Kretzmer stared at him.

'I suppose you had better take him with you. Though frankly, I'd rather leave him in the carriage. It would save a lot of trouble if he caught a stray shot.'

In truth, he was half-tempted to shoot the man himself and pretend it to have been enemy fire. But there was no time for that. Steel turned and ran back down towards the bridge. The firing had ceased and he presumed that the cavalry had withdrawn to regroup. As far as Steel was aware across the bridge was the only way into the town. It was a natural defensive position but he knew too that it would not be enough for his small force to hold off a troop of hussars and whatever infantry they had in tow. If they were to survive, his simple trap would be the only chance they had.

*   *   *

Major Jennings had also made a plan. Moving from house to house up the hill, parallel to the main street, he had now reached the square. In his hand he held a short infantry sword, a side-weapon borrowed from Stringer. He had but one purpose in mind. He had heard the crack of musketry from the bridge below and the cries as the redcoats engaged the French. Had watched the cavalry charge from an upstairs window. The arrival of the hussars had been a real stroke of luck. Oh, he knew now why they were here. He had guessed that the white-coated Grenadier Major, whoever he might be, was after the package that he himself was so determined to have from Steel. But his presence was an irrelevance, although it did imply that the hussars might have infantry support. Even without it, it was clear to Jennings that their small force was about to engage in a desperate fight. And that, he realized, was all the opportunity he needed. Why bother with the risk of slitting Steel's throat in his sleep when he could kill him in the mêlée, retrieve the letter and turn a bungled mission into a moment of glory? He saw the men drawn up in three ranks at the head of the street

215

and, moving to another of the lanes leading to the river, Jennings lengthened his stride and began to run as fast as he could towards the bridge.

* * *

The hussars, as Steel had predicted, had come at them in the only way they could. Straight across the bridge. The redcoats' first volley had dropped six of the horsemen and those behind, surprised by the fury of the fire, had fallen back. Now, though, they had re-formed and, advancing three abreast across the bridge, they came on in a dense column of snorting animals and jangling harness. There was no room for them to accelerate to a charge, they knew it would be bloody murder. But the horsemen were determined and Steel knew that however many more of them his men killed and wounded with the next volley, they would prevail through sheer weight of numbers. He cocked his fusil and rested it in the ready position.

'Make ready.'

Looking down the ranks he saw familiar faces and gauged their looks of apprehension and resignation.

'On my command you will give fire. Then run like bloody hell up that hill. Grenadiers. Present.'

The hussars were almost on them now. Still at a trot, but at any moment they would be able to fan out at the head of the bridge and then, if the Grenadiers held their fire too long, it would all be over. Steel paused. Still he did not give the command. He saw Slaughter steadying someone's gun and muttering words of encouragement.

'Steady. Steady.'

Then it was time.

'Fire.'

The air became a cloud of white smoke and ahead of them, just at the moment that the three leading hussars left the confines of the bridge, he saw eight or even ten of their number crash down in a heap of men and horses.

'Right. Retire. All of you. Run.'

Steel began to walk backwards, still gazing at the carnage on the bridge. Some of his men, the old sweats, did likewise but most of them were already running hell for leather back up the little street.

And then he was with them, running too, as fast as he could go.

Steel knew that it would take a few moments for the cavalry to disentangle themselves from the dead and dying. But he knew too that once they were clear, he and his men would be defenceless until they reached the reserve at the top of the hill.

Steel cast a nervous look back over his shoulder and saw, emerging out of the clearing smoke, the distinctive shapes of the hussars. And now they were free to charge.

'Run you buggers. Run.'

His boots slithered up the slippery cobbles, his heart thumping against his chest. He knew that a few of his men would go down. But this was their only hope. Ahead he could see now the three ranks of redcoats. He raised his hand, motioning them to the side.

With perfect precision they parted just in time to admit the remainder of the men in front of him. Steel was ten feet away from them now. From behind he heard a scream as one of the Grenadiers fell beneath a hussar's bloody sabre. The line had to close up or else they would all be lost. He raised his hand again, signalling them to move together. Unquestioning, the men did as ordered and he was caught between the crash of approaching hoofbeats and a wall of bayonets and muskets. He dared not look round again, but he could feel the hot breath of a horse on his back. Six feet to go now. Five. With an almighty effort, Steel threw himself at the line of redcoats and, sensing the presence of something cutting the air immediately behind his neck, slid on his back across the cobbles before crashing into the feet of two of the front-rank men. At that exact instant, above his head, the world became a storm of shot as the redcoats opened up. Steel pressed his head into the stones and prayed.

Still lying down, he turned his face towards where the cavalry had been. As the smoke cleared he saw six of the horsemen and four horses lying dead and dying in the street. He knew that it wasn't enough. Behind the shattered, blue-coated bodies he could see a block of hussars, riding knee to knee, advancing steadily towards him. The volley had merely skimmed the top of the column. They had not even bothered to re-form. Their commander had sent them forward in waves. The first had been annihilated, but here was the second. There might be time for one more volley. But then what? How could so few infantry resist? He clambered to his feet and edged to the rear rank looking around at the redcoats. He saw Slaughter, Cussiter, Taylor, Tarling, Hopkins and Tom Williams. Good. Though he wondered which poor devils had been left out there on the cobbles with the dead hussars. And where in God's name was Jennings? Stringer too had disappeared. Steel was damned if either man was going to be spared what looked as if it might be their last fight. He found Williams.

'Tom, go and see if you can find Major Jennings and Sarn't Stringer. Look everywhere. They're probably somewhere near the square. Hurry.'

He turned to Slaughter.

'Reload, Sarn't. How many rounds a man do we have?'

'Couldn't say, Sir, but it can't be many. There's always the grenades.'

'No. The cobbles would be blown to blazes. We'd kill as many of our own men as theirs. It's bullets this time, Jacob. And bayonets. Let's see how many we can take with us.'

Steel could see the hussars coming on again. His plan had worked but it had not been enough. He wondered whether Williams had found Jennings and Stringer. Whether they would reach him before the cavalry rode down the redcoats and began their butchery or whether the three officers might yet escape. Glancing across the square he saw the empty carriage and thought of Louisa. What would happen to her? He should have sent her away. But how? Too late now for that. He prayed that the French hussars would be more merciful than their Grenadiers. He turned to Slaughter and smiled. He was ready for it now. Listening for the hooves on the cobbles, for the battle cries that would come as the cavalry urged themselves on towards the guns and the bayonets, Steel turned to the redcoats:

'Make ready.'

Down the street the hussars still came on, boot to boot.

'Present.'

The cavalry were trotting at them now. He could see their faces and their piercing eyes. Heard the sergeants calling out commands in French. Pushing them on. They were packed too tight for a canter, but Steel knew that their sheer weight would be enough to push them into the infantry. The line of muskets held its aim on the advancing cavalry. Slaughter hissed at them:

'Steady. Wait for the command.'

Thirty paces out. Twenty.

'Fire!'

Steel yelled the word and as he did, squeezed the trigger of his own weapon. The volley filled the narrow street, half-deafening the infantry and covering the scene in thick white smoke. Steel peered towards the enemy.

'Prepare to receive cavalry.'

The volley had slowed the riders but he was sure that they would come on, regardless. Suddenly, from the white mist figures began to appear. To his left three hussars had managed to negotiate the piles of dead and broken men and horses and connected with the line. The first took a bayonet in the thigh and hacked down at his assailant, who ducked and, retrieving his bloodied blade, thrust it again and this time sent it clean into the cavalryman's unprotected side. The man clutched at the weapon and hurled himself from the saddle only to impale himself further. Next to him another hussar had had better success, parrying the thrust of one of Jennings' men and swiping down with his blade to flense off half of the man's face. Steel pushed aside the dying musketeer and before the Frenchman could defend himself, made a great sweeping cut with the broadsword, taking the tip of his blade and three inches of steel through the man's side and belly. The man dropped his sword and clutched at the awful wound. He tried to turn his horse and was brought down by a shot, fired from the rear rank. More figures were appearing through the smoke now. A voice from his rear made him turn. It was Stringer, eyes staring, bayonet bloody:

'Mister Steel, Sir. They've come round the flank Sir, up the next street. You must come, Sir.'

Steel turned to Slaughter:

'It's Jennings, he's in trouble. Take over. Re-form the men, Jacob. Reload if you can. I'll be back as quickly as I can. And find Williams.'

He ran after Stringer, who had already begun to run away, and down the narrow alleyway connecting the two streets like the spokes on a wheel towards the town square.

It was deep black between the high walls and, looking towards the light at the end, after a few yards Steel saw the Sergeant turn left into the main street and out of sight. He continued in pursuit. He had slung the empty fusil over his shoulder and carried his sword low now, in readiness for whatever might meet him. His ears were still ringing from the crashing volley and his feet on the cobbles sounded curiously dim against the general cacophony. Even half deaf, though, as he rounded the corner, Steel was aware that something was missing. The street was silent and before he could check his pace, he realized that he had not run into some desperate struggle, but merely into a trap.

Stringer's bayonet-tipped musket was pointed directly at his chest. Behind him, Jennings was leaning against the stone sill of a ground-floor window.

'Ah, Steel. Thank you. Once again you come to my rescue. This time though, I am afraid that it is not myself that is in deadly peril, but you.'

Steel stood staring at the Major, all too aware of the needle-sharp point that hovered dangerously close to his throat. God damn it. How had he not seen this coming? Another duel had been inevitable. Honour must be satisfied. But like this?

'Major Jennings. You can call off your terrier now. I'll fight you fair. But this is not the time. We're being beaten. We must act together for the sake of the army. We cannot afford to lose here. For pity's sake, man. This can wait.'

'But, Steel. Don't you understand? Have you no idea at all? I am doing this for the sake of the army. I am aware that we cannot afford to lose here. Not the flour. The real reason for your mission.'

Steel's eyes widened.

'I know what you have, Lieutenant. I know what it was that you bought from Kretzmer and its importance to Marlborough. But you see it is of equal importance to those who sent me here. No, not Colonel Hawkins but those who have Britain's true interests at heart.'

'You bloody traitor.'

Jennings grimaced.

'Now, now, Steel. Really, I expected better from you. You know I have come to have some respect for you over the past few days. You are a fighter,

222

though you may be a ruffian at heart. And you do at least know your place. Unlike our brave commander, the Duke, who can never be anything more than a jumped-up farmer. We need to be led by natural leaders, Steel. By the men whose ancestors led us at Crécy and Agincourt. With that letter in their hands they will be able to bring down Marlborough and restore the army to its rightful masters. And it is my duty to ensure that they have it.'

'You'll have to kill me first.'

'Oh dear. I did so hope that you weren't going to be heroic.'

Stringer, grinning, edged the tip of his bloody bayonet closer to Steel's throat.

'And sincerely, Steel, I would have loved to have given you a chance in a fair fight. But now you see, as you yourself are aware, time is of the essence. Now. Your weapons, please.'

Again the bayonet moved forward. Steel dropped the sword to the ground.

'And the gun.'

Steel hooked his hand beneath the sling of the gun and moved to let it fall to the ground. Just as it seemed that he was about to drop it though, he grasped the weapon by the barrel, and dipping down beneath the bayonet and musket, swung it up and drove it, butt first, with all his strength deep into Stringer's groin. The man yelped in agony, dropped his musket and fell to the ground, screaming and clutching at his genitals. Steel, still holding the gun, straightened up, but Jennings was quick.

Thinking fast, the Major made a copy-book lunge at Steel's side and struck home. He felt the blade slide into flesh and quickly withdrew it. Steel let out a hollow groan and turned, clutching at his side.

'Tut tut. Brawling with a senior officer, Mister Steel? You'll never find promotion that way. En garde? Oh, you are unarmed. Well, as you will then.'

Steel swung out wildly with the gun, but Jennings hardly had to move to avoid it. He lunged at Steel and cut into thigh, a few inches above the knee. The pain tore through the Lieutenant. Steel looked about for his sword and saw it, lying just a few feet away. If he could just get to it, somehow. Hurling the gun at Jennings, he reached wildly for the sword and grabbed at the hilt but before he could make contact, Jennings was on him again. Steel felt the burning stab as the tip of the sword just nicked his back. He turned and, his eyes filled with rage and pain, threw himself, weaponless upon the Major, wrenching his sword by the blade from his hand and in the process cutting his own down to the bone. Jennings, taken completely by surprise, dropped the sword and saw that Steel still had it by the blade.

To Steel's right, close to where the Sergeant was still writhing in pain on the ground, Jennings saw Stringer's fallen musket. In an instant Jennings was on it and, as Steel paused to move the sword hilt into his right arm, he brought the heavy wooden butt crashing down like a club upon the Lieutenant's skull, with a sickening crack. Steel's legs gave way and he slumped to the cobbles. He fell on to his knees, his back quite rigid and, as his eyes filled with a red haze, collapsed upon his face. Jennings, breathless, stood over him, the musket still raised in his hands. No, he thought. He would not beat the man's brains out. Nor would he spit him on the bayonet. He would finish him like a gentleman. But first. He dropped the weapon to the ground and, crouching down, reached beneath Steel's heavy body. He delved into the inner recesses of his coat and at last his fingers closed around a small square object. Smiling he withdrew his hand and looked at the package. It was tied with twine around brown paper. He eased the string to one side and read the first, faded page.

'Your Majesty,
You cannot know how my heart yearns for your return and how all Britain shall rejoice when once again our land is restored to its rightful monarch . . .'

Looking further down the small sheet Jennings was able to discern the signature:

'Your most faithful servant,
John Churchill.'

Jennings clasped the package to his chest before placing it deep within a pocket of his waistcoat. Then, still grinning, he stooped again to collect his own sword from where it lay beside Steel's limp hand. Now, one thrust and the world would be rid forever of this annoying upstart. Taking his time, Jennings stood over Steel's body, lining up his blade with the left side of his back, just at the point where the heart would be. He raised the weapon to strike. Now, and it would be finished.
'Sir! Major Jennings, Sir. What are you doing?'

Williams ran from the alleyway and stopped in his tracks. Jennings advanced upon him, his sword at the ready. The boy raised his own weapon but not before Jennings had time to lunge and slash his thigh with the tip of the blade. Williams yelped in pain but kept his guard.

The two men began to circle one another. Jennings whispered:

'Steel's dead, boy. He betrayed his country. Now put down your sword and we'll say no more of it.'

Williams noticed Stringer now and realized that Jennings might not be telling the whole truth.

'I don't believe you, Sir. You killed him.'

'I killed a traitor.'

'Mister Steel was an honourable man, Sir. He would never betray us.'

Jennings sighed.

'Ah well. I gave you your chance. Have you ever fought anyone before boy? One to one? Have you?'

Williams said nothing. But, to Jennings' surprise, he lunged and caught the Major momentarily off guard. The tip of his sword glanced against Jennings' left arm and drew blood.

'So. You've got spirit. I'll give you that. But spirit ain't enough for me, boy.'

Jennings lunged again and, as if he was using the boy to demonstrate his skill, as a fencing master might use a dummy, touched the Ensign less than an inch away from his previous wound.

The pain seared red-hot through Williams' leg and he was conscious of the fresh, warm blood dripping on to his reddened stocking. God, thought Williams, but Jennings is good at this game. So much for his costly fencing lessons at

226

Eton. What use now the classical moves on which he had spent so much time? This fighting was fast and brutal. No finesse here. Just kill or be killed. And at present, Williams guessed, he would not be the one who would be walking away with his life. He glanced at Steel's motionless form.

Jennings broke the silence.

'He's dead, boy. Quite dead. Come on, you're not scared, surely? That won't make you a soldier. Soldiers are brave, Mister Williams. But you're not brave are you? You're scared. Daddy wanted you to join us. You were good for nothing else. But you'll never make a soldier. You haven't the guts for it. Get out now, before it's too late. Before you're spitted by some Frog.'

He laughed to himself.

'Oh dear. I forgot. It's too late already.'

On the last word, he lunged and made contact with Williams' right forearm. The Ensign staggered backwards and slipping on the cobbles, slick with Steel's blood, lost his balance and went crashing to the ground, hitting his head on the sharp edge of the wide stone windowsill. He slumped to unconsciousness, trailing blood down the wall behind him. Stringer had managed to get to his feet now and was hobbling about, doubled over with pain.

Jennings looked at the Sergeant for a moment, then back at Williams and Steel, deciding which of the fallen men he should make sure of first. There was no choice. He crossed to where Steel lay and was about to raise his sword again when Stringer, looking down the alleyway, pointed and called out in a hoarse voice:

'Sir.'

Jennings looked round just as the tall figures of two of Steel's Grenadiers emerged into the street. He clutched at his arm and pressed on the cut, making sure they would see the blood seeping through his fingers. He feigned pain and screamed towards the two redcoats:

'Hurry men. The French are behind us. I've been hit. Mister Steel's dead.'

The Grenadiers rushed past him and Jennings ran up the street towards the main square. It was deserted, save for the carriage. Jennings ran across to it and moved to the front. There were two horses, both built for strength rather than speed. Jennings began to unbuckle the harness of that closest to him and then, leaving her in the shafts, turned back towards the door of the coach. The money, Kretzmer's payment for the flour and whatever he had from Steel, confiscated after his crime, had been placed in a strongbox on the floor of the carriage. It could not go to waste. Jennings pulled himself up into the compartment, opened the lid of the box and withdrew the two leather purses. He looped the strings of the two heavy bags around his belt and turned towards the door. Stepping down from the carriage, he began to lead the dray horse from the shafts. He was preparing to mount her when, from close behind him he heard an unmistakeable noise. It was the sound of a musket's hammer being cocked. Instinctively Jennings began to turn and as he did so, he saw a red-coated figure with a musket levelled directly towards him. Dan Cussiter was standing a few paces away from the door of the coach. The Private stared at him with venomous, vengeful eyes, his mouth curled in a tight smile.

'Now, boy, don't be hasty. I can explain everything.'

Cussiter said nothing. He tucked the musket deeper into his shoulder and Jennings knew that it was ready to fire. All he could hear now was the beating of his own heart.

'Don't be foolish, boy. You know what punishment feels like now. You've felt the cat. Imagine what they'll give you for killing an officer. Put down the gun. Be sensible. I'll speak for you.'

He extended his hand. Cussiter's finger played with the trigger. His eye looked straight down the barrel of the musket, straight at Jennings' forehead. He began to squeeze and Jennings waited for the flash. It came but as he closed his eyes and flinched away he sensed no more than a slight burning sensation on his head, as if he had been touched by a sudden, fast breath of hot wind. Opening his eyes he saw that the puff of smoke had gone high into the air and with it the musket ball, which had evidently done no more than nick his head and part his wig. He looked back at Cussiter and saw him sprawled on the ground, locked in a desperate struggle with Stringer. Evidently the Sergeant had hurled himself at the man at the moment his finger had pulled the trigger.

Jennings did not wait. Stringer might have saved his life, but he had no time for thanks. The Sergeant was no longer necessary to his plans. With no time to take the horse, he turned and he ran as fast as he could for the corner of the nearest house. Behind him the space had filled with soldiers. He did not look back. Ahead of him, at a crossroads of back alleys, a dead French hussar lay

229

sprawled on the ground, his hand still tangled in the reins of a bay mare who stood close by chewing at a patch of scrub. Not wasting a moment, Jennings ran to the horse, snatched up the reins and pulled them from the dead man's hand. Then he was up and in the saddle. He whipped the animal quickly into a canter and then a gallop and drove her fast through the narrow streets, and then down and over the bloody bridge and out into the fields. He was exultant. He had the papers. The papers that would bring down Marlborough and guarantee his own passage to untold influence and prosperity. But before any of that could happen, he would have to carry them to safety. And after what he had just done, he knew that at this moment, safety lay in only one direction. Aubrey Jennings pressed his spurs deep into the horse's flanks and rode as fast as he could towards the French.

* * *

Steel coughed blood and felt a loose tooth in his mouth. He spat it on to the cobbles. His head felt as if someone had laid about it with a hammer. He put his hand up to touch it and felt the blood. He coughed again and retched. Looking up, he could see Williams getting to his feet. His face was covered with rivulets of blood and he was standing as groggy as a drunk. One of the Grenadiers, Mackay, placed a hand beneath the Lieutenant's arm and Steel tried to stand. As he put the weight on his right leg a searing pain shot through his calf. He looked down and saw for the first time the extent of the damage done by Jennings' blade.

230

'Bugger.'

He looked at Mackay.

'Where is he?'

'Who, Sir?'

'Major Jennings, man. Did you get him?'

'He's gone back to the fight, Sir. Told us the Frenchies had killed you.'

'Like hell he has. Major Jennings is a traitor.'

So, Jennings had escaped. Steel panicked. He reached inside his coat for the packet and, as he had known he would, felt nothing. He had known Jennings to be bad, but a traitor on this scale? It had not entered his wildest imaginings. Through the mist of his agonizing headache he heard the sounds of battle. Christ almighty. They were still fighting the French. It began to come back to him.

'Williams. Are you all right?'

The Ensign was sitting on the window ledge, swaying slightly, staunching the flow of blood from his head and leg.

'I think so, Sir.'

'Stay there. You, Tarling, stay with him. Mackay, you come with me.'

Steel picked up his sword from where it lay on the ground, grabbed the gun and limped off with the Grenadier along the narrow alleyway. Ahead of them the sounds of fighting grew ever louder. It was true. God alone knew how, but they were still holding out.

As he approached, Slaughter caught sight of him.

'Told you I was going nowhere, Sir.'

Steel looked down the street over piles of dead and wounded, mostly hussars. Body parts lay strewn upon the cobbles and blood had spattered the walls of the houses on either side. In three places the road surface had disintegrated.

'Don't tell me. You used the grenades.'

'Like I said, Sir. I wasn't going anywhere. Besides, Thorogood here used to play cricket for his parish. He threw the bombs when the hussars were forty paces off. Should've seen it, Mister Steel.'

'Can we do it again?'

'Only three bombs left. Reckon one more time if we need to. If we're lucky. What happened to you, Sir? You look bad.'

'Major Jennings.'

'The Major? Was he hit? Is he dead?'

'It was the Major who did this to me, Jacob. He's a traitor.'

'Well I'll be buggered. I always knew he was bad, mind. But that. By Christ.'

Their conversation was interrupted by noise from the street below. Wearily the remaining men in the firing lines finished loading their muskets and made sure their bayonets were secure. Leaning on his gun as a support, Steel strained to see what was going on beyond the dead. He could make out nothing and the light was beginning to fade.

'You'd better get those grenades ready, Jacob. They're the only chance we have now.'

He waited for the jingle of harness and the clatter of hooves that would announce the coming attack. But it was neither of those sounds that he heard. From the bottom of the street, beyond view, came the clash of steel on steel. Ahead of him he watched as the leading two ranks of blue-coated hussars, now a mere fifty feet away from them, turned on command and began to trot back down the street, before vanishing around the bend.

Steel looked at his men. At Thorogood, a bomb in each hand, waiting to light the fuses. At the guns held steady at their shoulders, eyes aligned with the barrels. The natural inclination was to fire at the retreating cavalry. But Steel knew that it could easily be a trick intended to draw their single volley before the hussars simply turned and rode straight for them.

'Hold steady. Hold your fire.'

Still the din came from the river. What the deuce was happening? The tumult grew louder and then quickly died away. Steel could hear some shouting yet, and the sporadic crack of muskets and carbines. But the distinctive sound of blade on blade had gone.

He saw a horseman appear around the bend in the street. This was it, then. He looked again at the ranks. The men were sweating hard with the exertion of keeping their muskets level.

'Steady. Keep the present. Prepare to fire.'

Steel looked again towards the river and his mouth dropped open. The single horseman continued to approach. But this was no hussar. The man wore a black tricorne hat and a red coat. Whose red was it, though? Another trick?

Steel pushed gently from the rear of the line, passing between the files and stepped out in front of his men, ensuring that he could be plainly seen. He saw that the man's sword was soiled with gore. At twenty yards out the rider pulled up his horse and stared.

Steel stared back, straight into his eyes. He half turned to address his men: 'Hold your fire,' then yelled down the street: 'Who are you?'

'Captain James Maclean, Hay's dragoons. Who the devil are you?'

'Steel, Sir. Lieutenant, Farquharson's Foot. We thought you were French.'

'Not us. Scots, old chap. Like yourselves. You look as if you've had a bit of a time of it.'

'You could say that, Captain. A bit of a time. Thank God you're here. How did you find us?'

'Oh, it was no trouble really. We just followed the sound of the guns.'

'You heard our fire?'

Maclean laughed. Pointed towards the bridge.

'The Duke himself will have heard your fire, Lieutenant. The entire allied army is encamped but three miles down that road.'

EIGHT

Steel groaned. How much longer could this possibly take? Clad in just his shirt and waistcoat, breeches and stockings, he sat in his tent within the allied lines, with his right leg hoisted up on a hay-filled forage bag. Before him Corporal Taylor crouched over the wound that had been inflicted fifteen days ago by Jennings' filthy sword, while above both men, Sergeant Slaughter stood gazing on, half in admiration, half in sceptical curiosity. Steel drummed impatient fingers against the small table beside him and sighed:

'Taylor. You're quite certain that this is absolutely necessary?'

'Please, Mister Steel. Do try and remain still,

234

Sir, and I'll be finished with you in an instant. This is the last time I'll have to do this. I swear, Sir.'

'What the devil are you putting on me this time? Not more rancid pumpkin flesh and stale meal, surely?'

'No, Sir. This is the final stage. Just finishing you off nicely. Brown sugar, lees of wine and linseed oil. My own recipt.'

'Sounds rather as if you're preparing me for the kitchens. And it doesn't smell any better.'

'That's the matter from wound that's smelling so bad, Sir, not my poultice.'

Slaughter coughed: 'Smells something awful, Sir.'

'Thank you, Jacob. I'm as aware as you of the stink. Corporal Taylor here assures me that this is the only way to ensure that the wound will heal by the time we fight the French. And after all that has happened I do not intend to miss the moment we have been seeking these four months.'

'All the same, Sir. It don't half reek.'

Taylor glared up at the Sergeant.

'But at least, Sarn't Slaughter, it's not infected any longer.'

He pointed proudly at the pink, glistening, puckered scar, a small section of which still lay open.

'See all that slough running down off your leg, Sir? That there's the last of the matter to come out of the wound. I promise you, you'll be fine within the week, Mister Steel.'

'Thank you, Taylor. I really am much obliged to you. But I intend to be fine within the day. The Frogs are just over that hill and I promise you that very soon, sooner than you think, we will be at them.'

'Oh, Jack, what is that horrid smell.'

The sound of a woman's voice turned all their heads towards the tent flap. Louisa Weber stood framed against the day, the pale afternoon sunlight catching the golden strands which ran through her pale yellow hair.

'It's like you have a ham cooking . . . in honey or something.'

'It's my leg. I'm sorry.'

She grimaced, then laughed. Ten days of nursing Steel had inured her to the sights of a field hospital. If not the smells. She entered and Slaughter smiled and left. Taylor was lost in his work, carefully winding a clean bandage around Steel's leg.

'Corporal Taylor is a fine doctor, Jack. He looked after me so well.'

Even through his stubble, Taylor's deepening colour was evident. 'It was nothing ma'am. Just did what I could.'

'Nonsense. You are a treasure. Don't let him go, Jack.'

'No danger of that.'

Steel looked hard at the Corporal:

'Aren't you done yet, Taylor? Go on, get on now. I'm sure that'll do it.'

Taylor tucked in the end of the bandage to secure it and gathered up his ointments, placing the glass phials with care inside their leather bag.

'Good day, Miss. Mister Steel, Sir.'

'Good day, Taylor. And thank you.'

As Taylor left the tent, Louisa bent to kiss Steel on the forehead. He pulled her down on to his knee.

'Jack. Be careful. Your leg.'

'My leg is as good as new. Your Corporal Taylor told me so. Where have you been?'

'I was visiting the wounded. One of them died in the night. A young boy. He had asked for me. I came too late.'

She stared at the ground and began to rub at the balls of her fingers, as if she was trying to eradicate some dirt. Steel had noticed the habit before and knew that she did it to stop the tears.

'How's Mister Williams coping with his duties?'

'He looked very busy. He wears his head bandaged up and he has taken to walking with a stick for the sake of his poor leg. He looks very . . . dashing. He was marching with some of your men beside the wagon park. He smiled at me.'

At least they could be thankful that Williams had not been killed.

Steel could recollect little of the immediate aftermath of the fight at Bachweiden. But gradually he began to remember details. The fight with Jennings. Their timely rescue by Hay's dragoons. Most pressingly the fact that Jennings was now in possession of the papers.

Louisa, freed from Jennings' threat, had revealed the true identity of her attacker.

Steel had offered an apology to Herr Kretzmer, who, thankful for his lucky escape from the noose and the bullet, had been only too happy to accept the offer of an escort to Augsburg. Of course they had been obliged to make good the payment for the flour. Jennings' deceit had cost them all, dearly.

Now Steel would not rest until Jennings was dead. How had he not seen through the man before? A rapist and a traitor. The wound had kept him confined to bed and it irked him not to be in pursuit of the Major.

After their rescue, Steel and his Grenadiers had remained in the British camp at Neukirk to join the rearguard, while the bulk of the army had manoeuvred further still into Bavaria. Then the army had returned and together they had made the short march north. Yesterday they had arrived here, just to the south of the town of Rain, which had been taken by Marlborough shortly after their departure some three weeks past. What there was left of the precious flour had been gratefully received. As to the more vital part of Steel's mission, though, little had as yet been said. Now he awaited Hawkins' arrival.

Steel knew that soon he would have to account to Marlborough. He had failed. Of that there was no doubt. And whatever might be his punishment for such failure, it remained to be seen how, if at all, it might yet be remedied.

First though, he must be fit. He had been surprised at the gravity of his wounds. The blow on the head had very nearly cracked his skull, but it had been the leg wound from Jennings' blade that had caused him the most severe discomfort. Having at first considered it no more than a scratch he had had it dressed. But then it had begun to throb and soon to stink. For six days he had lain in a fever. That he had not died was due entirely to the ministrations of Corporal Taylor and Louisa.

He gazed at her now as she attempted to tidy up around him. At her slender waist, the pale beauty of her half-covered shoulders and her delicate profile. He wondered at her resilience. At how quickly she had seemed to recover from her ordeal.

Again he played in his mind with the possibilities of their relationship. If there was ever a woman who might grow accustomed to the life of an army wife, then surely it was Louisa. But was she suited to it? Or indeed suited to him? For what did she really know of him? And what, he wondered, of himself? Was this what he wanted? Arabella was a distant memory and many, many miles away. Louisa was here and now and Steel wondered whether what he felt for her was what men called love. For an instant he caught the word on his lips, then stopped himself. Louisa turned to him and smiled.

'What?'

'I. Nothing. I was just . . .'

She seemed about to say something when the tent flap opened and Henry Hansam entered, followed by Colonel Hawkins.

Steel attempted to stand but the Colonel waived him down.

'Jack. I am very much afraid that I come bearing a summons. You are ordered at once to the Commander-in-Chief.'

He noticed Louisa and removed his hat.

'Good day, Miss Weber.'

Hansam followed suit. Like the rest of Steel's fellow officers he had accepted her presence in his friend's tent as readily as they had all welcomed the return of Steel himself. Women in camp were no great novelty. Though for the most part of course they were found among the other ranks. But with Steel, as they all concurred, anything was possible. It seemed only natural that the maverick officer should return to the camp with this beautiful Bavarian angel as his consort. For if Steel was not yet decided as to their future, to his comrades it seemed to be a foregone conclusion.

Steel pushed himself up off the chair. Louisa moved to help him to his feet. She buttoned his waistcoat which hung open and draped his red coat across his shoulders before helping him insert his arms. As, with Louisa's assistance, he pushed his feet into his boots, Steel ran a hand around his recently shaved chin. He peered at himself in the small piece of mirror-glass propped up on a folding table. Hawkins smiled at him.

'You hardly present the very perfect picture of an officer, Jack. But I dare say you'll do for Marlborough.'

'Colonel. I am not back yet ten days and you goad me.'

He pointed to his leg.

'I am a sick man. Have you no pity?'

Hawkins laughed. Louisa handed Steel the stout ash stick that, to avoid putting pressure on his leg, he had been using for the past few days to help him walk, and held back the flap of the tent as he lowered his head and felt the touch of the balmy evening air. Hansam held the tent open for Hawkins and Steel who, as he left, turned back to Louisa.

'Wish me luck, both of you. I suspect that I may have need of it.'

*   *   *

Marlborough's tent, illuminated by the light of two

240

dozen candles, was empty when Steel and Hawkins entered, save for the General's soldier-servant who was busy pouring three glasses of wine. Hawkins handed one of them to Steel before he spoke:

'Truly, Jack, I did not expect this to happen. I knew nothing of Jennings' intentions. Of course I learnt of his departure, but assumed that Colonel Farquharson had dispatched him. There is no doubt in my mind as to who might be behind this. It is common knowledge that the Margrave is opposed to Marlborough's strategy. We can surmise that one of his commanders must have stumbled upon our plan. There are Tories in the army but I had not been aware that Major Jennings was of their persuasion.'

'Nor I, Colonel. Although I did perceive that his way of waging war might be somewhat different to that proposed by our Commander.'

Hawkins looked grave.

'It is clear that the French Grenadiers, their officer in particular, were pursuing you with a specific prize in mind. Otherwise they would not have dared venture so close to our lines. I can only wonder if Major Jennings is now with the French; whether he has yet been discovered by your Grenadier officer. I do not suppose that he will be very comfortable in his new billet, either way.'

'A turncoat he might be, Sir, in his loyalty to the Duke, but I cannot believe that even Jennings would turn traitor to his country. Although I am afraid that Colonel Farquharson cannot now bring himself to talk to me, so mortified is he by his relation's behaviour.

'But whoever it was alerted the French to my mission, it seems now that Jennings has done their work for them. And in truth, it is I who am at fault, Colonel. I should have been suspicious at his arrival on the march. I should have seen his true purpose. Above all I should not have allowed him to catch me off guard in the heat of battle. I am truly sorry.'

'I believe, Steel, that I know who may have brought in the French. Jennings had a Sergeant did he not?'

'Stringer? An accomplice?'

'The Sergeant, it seems, has been running a racket with the French and selling them supplies. He was dealing through one of the commissaries. Jennings must have let him in on the reason for their expedition and naturally, seeing that there's money in secrets, he tells his go-between who, for a price, tells the French. It's not until the second ambush that Stringer realizes he's signed his own death warrant. Of course the French don't get him, thanks to you. But the hangman will. Man's a born traitor. We've already arrested his friend. He admitted everything and he'll swing for it tomorrow.'

'But not Stringer? You haven't taken him.'

Steel looked desperate.

'You must know, Colonel, that Stringer is my chief hope of finding Major Jennings.'

Hawkins placed a hand on his shoulder.

'Don't fret, Jack. I guessed that you might have plans for him. Sergeant Stringer believes that he's got away with it. He'll be nervous, but that just might make him all the more eager to keep you sweet. He's yours until you find Jennings. Then he belongs to me.'

There was a cough and both men turned. 'Let us

hope, gentlemen, however we catch our fox that we are not too late to undo the wrong that has been done.'

The voice belonged to Marlborough, who, as they had been talking with their backs to the entrance, had quietly entered the tent. He was alone and Steel turned and met his gaze, giving a short bow.

'Your Grace. I was not aware . . .'

'No, Lieutenant Steel. Indeed. I hear that you have been sorely tried. Two engagements with the enemy. Infantry and cavalry. Hussars if I am informed aright. How did you find them?'

'They are fine horsemen, Your Grace, but I am of the opinion that too much of their reputation rides upon their appearance. We gave them a good licking, Sir.'

'And were damn near licked yourself in the process. You were only saved by John Hay's dragoons. Am I not right? But I do hear that you fought valiantly, Steel. And at least you are safe, eh? How are your injuries?'

Marlborough gestured at Steel's leg.

'Have you the proper attention? I have a doctor.'

The icy, grey-green eyes stared deep into Steel's soul.

'Thank you, Sir. I have the best of care. And it was no more than a scratch, Your Grace. And a knock to the head.'

'Given you, I believe, by our friend Major Jennings.'

Steel was at a loss for words. He wondered exactly how much Hawkins had already told the Duke. Marlborough continued:

'You did everything that was in your power to secure those papers. Everything. Indeed you had them in your very possession. You were not to suspect that Jennings would prove turncoat. You looked at the papers?'

Steel was unsure how to reply but decided on the truth.

'Yes, Your Grace.'

'So you know their content?'

'I saw an address, Sir, in France. The date. Your name. Nothing more.'

'My signature. Yes. And the name of the . . . Of another man. You recall the date?'

'1696. November, I believe, Your Grace.'

Marlborough paused. He seemed for a moment unaware to whom he was speaking.

'Yes. That was the date. I was asking for King James' pardon. For a wrong I believed I had committed against him and his house and against my own honour.'

Marlborough recovered himself and looked again at Steel.

'It was a foolish notion. Another time. Another country. I was another man.'

He walked over to the table, where the servant handed him a glass of wine. He took a long drink and set it back down.

'And so, God bless the Queen. Nevertheless, gentlemen. Now I think that we should all be very much afraid for I am quite exposed. Open to destruction. My future and the fate of this army, whether or not we prevail in the coming battle, now hangs on the actions of Major Jennings. It was not your fault, Steel, but as I intimated before your departure, should you fail, then we are undone.

244

And I am very much afraid that now that moment is come upon us. What, do you suppose, are we to do? Where will we find the Major?'

Steel was about to speak when Hawkins cut in:

'Your Grace, we must on all accounts remain calm in this matter. We know that Jennings rode towards the French, he did not ride directly for Flanders and the coast. It should be some consolation that he is still in the country and on the continent.'

Steel spoke:

'He is with the French, Your Grace. I am quite sure of it. He dare not return to the army at present.'

Marlborough let out a mocking laugh.

'Ah, I know what you will now tell me, Mister Steel. I have had it before today, from Hawkins. And from my Lord Cadogan and Cardonell. You will tell me that a lone English officer was spied riding on a French cavalry horse by a patrol of our dragoons. That he rode through the French picquets and into their lines. And I dare say that it was Jennings. But that was five days ago. Why, the man could be on his way to the Channel ports by now.'

Steel shook his head.

'No, Your Grace. With all respect, Sir, I know that he is not. I know it. Look at it from the French point of view, Sir. An English officer gives himself up to them. Tells them he has information that will bring down Marlborough and that he must be given an escort to the coast. Ask yourself, Sir, what you would do. You are about to engage in a battle with your entire force. A momentous battle which will decide the entire campaign, the war perhaps.

That is now the sole focus of your attention. Whatever this English officer does now will not change the inevitability of that encounter. Of course, you would like to believe him. But would you? Surely, Sir, your response would be to keep him with your army—on parole—until after the engagement? And then, if you win, send him back to England to offer terms. And if you lose, then you have a secret weapon on which to fall back and wreak catastrophic revenge upon a commander who thinks himself the victor.

'Surely, it would seem to any French commander that providence had indeed smiled upon him in delivering Major Jennings. Believe me, Your Grace. Jennings is with the French. And that is where I will find him.'

'Pray do not tell me, Mister Steel, that you propose that you should infiltrate the French camp? We are barely a day away from the fight. Attempt such a foolhardy enterprise and not only would you place yourself in mortal danger but we would be without one of our ablest officers.'

'No, Your Grace. And you flatter me. But I do agree, Sir, that would be foolish. No, I intend to find Jennings in the course of the battle. And when I have found him then I shall kill him—and retrieve the papers. You have my word on it, Sir.'

Marlborough turned and began to toy with the silver-mounted coconut shell, his favourite drinking cup, which stood on the table in the corner of the tent. At length he turned back to Steel. His face looked ashen.

'Very well, Mister Steel. Although I shall send out scouts to scour the country for the man. And, Hawkins, you must find his accomplices. But I believe that the principle suspects may already have left us. Tomorrow our army will join with that of the Imperial forces under Prince Eugene. Our friend the Margrave of Baden has departed for Ingolstadt with 15,000 men. Do not look concerned, Steel. In truth his departure is a blessing to me. The man was ever a hindrance. And now, with him happily diverted in a siege, we are free to get to the real business of this campaign. As we speak, Prince Eugene's army is marching towards us. An army 20,000 strong, gentlemen.'

His eyes ablaze now, Marlborough moved across to the easel which held the tattered cloth map. He smoothed his hand across its surface, narrowing his distance to sweep the road between Münster and Hochstadt.

'With Prince Eugene's men, our army will consist of 160 squadrons of cavalry and 65 battalions of foot. Over 50,000 men. Tomorrow we move to join him at his position at Münster. I have this very night despatched twenty-seven squadrons under the Duke of Würtemberg and twenty battalions under my own brother to his aid. My spies tell me that Marshal Tallard has been joined by Marshal Marsin and the rather smaller forces of the Elector. Perhaps some 60,000 in all. Yes, they have an advantage of numbers, but their troops are inferior and their command divided. They occupy the ground around the village of Hochstadt, enclosed by marshes. But I know that we shall lure them out. They must be drawn. They cannot resist the urge to have better knowledge of their enemy. Tallard may wish to defer and delay, but Marsin believes my army to be in retreat. The Elector too is convinced that he has the upper hand. In their eyes we have ravaged all Bavaria and will retire now to harry the Moselle.'

He cast a glance at Steel.

'But you may be sure, Mister Steel, that we will stand and fight them . . . here.'

Marlborough ground his fingernail into the map at a spot almost equidistant between Münster and Hochstadt. A village flanked by the broad blue line of the Danube. Steel squinted to see a name, but was unable to read it. Marlborough continued, talking, it seemed to Steel, as much to himself as to the others.

'Be aware that this battle, when it does arrive, will be decisive. It will be bloody and it will, I am certain, be something of which you will tell your grandchildren. As I, please God, will live to tell my own. And now, please leave me. Forgive me, gentlemen, I feel the headache returning. There is much to do. Leave. Please.'

As they walked away from the tent, back towards the lines in the slowly lowering light of the evening, Hawkins turned to Steel:

'You're a lucky man, Jack. There aren't many infantry Lieutenants whom Marlborough would speak to in that way. Nor many whom he would trust with such a mission after they had apparently failed him.'

He felt Steel wince at the word.

'Oh. You failed, Jack. But he's right. And he knows, as I do, that if any man can do it, you will find Jennings. And he's willing to offer you another chance to retrieve the papers.'

Hawkins stopped walking and turned to Steel.

'Jack, I will tell you what few men yet know.

248

Marlborough has embarked upon a desperate undertaking. He and Prince Eugene plotted most deliberately together to send the Margrave off to take Ingolstadt purely in order that they might exercise complete control over their combined armies. They knew that Baden would never agree to fight the French here, or anywhere it would seem, in his present temper. He is over-cautious and after the Schellenberg sees Marlborough as too happy to squander the lives of his men. Prince Eugene however, like Marlborough, is now fully convinced that battle has to be given and given soon if all Europe is to be saved entirely from the power of the tyrant Louis. Your losing those papers was the worst thing that might have happened. The poor man was already gambling his all. Now he is utterly driven down. And, God knows, over the coming days, if we are to prevail, he will need to summon up every last ounce of his strength that remains.'

They passed along 'the street', the twenty-foot-wide dirt road which ran through every camp, however temporary, marking off the officers' tents and those of the staff from those belonging to the ordinary men of each battalion and squadron. While on the officers' side of the thoroughfare, chatter, song and candlelight revealed that supper parties were evidently still in progress, to the left as they walked, most of the men were starting to turn in for the night. Small groups lingered around the campfires and from time to time Steel caught a few bars of a tune. Not now the swinging, jubilant marches with which the army had come down the long road from Flanders. But songs of a more gentle nature. Slow ballads that told of home and

249

lost loves. Of unfulfilled dreams and desires. Simple, lilting melodies that cut the conversation dead and had the hardest of men staring deep into the glowing embers.

Further along the lines they watched as a red-coated musketeer swilled out the filth from his meagre quarters. As he did so, from across the street a whoop of laughter echoed through the officers' bivouacs. The man raised his head and cast a sneering glance across to the revelry. Hawkins laughed quietly as they walked on.

'It was ever thus, Jack. No matter how good an army might be. No matter how even-handed its commander-in-chief. For every officer beloved of the men, you will find one they would sooner see laid in earth. Trust me, Jack, you will not be alone in our army in having a personal score to settle in the coming battle. How many of our own officers will die I wonder, what their families will be told was a hero's death, with a bullet in their back that was made in London?'

He thought for a moment.

'Although perhaps this time the men will be more set on the matter in hand, than personal vendetta. For in God's truth I've never seen an army so utterly resolved to its purpose. This is no gentleman's war any longer, Jack.'

'With respect, Colonel, it never was. And you most assuredly have no need to remind me of that.'

'I'm sorry, dear boy. Of course. That dreadful affair in the village. Women and children too. And you know that it will surely have consequences. You know that we have now burnt close on 400 villages. The Dutch and the Danes have thrown

250

whole populations out into the night. All done on Marlborough's orders most certainly. But the massacre at Sattelberg is a very different matter. Of course the French have done such things before. Think of the Palatine states. Of the poor Camisards in France. Their own people, for God's sake. But to bring such practices to our war, Jack. To revisit such evil upon these people. This is something new. It was done with the simple, malicious intent of blackening the good name of our army. This is a new kind of warfare. A warfare that plays deliberately upon the mind. Terror and infamy are its weapons. And that is another reason why you must find Jennings and kill him. An English officer who can attest to having seen such a massacre, without firmly ascribing it to the French, can only increase any case against Marlborough.'

He suddenly drew to a halt.

'My row, I believe. And now, Jack, I'll bid you goodnight.'

As Hawkins walked towards his tent, which was set some distance further towards the rear of the officers' encampment, Steel lifted the flap of his own and ducked his tall frame to enter. Louisa was sitting at the little table, reading from her Bible, one of the few possessions she had brought from the inn.

She smiled up at him. 'Was it bad?'

'No, not bad. Just hard to admit failure.'

'Will you fight your battle now?'

'Tomorrow perhaps. More likely the next day.'

'Can you fight, Jack? Your leg is not good.'

'It's good enough. And I have to fight. I am commanded to fight. I have to find the papers. To kill Jennings.'

She froze at the name. 'How? How will you find him?'

'I'll know precisely where he is. I know a man who can sniff him out. Jennings had a Sergeant, a nasty piece of work. And if anyone can find him you can be sure it will be Sergeant Stringer. He'll do anything to save his neck. Believe me, Louisa, I'll find him. And then I'll kill him.'

'No.'

'No? You don't want him dead?'

'No. I don't want you to kill him. It is my right.'

Steel could not help but admire her passion.

'And how do you intend to manage this?'

'In the battle. With you. You will find him and then I will shoot him.'

Steel laughed, but quickly stopped, aware that he might hurt her feelings.

'My dear, darling Louisa. If you are by my side where the battle rages you'll be lucky if you come away with your life. There will be 100,000 men on that field.'

She was silent. It was true. An absurd idea. But with every fibre of her being Louisa knew that if Jennings was to die then she alone had the moral right to kill him. She looked up at Steel, her pleading eyes brimming with tears.

He gazed at her. Feeling her emptiness as the hurt surged through her. He reached out and touched her waist.

'Will you do it? Jack, please. Take me with you in the battle. Take me to Jennings. Let me kill him. Then I will be free.'

'I cannot. You might be killed. Or maimed. I could not live with that.'

252

Steel shivered.

'You're cold? Perhaps the fever has returned?'

'No. It's nothing.'

Louisa gripped him around the waist and rested her head against his chest.

'How will it be, the battle?'

'It will be noisy and hard and very bloody. It'll be like nothing you ever saw before. Or the like of which you will ever want to see again.'

Steel looked down at her. He had become so used to her in such a short time. Love or not, they had become lovers and shared these last few days and nights, released from care, in each other's arms. They still had this coming night and whatever tomorrow would bring. She smiled at him again and very gently began to pull him down on to the little folding bed.

*　　　*　　　*

Aubrey Jennings had ridden south at first, on the only road out of the town which led away from where he knew the allied army must lie. He had ridden hard for two days until he had reached the outskirts of Augsburg. There he had thought that surely he must find the French. But instead he had stumbled upon a party of retreating Bavarian infantry who, seeing his red coat, had fired upon him. After that he had thought it prudent to go across the river and head north-west. But without a map he had become hopelessly lost. The countryside had become increasingly wooded and Jennings found himself constantly wandering into bands of dispossessed peasants. He had bought food and beer from them, but again his coat had proved more of a hindrance and ultimately he had turned it inside out, presenting a white uniform closer in appearance to that of their French allies. But the ornate buttons and lace, now worn on the inside, had proved a constant irritation and on the tenth day of his wanderings in the great forests he had turned the coat back to British red. It was sheer bad luck of course that on that very day he should have been spotted by a party of what he rightly took for allied cavalry. The dead hussar's horse though had proved an infinitely superior beast to their plodding supply mounts and he had outridden them with ease. On the twelfth day it had begun to rain hard and, starving and dehydrated, Jennings had resolved that his only option was to break cover. He had found himself in the town of Offingen and there, taking a welcome drink in an inn, had readily given himself up to a patrol of blue-coated French dragoons. How astonished they had been at his evident pleasure in encountering them and his willingness to surrender.

That had been two days ago. Jennings looked at his tired face now in the small, elegantly framed mirror that stood on the campaign chest in the small tent provided as his temporary quarters. He winced as the barber who had been sent to shave him pulled the skin of his cheek tight, while he dragged the blade of the razor clean down over the stubble. How very civilized the French were. Perhaps, he thought, when he was back with his own army, once Marlborough had been dismissed, he would suggest certain changes suitable for a truly modern fighting force. Those little touches of style that at present gave the French officers their edge. At his side, the servant rinsed the blade in the bowl of dirty water and handed Jennings a soft towel before leaving. As he dabbed at his face, the Major reflected on the past few weeks. At how very different his position was now. On the one hand he was a fugitive. He presumed that the survivors of the fight at Bachweiden would by now have reached the army and given their account of his part in the affair. Cussiter had gone to shoot him but then the man had a personal grudge against him. Of course Louisa would have told them now of who her real assailant had been. But what was the word of a Bavarian peasant? Jennings smiled. Who else could speak against him? Sergeant Slaughter? What would he say? Had he not discovered Kretzmer with Louisa. In Slaughter's eyes, surely, Jennings must be a hero. In truth there was no one left to testify against Jennings. The only evidence against him was his flight itself. He pulled on his coat and checked inside the pocket for the package. He felt the string and the paper.

For the hundredth time he rehearsed again how, once back in London, he would relate his intrepid tale. How he would tell of his ingenuity in outwitting Steel, the traitorous Scot, sent by Marlborough to rescue the incriminating documents. How he had survived numerous attacks by both the French and treacherous redcoats. How he had even braved the French lines to bring his Tory friends the evidence they needed. Then Marlborough would be sent again to the Tower. And this time he would not escape, just as Steel had not escaped. He still regretted not having had time to make that final thrust. Had he

255

done so he knew that his own fate would have been very different. He was certain that no one could have survived the blow he had dealt Steel. Jennings had heard his skull crack like a walnut. And the wound to his thigh alone might have been mortal. No, Steel was dead. That much was certain. Marlborough would be sent to the Tower and he would become a rich man. A Colonel at the head of his own regiment of foot. He was gripped by a vision of himself covered in gold lace and glory. He smiled at the prospect.

A discreet cough preceded a gloved hand on the entrance flap of Jennings' tent. A junior officer of French cavalry entered. Jennings stopped grinning and assumed an air of gravity.

'Major Jennings?'

'Lieutenant?'

'You will please come with me, Sir. My Colonel would speak with you.'

Jennings donned his hat and followed the boy from the tent into the warm evening. Around him lay the entire Franco-Bavarian army. Tens of thousands of men and horses, encamped as far as the eye could see, it seemed, upon the plain of Hochstadt. Their camp he had not thought at first very different from that of the allied army. On closer scrutiny though he saw its full extent. Beyond the immediate infantry lines lay row upon row of ammunition carts. More than he had ever seen in one place before. Close by them thousands of dray horses stood tethered in a vast field, like some country horse fair, and next to them he caught sight of elaborate field kitchens, at one of which a whole ox was being roasted on a spit. Ahead he could see three huge tents, buildings rather, at whose doors stood dozens of French officers, as if at a royal assembly.

As the aide led him towards them, past the cavalry, he glimpsed off to the right the interior of one tent in which several hussars seated around a table were being entertained by a half-naked dancing girl. She shrieked with excitement as one of them reached out and tore off her skirt.

It was as far removed from a picture of Marlborough's army that he was able to imagine and Jennings wondered, with a shiver of concern for his own future, which of them might emerge victorious from the coming battle. At length the two men reached the end of the lines and arrived at a sturdy, four-sided marquee, topped with a small flag bearing the fleur-de-lys and set slightly away from the body of the camp. The aide-de-camp held open the long entrance flap and motioned Jennings to enter. It felt strange to be so accepted here, among the enemy. A curious half-life, thought Jennings, with sudden and unexpected self-loathing.

'Major Jennings, Colonel.'

'Thank you, Henri. You may go. Major Jennings, allow me to present myself. I am Colonel Jean Martin Michelet of the regiment d'Artois. I bid you welcome.'

He narrowed his eyes and attempted to get the measure of this curious Englishmen. He tried to ascertain from his appearance and manner whether this turncoat was the genuine article or simply one of Marlborough's many spies.

'Any enemy of Lord Malbrook is a friend here. Please, sit with me. A glass of wine? It has just arrived from France.'

Jennings smiled at the Frenchman's inability to pronounce Marlborough's name, a common failing with his countrymen. Michelet was of medium build with a handsome, tanned face and a slim moustache in the Parisian fashion. His only distinguising mark was a thin scar which ran from the right side of his face, far under his chin.

'Now, Major Jennings, I understand that you gave yourself up to my gendarmes of your own volition. That you say you have something of great importance to our cause.'

Jennings sat and accepted the goblet of wine.

'But, Major Jennings. You are an officer in the English army. You are surely not confessing to being a traitor?'

He laughed.

'D'you have French blood?'

'No, Colonel. And I am certainly no traitor. But I am in the unique position of being able to do a great service both to my country and your own. I have certain information in my possession. Information which will bring down Marlborough and his friends.'

'You interest me, Major. This information. I think that perhaps you will tell us when Lord Malbrook will attack and where? You will point out his dispositions? His elite regiments? His weaknesses?'

'No. As an officer in the army of Queen Anne, and a gentleman, I cannot betray my countrymen. But I can offer you something much more precious. I have in my power the wherewithal to discredit the Duke forever. Papers with which to indict him as a Jacobite. A traitor to the crown. Naturally, they must be transported safely to

258

England on the person of an English officer. Myself.'

Michelet smiled. 'Yes, Major. We knew of these papers. It was a curious case. A man who had been dealing with my supply officers brought them to our attention.'

He laughed again.

'A little less mundane than the shoes they had been used to getting. Very good shoes by the way. English made. The man told me about these papers and that a merchant had them. That he had planned a rendezvous with a British officer. Your name was mentioned. Naturally, we paid him for his information and I sent a force to recover the papers. Grenadiers and hussars, under one of my finest officers. Your party ran into them in the village of Sattelberg and again at Bachweiden. You saw there how very efficient they can be. For that I am truly sorry. It was never my intention that these men should kill innocent civilians. Major Malbec is . . . his own master. It was . . . a real tragedy.'

He smiled and called for more wine.

'But, tell me, Major Jennings, the last that I heard of the papers, they had disappeared. Malbec was beaten off. I had thought them to be lost. If you really have them this is most welcome news.'

Jennings knew that now was the time to state his own position. To emphasize the important part that only he could now play in making use of the incriminating letter.

'All I ask is safe passage to the coast and an escort. If I can assist you by any other means of course, I would only be too happy. Although of course, I cannot take up arms against my own countrymen.'

259

'Naturally. Who would ask any officer to do such a thing? But by the same token we cannot release you back to your army. Even if you should wish to go, which I perceive you do not. Tomorrow or perhaps the next day we will fight a great battle. Marshal Tallard prefers to sit on his arse and wait. But I know that Marshal Marsin's argument will prevail. Tallard is no more than an old woman. His is not the way to lead an army of Frenchmen. I know that we will fight. And you, Major, will have a ringside seat for the spectacle. And then, after we have beaten your army and your Lord Malbrook, then we will give you safe passage to the coast. Now come. I perceive that you are an educated man, no? I shall have my clerk draw up your papers of parole. You will sign them and in the meantime have a little more of what I'm sure you will agree is a truly excellent Moselle and then perhaps you will join me and a few fellow officers for a little light supper? We have just imported a cook from Paris and this evening he has promised me a soup and a fresh chicken, with a few roasted vegetables. We have a really excellent cheese to follow and some fine brandy. It's not much, I know, but then we cannot be too fussy. For once we have other cares than our bellies. Tomorrow, Major, we have a battle to win.'

*   *   *

Steel lay awake in the darkness, listening to the flies as they buzzed about the tent. He watched as two of them settled on the grease congealing on the pewter plates from which he and Louisa had eaten their meagre supper of bread and beans, and which now awaited Nate's attention before the army broke camp. He had excused his soldier-servant his evening duties as was his custom on what might be the last night before a battle. He picked up one of the tin cups which stood beside the plates, brushed another fly from its rim and took a deep draught, determined to drain what he could of the dregs of the evening's wine. Steel looked across at Louisa's sleeping form and allowed his eyes to follow the gentle contours of her body beneath the blanket. He listened to her breathing, shallow and rhythmic. From time to time she would mumble in her sleep. Words he did not understand. He knew now how troubled she really was and he hated himself for having forbidden her to seek out Jennings herself. But how could he possibly allow this girl, the one girl since Arabella for whom, he now reasoned, he felt true feelings, to experience a battle. How could be expose her to that horror, that circus of death, where only fate governed who would perish or survive?

With difficulty, and taking care not to wake Louisa, Steel swung himself from the bed and managed to get to his feet. Pulling on his breeches and wrapping himself in the scarlet coat, he fastened a single button and walked barefoot to the entrance. Stepping out into the cool night, he looked up into the clear, cloudless sky. The moon sat low and against the black firmament Steel could make out the constellations which, since boyhood, had exercised his mind and stirred his imagination.

There was the Pole Star, shining high in the north, at the head of the Plough and beside that

261

the Great Bear. He turned towards the south and, as he had known he would, saw Orion, a great sword hanging from his belt. The Greeks, he knew, believed the moon's pale light to represent the grief of Artemis, Orion's lover, fooled into killing him by her brother Apollo. Steel prayed that tomorrow would not see two more lovers touched by tragedy. The form of the hunter hung in the sky over the silent camp: a sea of moonlit canvas, beneath which the men were getting what rest they could before the coming day's march to join the Imperial forces.

From his left the sound of hooves and a jingle of horse harness announced the approach of a group of riders. Instinctively Steel grabbed for where his sword would have hung. He found nothing and felt relief when, peering into the night, he heard English voices. A lone sentry had challenged the riders and, as he snapped to attention, they rode on towards Steel. There were perhaps ten men, most of them in red coats, the remainder in blue. As they drew closer the moonlight caught their features and he recognized the foremost horseman. Marlborough spoke:

'Mister Steel. You keep late company. You'll have no time for sleep, we rise at two of the morning, in but three hours' time. You'd best find some rest. I see that your Sergeant has already taken my advice. I bid you goodnight, Lieutenant.'

As the Duke and his entourage rode off down the lines, Steel looked across at Slaughter, who, wrapped in a blanket, was snoring gently across the entrance where he had posted himself throughout the evening lest anyone should attempt to disturb Steel and Louisa. A footfall behind him made

Steel turn. Tom Williams smiled at him through the darkness.

'Tom?'

'Couldn't sleep, Sir. Don't know why. It must be the battle I suppose. I can hardly wait. I have thought of it in my mind, so many times.'

'It'll be here soon enough, Tom. Then you won't need to imagine. Remember, whatever you do, try to keep your eyes on me. Look to your men, but do as I do and all will be well.'

Steel thought back to his own first real battle. To a young Ensign, barely eighteen, standing beneath the billowing crimson colours of the Foot Guards on the windswept plain of Steenkirke. August the third, 1692, as the army of King William surprised the French after a bold night march. He could almost feel again the bite in the air and the sense of astonishment and terror as the morning mist rolled back to reveal thousands of white and red clad infantry; Frenchmen and Swiss mercenaries in the pay of King Louis, standing before him in a mirror image of their own lines. He saw the cannonballs, visible at first as black dots, quickly accelerating in speed and growing in size to sear through the files in gouts of blood and flesh. No glorious victory that day, but a headlong retreat. But then they had not had Marlborough at their head. Tomorrow, he knew, or the next day, whenever they found the French, would be very different.

'D'you really mean to kill him in the battle, Sir. Major Jennings?'

Williams' voice brought him back to the present. Steel nodded.

He knew that somewhere in that hell of glory

263

and destruction he would find Jennings. He had made sure of it.

'You're sure that Sergeant Stringer will lead you to him?'

'Tom, if there's one thing that little man's good for it's sniffing out vermin. He's got a nose for rotten flesh. And Jennings is as rotten as they come. And besides, he only has my promise of a pardon until the job's done.'

He thought of his conversation earlier that day with Stringer. Understandably, given the unpleasant wound Steel had given him in Bachweiden, the Sergeant loathed him. The man's company was equally odious to Steel and he had made it as quick a meeting as he could. With an eye to the future, Steel had not yet revealed to anyone Stringer's part in Jennings' attempt to murder him. For the moment he could make good use of the man's prodigious talent for deceit. He knew that Stringer, the lapdog turned Judas, knew no shame. Perhaps he thought that Steel might make a new master. But in that he could not be more mistaken.

'I hope you find Major Jennings, Sir, and that you kill him.'

'So do I, Tom, and now you'd best try to get some rest. Don't want you falling asleep in the middle of your first battle, do we?'

Williams limped back to his bivouac. Somewhere in the distance a dog was barking. Steel walked slowly to the tent. He had discarded the walking stick now. He had no use for that in a battle. His leg felt firm. Firm enough anyway to carry him to the French.

Reaching the tent he lowered his head to enter

and ducked inside. He looked down at Louisa, her golden hair fanned across the pillow. Sensing his presence she opened her eyes, smiled and turned back the blanket.

Later, as he held her in the ebbing blackness of the early morning, Steel felt her body move alongside his, disturbed in sleep by the irresistible rhythm of the waking army. Clinging to her harder now, he strove to shut out the insistent rattle of the drums and, closing his eyes again, tried in vain to wish away the dawn.

NINE

The mists that had hung low across the Danube marshes throughout the night were gradually being burnt off by the morning sun of what promised to be a more than usually hot August Sunday. Slowly the French cavalry scouts began to see that what they had thought to be the outlying troops of an army on the march, were nothing of the sort. From his vantage point on the rising ground to the north of Blenheim village, Marshal Tallard now found himself gazing in stupefaction upon the battle lines of the entire allied army, drawn up before him at a distance of just under a mile. At first his generals began to count the standards to estimate the number of battalions in the field. But as the numbers grew they began to realize the extent of the force and thought at last to rouse their men. At nine o'clock Tallard, panting from his exertions, joined Marshal Marsin and the Elector up in the church tower at Blenheim and the three

265

commanders began to discuss how best they might complete their victory. For there was no doubt in any of their minds that this extraordinary action of the English milord could only bring about the utter destruction of his army.

Across the plain, Marlborough, mounted on his favourite grey mare, and accompanied by a small entourage including Cadogan, Cardonell, Hawkins, and all his principle generals, continued his progress along the long lines of red-coated infantry. He moved with deliberate slowness, inspecting the men closely, making sure that as many of them as possible would have a clear view of him. They knew him well by sight. The grey horse, the rich red uniform with its abundance of lace and most distinctive of all, the blue sash of the Order of the Garter.

This battle, a battle for his own survival as much as for the fate of Europe, would depend, Marlborough knew, upon the individual morale of every man. He looked at them with a genuinely personal interest. At their ragged hair and the week-old growths of beard. Their uniforms at least, while hardly the thing of a Horse Guards parade, were as fresh as they might be, given all that they had come through to arrive at this conclusion of the great adventure that had begun three months back in Flanders. Their shoes, too, he knew to be recently replaced and free from wear, their muskets clean and their powder dry and cartridges plentiful. They were well fed too. Bread and beer. Such were the things that made an army fit to beat the enemy. And now that day had come at last.

Marlborough had ridden with Prince Eugene

out to the village of Wolperstetten in what he planned to make the centre of the allied line. They had climbed the church tower and through their spyglasses surveyed the enemy camp. Their conversation had been short and to the point. God, he thought, must surely have blessed him with this man for an ally. For Eugene was everything that Baden was not. Decisive, daring and above all, receptive to Marlborough's plans.

Now, as the little party neared the final company of Colonel Webb's regiment, the Duke turned to Hawkins and Cadogan, who rode close beside him.

'Prince Eugene assures me that he will hold the right flank against whatever the French and the Elector might throw at him there. He will thus leave us free to attack them in the centre. Just there.'

He pointed across the plain, towards the extensive open area behind the village of Unterglau.

'The key to this battle, gentlemen, are the villages.'

He drew his finger in an imaginary line from left to right:

'Blenheim, Unterglau, Oberglau and Lutzingen. Take the villages and you take the field. They must be ours at all costs. At all costs, gentlemen. I do not use those words lightly.'

They heard a village clock striking the hour. Eight o'clock. And as if on cue, on the French right flank a cannon opened fire. Its thunder was echoed by another and then another as the shot came flying in with terrible ferocity. Marlborough gazed coolly at the enemy guns.

267

'So, it begins, gentlemen.'

A roundshot flew directly towards the group of staff. One of them, seeing it coming had the sense to duck. The ball though fell short, and hit the recently ploughed earth to the left of Marlborough's horse, throwing up clods of soil and covering his saddle and breeches. Feigning indifference, he ignored it and rode on. Instantly the regiment nearest to him—Meredith's—began to cheer.

Marlborough raised his hand and acknowledged them. Smiling he turned to a runner, one of several athletic, blue-coated boys that he habitually kept about him. The runners, dressed in their distinctive peaked skull caps, formed his principle means of communication with his commanders across the battlefield.

'Take a message to Prince Eugene. Ask him whether he is now ready to advance. Tell him that it is of the utmost urgency. We shall, I perceive, very imminently be hard-pressed by the enemy cannon.'

The boy took off at a sprint and as he did so another cannonball flew over the head of General Orkney and did its deadly work among the cavalry drawn up to the rear, bisecting one mount and taking the hind legs of another as well as the foot of an unfortunate trooper.

Cadogan spoke:

'You are quite set on this plan of action, Your Grace? We run a dreadful risk if we do this, Sir. The enemy is heavily fortified and despite our best efforts, appears to have us at an advantage in numbers.'

Marlborough smiled at his friend, and turned to

Hawkins.

'You may be surprised to learn, Hawkins, as was George, here,' he smiled at Cadogan, 'that I am quite well acquainted with the lie of this land. Major-General Natzmer, who commands a brigade of horse under Prince Eugene, fought here only last year. On the opposite side of that slope. Sadly, he was defeated by the French, but he has detailed knowledge of the ground to the rear of their position.'

Orkney spoke:

'That is as maybe, Your Grace. But from where I stand, the French appear to have placed themselves in an eminently strong position. Do you really think it wise to attack them here and when we are so evidently outnumbered?'

Marlborough pursed his lips:

'My Lord Orkney, now is not the time to reconsider whether we should attack. Merely how. Yes, I grant you this is a strong position. As strong as any I have ever seen. But I tell you, we shall yet have the best of them.'

He looked directly at Hawkins and Cadogan.

'Have any of you yet noticed his mistake? Have you found Tallard's Achilles heel?'

The generals craned to see across the plain.

'You do not need to peer, gentlemen. It's obvious enough. Observe the centre of the line. Tallard and the Elector have camped not as one, but as two separate armies. With the horse on either wing of each. See how their horses are placed boot to boot in the centre of the field.'

Orkney demurred.

'Perhaps it is their intent. That is fine ground for cavalry. No hedges or ditches and the corn ready harvested.'

'That may be so. But even if it is a premeditated move, you cannot deny that it has presented me with an opportunity. Tallard has placed how many, eight perhaps nine battalions of infantry in the centre. Gentlemen, it may well be a fatal error.'

As he spoke the words, a shot came spinning through the air from the French lines and hit the horse of one of his aides, a cornet of Lumley's Horse, square on. It sheared the animal's face and jaw clean off and carried the bloody remains on into a regiment of infantry standing close behind. Hitting the front-rank man in his chest the shot passed through his body and took the man to his rear in the stomach and the man behind him in the groin. It eventually settled some fifty yards behind the regiment, its trail marked by a grisly red streak. As the aide collected himself and attempted to disentangle his legs from the saddle of his beheaded horse, Marlborough turned back to the staff.

He sought his brother, Charles Churchill, who commanded a brigade and had been on the field since early that morning.

'Charles. I think it would be a good idea now if the infantry were to lie down. The sun is somewhat warm and we cannot have the men over-heated before time.'

Within seconds, along the allied lines, officers and sergeants began to issue the command 'lie down'. A train of artillery rattled past the knot of staff, on its way to higher ground. Marlborough watched it go:

'Observe, gentlemen. Colonel Blood has an unerring eye. We may be outgunned by the French in numbers of cannon, but we will most certainly not be out-shot.'

They looked across the field, following the rain of black balls now hailing down upon the French forces. It was possible to mark quite clearly where they fell. Where the neat, white ranks were suddenly cut through with a passage of dirty red.

Seeing another cannon being heaved past them, over the undulating scrub, Marlborough motioned to the staff to follow him. They rode to the heights above Unterglau, almost exactly at the centre of the line and soon neared the place where the battery had set down and was busy unlimbering. Marlborough dismounted, gave his reins to a groom and approached the battery commander, a man of medium build in his early thirties whose bronzed features and large, calloused hands bespoke his profession.

'Who are you?'

'Jonas Watson, Your Grace. Major of artillery.'

'Well, Major Watson, where do you suppose to direct your fire?'

The man smiled. He turned and pointed with deliberate precision towards the French.

'Directly towards that large formation of horse, over there, Sir. Colonel Blood's specific orders, Your Grace.'

The man indicated a mass of several squadrons of French cavalry, dressed in pale grey coats distinguished by black cuffs.

'Yes. I do believe that you are right. And what trajectory would you employ to hit that target?'

'No more than eight degrees, Your Grace.'

'Let me see.'

Marlborough walked across to one of the great

brass-barrelled twelve-pound cannon. He leant over it and aligned his eye with the five-foot-long barrel.

'You need to depress your angle of fire by two, no, one degree only, Major Watson. There, that will take your shot directly into the heart of the enemy. Carry on, Major.' He remounted his horse and rode back to his position, the staff following, leaving the somewhat bemused gunnery officer to his duties.

'You see, Hawkins, how the men do love my becoming involved in what they do? They value it, as I do. It is what marks the good general out from the bad.'

Marlborough stared out towards the French and reassessed the situation. He spoke to no one in particular.

'We must cross that stream before he realizes what we have done. You can be sure that if Marshall Tallard is anything of a general, he will attempt to prevent us. It is vital that we establish ourselves beyond the soft ground before he has time to mobilize his horse. Pray God that Prince Eugene is ready soon.'

*　　　*　　　*

Music was drifting over the plain now. Cacophonous for the most part and indistinct from the French side. But from time to time a tune could be discerned. The music of King Louis. The soaring voice of the Sun King's imperialist aspirations.

Marlborough rubbed at his ear, as if in pain. He squinted and shook his head and turned to

Cardonell.

'What is that noise? I think that we can manage better than that, Adam, do you not? Have the bands strike up. Let them play what they will. Something rousing. "Lillibulero", "Over the Hills and Far Away", "The Grenadiers' March". A tune to stir the soul.'

He looked across to Hawkins.

'Music is the thing now. It will cheer the men, and it may also unsettle the French.'

As he spoke another salvo of artillery fire broke about them, the heavy iron balls smashing into the earth with horrible ferocity before ricocheting up to land among the ranks of prostrate redcoats. Even though they were now lying down, still the cannonballs found their target.

*   *   *

At that precise moment, 500 yards away to the left, on the low-lying land towards the steaming marshes, exactly the same thought was beginning to gnaw at Steel's mind. He looked out towards the enemy, across the sun-drenched field, his head heavy from the previous evening's wine, his senses still filled with Louisa's distinctive, musky scent. They had come here yesterday, Saturday, posted on picquet guard to the village of Schwenningen with other units from Rowe's brigade and orders to protect the narrow pass whose passage would be so vital to the approach of the army. Ahead of them the pioneers had gone on to ensure that the roads would be managable and the day had been wrought with alarms as the picquets of both sides found each other and played out their deadly games.

At around six o'clock in the evening, they had been approached by a great body of French dragoons. But ranged in line and calling on a little assistance from the Foot Guards, the allies had seen them off. And then all had been peaceful.

For once his men had slept under cover, taking their pick of the houses in the abandoned village. Steel had taken Louisa off to a small, humble dwelling on the outskirts where she tended the garden every day. Her father, who until now had been a guest of Henry Hansam, had gone with them and was soon sleeping soundly in an open cot before the fire. The couple had sat close to each other at the simple table of the peasant cottage, Louisa clad only in her loose shift, looking as beautiful as he had ever seen her. Black bread and ham and cheese had been their food, and more than one bottle of the local wine, which Hansam had discovered in another of the houses. And afterwards they had enjoyed what both of them knew might be their last night together.

Their sleep had been brief, and at a little after three in the morning, the army had come to them. It had crossed the Kessel on pontoon bridges, moving in eight great columns towards the west, between the wooded hills and the marshes that flanked the Danube to their left. Together they had watched the squadrons and battalions as they spread like the arms of a fan on to the plain. And then, all too soon, it was time for his own brigade to swing into line and join the general advance.

They parted without a word. Held each other until the last moment. And then, as the motion of the great machine swept him on, from high above the column of marching men, Steel kept his eyes upon hers until he could see her no more. Then, turning to the front, he was a soldier once again.

Now, as they formed on the field, Steel began to see Marlborough's grand design unfold. To the right, the Imperial troops under Prince Eugene— Danish and Prussian infantry and a mixed force of cavalry from Imperial states—moved steadily and slowly across the rough ground towards a far distant village. On the left wing Marlborough had concentrated his English troops along with the Dutch, the Hessians and the Hanoverians.

Across the position insistent drum rolls called the army to order. The pop of muskets being discharged into the air told of weapons being checked and made ready for the coming day. In the pans any trace of damp powder was carefully scraped out with the tool every soldier carried for just that purpose. There would be no second chances today. Every shot had to count and misfires, an all too common occurrence, would soon be a matter of life or death.

*   *   *

Sword clanking against his thigh and fusil slung over his back, Steel marched along the track at the head of the company, in column, three abreast. At his side walked Hansam and behind them Tom Williams.

At the head of the column, Sir James, with Frampton, who had now replaced Jennings as the Adjutant, turned off towards the left and led the regiment into a field whose dew-laden grass covered their new shoes with a glistening sheen.

Behind Steel the company sergeants barked their commands to change direction and gradually the red caterpillar of Farquharson's Foot moved across the fields to take up its allotted position.

Hansam spoke:

'What think you of this, Jack? We have a river to our left and a forest to our right. There remains but one direction in which to move.'

Steel smiled at him. It was, he thought, a good enough place to stand and fight. A wide, level plain which stretched for four, perhaps five miles, from the Danube to the dark, wooded hills of the Swabian mountains. As far as the eye could see it was covered in rich cornfields. Across the middle of the plain ran a little stream, the Nebel, which flowed north to south into the Danube. On either side of it the armies had deployed and it was here, in a patch of dead ground just to the front of this stream, close to where it divided into two, that the regiment came to a halt. Slaughter gave the command:

'Form line.'

With a swift, if not altogether fluid movement, the red column began to split into smaller sections. Men turned inwards as they had been taught to do on the drill ground and within a few minutes the marching formation was transformed into a line of battle. Steel found his position in the centre of the company, four paces to the front of his men, and looked to his left:

'I can see, Henry, what His Grace intends for us. He believes that we can carry all once again in a frontal assault. We shall have to prove his confidence.'

Steel looked past Hansam, who was standing to

276

the left of the Grenadiers, next to the two nervous-looking drummer boys. Past them, along the line to his left, Steel could see McInnery and Laurent standing beside the first and second companies of the regiment, laughing and calling unintelligible comments to one another. Beyond them, past numbers three and four companies, towards the centre of the battalion, were the colours: the red silk of the regimental colour and beside it, the azure and white Saltire of Scotland, fluttering proudly above the battalion, held firm in the hands of the two most junior Ensigns. Behind them stood the familiar bulk of Sergeant Macwilliam, his halberd placed firmly on the ground, ready to be used as a quarter-staff should anyone in the ranks consider dropping back as much as a few inches. And mounted behind him, to the front of the pioneers, on his bay gelding, sat Sir James Farquharson. It was hard to tell from a distance of a hundred yards, but to Steel it seemed that his commanding officer's face wore an expression that was part pride, part sheer terror. Steel poked a finger under his collar and scratched again at his neck. The lice that plagued all of the men, officers and other ranks alike, had been heated by the march and were on the move. Slaughter spoke quietly, smiling:

'Old trouble, Sir?'

'Same old trouble, Jacob. I'm damned if I know why, but the little beggars always seem to get more active just as we're about to go into action. Christ knows if I'll ever have my clothes to myself again.'

'Must be your blood, Sir. It'll be more heated at the present, if you see what I mean. Before a battle that is. You know, Mister Steel, you should talk to

Taylor about it. He swears by lavender and almonds, Sir. Rub it on your self, you do. You'll never see another of the little bleeders again, he says. Don't you think that after we've finished this business and done for the Froggies, that you might not just have a go at letting me get rid of the little bleeders once and for all? Jesus, Sir, I really thought that Miss Louisa might have cured your bad ways. If I might be so bold as to suggest it, it doesn't do for an officer like yourself to be scratchin' all the time.'

'No, Jacob, you may not be so bold and you know as well as I do, Sarn't, that these vermin are not particular with their attentions. Why the cleanest of men are regularly infested. The late King himself had a dreadful time of it on campaign.'

Williams laughed. That had been Slaughter's plan and Steel knew it. It was the same with any new blood in the regiment on their first time in action. Laughter was the answer. It released all the tension. That was what to do. Laugh. And talk about other things. About anything other than the imminent prospect of death and mutilation and unthinkable pain.

Trying to ignore the irritating itch, Steel looked still further down the line of men that stretched away to the left in an apparently endless river of red.

'So, Tom. What d'you think of your first set-piece engagement? D'you see all the regiments. You can tell them from their colours. There's Lord North's with its yellow, then the Duke of Marlborough's own regiment under their cross of St George. That next, you see, the blue ground, is

Ingoldsby's, mostly Welshmen there, and lastly you have the red duster of Brigadier Rowe's Yorkshiremen. The whole brigade drawn up for battle and you won't see better away from the Horse Guards.'

'It is a magnificent sight, Sir. If I were a Frenchman I should be shaking in my boots.'

Steel lifted his gaze across the plain towards the enemy. He wondered how many Frenchmen were doing just that.

He had been astonished to find, as the mist began to clear, that the tents of the French camp were still pitched. Had they not heard the drums, the trumpet calls, seen the approaching columns? Now, though, the tents and the baggage had been sent to the back and the French and Bavarians stood arrayed before him. It was an impressive sight. Seventy, perhaps eighty battalions and twice that many in squadrons of cavalry with more cannon, he thought, than he had ever seen before on a field of battle. Eighty or ninety guns in all and some that looked like huge siege weapons. It was a strong position too, well chosen. Other commanders would not have dared to contemplate an attack on such a position. But Marlborough was no ordinary commander. And this, he told himself again, was as good a place as any to stand, and perhaps to die.

Steel realized that Hansam was standing behind him:

'You see, Jack, from the colour of their uniforms, how they have deployed by nationality. French white and grey predominately to their right and Bavarian blue on the left. It is a wise precaution, d'you not think. One perhaps that

Marlborough might emulate, given the polyglot nature of our own force.'

'I do not believe that is in His Grace's mind at all, Henry. He means to mix us up. Have you not seen that in our own division General Cutts deploys us in six lines of attack. Four of infantry with two of horse behind. D'you see? He has on purpose interspersed the English and Scots with the foreign troops and mercenaries. Behind the first line of Rowe's English he has ranged a brigade of Hessians and behind them another English brigade, that of Ferguson. Finally, in the fourth line he places our Hanoverian friends.'

In truth, Steel had been wondering all morning about their deployment. In the column of which Farquharson's was a part, under Lord Cutts, the cavalry were positioned to the rear, as was generally the rule. But across the remainder of the field, as far as he could tell, Marlborough had deployed with one line of foot, followed by two of horse with another of foot in the rear. It was an unusual formation and he wondered what it meant. In all, thought Steel, we have some 12,000 men, almost a quarter of the army and the better part of the infantry, with us here on the left flank. The centre of the enemy line he could see was filled with cavalry and Marlborough appeared to have matched them. But here, before Blenheim, he realized, it was the infantry who would carry the day. He saw too now, with a hollow feeling in the pit of his stomach, that for the Duke to succeed he would have to send his army on to the plain in full view of the enemy guns before finding some means of traversing the surrounding bogs. One thing was clear. This would be no easy victory.

In front of him the parched grass was already littered with an ugly harvest of corpses from the forward ranks. For over an hour now the French artillery had been pouring in a steady fire. Recently though it had intensified. And still the order to advance did not come. Word was that they were still waiting for the troops under Prince Eugene to reach their allotted places on the right wing.

Slaughter too had been surveying the position:

'It's bad ground, Sir. Bad at least for whichever one of us means to attack.'

He tested the ground with his feet.

'Look, Sir. See that. That's right boggy ground there.'

He pointed in the direction of their intended advance.

'And you see the way the ground slopes up? You can't hardly make it out. But look really carefully and you can see. I tell you. Boggy ground and we'll be marching uphill an' all.'

The cover of their earlier position had afforded the regiments the chance to re-form. Now though, even as the shot flew over their heads, they had adopted a looser formation. At the head of the regiment the padre, a small, pale man, with an oversized nose and a mop of lank, black hair, was conducting a drumhead service. The men had created a clearing in their ranks to act as a temporary chapel. The front rank had turned about, while the rear two acted as the nave and chancel. The priest had laid his gold embroidered altar cloth across the top of six drums that had been stacked together, and had given his long gold cross to one of the regimental drummer boys. On top of the topmost drums they had placed two tall gold candlesticks, with unlit candles. The padre began to speak, in the flat and uncharismatic voice of the Oxford-educated clergyman, made the more comical by the fact that he had a slight lisp.

'We are but dust and to dust we shall surely return.'

From behind him Slaughter coughed and muttered.

'Christ almighty. Do we need you to remind us of that? We'll all be going there soon enough.'

Steel admonished him.

'Jacob.'

Hansam shrugged and looked at Steel.

'I don't care for all this stuff much myself, do you? The men seem to find it comforting, I suppose.'

'No, Henry. Can't say that I do either. Each to his own, though.'

Several of their brother officers were kneeling now at the front of their men, before the improvised altar. Among them Steel could see McInnery, the inveterate gambler, particularly with other men's money, and beside him the Huguenot, Laurent, who if the truth were known, had a wife in more towns in Flanders and Spain than he might care to remember. Still, if such men felt at ease with their God, then that was no business of his. For a fleeting moment though Steel felt himself strangely caught up in the mystery, as the men began falteringly on the first line of a familiar hymn to intone a psalm. There was after all, still a small part of him that recalled the Sunday services in the little church near his family's house. The jovial minister, the Reverend

282

McLuskey, and the dreadful choir, mostly conscripted from farm labourers. And most particularly, his mother, young and serene and beautiful, listening so attentively to the sermon in the family pew, beside his snoring father. How very different it all was to the pasty faced, terrified young divine who now stood before them. But that, he realized, was surely more a longing for the past than a desire to believe. Yet he could not deny that he had felt something in the church at Sielenbach, before that gaudy altar, with its grim statue of the dead Christ. Perhaps it was all getting too much for him. Louisa. Jennings. The approaching battle.

He watched the redcoats singing their hearts out in a despair born of imminent death and even as their shrill notes reached to the heavens, the shot began to fall among them.

The first of the cannonballs ripped a bloody hole through the single rank standing facing inward behind the altar. Hurling men and body parts into the improvised nave.

'and deliver us from evil . . .'

From their rear within the second brigade of Cutts' division, a Hessian regiment began to intone a Lutheran psalm, their flat, Teutonic voices carrying forward on the wind. Yet for all their coolness, Steel thought, there was just as much passion in the Germans' singing as there was in their own lads' lusty rendition.

The padre's efforts at conducting his divine ministry were becoming increasingly interrupted now with cries of pain as the cannonballs carried away arms and legs. As Steel watched, a musketeer's head, its tricorne hat still attached, flew up from the ranks and past the poor man's face, spattering him with traces of blood and brains. The padre managed to mutter the last few words:

'*et spiritu sancti*. Amen.'

White as a sheet now, he closed the great black Bible with trembling hands, made the sign of the cross and, leaving his cloth and candles for his temporary altar boys to gather up, quickly began to walk to the rear of the brigade.

Slaughter grunted:

'And goodbye and amen to you, an' all.'

'Now, Jacob. And I thought you were a God-fearing man.'

'Oh yes, Mister Steel. I do fear our Lord, Sir. But I tell you, I fear his ministers more than the great man himself. I've always found that when you're on a battlefield there's never anywhere half so dangerous to be as around a man of God. War, you know, Sir. Well, it is the devil's work, isn't it?'

'I dare say it is, Sarn't.'

As Steel spoke, a French cannonball flew into the front rank of number two company and carried on through, destroying the bodies of a half-dozen men. Three were killed outright. The others, though, were not so lucky. As the sergeants took care to close up the files, one of the wounded, a boy of no more than seventeen, began to drag himself to the rear. Both of his legs had been carried away by the shot and apparently unaware of the fact, he was using his one good arm to crawl across the baked grass and ragged earth. Steel could bear to look no longer and averted his eyes. Yes, Jacob, he thought, this is the Devil's own work, and this place is surely as close as you may find anywhere on earth to hell itself.

*   *   *

It was very nearly midday now and still the cannon crashed out from both sides of the battlefield. Marlborough peered through his spyglass from his position on an escarpment at the southern edge of the village of Unterglau. There could be no doubt as to the full extent of the devastation currently being wrought upon Cutts' division. He turned to Cadogan.

'George. Ride and find Colonel Blood, wherever he may be. Tell him, if you will, that we will need at least six, no eight cannon in the vicinity of Blenheim village. He must give supporting fire immediately to General Cutts' attack on that place. Make haste. We must give the infantry support before they are cut to pieces.'

Marlborough stared down at the plain then turned to Hawkins:

'Why do you suppose Marshal Tallard has not yet attempted to stop our advance. The Nebel stream is the key to the field. You heard Natzmer's report. Why did the Marshal not attack our troops as they crossed it, with their columns still disordered? Why, James, a few squadrons of French cavalry could quite easily have wiped out the entire attack.

'Perhaps, Sir, he has other reasons. Although in truth I am confounded as to what it might be. It is against all the principles of good generalship.'

Orkney spoke:

'I cannot understand it, Your Grace. He has not moved. My first action would have been to attack

285

us in the stream. But look.'

As they spoke they could see the last of the redcoats re-forming on the far bank of the Nebel. Marlborough dismounted and signalled to the attendants to bring up a large oak table and several chairs.

'Gentlemen. I think we shall eat now. Join me, please. Adam, send word to all the brigades. Have the men eat their rations. They may sit or lie down, as they wish.'

Hawkins began to wonder whether Prince Eugene had yet reached his appointed position. Surely, he thought, they should have heard from him an hour ago.

Across the allied position small parties of men began to make fires on which to cook their meagre ration. Still though the French shot crashed into the ranks and men stirring pots and cutting bread were suddenly blown to atoms.

To the right of the general staff a regiment of combined Dutch and Swiss infantry was being decimated by cannon fire. Marlborough caught sight of them for a moment.

He saw one of the officers give the command to lie down and, as he did so, have his head carried off by a roundshot.

Cadogan rode up, breathless, his horse flecked with sweat.

'Your Grace. I have a message from Prince Eugene. He is very nearly ready to attack, Sir. He says to you that he will send word as soon as he possibly can.'

Marlborough looked his friend directly in the eyes:

'And the bridges? Tell me, George, have the

286

pioneers done as I commanded?'

'Aye, Sir, all ready. As you instructed them.'

'Then all that we await is Prince Eugene's signal.'

Marlborough sat down at the table and called for wine. He broke bread and picked at a leg of chicken, smiling at his generals.

'Wine, George? Charles? General de Luc? Pray gentlemen. Rest while you may. We can do nothing until His Highness Prince Eugene indicates that he is in a state of readiness.'

He raised his glass. 'Gentleman, I wish you joy of the day.'

As they returned the sentiment, an aide rode up on a horse flecked with sweat. He spoke in a soft German accent:

'Your Grace. His Highness begs to inform you that is ready to give the signal for the attack in one half-hour. At half past twelve, Sir.'

Marlborough nodded. He took another long drink and wiped his mouth carefully on a white lace handkerchief, then turned to Hawkins and spoke in a whisper:

'Waiting. Why this waiting, James? What is Eugene doing? Surely it cannot take so long to reach his position?'

'It would be imprudent to send to him again, Sir. You must preserve his friendship.'

Hawkins looked across to a battalion of English foot and along the ranks of red. He wondered at the fortitude of the men. Wondered what it was that kept them there. What stopped them from running away from the hail of shot that had been falling upon them for so long. Of course, he knew the answer. Marlborough. It was their commander.

He had created this army and he alone would preserve it. Without him the army was nothing. But it was the men too. Cutpurses and guttersnipes to a man, but by God, he knew he would rather go into battle with ten of these men behind him than 10,000 of Tallard's French.

From the corner of his eye he saw George Cadogan ride up again. The Brigadier reined in, leapt down from the saddle and ran across to where Marlborough was sitting, the tails of his long red coat flapping out behind him. As he approached, the Duke threw the chicken leg on which he had been gnawing towards one of Cardonell's dogs.

'I know, George. I know.'

'Your Grace. He's ready, Sir. Prince Eugene has drawn up his infantry in two lines on our right with his cavalry to the left. He signals that he is now ready to advance, Sir.'

Marlborough nodded and rose from the table.

'Now, gentlemen, it appears that our time is come.'

He turned to his brother.

'Charles. I think we might have the infantry rise up now.'

He clicked his fingers to summon an aide, who came running.

'Send word to Lord Cutts. Tell him to have his infantry brigades press forward now with the utmost haste. Tell him that he shall have all the cavalry support that he needs. I have fifteen squadrons ready to follow him.'

Now they would see how well the French had prepared Blenheim's defences. What lessons they had learnt. Hawkins watched as Marlborough turned to the press of his generals.

'Gentlemen. To your posts, at once. Follow my plan to the letter and the day is ours.'

*   *   *

Sitting on a small mound beside the Nebel, Steel stopped chewing on the piece of black bread which had formed the greater part of his lunch. He listened again. The bands had stopped playing. So now it started. Now it was time for the bandsmen to return to the ranks. To become part of the attacking force. Save of course the drummer boys, who steadied themselves now to begin the long and bloody march that would carry their regiments into the French lines. Finishing the bread that he had crammed into his mouth, he looked along the line. The Grenadiers, as was their privilege, had been positioned originally at the right of the battalion, next to number one company. In the past half an hour though, just before they had sat down to eat, Captain Frampton had ridden down the line telling-off the companies into their pre-designated firing platoons. In accordance with the manual, Hansam had taken his half-company of the Grenadiers off to the left flank, while Steel had closed up with the remainder of their men so that the battalion now had a complement of Grenadiers on each of its flanks. This was the formation required for the revolutionary platoon firing system which, it was generally held, was proving to be the undoing of the French.

Now Steel stood at the extreme right of the first rank, with Slaughter close behind him. For three hours they had endured the blistering French

289

cannonade. Behind them all stood Tom Williams, grinning broadly, with his sword drawn.

He called to Steel: 'Sir. Do you really think we shall attack very soon?'

'Soon enough, Tom. Don't be too impatient. The French will wait for you. They're not going anywhere.'

Hansam wandered across to him.

'What think you to General Cutts, Jack? They say he is as brainless as the sword that hangs at his side.'

'Brainless he may be, but I dare say that he's also quite as sharp. He is certainly known for his bravery, Henry. And his boldness. Perhaps we shall see today.'

Slaughter spoke up:

'Aye, Sir. That much is for certain. We'll be at them soon enough, God willing.'

Hansam laughed.

'You're in fine spirits today, Sarn't. Impatient for the battle?'

'Always like a good scrap, Sir. Specially with the Monsewers.'

Steel raised an eyebrow:

'I shouldn't be too complacent, Sarn't. You know that they call Cutts the "Salamander", Henry, on account of his always liking to be in the hottest part of the fire. You realize that we are now standing in the most perilous part of this battlefield.'

'Well, we are Farquharson's Grenadiers, Jack. What else did you expect?'

Looking to their left, the officers noticed a group of horsemen approaching along their front. Hansam touched his hat.

'I sense that I must return to my post. I suspect that this might mean we are about to move. Jack, Sarn't Slaughter. Good luck to you both. Until we meet—in Blenheim.'

As he walked back, the horsemen grew closer, stopping close to the centre companies. At their front, Brigadier Rowe stood up in his stirrups.

'Good luck, my boys. I am certain that we are sure to take the day. It will be as hard going as any you have seen, but I have no doubt that we will come through it together. Keep me in your sight, my lads. For I shall be the first at those wooden walls. And mark me well. You are not to give a single fire at the enemy until I myself have struck my own sword upon the palisades.'

Rowe turned his horse and rode back along the line.

Steel heard Sir James' tremulous voice sound high above the guns:

' 'Talion will prepare to advance.'

He drew his sword and raised it high above his head. Now, thought Steel. Now, you foolish, brave old man. This is the moment for which you have waited. The reason that you raised this regiment. I wish you luck and joy of it.

Sir James' voice rang out again:

' 'Talion. Shoulder arms. Forward march.'

As the sword came down to rest on his shoulder, the drummer boys struck up a thunderous roll and followed it with the crashing rhythm of the 'advance'.

The ground was soft and boggy and as they walked forward Steel could see the mud pulling down stockings and sucking off shoes. He gazed across the ground at their objective. It was he guessed 200, perhaps 150 yards away. Before them lay the smaller tributary of the Nebel, some seven feet wide. The banks looked dry enough but as they approached the ground became increasingly marshy. Ten paces more and puffs of smoke began to erupt from the smaller of two wooden water mills which spanned the stream. Musket balls began to patter around them like hailstones. One man of his company went down, hit in the leg.

Cussiter exclaimed:

'Christ, Sergeant, I thought the pioneers had cleared out them houses.'

Slaughter hissed in his ear.

'Them's not houses, Cussiter. Them's mills. And never you mind about the pioneers. Just keep moving forward. Look to your ranks.'

As they watched, the French snipers in the mills ran from the buildings and back towards their lines. As they did so, with a loud crackle the mills' wooden timbers simultaneously burst into flame.

Glancing to the left Steel could just see the Foot Guards, his old comrades, going into their own attack beneath the huge squares of crimson silk.

The Guards' objective appeared not to be the village of Blenheim itself, but a long line of overturned carts that linked the furthest most cottages to the marshes at the edge of the Danube. There were Frenchmen behind that barrier for certain but in what strength and of what quality Steel could not be sure. Well they would find out soon enough. By a curious quirk of sound, above the noise of the drums and cannonfire, he heard the distinctive sound of his own regimental colours snapping in the breeze. The French cannon were firing more fiercely now. Suddenly Steel looked to his left and flinched away as a huge iron ball tore into the front-rank man two down from him and obliterated him in a mess of flesh and bone.

'Christ, Jacob, what was that?'

'I don't know, Sir, but whatever it was I don't want it near me.'

The French had opened up with their heavy guns. Twenty-four pounders. The calibre of artillery more normally employed for siege warfare than against infantry. You could blast a hole a yard wide in a solid stone wall with one of those cannonballs. Against flesh and bone the effect was devastating, particularly when used at such short range. Another of the balls came hurtling into their ranks carrying away an entire file of men and leaving in its trail the wounded and dying. Their shrieks coloured the air.

They forded the shallow stream and began to climb the apparently gentle slope on the other side. Steel knew what they would see at the top. But he wondered quite how they would be met. It was surprisingly hard going here. Reaching the crest of the escarpment they had an unrestricted view of the village from about 120 yards out. They could see, too, the source of the deadly barrage which had rained down on them for so long. On a small hill to the right of Blenheim stood six of the largest cannon Steel had ever seen. Further down the allied line, as he watched, the English pioneers, themselves under heavy fire, were finishing the bridges of fascines which would carry the centre of the allied army across the Nebel.

The drums were building to a crescendo now, hammering out their rhythmic beat to drive the men on. He looked about at his own command,

and tried to account for as many faces as he could before they continued their advance. Mackay, McNeil, Tarling, Cussiter, Taylor, McCance and the rest. All of them grim faced now. Slaughter began to dress the lines.

Steel saw Sir James as he rode along the rear of the re-forming battalion. He watched as the Colonel dismounted and gave his horse to a servant before walking slowly to the centre front of the regiment. Yes, he thought. You do have it in you, old man. Now, seize the moment and take your men into battle.

Farquharson raised his sword high above his head.

'Now, my lads. For Queen Anne and the glory of Scotland. Follow me to victory.'

The drummer boys, red faced and tiring as they were, beat up the pounding, insistent rhythm of the attack march:

Rum dadada rum dum, rum dadada rum dum, rum dadada rum dadada rum dum dum.

Over and over it echoed across the field and there was no resisting it.

Steel stepped out to the front of the half-company and found himself a few paces in front of one of the newer arrivals, Henderson, a Borders lad. Fond of fishing. The boy was shaking and Steel clasped his shoulder, speaking quietly and fast.

'Don't worry. You'll be fine. We all feel the same. Just stay with me.'

He turned to the men.

'Grenadiers. Follow me.'

All along the battalion line now he knew that the other company officers, Laurent, McInnery,

Frampton, all the familiar faces from the mess, would be mimicking his actions and his words.

He saw Slaughter close behind him and Williams, his sword resting on his shoulder. Steel looked back towards the enemy and felt the familiar emptiness. The dryness in his throat. The sweat creeping across his body beneath the heavy red coat that seemed to drag him down with every step. He could hear Slaughter now:

'Steady. Keep your ranks. Hold steady now.'

Eyes fixed resolutely on the objective to his front, Steel began to increase his pace and gradually, with relentless, unquestioning certainty, the great red-coated mass of men that was the regiment began to move forward, taking the battle to the enemy.

*　　　*　　　*

For the last two hours Aubrey Jennings had been wandering the ranks of the French army, interested to see what they made of this turn of events. Michelet had told him that there might be a battle, but the general opinion among the officers he had met at the dinner table had been that Marshal Tallard preferred not to fight. That Marlborough would take his army north, under their noses. And so he had gone to bed, hopeful now that he might reach the channel and England without having to stand and watch with mixed emotions as his countrymen were blown to pieces by the French.

All that was changed. He had spent the night in a barn on the east side of the little village the French called Blindheim. Now he stood on a slight rise in the ground not far from the barn, from which he was able to observe the conduct of the opening moves of what promised to be a full-scale battle. Marlborough seemed to be about to attack and Jennings heard the familiar beat of the English drums driving the men on. He saw the colours moving to the centre. The officers to the front. He scanned the field and took in the light blue horde of the Bavarians on the left wing. The cavalry massed in the centre and the Dutch, the Hessians and to their left, the Guards. And there, over to his right, a little distance out from Blindheim, he saw the Saltire standard and red facings of Sir James Farquharson's Regiment of Foot.

A nagging doubt within him told him that that was where he belonged. Over there. On the opposite side of this soon-to-be-bloody field, with his men. For he was above all things, a British officer, loyal to his country and his Queen, if not to all her ministers. But no sooner had the thought come to him than another part of his conscience absolved him of his negligence of duty. Told him that what he had done was right and proper. That it was the only thing possible for a man of honour to have done. It would be the saving of his nation. Now he began to see just how unlucky he had been. How it was his great misfortune—a truly great sacrifice—to miss this experience among his own men. There would no doubt be other battles under other commanders. Jennings thought of the years to come. The campaigns in Spain in which the war would be decided as it should. Glorious victories to be gained far away from this sodden German plain. But still his heart was torn. He wished on the one hand for Marlborough's disgrace. But somewhere within his tortured soul a voice still cried out that there should by right be no victors on this day save the British.

TEN

They were fifty yards out from the enemy now. No, forty, and still the French infantry in Blenheim had not opened fire. At the right of the line of the advancing battalion, Steel looked down its length. It was ragged now, showing the effect of walking over the rough ground. The men had fallen into their natural gait and sergeants moved along behind them, using their spontoons to coax the line back into order. At any moment now, he guessed, the French would open up and in the face of a volley of musket balls a disordered formation could easily crumple into a formless rabble. He waited for the spout of flame, the smoke and then the hail of death. Steel tried not to think about it but studied the objective.

It was a sizeable village of perhaps 300 houses, some surrounded by what appeared to be small walled gardens. In the centre he could see the tower of a tall stone church. That, no doubt, would be the core of the French defensive position and would, he presumed, have a walled graveyard. The perfect improvised fortress.

Looking to his left and right he could also see a small stream that ran through the village. That too would provide the defenders with a useful obstacle. His earlier presentiments that the French

297

would have spent some time strengthening their position now proved horribly justified. Before him he could see the shapes of basketwork gabions and *chevaux de frise*—tree trunks on to which bayonets and swords had been fixed to create ghastly, impenetrable obstacles. Alongside them barriers had been constructed from anything that the defenders had been able to call into service. Upturned carts. Wooden packing cases, logs and branches of trees. And anything they had been able to pull from the houses, whose inhabitants were now long gone: tables placed upon their sides, a chest of drawers, a piano and the ubiquitous grandfather clocks. He saw the glint of sunshine on metal and realized that the French were poking their bayonets through the improvised embrasures they had punched through their wooden defences. It might have taken them time to realize the enemy's presence, but the French had been far from idle.

Most worryingly, they had erected stout-looking wooden palisades before every entrance to the village and continued the line until it formed a curtain wall that stretched past the village itself down to the river.

Slaughter was at his side:

'By Christ, Sir. How in the name of God in all his Glory are we going to take that? And without any support from the guns?'

'I wish I knew, Jacob. I can only presume that Lord Cutts considers that we must be as fiery as he himself. Perhaps he intends to burn it down with his salamander breath.'

They were thirty-five yards out now. Still the drums gave out their relentless beat. He could hear those of the French now, answering. Curious, he thought how utterly different the sound. The timbre and the rhythm instantly recognizable as something quite un-British.

Still the muskets did not fire. The going was devilishly slow and he saw one of his men stumble:

'Come on there, McLaurence. Get on, lad. They're waiting for us.'

He was suddenly aware that the French cannonballs were no longer falling on his company, or indeed on any of the brigade. Williams came up by his side.

'Why don't they shoot at us, Sir? It seems very strange.'

'It's not strange, Tom. They're just holding their fire until we get nice and close. Close enough to be sure that they don't miss. Don't worry. They will.'

Of course he was lying. What else could he do? What use to them was a terrified boy with a sword. He had to keep Williams convinced of his own immortality. Always believe in that. I cannot be hit. It will not be me. But he knew in his soul that somewhere there was a bullet which would one day find its way straight to his heart.

Williams spoke again:

'But what about their artillery, Sir? The siege guns up on the hill. Their shots are all falling behind us. Far behind. They seem to be over-shooting, Sir.'

'No, Tom. It's just that they daren't fire directly at us any more for fear of hitting their own men in the village. And even if their men are expendable, one of those big buggers falling on the French defences and we'd have a ready-made breach.'

It was a blessed respite from the harrowing

cannonfire they had endured for the last three hours. But Steel knew that at any moment an equally deadly fire was about to pour out on them from behind the defences. He could see the French infantry quite plainly now, their light grey coats and the red waistcoats. Who were they? The Navarrois, he guessed. Or the regiment d'Artois. He saw too the gleaming brass bands around the musket barrels, poked menacingly through the wooden walls. Come on, he thought, you must open fire now. Fire, damn you. In answer, almost immediately from behind the barricades, at just under thirty yards, came the first crack of musketry. The red-hot, half-inch diameter lead balls flew into the line of redcoats. Too many found a target. Steel saw men plucked from their positions as if by some unseen hand and thrown back against the advancing tide.

A musket ball shot past Steel's head and hit the man to his left in his first rank, McLaren, clean in the temple, killing him outright.

And still the gaps in the line were swiftly closed up by the cool-headed sergeants. The Grenadiers kept their ranks. They stared straight ahead, stepping over their dead and dying comrades. Slaughter was right. This was madness. To storm such a heavily fortified position in full view of the enemy, with unsupported infantry. The guns were giving what fire they could. But the range was too distant and Marlborough had other pressing concerns. It was worse even than the Schellenberg. There they had cut and run. Here though he could see the press of men at the ramparts. They would not run here. Could not. They would stand and give fire until the redcoats were upon them. If we

300

make it that far, he thought. He could hear the French officers issuing commands now. Their own drums fell silent and the drummers moved to the rear and in that instant he heard distinctly above the noise a single French voice:

'*Tirez.*'

Then all hell broke loose again as a fresh volley struck them with full force. To his left Steel saw one of his men instinctively raise his hand to his face as if sheltering from the rain. He vanished in a hail of lead. The French will not break, he thought. They will stand. Even against us. The finest troops in Marlborough's army. Any army. Ingoldsby's, North's, Hamilton's, Orkney's and the Guards. Oh, yes, the French will stand. But we will make them pay.

Fifteen yards to go and he turned his head towards the half-company:

'Light your fuses.'

Quickly, the forward-most Grenadiers each drew a single bomb from their ammunition pouches and touched its fuse to the glowing slow match fastened to their crossbelts.

And then they were there. Up against the palisades. Steel saw Brigadier Rowe to his left strike hard against the wooden fence with the hilt of his sword. At the commanding officer's signal the entire first line of his brigade came to a halt.

Steel yelled above the din:

'Grenadiers. Throw grenades.'

As one, the leading men of the company hurled their bombs across the defences, then stepped back as the black metal spheres landed in the midst of the French. He counted eight explosions and heard the screams, but the grenades, though lethal, had fallen beyond the defences and failed to make any impression on the walls. Looking to his left, he caught sight of Rowe again now. Saw his sword strike once more against an overturned wagon which had been carefully incorporated into the complex fortifications. Those Grenadiers who had not thrown their bombs now took a pace to the front. Slaughter gave the command:

'Make ready. Present.'

As one, the entire brigade raised ready-loaded weapons to their shoulders.

'Fire.'

A ripple of flame eddied along the line and the world became an airless explosion of heat and smoke as close on 3,000 muskets crashed out against the French defenders. As the smoke cleared Steel knew what he must do next.

'Grenadiers. Charge your bayonets. Follow me. Charge.'

Not bothering to look to see who, if anyone, was following, his sword raised high in the air, the gun still slung across his back, Steel dashed forward against the wooden barrier. He sensed bodies behind him. Redcoats, their hands pushing past him to grasp something, anything of the wall, or in desperation the barrel of a protruding musket. Heard the curses close to his ear. He looked quickly for any purchase and found a narrow foothold on the axle of a cart. Steel managed to hoist himself up on it and propel himself across the top of the wickedly sharp points of the palisades and landed with a thump in a knot of Frenchmen. Five of his men had followed him, and another six behind them. Before him a French private raised his musket, bayonet at chest-height. Steel cut

302

against it, parried it to the left and followed through with a quick lunge which took the man by surprise and pierced him in the heart. Withdrawing the big blade, Steel spun to the right where he was instantly conscious of movement and just managed to deflect another musket coming against his side. But this man was more quick-witted and circled around the great broadsword. Steel however had anticipated his action and cut again, feinting to the left this time, before making his genuine attack to the right, slashing deep into the man's forearm, which fell hanging by a single ligament. Steel did not bother to observe his fate. The French were everywhere, packed into the defences in a milling crowd rather than anything resembling a discernable formation. He knew at once that there were simply too many of them and turned to the man closest to him.

'McCance. We must retire. Tell the others. Follow me.'

Backing up to the wooden wall, Steel made one final cut at an officer who lunged forward too far and suffered a deep cut across his eyes for his pains. Then, as the blinded man fell back into the throng, temporarily blocking their way, Steel leapt to the top of the fence and jumped down on to the other side. Seven of the eleven Grenadiers who had followed him managed to do the same. The fate of the others was only too evident.

But even as Steel and his men made their escape, fresh French troops poured into the gaps in the defenders' ranks and he had to move to avoid the points of two gleaming bayonets that thrust through the defences. It was beyond hopelessness. There was no way to get enough men into the defences at any one time to take on this many French.

He saw Cussiter and Mackay attempting to tear down the wooden pales with their bare hands. Two more Grenadiers were with them, trying their best to keep the French at bay by thrusting their bayonets through the gaps. Looking to his left Steel heard a groan and watched as Brigadier Rowe fell, blood gouting from a long wound in his leg. Two of the General's staff officers—Colonel Dalyell and Major Campbell—Scots whom Steel recognized, rushed over to retrieve the body. More muskets crashed out and almost simultaneously the two officers fell on top of the body of their dying Brigadier, their coats torn with more bullet holes than he could count at once. Somewhere in the thick white smoke he heard an officer's voice shouting:

'Retire. Pull back.'

In an instant, the cry had been taken up along the length of the line. The men too began to shout:

'Retreat. Save yourselves.'

The Grenadiers looked to their front. Slaughter, his face covered with grime, looked to Steel, pleadingly but said nothing. The men stood their ground. Another French volley crashed out. Within the village the enemy had re-formed now, he thought. Stay here and we are dead men. Steel knew that there was only one thing they could do:

'Grenadiers. Fall back on me. Retire.'

Slowly and reluctantly the men pulled back from the defences. They edged backwards, still facing the enemy, over the ground which only a few minutes before they had taken at so dear a cost. The French, heartened by the sight of so many retreating redcoats, pushed forward. Some leapt from the firesteps and jumped on to the other side of the palisades in pursuit.

Steel saw them: 'Keep going. Don't bother with them. Regain your positions. Retire to the lines.'

He moved away from the wooden stakes with what was left of his party, retracing the line of their advance, their backs now to the enemy. He had to make as much ground as possible before any pursuit. Before the guns opened up again. The scrubland over which they had attacked was littered with red-coated bodies. Among the dead were scores of wounded men. Some, maimed beyond redemption, lifted their arms and called for aid. There was no time. At around a hundred yards out from the walls Steel stopped and turned to face the enemy. Looking back at the walls, he could see Brigadier Rowe, lying where he had fallen. Trapped beneath the bodies of the two dead staff officers, he too had long since ceased to move.

Steel wondered who now was at their head and tried to see what remained of his own command.

'About face. Close up.'

He found Slaughter:

'What are our losses?'

'Four left inside the walls, Sir, and there's another four lying out there as won't get up again. Then there's Tarling and McLaurence. Both hit, Sir, but not so bad. That's ten all told. And Baynes is missing.'

Eleven men down out of his thirty-three. Exactly one in three. He looked along the brigade and guessed that it must be a similar tale with every company and regiment. He saw that beyond them, even Ferguson's men had not taken their objective. The Guards he could see quite plainly, streaming back through a small orchard, their crimson colours shot to tatters. Surely they would not send the brigade in again to take the village. He knew that they could not manage it without artillery support. Cutts must see how impossible it would be.

He had expected the French to open fire again almost immediately and waited every moment to feel the burning stab of a musket ball. None came. Aside from a few sporadic shots the French infantry had fallen silent. Those men who had sallied out of the defences had also now climbed back. He wondered too why the French artillery had not opened up on them with renewed fury.

Slaughter put his thoughts into words: 'Have you noticed, Sir? How they've stopped firing. All of them. I mean it's too far for the infantry. But you'd have thought as the guns on the hill would have tore into us again. What's going on, d'you think? They're never giving up?'

'I hardly think do, Sarn't, do you? I wonder what we do now?'

All too quickly, his question was answered. Towards the rear and slightly to the right of the battalion, he felt the ground begin to tremble. Supposing at first that this might herald the arrival of the longed-for supporting artillery, Steel looked around and stopped dead. For it was not artillery that met his eyes, but horsemen. They wore red coats and they came from the direction of the allied lines. But instinctively Steel realized that these men were no friends. And then he saw that they were closing very fast. He turned to the men.

'Ware cavalry. Cavalry on the flank. Right flank turn, form line. Prepare for cavalry.'

Williams ran into action, trying to remember his all too brief training:

'Prepare to repel cavalry.'

As Steel watched the cavalry accelerated into a gallop. There could be no doubt now. They were French and they were making directly for the exposed right flank of Rowe's disordered brigade. Straight for the regiment. For him. He tried to count them. Six, seven, eight squadrons. Too many. Perhaps 1,200 men. And as they drew nearer he began to recognize their uniform. Red coats with elaborate lace trimmings that stretched across the entire front. Silver lace adorning the hat of every man—irrespective of his rank. They wore vividly coloured crossbelts, a different hue for each company: yellow, violet, green, blue and that curious colour that only the French army wore: aurore, the colour of the dawn.

These were the French army's elite cavalry. The Gens d'Armes. The gentlemen soldiers of France. The successors to the knights who, as every British schoolboy learnt, had fought against King Henry at Agincourt and who had famously died in a hail of arrows. These men, though, looked as if they were determined to avenge their slaughtered ancestors in this one brief moment.

He shouted again to the Grenadiers.

'Square. Form square. To me.'

Slaughter too was fully aware of the danger now:

'Christ almighty, Sir. Square. Form a square.'

Had they had the time and seen the cavalry from a distance, this would have been a parade ground manouevre in which the four grand divisions of every battalion would have faced the rear by the 'right about', the second and fourth wheeling in to form the left and right faces and the other two the right angled sides. The two Grenadier platoons would then have either been used to strengthen the corners or as a central inner square, around the colours. Then on the command 'face square' all would have turned outward to the enemy. But the square that Steel now formed was something very different. This was a rallying square, an instinctive defensive block formed from his own half-company, reduced now to barely twenty men, joined by the remants of two other line companies. In all he thought there were probably close on a hundred men. They stood not in the prescribed three ranks but only two deep. The first, kneeling, had embedded their musket butts into the soft ground so that the bayonets pointed upwards at an angle designed to pierce a horse's belly. Behind them another rank stood with fixed bayonets, ready to fire. Used properly, even without the third reserve rank, such a formation was impregnable to cavalry. But if at all ragged, it would falter and open and, once inside, the horsemen would simply ride about in a spree of killing. Slaughter and the other sergeants and corporals barked commands. They waited for the impact.

'Dress your lines. Close up. Keep it tight.'

Standing inside the hollow square, Steel looked about. Over there stood Tom Williams. He noticed that Laurent was with them, but there were no other officers to be seen. He peered outside the formation. Had the others managed to rally?

Where were Sir James and the colours? Slaughter's voice rang out.

'Prime your weapons.'

As one the Grenadiers raised their guns and, half-cocking the locks, poured a little powder into the frizzen pans, before closing them.

'Load your weapons.'

With well-drilled response, the men reached into their leather cartridge pouches. Extracted a cartridge and quickly bit off the end containing the ball, being careful not to swallow. They carefully tipped the black powder down the muzzel of the gun, then spat in the ball and folding up the paper case, pushed it too into the hole. Eager hands drew the wooden ramrods from their metal holders and pushed the wad down the barrel.

'Make ready.'

The guns were brought up to chest height, as thumbs simultaneously pulled back on hammers. Still looking to the right, Steel could make out at least one more square of red. But too many of the men were still adrift, out of formation and horribly exposed. The French horsemen were almost upon them now.

'Present.'

The men along the side of the square closest to the cavalry raised their muskets.

The big horses were bearing down on them hard.

'Wait for it. Wait. Steady.'

Twenty paces out and Steel saw the blades, shining in their evil, razor-edged beauty.

Now.

'Fire.'

The side of the square opened fire. Twenty-five

muskets at close range against the ragged ranks of a charging troop of cavalry. He heard the balls make contact through the smoke. The weird plop as they sank into flesh. The whinnying horses and the screaming men. On either side of him horses and cavalrymen crashed into the redcoats. Their swords though did little damage. The men and in some cases the beasts were dead or dying by the time they hit the line. Nevertheless the impact of the sheer weight of cavalry was enough to topple several of the infantrymen. Three men away from him, one of the horses, huge and black, had gone careening straight into an angled bayonet which had ripped into its chest tearing apart flesh and muscle. The beast collapsed heavily upon the weapon and its owner, a Grenadier, dropped it just in time. Then, quick-witted enough to draw his short sword, he stabbed towards the rider, still in place on his saddle, and plunged it straight into his chest.

Steel shouted across to him:

'Well done, Morrison. Keep it up.'

As the smoke began to clear it became evident that, with extraordinary luck, almost every one of the bullets from the volley had struck home. Before the square the ground was a mess of fallen men and horses. Most of the horses that had been hit were not yet dead and lay in agony on their riders. Few of the cavalrymen were moving. One though, bleeding from a wound in his stomach, was endeavouring to drag himself away. Behind the wounded the rest of the attackers had reined up and were pulling back. For the present at least they appeared to be safe.

But Steel's relief was short-lived as, to the right

of his square, another troop from the same unit now caught his attention. He watched, intrigued, as a third and fourth squadron of the red-coated horsemen swung into the retreating infantry who had not yet found shelter in a square. He heard forlorn cries as small groups attempted to form square. Saw the sabres slice down again and again. Heard the whoops of exultation as the blades came down upon the heads and shoulders of the terrified redcoats. Steel saw one man running blindly. He had lost his right arm and, still on his feet, was making for one of the squares, the men in its ranks calling to him, urging him on. It was a useless gesture. As he watched a huge Frenchman on a black horse rode up behind the maimed man and with a single chop of his sabre sliced him through the head so that it fell apart like a ripe fruit, spilling the man's brains. The men in the square jeered and raised their muskets as the Gen d'Arme rode off to find easier prey.

Steel searched the squares with desperate eyes and tried to see what had happened to the rest of the battalion. He thought that in one of them he saw Colonel Farquharson. Of the colours though there was no sign. Then he saw them. Only one Ensign remained with the precious symbols of the regiment's pride, a boy of perhaps sixteen, newly joined, clutching the ragged red Colonel's colour. The bright red Scottish Saltire was held now by one of the senior sergeants. Steel saw that with his other hand he was steadying the ashen-faced Ensign. Saw him whisper something in his ear. A small group of men from the battalion had formed about them and Steel saw that it included two Grenadiers, Royce and one of the younger

311

recruits, Ritchie, he thought.

The little group appeared to be edging carefully away from the cavalry, attempting to find safety in the squares but they had not gone ten yards when they were spotted. With cries and huzzahs all of a troop of cavalry charged towards them. Steel watched as the infantrymen, perhaps a dozen of them, made ready as best they could. Two of them fired a desultory shot and then the cavalry fell upon them. He saw one of the line company men skewer a Frenchman with his bayonet under the armpit, only to be cut down in turn by the rider's side man. The Ensign, his thin standard issue sword raised high above his head, made a clever cut at a cavalryman's thigh and hit home with surprising force. The man recoiled, clutching at his bleeding leg, but behind him another man took his place, only to be parried by the boy. But there was nothing that the Ensign could have done about the third man, who came at him from behind and cut down hard and fast straight through his shoulder and deep into his upper body. Steel saw the poor boy's face contort in the agony of the moment and then noticed his eyes widen with shock and despair. Then he sank to the ground in a heap of bloody flesh and splintered bone and the smiling cavalryman reached out and grabbed the falling colour from his dying hands. Holding aloft the bright, blood-soaked banner, the Frenchman gave a shout of joy and rode away from the infantry back towards his lines.

It was too much. Steel grabbed Slaughter.

'Jacob. The colour.'

'You can't be serious, Sir. We don't have a chance. It's suicide.'

'Are you coming or not? It's now or never.'

He looked for Williams.

'Tom, tell Captain Laurent I'm taking the Grenadiers. He's in charge.

Steel unslung the gun from his back and, still grasping his sword, began to push through the side of the square nearest the French cavalry.

'Grenadiers. Follow me.'

The half-company and a few of Hansam's men began to file out of the safety of the square, followed by Slaughter.

'Bloody hell. Here we go. Hold on, Sir. I'm here.'

Advancing in perilously open order and aware that at any moment they might be seen by the French cavalry, they walked across to the right of the field, towards where Steel had spotted a battalion of blue-coated Hessians. Up to now the Germans had been lying down in the marshy ground to avoid the cannonfire.

As Steel and his men drew closer the German officer barked a command to his men and they rose up as one and, to Steel's astonishment, quickly and efficiently formed a perfect defensive company square. They were Grenadiers. Steel's precise equivalent in the army of Hesse-Kassel. They wore elaborate mitre caps with detailing even richer than that of Farquharson's men, high-fronted in gold-embroidered red cloth with a red bag to the back, piped in white. Their dark blue coats were lined and cuffed in red and most distinctive of all their stockings were a shocking shade of scarlet. For the first time too Steel noticed that every single man, without exception, wore a moustache. He advanced towards the

313

commanding officer of the company and gave a short bow. The German returned the courtesy.

'I'm afraid that I don't speak German.'

'I speak some English, Lieutenant. That will do for us. Hauptman Rodt. Grenadiers of Hesse-Kassel.'

'Lieutenant James Steel, Sir. Sir James Farquharson's Foot.'

'Tell me, Lieutenant. You are doing a strange thing. You leave your square to come to us. What do you intend?'

'I was wondering, Captain, if you might oblige us with a little help. You see, those gentlemen over there have taken our colour and I intend to take it back.'

The Hessian peered through the smoke towards the French cavalry who were still happily engaged in riding round some of the detached survivors of Rowe's brigade, hacking them mercilessly to death where they stood.

'They have your colour? Of course you must take it back and of course we must help.'

He turned to his company and barked an order. Instantly the Germans took a single pace forward, opening the ranks of the square as they did so.

'And now, Lieutenant, if you would care to join us. I would be happy to have your men within my square.'

Warily, but with encouraging smiles from Slaughter and Steel, the Grenadiers began to move into the Hessian ranks, intermingling as best they could. Steel and Slaughter joined the Captain in front of his men. From the left Tom Williams came running, grinning, to join them. Somewhere, he had finally lost his hat. He saluted first Steel, then the Captain and moved to stand to the left of the little group of officers. Rodt raised his sword arm and brought it down straight out in front of him.

The German roared a command, shouldered the blade and the company began to advance towards the French. Slaughter half-turned his head to Steel:

'You know there's part of me, Sir, that says this is just plain madness. Infantry attacking cavalry. And the pick of the Frog cavalry at that.'

'I dare say that part of you is right, Sarn't. But there's a part of me that says that we are duty bound to retake that colour.'

After fifty paces Steel knew that the cavalry had seen them. Rodt knew it too. They halted. Steel lifted his voice above the guns:

'Grenadiers. Prime and load.'

The Gens d'Armes, bored with their bloody game, began to turn away from the wreck of Rowe's brigade. Here was an altogether more tempting target. A small body of Hessians, with what looked like a few redcoats among them and a colour party in the rear. They had one standard already to lay at the feet of the Sun King. The prospect of two was irresistible. Purposefully the Frenchmen began to re-form and within a minute Steel saw that they numbered close on a hundred. He knew that at any one time the maximum number of guns from the square which could be brought to bear upon the enemy would be no more than twenty. He knew too that the French would have worked out the simple arithmetic. But there was something, he thought, with which the gentlemen of France might not have reckoned.

Steel and the others had moved behind the ranks now to just within the square. Looking between the Hessians, he could see the French quite clearly. And there in their midst he saw the captive colour. It was better than he could have hoped. All the logic of war dictated that whoever captured an enemy colour should instantly return with it to the rear to present it to the commander and receive the deserved honours. But the Frenchmen were carrying it back into battle. Steel looked for Slaughter.

'Jacob? We have one chance.'

The Sergeant smiled. Steel turned to Rodt.

'Captain. I have an idea.'

*   *   *

The French, advancing steadily now, were confident of an easy victory. A square, properly formed, might hold off cavalry of the line or irregulars. But they were the king's men, the Gens d'Armes of France, and such squares as this, poorly formed and half their size in number, was no great challenge. They would advance towards one side of the square only and once within twenty paces of its face would pull up and wheel round as if they were fleeing to the rear. At this stage of course the square would open fire and perhaps five of the cavalry would fall. But then, at a given signal the survivors would turn and, with the infantry busily reloading, they would charge straight into the men and with another wave close behind them, ride down the side of the square. The rest would be as easy as sticking pigs.

As the cavalry grew closer, to within twenty-five

paces, Captain Rodt ordered the 'Present' and twenty Hessians raised their fusils to their shoulders.

Steel followed suit.

'Grenadiers, make ready.'

But instead of presenting their weapons, each of the redcoats delved into their pouches for a small black orb.

'Light grenades.'

They touched the fuses and the bombs sputtered into life.

Some of the French cavalry saw what was happening and, almost at the moment at which they had been intending to make their feint, turned to retreat. It was too late.

'Fire!'

With a crash the line opened up. And as it did the twelve British Grenadiers hurled their grenades, full toss. There was a brief instant in which the world seemed to stand still. Then the bombs exploded and the pride of the French cavalry dissolved in a sea of flame and blood.

Through the smoke Steel saw the carnage. Horses falling on one another and crashing into those in front. He turned to Slaughter.

'Come on.'

Together the two men ducked between the three ranks of the front of the British square and waded into the nightmare. Now the jubilant Frenchman who had taken the colour and slain the Ensign lay trapped with his prize beneath his disembowelled horse. Panic had seized the highly strung mounts of the Gens d'Armes, who yet remained unhurt, and they were galloping in every direction, unseating their riders and flailing wildly

317

with lethal hooves that broke skulls and shattered limbs, indiscriminate of their uniform.

In all the unfolding misery though, Steel's attention was only focused on one man. He stood over the Gen d'Arme and saw the despair in his eyes as the great blade of the Ferrara sword swung upwards and cut the Frenchman through his upper arm and deep into his chin, cleaving his face in two. Putting his other hand to the bleeding wreck, the cavalryman dropped the standard and was finished by Slaughter with a blast from his gun. Steel picked up the fallen silken square on its pole and clutching it to himself ran back towards the lines. Another Frenchman rode out of the mass and reached to cut at Steel's back, but Slaughter had seen him and, thrusting up with the short sword, skewered him through the belly. More Grenadiers were with them now, deep in the mêlée and pulling the horsemen from their saddles. But Steel knew that was no time to get carried away.

'Grenadiers, to me.'

They followed instantly, as one, not hesitating to question his command. Secure in their faith and trust. Racing for the lines, Steel, Slaughter and the men who had rushed out to help them, reached the safety of the Hessian square. The ranks opened barely wide enough to admit them and had only just closed when Rodt barked the command:

'Fire.'

Another volley sang out and what remained of four squadrons of the cream of the French cavalry turned and fled, leaving their dead and dying strewn on the ground before the breathless British and German infantry. From his right Steel heard hoofbeats and the echo of a hurrah. Into his line of sight erupted more red-coated cavalry, unmistakably English this time, General Wyndham's Horse, five squadrons of them, charging across the scrub in pursuit of the broken Gens d'Armes. The French still outnumbered them by almost seven to five, but for all their boasted pomp they were no match for the British horsemen. It was a perfect display of the power of disciplined use of the cavalry. The British allowed the Frenchmen to outflank their three centre squadrons and then came at them from three directions, broke and routed the flanks, and then smashed into the centre.

Steel watched as they closed with the stragglers, taking them in the back with their long swords, keen to the battle and hungry for blood. On and on rode the English dragoons until, coming under fire from the village, they were forced to retire.

Steel, still recovering his breath, sheathed his sword and took his leave of Captain Rodt. Then, cradling the bloody colours in his arms, he left the Hessian square, followed by Slaughter and the Grenadiers, and walked across the allied lines towards the reformed remains of Rowe's brigade. He found Sir James Farquharson, nursing a slight sword cut to his arm, in agitated conversation with Charles Frampton. As he approached, Steel saw Farquharson's incredulous gaze fall on the bundle in his hands.

'This is yours I believe, Sir.'

He offered his Colonel the colour.

Farquharson took the tattered square of red and gold embroidered silk and looked at Steel.

'Lieutenant Steel. My word. Indeed. 'Pon my word. You are a hero, Sir. An honour to the regiment. To the army. The Captain-General shall hear of this. Well done, Sir.'

He shoved the bloody rag at Frampton.

'Frampton. What say you? Mister Steel has rescued the colour.'

Frampton smiled.

'Yes, Steel. Well done. Very well done.'

He turned back to the Colonel.

'As I was saying, Sir James, we must re-form. Lord Cutts commands that we must attack the village once more. He promises artillery support when it can be got but the ground is too infirm. We must go again, Sir.'

Leaving them, Steel regained the ranks of the Grenadiers, who had now re-formed as a single company. The men had formed two ranks and Slaughter was taking a roll-call. Close by he found a smiling Henry Hansam, his head wrapped in a bandage, improvised from a torn shirt, and Williams, who had taken a sword cut to his hand.

'Are you hit, Tom?'

'No sir, merely a scratch. I got the blaggard though.'

'Well done. You had better bind it up. We're going in again.'

Hansam shook his head.

'Surely not, Jack. Not without covering fire from our guns?'

'I'm very much afraid so, Henry. Cutts' orders. Though I cannot see an outcome any different from the last. It would seem, gentlemen, that we are to be sacrificed to divert the enemy's attention from whatever the Duke intends to be his real *coup de main*.'

From the rear came the sound of the drums

beating the 'stand-to'. Frampton's voice rang out.

'The battalion will form line of attack.'

Steel saw him, standing with Sir James beneath the tattered colours, held now by the only two Ensigns of the regiment, apart from Williams, who still remained unhurt. As the ragged lines came together, Steel turned to the company.

'Grenadiers. Right of the line.'

He looked across to Hansam, Williams and Slaughter.

'Good luck, all of you. We're surely going to need it.'

*　　　*　　　*

Six hundred yards away to the west from Steel's position a red-coated officer stood on the short ridge that ran from above the village of Sonderheim to the banks of the Meulweyer, the little tributary of the Danube that flowed through Blenheim.

For the past hour, just beyond the range and trajectory of Marlborough's cannon, Aubrey Jennings had watched the British attack come in. Had seen the full extent of the slaughter inflicted by the batteries of twenty-four pounders directly below him and the white-coated infantry packed into the village. He had watched Rowe's men go down in droves. And he had known. Farquharson's was not an easy regiment to miss and at one point he had even picked out Sir James himself leading his men into battle. That, he had to admit, had been something of a surprise. He had always thought the man something of a coward. But then this had been a day of surprises. For peering down into the smoke-filled plain, he had found the Grenadiers and there, at their head had seen the distinctive, bareheaded, unlikely figure of Jack Steel.

It was hard at first to think that he could be anything more than a ghost, so well had Jennings convinced himself that Steel was dead.

That initial shock and fury had been tempered by the realization that Steel's death could never have been as easy as he had imagined. The man was charmed. As much was evident from the way he lived his life on a knife edge and survived. Damn his luck.

Now Jennings had watched the scene before him play out with a more particular interest. He looked carefully as each of the small red figures went down and tried to see if Steel was among them. He lost him in the smoke of another French volley and then found him again at the very gates of the village. The man was indestructible. Surely though, his luck was wearing thin. How many could withstand the fury of such fire?

Jennings had watched the ebb and flow of the battle on the French right wing, casting the occasional glance across to his left where he was aware that the Imperial forces had taken the attack deep into the army of the Elector.

He had seen the redcoats retreat from Blenheim, or Blindheim as the French insisted on calling the village. And, as the smoke had increased in volume, it had grown increasingly hard to discern any of the individual units, let alone a single man. When the French cavalry had gone in he had thought at first that the entire wing of the allied army must collapse. That French

322

victory might come sooner than even he had imagined. But that had not happened. The French cavalry had come streaming back and once again the conflict might go either way. And whatever happened, he was powerless to play a part.

Jennings was roused from his worries by the approach of four white-coated horsemen. Colonel Michelet, with two of his regimental officers and a trumpeter leading a riderless white horse, had ridden up on to the ridge from their position to the left and rear of Blenheim. He hailed Jennings.

'Major. Good morning. I presumed that I might find you here. I trust that you slept as well as I. There is simply nothing to equal a fine cognac as an aid to the digestion, eh? I see that you have been watching our display of strength. I am afraid, Sir, that it does not go well for your army.'

He wore a wide grin:

'Look now. Your valiant redcoats intend to attack again. Don't your commanders realize that it is quite futile? How can they prevail against such an army as ours, in such a position as this? You must find it very galling.'

Jennings smiled.

'My dear Colonel. I am touched by your sympathy. But really, it is quite unneccessary. The greater the number of our men that fall today, the speedier will be Lord Marlborough's fall from grace. It is the price that we must pay for salvation.'

'Oh, you English. Always you must bring your Protestant moral ethics into everything. Surely, the papers that you carry to England will be sufficient to engineer Lord Malbrook's destruction?'

'I am quite certain of it, Colonel. But as *un*

323

gentilhomme militaire, you must surely appreciate that it can never do any harm to have the reassurance of a reserve?'

The Colonel laughed and patted Jennings on the shoulder.

'And now, my friend, to business. The reason that I have sought you out. My General, the Marquis de Clerambault—I believe you met him yesterday evening—would ask you for a small favour in exchange for our hospitality. It is evident from your conversation with him that you are a man of some standing. That you are perhaps privy to the dispositions of your army?'

Jennings grinned nervously and tried to recall his boast of the previous evening. Exactly what he had told the pompous French General who reeked of brandy and stale eau de cologne.

'Colonel.'

Jennings guessed what was coming next.

'Here to your front, I perceive from your demeanour, is your own regiment. You will surely know with whom it marches. In which brigade. You will know which of these regiments are the strongest, the elite, and which the most likely to break. My General would be most grateful if you would ride to him—we will provide you with a horse—and advise him if you would of every such thing that you know. We are sending in another ten battalions to Blindheim. We believe your Lord Malbrook's attack to be a double bluff. He intends us to think the attack here is a feint and that he will come at our centre. But we believe that it is Blindheim that he will make the real focus of his assault. You, Major, have the knowledge to tell us whether that is indeed the case.'

Jennings shook his head.

'I am sorry, Colonel. You cannot persuade me to betray my countrymen. You may continue to try, but I shall only continue to refuse. Horse or no horse. But let me ask you something. Are you quite certain that it's wise to place twenty-seven battalions in so small a village?'

Michelet laughed.

'It is our way, Major. If we believe in a plan, we stay with it to the end. We reinforce in strength.'

Jennings smiled at the Frenchman's bluff arrogance.

'How can you be sure that I will not break my parole? Any British officer who vouchsafed such information as you have just told me would now be honour bound to ride back to his own lines and alert his commanding officer.'

'But, Major Jennings, you and I have the measure of one another and I think that we are both aware that you are not "any British officer". You are a particular type of officer. The sort of officer who might not be bound by honour, if the "salvation" of his country, and his own advancement in particular, might be served by a course of action which might otherwise be seen as "dishonour".'

Jennings stared at the man. He was tempted for an instant to call him out. But then he remembered where he was and it also began to dawn upon his clouded mind that Michelet was right. In doing all that he had done, he had overturned the accepted code of honour and replaced it with one of his own making. A moral code for the modern age. He knew now that there could be no going back. Michelet made to ride off and then turned:

'Oh, Major. I do have one other small request. I know that you will not take up arms against your own countrymen. Nor would I expect that, even from you. But we have a problem that perhaps you can help us with. In the fields to the rear of Blindheim there is a unit, a company, of what you might call "turncoats". Deserters from your army. They are mostly English, Irish and Scotchmen. I would be obliged, Major, if you would take them under your care. Bring them out of the village and advance them to the centre of the line, but well back. Out of danger. I assure you that there, according to the current dispositions, you will merely have to fight against Dutchmen and Prussians, if at all.'

Jennings nodded his head and smiled at the irony that he should be asked to command a detachment of deserters.

'You are a clever man, Colonel. Of course I shall do as you ask. What else could I do? It is a small price to pay for victory. And anyway, from what you say, Colonel, the battle is as good as won.'

Michelet laughed.

'Yes, Major. I do believe that there can now be no doubt about it. We are winning.'

ELEVEN

Marlborough shook his head and looked to Cardonell.

'Adam, ride to General Cutts if you would. Tell him most expressly that he is not to attack Blenheim again without my specific orders. He is to retire to . . . eighty yards and maintain a steady fire. He must keep the French pinned down in their positions within the village. Tell him to do so by moving forward his platoons in succession to give fire and then to retire each of them out of range of the French. In so doing he will subject the French to a constant, rolling fire. On no account is Lord Cutts to attack the position. He is merely to keep the enemy occupied and to prevent them from leaving. You understand?'

'Entirely, Your Grace.'

As Cardonell rode off, Marlborough turned to Cadogan.

'You see, George, that way we will be able to occupy close on a half of their entire force. Tallard must have 25,000 men in there. And we shall keep them there while expending but half their number.'

The Duke stared down at the carnage unfolding before him. He turned to Hawkins: 'I think, James, that we can leave General Cutts to handle Blenheim. He has his orders.'

Hawkins pointed towards the right wing where the rising palls of white smoke rose against the sky:

'Prince Eugene it would seem also has a fight on his hands, Your Grace.'

'His purpose is to occupy as many of the enemy as possible. He is quite aware of that. I am sure that he will not falter.'

Marlborough looked towards the centre of the enemy line. It was hard to make out how the fight was progressing.

'What think you, James. Is the village ours?'

Hawkins put a glass to his eye and looked out towards Oberglau. Against his advice, Marlborough, bound by his alliances and promises, had given command of this crucial attack to the young Prince of Holstein-Beck, a strip of a lad who had arrived with them only yesterday. As far as both men were aware, he was utterly inexperienced as an officer. From what Hawkins could see it seemed that events had not gone as he had planned. The French had advanced out of the village and at their front both men watched as one of their battalions went crashing into Holstein-Beck's brigade. Again Hawkins put the spyglass to his eye and looked closely at their standards. Three in particular caught his eye. A white cross with opposite quarters of green and yellow inset with crowned golden harps.

'Irishmen, Your Grace.'

Marlborough grimaced. These were the famous 'Wild Geese', exiled Jacobites, who for the last twelve years had fought in French service. He knew well to beware of them and their burning need to atone for their countrymens' flight at the Boyne, but this was beyond what he had expected from even these desperate men. As he watched the red-coated Irish infantry continued their advance directly into the two leading Dutch battalions, who instantly fell back in disorder.

A courier rode towards the Duke. A Dutch cavalry officer.

'I bring word from the Prince of Holstein-Beck, Your Grace. He is in grave need of cavalry, Sir. He asks me to tell you that he asked General Fugger some time ago to send cavalry. But, Your Grace, Fugger will not send the men. He says that he cannot make any new dispositions without express word from Prince Eugene.'

Marlborough put a hand to his head.

'It was as I feared. While Prince Eugene and I have the strongest of understandings, his generals will take no direct orders from mine.'

Cadogan spoke:

'We must act at once, Your Grace. The Irish and the French to their rear will break our centre. The line will be cut in two.'

Marlborough called for paper and pencil and began to write. He thrust the note into the Dutchman's hand:

'Quickly. Take this to Prince Eugene. Direct from me. Make sure that he reads it. It orders him to send Fugger's cavalry directly to Holstein-Beck. Then ride and tell Holstein-Beck that Fugger's Cuirassiers are on their way. He must needs hold the line only until they arrive.'

As the man rode away Hawkins prayed that it would not be too late. Then, turning back to re-appraise the struggle in the centre of the line, he gasped and clenched his hands tight together about the pommel of his saddle. For the sight that now met his eyes told quite clearly that, for Holstein-Beck's brigade at least, the promise of Fugger's cavalry could no longer be of any help.

As they looked on, Marsin's cavalry began to

pour through the gap created by the Irishmen. Hawkins tried to determine numbers. Marlborough too:

'James. How many of their squadrons do you count?'

'Thirty, Sir. Possibly more.'

Thirty squadrons. Everywhere the blue- and red-coated horsemen were chopping down at the heads of the allied infantry. Within just a few seconds Holstein-Beck's brigade had simply ceased to exist.

Cadogan saw it too.

'Good God. They've broke our centre. Sir, the line is broke. D'you see?'

Marlborough spoke, still staring at the slaughter taking place down on the plain as the French cavalry whooped and hollered and cut without mercy into the dying Dutch and Swiss.

'Yes, I can see, George.'

Now their entire centre was open and exposed. Within moments it seemed possible that the enemy might be about to drive a great wedge between the two wings of his army. They were about to lose the initiative. It was beyond doubt. The French were winning. There was only one thing to do and the Duke too could see it.

'Follow me.'

Spurring the grey horse into a trot and then a gallop, Marlborough picked his way, followed by the six men of his staff and retinue, down the slope to one of the bridges built earlier that morning by the pioneers, and rode across the Nebel.

An officer rode up, covered in blood.

'Your Grace, Holstein-Beck is wounded, and captured. All is lost, Sir.'

330

Marlborough turned away from him, to an aide.

'Charles, bring forward the Hanoverians from the reserve. All three battalions. The Danish horse too. As many squadrons as you can find. And have Colonel Blood bring a battery, no, two batteries of cannon, across that bridge. Tell him not to worry. It will bear their weight.'

Even as the man rode off, there was movement to the right as Fugger's Imperial Cuirassiers at last made their advance. The huge men, in their distinctive buff coats and shining silver-black cuirasses and lobster-tail helmets, mounted on horses chosen for their stature, rode down the slope from the right wing. Before their eyes all twelve of their squadrons crashed into the left flank of Marsin's massed cavalry, taking them in that place that every cavalryman feared most, on his bridle-arm side, his most vulnerable area where his own sword arm could not swing to full effect. For a moment, Hawkins thought, it was as if a wall of steel had come up against a great blue and red rock. And then the rock began to give way, pushed back by the Cuirassiers clean into the centre of the French army. Marlborough turned to Cardonell.

'That, Adam, was probably the most selfless and courageous act by any general that you will ever witness. Prince Eugene's wing is sorely pressed, yet he sends me all the cavalry I desire and doing so saves the day. I thank God for his friendship and loyalty.'

It was three o'clock and they had been fighting now for near on six hours. It was clear that the immediate threat to the British infantry had been forestalled, but Hawkins, like Marlborough, was also profoundly aware that what he was now experiencing was that moment of crisis that lay at the heart of every battle. The epicentre around which everything hung. Marlborough echoed his thoughts:

'We must contain the enemy infantry in Oberglau. Lord Cutts prevents their leaving Blenheim. We must do the same in the centre.'

Hawkins surveyed the field. Everywhere troops appeared to be locked at a standstill. Ahead of them the long lines of cavalry faced each other, neither prepared to make the first move, while on the right wing, Eugene's advance too had come to a grinding halt. If we should leave the field now he thought, they would say at home that the army had been licked. But the Colonel knew that was not Marlborough's way. The Duke had one more hand to play and Hawkins had an inkling as to what it might be.

*   *   *

Jennings stood in the garden of a small half-timbered house on the north-west side of Blenheim village and inspected the group of dishevelled and surly men whom he had been appointed to command. While most wore the red coat of Britain, within the ranks he could also discern Prussian blue, and Austrian and Danish grey. There were around fifty of them, all told. Unshaven and poorly equipped. Most had lost their hats and they carried a risible assortment of weaponry, ranging from standard issue English Brown Bess muskets to fusils, dragoon carbines, swords and axes. The men were about as far from Jennings' idea of soldiery as it was possible to get.

But for the next few hours at least, his life was inexorably tied to theirs.

From the direction of Sonderheim a knot of riders appeared.

At their head rode an officer of some rank and he looked vaguely familiar. He was slightly overweight and his blue coat was more heavily embroidered with more gold on the lapels and cuffs than on any uniform to be found in the British army.

As they rode past Jennings and into Blenheim through the only road still open that led directly from three French lines, the officer reined in. He looked at Jennings.

'Who are you?'

'Major Aubrey Jennings, Sir. Late of the army of Queen Anne. I am prisoner of your army, Sir. I have given my parole.'

One of the officer's aides rode forward to Jennings:

'Allow me to present His Highness General le Marquis de Clerambault.'

Jennings recognized his drinking partner of the previous evening. He removed his hat and bowed. The General continued.

'And who are these men, Major?'

'Deserters, Sir. They have been placed in my care. But I believe, Sir, that I already have the pleasure of your acquaintance. We met if you recall only yesterday evening in the camp at . . .'

Clerambault, whose recollections of their after-dinner conversation were evidently not as good, cut him short.

'And what exactly do you intend to do with them?'

'I have orders from one of your officers, Sir. Colonel Michelet of the regiment d'Artois, to conduct them to the centre of the line where they will fight for your cause.'

'Have you now? Orders, eh?'

He turned to the aide.

'Michelet. Did I give any such orders?'

'No, General.'

'No indeed. I did not give any such orders. These men may be deserters, but they are here in my sector of the field and here they will stay, Major. You observe, I cannot afford to send a single man elsewhere.'

'But, my dear General. What then must I do? You cannot expect me, an Englishman, to fight my own countrymen, which I must surely do should we remain here, in Blenheim.'

Clerambault thought for a moment.

'Well, I do see your point, Major. But I am afraid that there is nothing that I can do about it. Here you must stay. Move from the village and I shall consider it a sign that you have broken your parole. And then of course, we will have no alternative but to shoot you.'

Jennings knew when he had been beaten. He smiled at the General and nodded his head. Clerambault looked as smug as his habitually self-satisfied expression would allow.

'Good day, Major. I wish you joy of it.'

Jennings gazed after the little group and called down a curse upon the General, then turned back and gazed again on his company of misfits. He could not now lead them away from here and yet he could not lead them to battle against Englishmen. He found a sergeant, an Irishman, in

334

the uniform of Orkney's regiment.

'Sarn't. See that the men are, erm, well rested. Find them some water if you can. I'm going to see if I can get a better view of the battle.'

The man did not move.

'Sergeant. Did you hear me?'

'If you please, Sir.'

There was an unpleasant inflection on the final word.

'The men aren't inclined to take orders from no one any more . . . Sir. Seeing as we'll all be shot for desertion if we're captured, and the easiest way not to get captured as we see it is to stay at the rear, Sir.'

'Very well. We shall stay at the rear. But you'll take your damned orders from me or you'll end up at the front line. Now, just do as I ask. Keep a watch on the house. Keep the men together and keep them happy and I'll make it worth your while. Understand, Sarn't? There's a quart of rum in it for any man who'll obey me. I promise not to get you killed if I can help it and I'll do my best not to get you captured. If you want me to, once this is all over and I'm in power, I'll even get you a pardon. What d'you say?'

The disgraced Sergeant, summoning every ounce of what military spirit he had left in him, pulled himself up and snapped to attention. He turned to the men and began to bark orders. To his surprise, Jennings saw that they obeyed. They too, he realized, must now live only by their own code of conduct.

He walked towards the house and, pushing open the door, took a final look at the deserters. One of them, though, he did not see. A small, weasel-faced man who had been standing in the shadows behind the rear rank as the new commander had approached them and who, with a skill learnt as a child in the alleyways of Holborn, had slipped away quickly and quietly through the backstreets before climbing down to the stream. There, stepping over the bodies of the wounded who had crawled there to die and colour its waters with their blood, he had cast off his coat and plunged in, intent on swimming across to the allied lines. For he had a message to deliver.

* * *

Steel rubbed at his face with his hands and tried to summon a glimmer of hope. As he had known it would, their second attack had foundered. Oh, they had pushed the French back from the ramparts. Had even in some cases penetrated the streets. But it had been in vain. Blenheim was a curious, straggling village. More a collection of individual farms, set side by side, each with its own yard and grounds, and each one making a highly defensible position. The place was packed with French infantry. There had to be 20,000 men in there. Faced with sheer weight of the enemy and too many strongpoints, there had been no alternative but to withdraw. And so they had pulled back to nurse their wounds and count their dead. Their casualties had been even worse than previously. The Grenadiers had begun to lose heavily. A total of seventeen were down now, of whom ten were certainly dead or dying. Worst of all, Nate Thomas had taken a ball in the chest and was dying slowly and painfully.

Sitting on the grass, in a hollow of ground that afforded them protection from the musket fire that poured constantly from the village, and surrounded by the remnants of his half-company, Steel looked down towards the Danube and wondered how long this respite might last.

Slaughter's respectful cough brought him back to the present. The Sergeant was accompanied by two Grenadiers and between them stood what appeared to be a prisoner.

'Mister Steel, Sir. Thought you might be interested in this one. Caught him down by the water, Sir. He was asking for you by name.'

The Sergeant, who Steel now saw to be grinning, stepped aside and he looked at the man they had brought in. He was dripping wet and clad merely in his shirt and breeches. Steel looked at his face and knew him instantly. There could be no mistaking Sergeant Stringer's smile.

*   *   *

Marlborough too was smiling. And so he might. On the stretch of ground between Blenheim and Oberglau he had managed to assemble a full eighty squadrons of horse, principally English, and no less than twenty-three battalions of foot. And some of the finest of them at that. He scoured the French lines with his glass then handed it to Cardonell.

'Tell me what you see, Adam.'

'I see cavalry, Sir. Around fifty squadrons. And infantry, Your Grace. Nine perhaps ten battalions.'

He handed the glass back to the Duke who snapped it shut and smiled.

'Gentlemen, I believe that we have them. They are outnumbered by two if not three to one in the centre. There is not a moment to lose. Cadogan, give the order for a general advance.'

Slowly and deliberately, the great lines of horse and foot which the Commander-in-Chief had so carefully marshalled between the villages, began to move across the plain. And the French, who had thought themselves to be in the ascendant, instantly saw that their fortunes had turned. The great mass of red and blue continued its march across the plain and up the slight slope towards the French lines. Marshal Tallard, back at last in the centre of his line after a protracted conference with Marsin, saw them come. He called for reinforcements, looked to his rear and saw nothing. Marsin turned to one of his aides. Where, he asked, were the reserves? Those twelve battalions of infantry he had earmarked specifically for this task. The aide looked at him and raised his eyebrows. He pointed and uttered but one word: 'Clerambault'. Tallard followed the line of the man's arm, down towards the right flank, towards the Danube and the little village of Blindheim. And in that single moment he knew that the battle was lost.

*　　　*　　　*

Steel could hardly credit his good fortune. If Stringer was to be believed, and there was no reason to doubt a man who would have bargained away his own mother for a tot of rum, then Jennings was in Blenheim.

'And you saw him, Stringer?'

'Clear as day, Sir. He's there all right. Major Jennings in the flesh. They've given him a command too. An' if I know him he'll take it. He's nothing but a liar, Mister Steel, Sir. Beggin, your pardon. But he lied to me, told me as you was a traitor, Sir. As I should kill you. It was never my idea, Sir. He lied all along. An' I won't be lied to, Sir. Not me.'

Whatever his motives, and despite the fact that in their recent encounter, Steel had almost emasculated him, Stringer had done as he was bidden by the Lieutenant and betrayed his former master.

'You have give me what I need Stringer. No more will be said.'

'Thank you, Sir. Thank you, Mister Steel. If there's anything else I can do. Anything at all. Any way I can be of service . . .'

Slaughter cut in.

'That's enough, I think.'

Stringer looked at him, his eyes filled with hate. He clasped the bag of coins to his sodden chest.

Steel beckoned to Slaughter to come close as the two Grenadiers marched away, and Stringer moved apart from them in the cover of the knoll, counting his money.

'Wait until he's finished counting it, Jacob. Two minutes. Then, quick as you can, put him under arrest and have him taken to the rear. Colonel Hawkins' orders.'

'My pleasure, Sir.'

Slaughter walked slowly across towards the grinning, sodden Sergeant.

Steel needed to get into the village now. When, he wondered, would they go in again? For the last

339

two hours they had played a frustrating and costly game of cat and mouse with the French defenders. The British and Hessians would advance by platoon and fire before retiring, while the French would periodically attempt a sortie, only to be spotted and beaten back. The ground before them was littered with red-coated corpses. But for half an hour now some of the allied cannon had also been playing upon the village, and God knew what conditions were now like behind those ramparts. It was a siege in miniature. A war of nerves. And Steel was beginning to lose his patience.

Somewhere in those houses, not 200 yards to his front, lay documents vital to the allied cause and to the fate of his Commander-in-Chief. Documents too on whose safe retrieval depended his own future and his honour. And they lay with the man who had violated the woman he loved. Steel was not about to not let a few thousand Frenchmen stand in his way. Somehow, he was determined to find a way into Blenheim. To find Aubrey Jennings and to settle their quarrel once and for all.

*   *   *

From the position back on the eminence above Oberglau, among Marlborough's staff, Hawkins was able to observe the advance of the centre. The cavalry under Lumley and Hompesch were moving forward steadily in three waves at a smart trot, their ranks thigh to thigh, swords drawn as had been directed. Marlborough spoke:

'You see, James, how they have been forced to form square against our cavalry. Now we shall see wherein lies the true talent of Colonel Blood.'

340

As he finished a battery of nine English cannon opened up on seven large battalion squares of French infantry. It was a valiant stand, but even from this distance the results were clearly evident.

'Partridge shot at a hundred yards, James. By God, but that man is the very father of artillery. Look.'

Holcroft Blood, Marlborough's redoubtable Colonel-in-Chief of artillery, had loaded his cannon with partridge shot—a linen bag, containing dozens of musket balls or those more normally used in game shooting. The effect at close range was almost always devastating, killing and maiming scores of men with every shot. Two of the French squares, so bombarded, had now been reduced to little more than a rabble, attempting to form. The other had taken heavy casualties, but still appeared largely intact and was attempting to move to the rear.

Marlborough turned to Cadogan.

'Have you the time, George?'

'I believe that it is close on six o'clock.'

'Send a message to Lord Cutts. Ask him if he will oblige me once more by holding the enemy a little longer. He may, if he thinks it prudent, wish to make an assault upon the village. If he cares to look he will see that Blenheim will shortly be surrounded.'

He was right.

Looking across the plain Hawkins could see the first elements of the allied cavalry sweeping across the open ground between Oberglau and Blenheim, driving before them the ragged mass of Tallard's and Marsin's combined horse and dragoons.

Marlborough grinned.

341

'Gentlemen, I think now that I might allow myself to commune with the remaining squadrons of our horse as they take the field.'

For the first time that day, the Duke drew his own sword and raised it high in the air.

He turned his head.

'Trumpeter. Sound 'Charge'. Gentlemen, will you join me? We have a victory to complete.'

* * *

The order to renew the attack on the village had come as a merciful release. Like all of Cutts' beleagured infantry, waiting on the outskirts of Blenheim, Steel and the Grenadiers could hear the unmistakable ten rising notes of the cavalry charge flooding the battlefield as squadron after squadron poured though the ever-widening gap in the centre of the French line.

One of the youngest of the Grenadiers, Collins, a Hampshire ploughboy, tapped Slaughter on the arm:

'Look Sergeant. Look over there. The French are retreating. Look. It's a miracle, Sergeant.'

'If it's a miracle then it's His Grace the saintly Duke of Marlborough as is the miracle worker. That's no bloody miracle, lad. That, Collins, is just the British army doing what it came here to do. Murder the bloody French. Now stop looking, lad and get killing. This place is still full of the buggers.'

There was truth in Slaughter's brutal words. The centre might have broken, but the battle was far from over in the village. There was still plenty of time for men to die. Steel knew how many they might lose assaulting such a place. And yet, from what he had seen on previous forays, he guessed that now their losses might not be as crippling as they could have been. For if the French had fortified well then their infantry were in despair. He could not believe the folly. Their commanders had crammed men into every house and every street with the result that few of the infantry would be able to gain a clear field of fire to shoot at the advancing English.

He heard Frampton's voice at the rear of the battalion:

'Stand-to. Officers, take positions.'

This was it then. Once more and they would be in there. And then he would find Jennings. He looked across to Hansam.

'Henry, I'll take half the company to the left. We'll move around the south of the village. The Guards have taken the barricade and appear to be sweeping up the flank.'

Sir James's voice rent the air:

' 'Talion will advance. March attack.'

They had no drums to play them on now, for two of the drummer boys had been killed and the others who were not wounded had been detailed to collect and tend any wounded out of range of the French. As one, the regiment stepped off and immediately the French infantry in the village opened up. The musket balls came screaming in like a swarm of bees. Steel turned his head and shouted at the men, all of whom were advancing with their heads down as if in a rainstorm:

'Forward. Keep on. Come on, with me.'

Some had gone down, but there was no time now to see who. They must be almost at the barricades now. The French reloaded again and levelled their muskets. Steel kept his gaze focused on the wooden wall. Only a few more yards. They were running now, their great red tailcoats billowing out behind them, bayonets levelled in the headlong rush. He heard the crash of the French volley and saw the flash and the smoke. Feeling a sudden stinging pain in his left arm he looked, instinctively, as he ran. A musket ball had touched his upper arm, leaving a small, smoking hole in his coat. No time now. Push on. Five yards out. They hit the barricade with an audible thud and then they were on top of it. They knew where to find a foothold now and threw themselves off the top down into the white-coated defenders. Some of the Frenchmen turned and tried to run, but caught in the press of ranks behind them, were spitted in the back on English bayonets. Others stood their ground and thrusting upwards with their own weapons, impaled their attackers as they jumped. But now the tables had turned and Steel saw that in the first rush enough redcoats had managed to find a place within the walls. He shouted to Slaughter:

'Push on, Jacob. Just push forward.'

The battle became a struggle between individual men. A trial of strength in which musket butts cracked open skulls and bayonets, unseen at close quarters, struck home with surprise. Some men used their fists, while others gouged at their opponents' eyes and faces, tearing away flesh. Steel stood face to face with a French soldier. He could smell his breath and stared hard into the man's brown eyes as he ground his sword hilt hard into his jaw. He pushed with all his strength and

344

the man moved his head away for an instant. Steel did not miss the chance. Drawing back his sword arm he let fly a punch, using the heavy metal sword guard as a knuckleduster. It took the man square between the eyes and split his forehead wide open. He fell to the ground and Steel walked over his body to confront the man behind him. But the Frenchman did not stand. Turning, he pushed against the ranks behind him and urged them to retreat. From the rear of the disordered French infantry an officer's voice was shouting commands. Whether they were to stand or to retire Steel never knew, but suddenly, as one, the mass of Frenchmen before the redcoats gave way and began to move back. A moment later and they were streaming westward, abandoning the streets on the eastern edge of the village. Steel knew the danger of premature pursuit. He shouted to Slaughter:

'Sarn't. Take the first two streets. No further.'

*   *   *

Steel urged the men forward. They worked their way cautiously down the narrow street, half crouching to present the smallest target, as he had taught them and looking from time to time up at the windows for the merest sign of a musket barrel. They rounded the corner of the last house in the street and emerged into a small square. Directly opposite them stood another house, its yard enclosed by a four-foot-high moss-covered stone wall. It was lined with white-coated infantry wearing bearskin caps. Steel yelled:

'Christ almighty. Take cover.'

345

As the redcoats split left and right, the enemy, who in fact were almost as surprised as the British, opened up with a single volley from some thirty muskets. But his men had learnt well from Steel and moved fast. Just five of their number fell in the street, Cussiter and Collins among the wounded.

Instantly, Steel shouted.

'Now, Grenadiers, with me.'

He knew that such was the press of men that the French could not possibly bring forward a fresh line of fire and would have to reload before they shot again. Now was their only chance. As the redcoats emerged from their cover behind the houses to the left and right of the narrow street, Steel could see that the French, guessing his tactic, had been uncommonly quick in their action. Most of the men in white had managed to prime their muskets and as he watched were busily ramming home their charges. He reckoned that he would have at the most five seconds. Heart thudding, Steel began to run for his life, stretching his long legs as wide as they would manage. Loping across the cobbles towards the French line he noticed his men doing the same, despite their long and cumbersome coats. Steel heard himself shouting.

'Come on. On men. With me. Run. Into them. Charge.'

Thirty Frenchmen brought up their weapons. Two of them fired, one hitting at point blank the face of a British Grenadier who sank in a bloody mess, his eyes and nose blown away by the blast. But the other men of the Grenadiers Rouge were a split second too late. With a great leap, Steel threw himself at the low wall and crashed over it into two of the French infantry, sending their muskets pointing skywards. He heard the crash of gunfire and saw the smoke as more than twenty of the guns discharged into the air over their heads. Now the redcoats were upon them and in that crush of man against man, Steel knew that here as before, only two things would count. Your skill with a blade—sword or bayonet—and sheer bloody brute strength. He chose the latter, pretending to adopt the *en garde* position with a French officer. The man looked at him and grinned, before saluting. Steel recognized him as the officer he had seen at Schellenberg. The man who had commanded in Sattelberg.

Well, by God, no such cold-blooded murderer of women and children would take his salute. Steel growled at him:

'You heathen bastard.'

And instead of playing out the steps of a formal combat, he lunged and caught the man off guard with a single thrust of his blade that slid past his thigh, sending Steel cannoning into him with the full weight of his body. The Frenchman careered back into his men, but recovered surprisingly quickly and came at Steel in a rush. It was all the Lieutenant could do to parry his blade. But the officer followed through with the hilt and caught Steel a heavy blow on the chin with the curved brass, sending him flying back into Slaughter and two other Grenadiers who were locked in a desperate struggle with three of the French. Steel sank on to one knee. His head reeled. He moved his jaw and looked up and saw the French officer raising his sword—not the usual rapier, but a heavy cavalry sword designed for chopping deep

347

into flesh. Steel raised his own blade high above his head and took the full force of the downward cut on its glistening length. The Frenchman's sword cut a jagged notch in the cutting edge, but did not break the blade.

The man was good, thought Steel. As good as Jennings. But as good as himself? The image of the Major reminded him of his purpose. He had more than a battle to win. Much as he despised this Frenchman, Steel realized that now was not the time to become involved in a long and drawn out sword fight. But again the French officer came at him. A huge uppercut this time which Steel only avoided by jumping back and arching his spine so that the blade sang past his chest. In return he side-stepped and made a feint attack on the officer's left side and switched his blade across to the right, catching him off guard and nicking his shoulder. To the left and right he saw that his men were now using their muskets as clubs and drawing their hangars from their scabbards.

Unable to leave the mêlée, Steel's only choice was to attack again, but as he prepared to move, a huge French Grenadier joined his commander and thrust his bayonet towards Steel's stomach. Steel cut it away, and in a return of the same move parried the officer's sword that was heading for his chest. This was getting a bit too hot for his liking. Taking a half-step back, Steel watched as Slaughter, reduced to using his short sword, deftly knocked a Frenchman's gun from his hand and cut him deep in the forearm. A noise from the rear and right disturbed him. For a moment he thought it must be more French, but the French officer had also heard it and as Steel instinctively half-turned his head towards the noise, Claude Malbec too was distracted by the sight of the scores of red-coated reinforcements who had poured into the square.

The French officer realized in an instant that, whatever the rules of engagement decreed and no matter how much he might be relishing this encounter with the tall British officer, it was now time to withdraw. When Steel glanced back, his adversary had gone. The big Grenadier made another bayonet lunge, but this time his height worked against him and in over-reaching he exposed himself. Steel thrust fast and hard, up into the flesh below the man's chin and pushed his blade until it protruded through the back of his neck. The Frenchman fell, gurgling blood, and Steel drew out the sticky blade.

There were men in red coats all around them now. Dutchmen by the sound of them, whose comrades were evidently advancing along two neighbouring streets to join the attack. These, thought Steel, were not Cutts' men, but fresh troops from the centre of the army. And that could mean only one thing, Marlborough had carried the field. Steel knew that if they pressed hard now they could take the greater part of the village. Perhaps force a surrender. The French officer might have evaded him, but now he had other, more vital business to attend to. He turned to Williams and pointed, breathless, off to the left.

'Tom. Take your platoon and flush out every house along that street. I want any officers you find taken alive. Whoever they are. But keep on your guard and if they look as if they mean to try anything, kill them. Offer them no parole.'

He knew for certain now that he would find

Jennings here somewhere and he did not mean to give him even the faintest chance of escape.

*   *   *

Aubrey Jennings sat in the little bedroom at the front of the house in a street on the westernmost side of the village and poured himself another large glass of the cognac looted by his newly acquired Sergeant. He had stationed the man, whose name he had discovered was Saunders, with two more of the deserters on the stairs and was waiting for the fighting to end. The Sergeant was a reasonable man. Perhaps, thought Jennings, when I return to London, when a grateful nation bestows on me the honours that are surely my right and I attain my Colonelcy. Perhaps I shall take the wretch into my regiment. He would make a passable Sergeant-Major.

The allied attack had come as something of a surprise to him. But still there was no need for consternation. What hope would Cutts' 12,000, or whatever was now left of them, have against more than twice their number within such a heavily defended position? And the fight on the rest of the field he knew to be going well for Tallard. Jennings had just embarked on toasting his own health when the door opened and Sergeant Saunders entered.

'Major. I think you'd better come and have a look. Things is going pretty bad out there. I reckon the Frenchies have been licked.'

'Now Sarn't. Don't get so flustered. I'm sure that you must be mistaken.'

'There's no mistake, Sir. They're running away

350

all over the bloody field. And it looks like we're surrounded. There's bloody redcoats everywhere. What shall we do, Sir?'

Jennings thought for a moment. He stood up and straightened his coat and sword and then picked up the two beautifully engraved silver-mounted pistols which he had plundered earlier that day from the body of an officer of French dragoons. One of them he thrust into his belt. The other he kept in his hand, cocking the lock.

'Sergeant. You know it's at times like these that only an officer can see the way forward. The solution is really very simple.'

The Sergeant smiled, newly confident again of the old faith that he had once placed in his officers. And then the trusting smile turned to a frown. Jennings levelled the pistol and very gently applied pressure from his finger to the superbly tuned trigger. The man slumped to the floor, a black, smoking hole showing where the ball had entered his head.

There was only one solution now, thought Jennings, as he carefully reloaded the smoking pistol and rammed home a new charge. He would wait here until the battle appeared to be drawing to a close, shoot anyone unlucky enough to find him and then quietly slip away in the ensuing confusion. A horse would be easy to come by. He was dressed in the uniform of a British Major. A Major in what appeared now to be the victorious army. He still had the incriminating papers with which to destroy Marlborough and food enough for several days. With the French defeated no one would question his passage through the allied lines and back up to the coast. He had no reason to doubt that the Sergeant had not been right. He could hear English voices in the street below now.

The end would not be long in coming. He reached for the half-full glass of cognac and as he drank he stared at the lifeless body of Sergeant Saunders and the line of gore where the blown-away back of his head had slid down the door. Pity, he thought. Man would have made a good Sergeant-Major. No matter. There would still be plenty of willing volunteers when the time came.

*   *   *

Tom Williams knew now that had found his true calling. Moving through the village, from east to west, he directed his platoon of Grenadiers with the skill of a seasoned veteran as they kicked open the doors of the houses that lay on Blenheim's perimeter. They had cleared four houses now and taken more than twenty-five Frenchmen prisoner. These men had no fight left in them, but it had not all been easy work. The first dwelling had been still smouldering from the effect of a cannon-shell. Inside he had stumbled over the charred remains of a dead Frenchman. Two more, their flesh half-burnt from their bodies, they had left screaming in agony, unable to offer help, and reluctant to administer the coup de *grâce*. At the second house he had met stiff resistance and the little knot of sour-faced monsewers had only been subdued by language of bayonet and musket butt. The third house though had been filled with dispirited enemy infantry who had been only too happy to surrender. This was the soldiering that he had dreamt of. The stuff of boyhood tales which, when

352

his father had announced that he was purchased into the foot, had fired his mind with such ideas as his family would never know. To them he was a hopeless case. But if they could only see him now they might think again.

He led two of his men to the closed door of a house on the corner of a street on the extreme west of the village. Through an arched passage that ran beneath the village they could see out on to the meadows that led down to the Danube. The grass was choked with the bodies of dead French dragoons and British redcoats, killed in the first attack that morning. Williams turned to Corporal Taylor.

'Taylor. I think I'll manage this one. I'll take a couple of men. You keep going with the prisoners. Take them back to Mister Steel.'

He kicked at the door and was surprised to find it locked. One of the Grenadiers put his musket to it and it gave way. Inside the house appeared to be deserted. Not a sound came from within the cool gloom and the table, still laid for breakfast, had not been touched for days. As they watched, a rat jumped from a chair and ran out into the street. Williams turned.

'No one here McCance. I'll check the upper floors. You carry on. Have a look in that passageway.'

With his sword drawn, Williams began to climb the stairs. The house was clearly uninhabited and the owners had left in a hurry. He wondered what he might find in the upper floors. Steel had told him of the rich pickings to be had—quite legally it seemed—in abandoned dwellings. Once apparently, in Russia, he had found a pot of golden crowns that had bought dinner for the entire regiment. And on another occasion enough lace to make three petticoats for his mistress.

But it was neither gold nor lace that greeted Tom Williams as he opened the door at the top of the stairs.

There, sitting on the bed in his shirtsleeves, with one hand clutching a glass of brandy and the other a cocked pistol, was Aubrey Jennings. He was barely recognizable as the dandy of the regiment. His face was gaunt and covered in soot from the powder. On the floor close by lay two bodies. One looked like a British redcoat. The other was that of a French captain. Both men were dead.

It was hard to know who was the more surprised, Jennings or Williams. For an instant it seemed as if Jennings might squeeze the trigger. But regaining his senses, he carefully eased back the hammer and laid the gun on the table.

'I say. What a relief. I thought you might be another fellow bent on killing me. I was captured, d'you see? This Frenchie would have killed me. But the brave fellow here came to my rescue only to be slain himself. I had given myself up for dead. And now of all people, you come to save me. Tom, isn't it? Welcome, Tom. A glass of cognac?'

Williams was speechless. His mind could not encompass the situation. The last time he had seen Jennings had been when the man had been attempting to kill him. Yet now here he was, a known rapist, greeting him in terms of the most fulsome friendship.

'I. I don't quite understand, Major. I thought . . .'

'Quite so. I am well aware of what you thought,

354

Tom. But let me explain. I am truly sorry for the hurt I may have caused you on our last encounter. I trust you are recovered. Truth is there was no alternative. You see, Tom, I am a British spy. I answer to the Duke of Marlborough alone and no one else.'

'But the village. Miss Louisa. Mister Steel said that you . . . you.'

'Well Mister Steel was wrong, Tom. Mister Steel did not know the truth about me. Few men do. Yet, while you have been toiling on the battlefield I have been in here fighting this war from the inside. It is because of the information which I feed the Duke that we have won this day, Tom.'

He rose from the bed. Williams, still unsure, took a pace back and held his sword steady.

'Come now, Tom. Put down your sword. But I can see that you are still uncertain. What say you that we find Colonel Farquharson and then I shall take you to Marlborough. How pleased he will be to see me. And when I tell him it was you who found me, who knows what rewards, eh Tom? Promotion so soon in one so young? It has happened before. But, come. I need a weapon. These French pistols are all very well. But they disgrace an English officer. Now give me your sword. Can't you see that I'm anxious to get to the fight. You can't keep all the glory for yourself, you know. Your sword, Tom, and we'll be off.'

Without thinking, and carried away by the dream of promotion, Williams offered Jennings the thin weapon, and advanced towards the back of the room, holding it towards him by the blade. Jennings took the grip in his outstretched hand and smiled:

'It's not what I would have chosen, but it'll do the job.'

Williams stared at him, unsure of his meaning. But then Jennings extended his arm and brought the tip of the blade to rest on the young Ensign's chest. Pressing gently against the boy's white shirt, he turned slowly and forced Williams to do likewise, until the boy's back was hard against the room's back wall and he was facing the door.

'I am so sorry, Williams. But you see, the truth is, none of what I have just told you was quite true.'

Williams froze.

'And now that you know my little secret, you leave me no alternative. Goodbye, Tom.'

Williams could smell the cognac-soaked breath. Felt the tip of the sword begin to press slowly into his chest. But, as Jennings prepared to skewer the boy against the wall with the twenty-six-inch blade, he was suddenly struck by the glimmer of a smile in Williams' eyes. And then the room exploded with noise. A bullet whipped the sword from Jennings' hand and threw it to the floor. It also blew off the tip of his forefinger before embedding itself in the wall beside Williams' head. The Major paused in shock for an instant then let out a shriek as the pain bit in and he clutched at his bloody hand. Williams leapt at him with his bare hands, but the Major was faster and more experienced. Before the boy saw what he was about, he had brought up his heavy ammunition boot and kicked it hard into Williams' groin. Then, as Williams crumpled up, Jennings made a fist of his undamaged hand and punched it down hard upon his neck, pushing him to the floor, where he lay moaning. It was done in an instant. Jennings spun round and through the white smoke saw a familiar figure.

Framed in the doorway stood Louisa Weber. She was shaking and she held in her hand a smoking musket, topped with a bayonet. Jennings' face contorted with fury:

'You! You little bitch.'

Louisa stood frozen to the spot. She had expected the bullet to kill Jennings, or at least to drop him to the ground. But not this. She backed away, unsure as to what she should do now. The gun, though unloaded, was still a weapon, a length of wood topped by a lethal seventeen-inch bayonet. But Louisa had no idea how to use it. Tentatively, as she edged away, she poked it towards the Major.

'Stay . . . stay away.'

Jennings, scowling, drew a handkerchief from his pocket and bound it round the stump of his finger. He winced at the pain.

'How did you find me?'

Louisa smiled with satisfaction and steadied herself.

'I heard Lieutenant Steel tell his Sergeant he would pay your Sergeant to betray you. And he did. So then I paid Sergeant Stringer again and he told me where to find you.'

'You're telling me that you, a woman, crossed a battlefield to get here?'

Louisa spoke breathlessly but with a flat deliberance, 'When a woman wants something badly enough, you would be surprised what she can do, Major.'

Jennings moved towards her and she poked at

him with the bayonet. 'Get back. I'll kill you.'

'Don't be stupid. You're out of your depth. Sergeant Stringer knows where I am. You said so yourself. He's sure to be here soon. Then he'll slit your throat.'

Louisa thought for an instant and smiled again.

'The last time I saw Sergeant Stringer, he was riding for Augsburg with a saddle-bag full of my money.'

Emboldened now, she took a step towards him and Jennings noticed that, in doing so she had dropped the angle of the musket by no more than a couple of degrees. He took his chance. Springing to the side of the bed, he picked up the two pistols, one of which was loaded, the other left empty through his own arrogance. Which he wondered was which? It was of no consequence. He turned to face the bayonet and before she could move the unwieldly weapon, had used his injured hand to push away the musket barrel. At the same time he raised his other hand and brought the butt of the pistol down upon her head, knocking her to the ground, senseless.

A groan from behind told him that Williams was struggling to his feet. The sword still lay on the ground where it had fallen, its hilt twisted by the impact of the bullet. Seeing it, Williams reached out for it, but again, Jennings was faster and kicked the weapon across the floorboards to the window.

'No, Tom. Now, where were we? Ah yes. I was about to kill you.'

Williams had regained his breath:

'You bastard.'

'Now. That's no way to talk to a superior

358

officer.'

Williams said nothing.

Keeping the pistol in his right hand, Jennings bent down and retrieved the sword. Then he swopped hands and held the tip back against Williams' chest. Deftly, he flipped the pistol round in his left hand so that his finger closed around the trigger. 'There, now we're ready. So tell me how would you like to die. By the bullet, Tom or by the blade?'

Williams was shaking with fear. Jennings continued to hold the sword against him. He pushed it a little so that the tip began to penetrate the boy's flesh. A pinprick of red showed, spreading to a small circle. As Williams tried to back away into the wall, Jennings cocked the pistol and held it to the Ensign's head.

'Tell me, Tom. How shall I kill you? Shall I stick you through the heart or spatter the wall with your brains?'

Williams' eyes, wide with terror, seemed to focus for an instant on something beyond Jennings. The Major smiled:

'Now, boy. Don't suppose you can fool me with that trick. I won't be taken in again. Now come. I've given you a choice. What is your preferred way to die. Come on. I'm a fair man, but I don't have all the time in the world.'

'You, Major Jennings? You haven't any time at all for this world.'

The voice came from the doorway.

Jennings turned. Steel was standing over Louisa. In one hand he held the basket-hilted broadsword, in the other the second of Jennings' pistols.

'Ah, Steel. I wondered when you would turn up. I gather that Stringer betrayed me.'

'One traitor should never trust another, Major. Wouldn't you agree?'

Jennings laughed:

'You call me a traitor, again, Steel. How little you understand.'

'There is nothing to understand, Major. There are good men in this world and bad men. No guesses as to which camp you belong.'

Jennings spun round on the ball of his foot and, still looking at Steel, smashed his elbow hard back into William's ribcage, winding him. Then, in a classic fencing salle style, he executed a perfect *balestra* and lunged at Steel with the boy's thin sword.

Steel raised his own blade to parry and with a flick of the wrist took it around Jennings' and cut him across the upper arm. The Major yelped, surprised at his own carelessness, but managed to recover and brought his sword up, so that the point was level with Steel's eyes. Steel took his weight on his right leg and parried with a straight cut. But Jennings had anticipated him and dropped his blade, making its point run wickedly along the outside of Steel's forearm, leaving a six-inch-long gash. Steel winced with pain and backed off two paces, being careful to avoid Louisa. He began to edge round to the other side of the room, towards Williams, who had recovered and was now looking for a weapon. It was his only chance. He threw Williams his own sword. Williams caught the great blade and turned on Jennings just as Steel pointed the pistol towards the Major, cocked it and pulled the trigger. It snapped home with an empty click.

The gun was unloaded. Jennings extended his sword arm towards Williams who, having seen his skill against Steel, dithered now as to how he should best engage him. The indecision was costly. For in the next instant, seizing his advantage, Jennings raised his pistol in the direction of Steel and squeezed the trigger. The shot filled the room with noise and smoke and the ball struck Steel clean in the left shoulder. He fell to the floor, clutched at his wounded shoulder and attempted to struggle to his feet. Jennings rounded on Williams.

'Now, Tom, where were we?'

Deftly, he circled the slim infantry sword around the larger blade and with a single action whipped the broadsword out of the Ensign's hand, throwing it across the room. Then he brought his own blade back down to point directly at William's throat. He grinned.

But even as Williams watched, anticipating the end, Jennings' smile turned to bewilderment; his eyes widened and his mouth froze open. And then, with what seemed like an infinite slowness, a bloody blade began to appear from his chest. Jennings looked down at the bayonet that had punctured his back. He dropped William's sword to the floor and clutched with his maimed hand at the seventeen-inch-long blade and then quickly found it with his good hand too. But now the full length of the bayonet was deep inside him. Behind him, Steel let go of Louisa's discarded musket which now protruded from Jennings' back and walked round before him.

'That was careless, Aubrey. Forgetful.'

Jennings staggered backwards, trying to keep his

balance, despite the weight of the musket that threatened to pull him down on to his back. He groaned at Steel in breathy whispers:

'You. You can't kill me, Steel. Damn you. You're not worthy.'

'Not worthy?'

Steel pointed to Louisa.

'Was she worthy? And what about the army, and your country, Jennings? Were they worthy of you? You traitorous bastard.'

Jennings was gasping now, his face deathly white. His mouth cloyed with blood. He choked out the words:

'How dare you. I'll see you in hell, Steel.'

Steel grasped Jennings by the shoulders and forced him down on to the floor, hard against the length of the musket.

'Perhaps you will, Major. But not for a very, very long time, if I can help it.'

The wood splintered with a crack and the weapon split in two as the socket of the bayonet made contact with Jennings' back and pushed deeper between his shoulder blades. Despite the burning pain in his shoulder, Steel continued to push and Williams watched as the Major's stare widened to one of pure terror and his hands flailed wildly around the blade. For a moment it was as if they could not find it. And then they stopped. Frozen in space, they clawed at the air. Steel let go of Jennings' limp body and stood up. He turned and knelt by Louisa who had regained consciousness. As he cradled her head in his hands, she opened her eyes.

'Jack?'

'Tom, come and help Miss Weber.'

Williams eased Louisa to her feet and Steel walked over to Jennings' corpse. Bending down, he delved carefully around the bayonet, opened the expensive red coat, stained a deeper red now by Jennings' blood and, reaching into the right hand side, pulled out the bundle of letters. He wiped it clean of blood and opening it, scoured the contents before placing it snugly inside his own coat pocket.

Williams and Louisa were sitting on the bed. The tears were chasing each other down her face.

'Is he dead?' She spoke in a whisper.

Steel nodded.

'Quite dead.'

Louisa wiped her eyes.

'What did you take from him? Money?'

Steel shook his head and clutched at his wounded arm where he could now feel the real pain cutting in.

'No, not money. Something more precious than that. Something that no money could ever buy.'

He looked down into Jennings' lifeless eyes.

'A man's honour.'

EPILOGUE

Evening crept over the field and brought the pale summer moonlight to touch the bodies of the dead and dying. The air was thick with the smell of powder and the honey-sweet scent of death and the blood ran free in the furrows of the fields and coloured the waters of the Nebel and the little Meulweyer. Blenheim itself lay silent, save for the groans of the wounded and the crackle of the flames. Within an area of barely four square miles, 15,000 Frenchmen, 6,000 British, Dutch and Germans and 3,000 of Prince Eugene's men lay united in death. For once the corpses were spared the attention of the plunderers who usually descended on them after a battle.

Marlborough had ordered his army to 'sleep upon its guns' and everywhere, across the great plain of Hochstadt, the living lay down with the dead in the sleep of exhaustion and victory. Here and there the orange glow of a fire indicated where those still filled with the spirit of battle chose to celebrate. The bodies of the horses lay almost as thick as those of the soldiers. Those animals not yet dead neighed and snorted in their agonies. Cutts' division and the British left wing had lost over 2,000 men in the fight for Blenheim village and Steel had long since stopped trying to discover which men of his regiment still lived. He knew from Slaughter how many of the Grenadiers had been killed. At least a dozen for certain and seven more missing. He knew that Cussiter, Taylor, Hansam and fifteen others, though wounded, would fight again. And that McCance, Collins and ten others would not.

*   *   *

He stood on the high ground above the villages, on what had been the French lines. The enemy had left some 3,000 of their tents standing and those men who could—officers mostly—had commandeered them for the night. Standing in one now, with Slaughter and Louisa, Steel was looking at some of the personal possessions which its previous occupant had left on a small table. A book of verse, a letter to his wife, three bottles of red wine, a pipe, playing cards and all manner of foodstuffs. Vegetables and herbs of all kinds. Slaughter stood in wonder:

'What d'you make of all this, Sir? An' I thought we were well supplied.'

'This, Sarn't, is what is called living off the land. Your French soldier is a born plunderer. You can be sure that nothing here was paid for, all of it stolen from the poor peasantry. Still. We can't exactly return it now, can we? How are you as a cook, Jacob?'

'You know, that is something that I've just never got on with, cooking. Women's work I'd say.'

Louisa laughed.

'Oh, I can fricassee a nice piece of beef, or horse if needs be. Nice that is. And taters is taters, isn't that a fact? But anything else is lost on me, Mister Steel.'

'Truly, I wish I hadn't asked. Who's the company cook then, would you say? No, let me guess.'

366

'Well, I'm willing to bet that Corporal Taylor could get us up a nice ragout from all this.'

'Well, best find him then, Jacob. Mustn't let it go to waste.'

Henry Hansam, his right arm in a sling, stuck his head through the tent flap:

'Steel. Have you heard. We have taken Marshal Tallard and forty generals. Forty of them, Jack. And close on 130 of their colours. But there is better news still. The Guards have found a hundred oxen, ready skinned and delivered this morning to the French. I'm taking a party to see if I can liberate one.'

'You see, Jacob, I told you our luck was in. You'd better raise Corporal Taylor from his sick bed quick, Jacob. We'll have a nice French beef ragout tonight.'

Their laughter was broken by the arrival of one of Marlborough's running footmen:

'Lieutenant Steel. The Captain-General desires to speak with you, Sir. At once, if you will.'

*   *   *

Steel walked with the boy across the trampled stubble. From time to time a wounded man would stretch out an arm towards them, but so set was the messenger on delivering his commander's guest, that neither of them took the time to stop.

They passed the corpses of the nine battalions of French infantry who had sought to oppose Marlborough's centre, lying dead in square, mown down in parade-ground formation by the devastating bird-shot from Colonel Blood's cannon. Steel could not help but look at their faces in the soft light. They seemed incredibly young. Some of them perhaps just sixteen.

At length they came to the mill at the edge of Hochstadt that the French had used to store gunpowder and that the Duke had now commandeered as his lodging for the night.

The runner held open the door for Steel. The room was filled with pipe smoke, loud voices and senior officers: Germans, Dutch and men from the Imperial forces. He recognized Hawkins and a few others, Prince Eugene among them. In the centre of all stood Marlborough. General Lumley, the celebrated cavalry commander was in full flow:

'You never saw such a thing. The finest cavalry of France off like a bride on her wedding night. Full tilt and straight into the Danube. How many were drowned only God knows.' Marlborough looked stern:

'Yes, Lumley. It was a great tragedy that so many brave soldiers should have suffered such an ignominious fate.'

Colonel Hawkins coughed.

'Mister Steel, Your Grace.'

'Ah, Mister Steel.'

Steel came conspicuously to attention. Marlborough smiled and, walking across the room, took two glasses of wine from the silver tray on the sideboard with which, along with several other items, the Duke's servants had hastily furnished his new quarters. He handed one to Steel.

'A drink, Mister Steel. You saved your regimental colour, Sir, I am told by Sir James Farquharson. Lord Cutts here believes that your action helped to save his brigade.'

Cutts nodded in his direction.

'It was nobly done, Steel. Gentlemen, forgive me for a moment. I have a small matter to discuss with Lieutenant Steel.'

Leaving the Generals to compare their tales of the French defeat, Marlborough drew Steel to one side of the fug-filled room.

'You saved a colour, Steel, and the best part of a brigade and by God man, you have saved me. Colonel Hawkins gave me the papers that you retrieved. Don't worry, all are there. It was well done, Steel. And what of Major Jennings?'

'He is dead, Your Grace. I saw to it personally.'

Marlborough nodded.

'For that too you have my thanks. I am in your debt. Although perhaps I may do something now to repay your service.' He called across the room, 'Colonel Hawkins. I believe that you have a paper for Mister Steel.'

Hawkins, spilling wine from a brimming goblet, hurried over. 'Ah. Yes. Indeed.'

Reaching inside his coat, the Colonel pulled out a folded sheet of paper.

'Here we are.'

'Well give it to him, James.'

Hawkins handed the piece of paper to Steel who unfolded it.

Marlborough continued:

'You must know that your commission was not undertaken as I had originally understood, nor as I would have desired. But it was done. And it was done well, Mister Steel. Or should I say Captain Steel?'

Steel read the paper:

'His Grace the Duke of Marlborough commands that the undermentioned should immediately be gazetted Captain of Grenadiers in the regiment of Sir James Farquharson. Effective from this moment.'

It bore Marlborough's signature.

The Duke spoke:
'Of course any such field commission or promotion needs to be ratified by Her Majesty the Queen. But I should not concern yourself overmuch with that formality. And do not worry. You may retain your company of Grenadiers. They are your men. You are indeed a rare man, Jack Steel. One of the very finest to command in this army and as such I shall mention you in my letters to Her Majesty. I daresay that I shall have need of your services again, ere long. Eh, Hawkins?'
'Indeed, Your Grace.'
Marlborough turned back to the party.
'Gentleman. One more toast on this great and glorious day of victory. I give you Captain Jack Steel.'

HISTORICAL NOTE

The Blenheim campaign was one of greatest feats of arms in British military history. Acting entirely on his own initiative, Marlborough marched his entire army 250 miles, down from Flanders and into Bavaria. It was an astonishing *tour de force* and a masterpiece of logistical planning, particularly given the international nature of his force. Of sixty-five battalions of infantry and one hundred and sixty squadrons of cavalry, only fourteen and nineteen, respectively were British.

Marlborough today tends to be overshadowed by Wellington, but properly considered his true importance becomes clear. Marlborough's victory at Blenheim delivered a body blow to Louis XIV whose army had reigned effectively unbeaten in any major battle for fifty years. At a single stroke Marlborough save the Austrian Empire and drove the French onto the defensive. In real terms the allies killed or captured 40,000 French and Bavarian troops along with 1,150 officers, 60 cannon and 128 infantry colours. The allied losses ran to 6,000 killed and 8,000 wounded. The news reached London on 21 August and the city bells rang out to salute the victory.

Blenheim was the end of an era. In a single day of battle, Marlborough had elevated his queen to the unquestioned status of European monarch, demonstrated that a British-led army was fully capable of defeating the French and given Britain the confidence which would result in the forging of her Empire. In personal terms, despite the

371

inevitable attempts to use Blenheim as a vehicle for party politics, Marlborough's political enemies were confounded and the balance of power in Parliament moved dramatically away from the High Tories in favour of the Whigs. The Duke's future prosperity was also assured with Queen Anne's reward of the manor of Woodstock in Oxfordshire where he and his wife, Sarah, set about the construction of a magnificent palace which would bear the name of his victory.

*   *   *

The British element of the polyglot force that Marlborough commanded in 1704 was largely the army created by King William, who had moulded the diverse regiments which had come out of the wars of the Glorious Revolution into the basic form we might recognize today. But it was Marlborough who truly made the army his own. He concentrated on the ordinary soldier's welfare: his uniform, shoes, food and supplies. And in so doing he formed an army that was better equipped, supplied and led than any other in Europe. Part of Marlborough's effect on the army was to greatly increase its size. In 1697, following the Peace of Ryswick, the British army was truncated from 50,000 to barely 23,000. With the renewed outbreak of war with France, new regiments were hastily formed. By 1702 the strength had climbed to almost 32,000 men and four years later to 50,000. In 1709 there were almost 70,000 British troops in the field. It is to this new army, whose like would not be seen again until Kitcheners' 'new army' of 1915, that Sir

James Farquharson's Regiment of Foot belongs.

*   *   *

Although its officers and men came from backgrounds as diverse geographically as they were socially, Farquharson's was a Scottish regiment. At the time of Blenheim the treaty of union and with it the notion of a 'British' army, was still three years away and Queen Anne had not one but two armies: one English and one Scots. Similarly, there was as yet no Union flag (Union Jack) and thus Farquharson's Regiment fights under the Saltire of Scotland. Although the background to the book and the detail is closely factual, the regiment itself is an invention, taking its inspiration from the new line regiments and its traditions and style largely from the First Regiment of Foot Guards, with whom both Marlborough and Steel had served. I trust that today's Grenadier Guards will take any resemblance only as a compliment.

From the 1670s one company of the thirteen which made up the 'on paper' strength of every regiment, of English or Scottish Foot Guards was designated 'Grenadiers'. They were shock troops: the precursors of the German *sturmtruppen* of the First World War, the tallest men in the regiment, they were instantly recognizable by their headgear: a tall, mitre cap, like a bishop's headdress, designed to allow them to hurl the small grenades they carried in their packs. Such a hat was more suited to crowd-pleasing on the parade ground of Whitehall than the chaos and filth of a battlefield but the men wore it with pride.

*   *   *

Despite Marlborough's advance preparations, the supply of bread and flour was a serious problem for the advancing allies and such foraging parties as that commanded by Steel were of vital importance.

Marlborough did burn Bavaria, although, according to Sir Winston Churchill and on the evidence of the Duke's own correspondence to do so went very much against his own feelings. It was one of his few failures and, as in the book, did not have the desired effect of coercing the Elector into abandoning the French. It certainly enraged the populace and we know that bands of peasants roamed the countryside intent on taking revenge. It has, understandably, gone down in Bavarian history as an episode of infamy.

The places in the book are all taken from a period map and they still exist today, if sometimes with different names. Some specific topographical details, however, I have taken the liberty to invent or adapt, according to the requirements of the story.

Colonel James Hawkins, like the men of Steel's regiment, is an invention. The other officers of Marlborough's staff however and most of the Field Officers are based upon real characters. Of the French characters, only Clerambault is genuine, although the Grenadiers Rouge did exist and were made up from just the sort of dubious social mix described in the book. They did not, however, commit the atrocity at Sattelberg. That said, the French had, in the not too distant past, meted out similar treatment, as Hawkins observes, to the people of the Palatinate and their own countrymen.

* * *

While Marlborough was greatly admired by Queen Anne, he was not universally popular. While he was on campaign, Tory politicians in England, notably Lord Nottingham, Lord Rochester and Sir Edward Seymour who, keen to replace him with the Duke of Ormonde, constantly attempted to engineer his downfall. Steel's mission to secure the vital letters is an invention, but it is typical of these intrigues and inspired by a genuine episode involving a plot against William III contrived by Sir John Fenwick in the winter of 1696. Although his Jacobite sympathies were always denied by his biographer, Winston Churchill, other historians have suggested that Marlborough, attempting to hedge his bets, did appeal to the exiled King James for a pardon for his having gone over to William. Whatever the truth of this, he was implicated in the trial. Interestingly one of those who sought to have Fenwick denounce Marlborough as a traitor was Charles Mordaunt, the future Earl of Peterborough and the father of John Mordaunt of the Foot Guards, future hero of the Schellenberg. Bizarrely, Charles Mordaunt went on to become a close friend of the Marlboroughs, although a few years later he was again an enemy. Fenwick was executed in January 1697 and Marlborough was lucky not to suffer a similar fate. It is also possible that Marlborough was intriguing with the Jacobite court as late as April 1704, although again,

Winston Churchill dismisses this apparent contact as anti-Jacobite espionage.

The military account of the campaign and the battle of Blenheim are as close to fact as I have been able to make them. A regimental colour was taken by the Gens d'Armes in their attack on Rowe's Brigade and recaptured by Hessians. It was not, of course, the colour of Farquharson's, but that of Rowe's own regiment, subsequently the Royal Scots Fusiliers and the Royal Highland Fusiliers and today sadly, incorporated into the Royal Regiment of Scotland. For this licence I beg that distinguished regiment's forgiveness.

The Margrave of Baden's relationship with Marlborough is testified to by many writers. However, I have taken a similar licence in suggesting that Baden might have leaked information to the Tories.

For the detail in the book I looked to any first-hand accounts which I was able to find. I also relied heavily on the extensive research and published works on Marlborough's wars of the late David Chandler, with whom I was fortunate to enjoy a friendship when, as an army-obsessed schoolboy, I spent many weekends among the experts at Sandhurst, where he was then Head of War Studies. Astonishingly perhaps, the best straightforward accounts of the campaign remain those written in 1930 and 1933 by G M Trevelyan and Sir Winston Churchill, while for detail Charles S Grant's meticulous research into the armies of the period is also invaluable.

Marlborough's victory at Blenheim did not win the War of the Spanish Succession. Ahead lay eight more years of war in Flanders, Portugal,

Spain, Italy and the Americas and the bloody battles of Ramillies, Malplaquet and Oudenarde. Steel, Slaughter and all their comrades still have much work to do if Europe can ever be freed from the scourge of the Sun King. Blenheim was not the end, nor, to paraphrase Marlborough's illustrious biographer, was it even 'the beginning of the end'. But it was a truly glorious victory.

Iain Gale